9/20

PRAISE FOR *PRETTY GUILTY WOMEN*

"From the moment I started reading *Pretty Guilty Women*, I was completely immersed in the gripping, twisty, diffuser-filled world of a posh spa wedding, where four college friends reunite, each with old baggage and new. Sparkling with insight, wine, humor, and a drop of blood, the women in this book leapt off the page and straight into my heart. *Pretty Guilty Women* is a must read!"

—Susan Crawford, bestselling author of *The Pocket Wife* and *The Other Widow*

"Love the strong female characters and the dark underlying themes—a perfect summer read."

—Harriet Tyce, author of *Blood Orange*

"This smart, layered story built around relationships and public perceptions slowly reveals past and present conflicts from fertility to financial struggles to domestic abuse. More than one twist will shroud the truth of the man's death in mystery until almost the very end... Readers searching for their next binge read or book club selection will want to seek out this title."

—*Library Journal*

"LaManna's women are flawed and relatable, and oodles of drama keep the pages turning all the way to a genuinely surprising final twist. This is the perfect summer beach read."

—*Publishers Weekly*

"*Pretty Guilty Women* is a joy to read! LaManna's writing style is so engaging...and indeed difficult to put the book down. LaManna does a superb job."

—*New York Journal of Books*

"An easy, breezy beach read with a clever twist."

—*Kirkus Reviews*

"LaManna deftly unpacks her characters' baggage in this twisty tale."

—*People* magazine

ALSO BY GINA LAMANNA
Pretty Guilty Women

THREE SINGLE WIVES

A NOVEL

GINA LAMANNA

Published by Sourcebooks Landmark, an imprint of Sourcebooks
P.O. Box 4410, Naperville, Illinois 60567-4410
(630) 961-3900
sourcebooks.com

Library of Congress Cataloging-in-Publication Data is on file with the publisher.

Printed and bound in the United States of America.
LSC 10 9 8 7 6 5 4 3 2 1

For my two sweet boys.

PROLOGUE

The Day Before
February 13, 2019

M ore wine?" Eliza Tate raised a bottle of vintage merlot by the neck and gave it a tantalizing wiggle. When no one spoke, she lifted one dainty shoulder in a nonchalant shrug. "Well, I'm having another glass. I've earned it."

Eliza studied the room before her as she tipped a stream of deep-red wine gently into her Bordeaux glass. Despite the lackluster response from the three other women, she continued to pour. She topped off one of the other glasses and then the next, leaving the third empty for obvious reasons.

"Bottoms up," Eliza said once the last drop had been poured. "Marguerite, how do you feel about everything we've gone over? Anything else you'd like to cover?"

"Actually, I have one more question." Penny raised a reluctant hand. "Is that okay? Are we still allowed to ask questions?"

"Yes, please do," Eliza said. "That's the point of a rehearsal."

"Did you have a theme in mind before you wrote *Be Free*?" Penny leaned back in the chair, her eyes flitting quickly toward Marguerite before settling on the tattered copy of the book before her.

"It's not quite that simple." Marguerite Hill, bestselling author and self-help guru, leaned back in the sleek, violet-tinted chair before the unlit fireplace. Eliza's sitting room ascended around her with lofted ceilings and elaborate furnishings. Marguerite stroked a hand over the velvety fabric on the chair's arm and looked lost in thought. "There are several themes. Some more subtle than others."

"You were being subtle." Anne gave a reassuring nod. "So subtle I almost missed it."

"You missed it because you didn't read the book," Eliza said. "It's hard to notice a theme if you only read the back cover."

"Well, that too," Anne agreed. "But I have little kids. I don't have time to read books."

Eliza didn't bother to touch on the other issues in Anne's life that might have prevented her from reading a book. She was just happy to see her friend had managed to drag herself out of the house. Eliza wondered idly if there was a catch.

"The most important theme, I suppose, is what inspired the title. See, men have held power over us, over women, for years." Marguerite closed her manicured nails into a tight fist. "They have expected us to put our heads down, toil away, and obey their rules. We have been conditioned not to whine or moan, let alone put up a fight. We have never been truly free."

Penny nodded enthusiastically. Anne picked at her cuticles. Eliza watched the author as she gently stomped onto her soapbox—the soapbox that had earned Marguerite over a million dollars and far more than fifteen minutes of fame.

"It's time we take control of our lives and shape our destinies," Marguerite continued. "If not now, when? Will we let another generation slip away when we have the power to change this very moment?"

"But how?" Penny's question emerged softly, like a subtle flavor infused into the conversation. Her words were accompanied by notes of curiosity and naivete. Finished with bold undertones of determination. "To be free...don't we first have to escape?"

Marguerite's face underwent a transformation. An initial burst of surprise teetered into a stony, unreadable expression. *She's stumped*, Eliza noted. Stumped by the not-as-innocent-as-she-looks Penny Sands.

"I didn't give you enough credit," Marguerite said finally. "You're so young. I thought you might still be an optimist."

"Not anymore."

"In answer to your question, we must start boldly and close to home. Sometimes, toxic relationships are before our very noses." Marguerite's gaze turned curiously toward Eliza.

Eliza cleared her throat and dodged Marguerite's intense stare.

"But I mean *specifically* what can we do?" Penny persisted. "What actions can we take? For example, if I was in a toxic relationship, what should I do about it?"

Marguerite's polished lips curved into a tiny smile. "I think we need to give men a taste of their own medicine."

"Of their own medicine?" Penny echoed. "You mean have an affair or something?"

"An affair," Anne said with a scoff. "That's way too much work. I can barely handle one husband. The last thing I want is another man who needs to be fed and clothed and attended to."

Eliza gave a soft snort of agreement.

"Well, what if you found out Mark was having an affair?" Penny asked Anne. "What would you do about it?"

"I'd probably kill him," Anne said. "I don't have the patience for a long con."

The room fell silent.

"Oh, come on," Anne said with a groan. "I don't mean literally."

"Of course not," Penny said with a weak smile. "We knew that."

"You guys, it was a joke." Anne curled her legs beneath her on the sofa as she settled a few inches deeper into the lush couch. "Do you think I would actually murder my husband?"

Another uneasy silence slid around the room.

"Come on. I couldn't do that. I love Mark," Anne said. "I'm too queasy for *murder*-murder. I could probably pull off poison or something, but blood is too messy. Plus, my husband's a cop. His friends would sniff me out before he was cold."

"Well, if we're talking in hypotheticals, there's one man in particular I wouldn't mind running over with my car," Penny said. "Theoretically, of course," she added quickly.

"Of course," Anne chirped.

"I mean, I just get so mad sometimes," Penny said. "I'd be the type to explode. *Boom.* Like you read about in the papers—as awful as that is to say."

"What about you, Eliza?" Anne asked. "If good old Roman had to go, how'd you do it?"

"Yes," Marguerite said. "I'm sure you've thought of it, darling. I mean, Roman's not a saint."

Eliza stalled with a dainty sip of her wine. "I've never considered it."

"That's a load," Anne said. "You and Roman have been married for ages. He's got to push some of your buttons."

Eliza felt her hands tremble. The truth simmered just below the surface. If only they could peer through the hazy steam and sort through the lies, they wouldn't be asking such a touchy, touchy question. *Would Eliza kill her husband?*

"Maybe," she finally said, fueled by the cozy warmth of wine and the camaraderie of a group of women. "I suppose if I was angry enough…"

"Oh, doll, don't be modest. You'd make a statement." Marguerite winked at Eliza and followed it up with a devilish little chuckle. "I think a knife suits you. It suits Roman, too. He'd have to go out in style, bless his rich little soul."

"A knife," Eliza echoed. "You mean stab him? That's pretty brutal."

Anne shrugged. "Just play along, won't you?"

"I suppose," Eliza said, feeling a redness creep down her neck. "A knife would be one way to make sure he was dead."

"You do follow through on your promises," Marguerite said. "I can vouch for that. If you ever set out to murder someone…well, let's just say I'd hate to be on your bad side."

"And you, Marguerite?" Anne asked. "How would the self-help guru go about getting revenge?"

"I really don't think murder is the best way to handle your problems," Marguerite said, shooting Eliza a somewhat bewildered glance. "I hope you know that's not at all what I meant when I said we needed to give men a taste of their own medicine. Things spiraled for a bit there."

Eliza hid her smirk. They hadn't covered this in their PR briefing earlier in the day. It wasn't often Marguerite stumbled from her platform. In a way, it pleased Eliza to see her floundering. However, instead of savoring the moment, Eliza tossed a life vest to her client. Leapt in to save the day as usual. That's why they paid her the big bucks.

"Marguerite's far too clever for anything as obvious as plain old murder," Eliza said. "If she wanted to get revenge on a man, she'd probably off him in a big way, then frame all of us and get away scot-free, wouldn't you, Marguerite?"

TRANSCRIPT

The Court: Prosecution, you may call your next witness.

Prosecution: I call to the stand Anne Wilkes.

The Court: Will the witness please stand to be sworn in by the bailiff.

(witness stands)

Bailiff (to witness): Please raise your right hand. Do you swear to tell the truth, the whole truth, and nothing but the truth?

Anne Wilkes: I do.

(witness goes to stand and sits down)

Prosecution: Mrs. Wilkes, let's start with the night of February 13, 2019. What do you remember about that day?

Anne Wilkes: I met up with a few of my girlfriends for a book club event that afternoon.

Prosecution: Which girlfriends?

Anne Wilkes: Eliza Tate and Penny Sands. Marguerite Hill, the author, was there, too, but I didn't know her well at the time.

Prosecution: Which book were you discussing at this event?

Defense: Objection. How is the book club selection relevant to the murder case?

Prosecution: I will demonstrate its relevance if given the opportunity.

The Court: Overruled. You may continue, Ms. Clark, but make your point.

Prosecution: The book, Mrs. Wilkes?

Anne Wilkes: It was called *Being Free* by Marguerite Hill.

Prosecution: I'm not familiar with a book by that name. Not by that author. Do you mean *Be Free*?

Anne Wilkes: Er, yeah. Same thing.

Prosecution: This is a murder investigation, Mrs. Wilkes. Details are important.

Anne Wilkes: Sorry.

Prosecution: Is that or is it not the follow-up to Ms. Hill's nonfiction bestseller *Take Charge*, a smash hit that took the world by storm a year ago?

Anne Wilkes: Yeah. Er, yes. At our first book club in October, we read *Take Charge*. We liked it, so in February, we read the sequel.

Prosecution: What is the book about?

Anne Wilkes: I think the title is self-explanatory. Both of Marguerite's works are pretty typical self-help books for women. About how to take charge of your life and all that garbage. It's inspirational, or so I assume. I didn't actually read either book. There are hefty SparkNotes summaries online that are a godsend if you're looking to get the gist of it. I have four kids. How do I have time to read a book that doesn't involve pictures?

Prosecution: Where were you between the hours of 11:00 p.m. on February 13 and 2:00 a.m. the next morning?

Anne Wilkes: At a bar. Garbanzo's. Our book club, uh, didn't go as planned, so we went out to blow off some steam.

Prosecution: Were you with Eliza Tate during that time?

Anne Wilkes: Part of it.

Prosecution: Please explain what happened that night at book club.

Anne Wilkes: Now, that's a long story.

Prosecution: We've got plenty of time, Mrs. Wilkes. Why don't you start from the beginning?

ONE

W hole wheat bread. One and a half slices of ham. One squiggly squirt of mustard. Five Lay's cheddar cheese potato chips arranged carefully on the bread. Cut crusts off, insert into plastic baggie, draw permanent-marker heart on the front of the brown paper lunch sack.

Was Anne Wilkes in a rut?

Probably, she thought, looking at the sandwiches she'd prepared for her children while simultaneously spinning to yank the refrigerator open and place the ham, cheese, and mustard in their rightful spots.

She stared at her perfectly organized fridge. Even her fridge was in a rut. The same milk, the same yogurt (Activia because Mark suffered from indigestion and bloating), and even the same treats. One Lindt truffle per day in order to keep her ass smaller than Pluto. After four kids, two of them twins, it was a constant battle.

The fridge closed, and Anne gave an incoherent mumble into the phone that would keep her mother's stories flowing for the next few minutes. Jutting a hip against the counter, Anne snuck a few cheddar cheese crisps from the bag, figuring it counted as breakfast.

"Anne, are you even listening? I wish you would pay attention," Beatrice said. "I wish…"

Beatrice didn't need to finish the sentence. It didn't matter, because Anne knew where she was going with it. Her mother wished for a lot of things. She probably wished for a different daughter. After what had happened three years ago, Anne was officially an embarrassment to Beatrice Harper.

For a while there, Anne had been somewhat mediocre in her mother's eyes. She'd acquired a house, children, and a highly respected husband. Anne's marriage had been her crowning glory for the last fourteen years. Happily married to a handsome, decorated LAPD officer—formerly of the narcotics division, newly promoted to detective—she'd done one thing right in her life. Until she'd failed at her marriage, too.

"Mom, I've got to let you go," Anne finally said. She'd hit a wall and was unable to listen to her mother's latest drama about the country club for a second longer. "It's time to get the kids ready for bed."

"You really should hire a chef, or at least a nanny," her mother sniffed. "It's not good for you to be running around like you do. You'll get bags under your eyes. Then Mark will leave you, and you'll be all alone—an unwed mother of four children."

"Thanks, Mom," Anne said. "We'll see you in a few weeks."

From the other room, the sounds of screeching reached Anne's ears. She sighed. It had been too easy. The twins had gone down early, both sleeping peacefully in their cribs by seven thirty. A record of sorts these days.

It must have been Samuel, sneaking into the room to torture them again. At four years old, he was fascinated by his two younger siblings, though his fascination often walked the fine line between love and hate.

"Mom!" Gretchen, the oldest at seven and a half, yelled unhelpfully from the living room. "The twins woke up!"

"Right, I can hear that," Anne hollered back. "Go get your jammies on, will you? Help your brother, please."

Anne shoved tomorrow's lunches back into the fridge and

slammed the door. She did a super-quick cleanup of the kitchen and told herself it was good to let the twins cry it out for a little longer. A quick check of her watch told her the babysitter was due to arrive in under twenty minutes.

Mark had scheduled Olivia to arrive half an hour earlier than she needed to be here. It was her husband's way of checking up on her. Then again, scheduling the babysitter for extra hours wasn't Mark's only way of checking up on his wife. In fact, he orchestrated unexpected checks so frequently they were anything but subtle by this point.

There were Mark's famous "surprise" lunches where he'd pop home unannounced for a bite to eat. Mothers from Gretchen's school had taken to showing up with trays of lasagna for no obvious reason. Playdates with Samuel's friends appeared on the calendar on days Mark worked extra shifts.

He still didn't trust her, and that was beginning to drive Anne batty. She was fine, fine, fine. She'd been fine for almost three years now. *Mostly fine*, she amended, but only to herself. She still had her days.

With a sigh, Anne glanced at the clock again. She had time to speed-rock the twins back to sleep, change into a somewhat sexy outfit, and apply some concealer to the bags under her eyes that felt permanent. Maybe her mother had a point. If she didn't shape up soon, she'd be a single mom of four. As much as Mark drove her nuts some days, she was married to him, and she wanted to keep it that way.

Anne cursed as she made her way into the living room and tripped over a stuffed elephant. As she hopped over to the stairway, her anger found a target in Gretchen, who still hadn't moved from the couch.

"Turn the TV off," Anne barked. "Olivia will be here soon, and I want you ready for bed."

"I want Olivia to put me to bed," she moaned. "She reads me extra books."

"You're not getting any books if you don't get ready for bed. You know the rules."

Babying her stubbed toe, Anne made her way upstairs and found Samuel in his room, staring at a tablet. She made a note to discuss the overuse of screens in this house with her husband later tonight at dinner.

"Put it away," she snapped at Samuel. "Get your pajamas on. Now."

Samuel didn't appear to hear her. The twins' shrieks reached new levels of earsplitting. Anne's blood boiled in her veins. Mark should have been home twenty minutes ago. He'd promised to help get the kids ready for bed so Anne could bake the boatload of cupcakes that Gretchen needed for some fundraiser tomorrow.

If Anne didn't get them baked, they would have to pay for the volunteer hours Anne hadn't completed. Unfortunately for the Wilkeses, they couldn't afford to pay for the hours, so a shitload of cupcakes was the answer.

Easing into the twins' bedroom, she saw the source of their discontent. Her cell phone chirped with a missed call on the rocking chair tucked into the corner. She must have forgotten it in the room after tucking Harry and Heather in. If she was a betting woman, she'd guess there was also a message from Mark that he was running late.

The twins quieted, watching her as she grabbed the phone. It felt like they were mocking her, teasing her, playing a game that Anne would forever lose. At once, Anne felt guilty as she looked at her babies. Her eyes welled with tears.

"I'm sorry," she muttered, then grabbed her phone and disappeared from the room.

Once safe in the hallway, Anne expelled a breath. Her fingers worked the screen, unlocking it to find a missed call from her husband along with a text message to match. *Perfect*, she thought. Not only was he not home, but he was also the very reason the twins had woken up from their miracle early bedtime.

Anne opened the message from her husband, confirming what

she'd already expected. He wasn't on his way at all. As she read the text a second time, her scalp prickled with dismay. Her very core trembled.

Mark: Sorry, hon. Really behind at work. Tried to swing it but can't. Do you mind canceling with Olivia? We'll reschedule for next week. You feeling okay?

Anne briefly wondered what she would say if she told her husband the truth. Was she feeling okay? *Ha, ha, ha.* Poor Mark couldn't handle the truth. If only men knew what it was like—motherhood, the insane wave of chaos and hormones and sleep deprivation, along with new baby mouths to feed and hearts to love. She struggled while Mark floated through it all, oblivious, content to contribute happy little paychecks and consider his duties fulfilled.

Anne began to type a response then deleted it. She typed another one, deleted that. What could she say? Mark had sent the babysitter home twice in one month, and Anne would be an idiot not to be suspicious at this point. Especially when she'd called his partner last time at the office to see what the holdup was, and his partner had said that Mark had gone home early due to a stomach bug.

The doorbell rang downstairs. The twins screamed. Anne looked down at the blank message on her phone. She couldn't bring herself to respond, so she tucked her cell into a pocket and returned to the twins' room. She performed a Cirque du Soleil–type maneuver to get both babies secured in her arms before hustling downstairs to open the front door as the bell *dinged* a second time.

Those Vegas acrobats had nothing on her. After nursing two babies at the same time and singlehandedly maneuvering a stroller with several small children in tow through a grocery store, she deserved some sort of accolade. A trophy. At the very minimum, a big, fat gold star.

Harry spit up all over Anne's neck. She closed her eyes. That was the sort of accolade she was used to getting.

"Olivia," Anne gasped, unlocking the screen door so the young woman could let herself in. "Actually, I'm so sorry. Mark is not able to—"

Olivia's face began to fall. "You don't need me...er...again?"

Without waiting for a response, Olivia reached for one of the twins. Anne handed Harry over and sighed with relief. The silence, the simple pleasure of having to hold only one child at a time swept over her as she studied the young college student.

"Actually..." Anne spun around and saw Gretchen on the couch. She could hear Samuel on his tablet upstairs. Suddenly, she didn't want to deal with any of it. She wanted to tuck her children (safely) into someone else's arms and disappear. For a long, long time. But that would be impossible. She couldn't run away and not come back. He'd find her.

Anne cleared her throat. "I was just going to say that Mark's running late, so I'm meeting him at the restaurant."

"Hooray!" Olivia's face brightened. "I was looking forward to babysitting. Plus, I imagine you could really use a night out."

"I suppose I could," Anne said.

But the truth weighed heavier on her. A night out was too small. Anne dreamed bigger.

"Let me just get the kids—"

"Stop!" Olivia raised her free hand, waved Anne away. "Go get ready. You've got spit-up on your shirt, and we can't have that for your romantic dinner."

Anne snorted with the irony of it all. Olivia merely smiled, missing the funniest part of the joke.

When Anne had married a cop, she'd known the drill. The long hours, the weekend shifts, the lifestyle that came with it. But after twenty years on the force, Mark had finally gotten enough seniority at the LAPD to move to day shifts. That meant he was supposed to be home at night.

Olivia set Harry down, took Heather from Anne's arms. Olivia was an olive-skinned beauty with long, dark hair and gorgeous almond-shaped eyes. Better yet, she was a magician with the children.

Heather and Harry each latched on to one of Olivia's fingers. Gretchen peeled her skinny limbs from the sofa and finally managed to find the Off button on the television remote. From upstairs, the sounds on Samuel's tablet went mute.

Samuel's curious voice called down, "Is that Olivia?"

"Only if you're in your pajamas," Olivia called back, tittering with laughter. "And what about you, ma'am? Those don't look like jammies to me."

While Gretchen heaved with laughter, Anne shot a grateful look over her children's heads to the babysitter. Olivia tilted her chin up, directing Anne upstairs to get changed.

Anne did so, taking a luxuriously long shower. It was seven minutes in total, start to finish, including time for shaved legs, plucked eyebrows, and the removal of one nasty ingrown hair. She spritzed her best perfume onto her bare skin and studied her reflection in the mirror.

Anne wasn't gorgeous by any right. She'd been cute, once upon a time. But her long, chestnut hair had since been chopped into a bob, and her once-plump hips now carried an extra twenty pounds that were no longer cute but quite saggy. Her breasts had also joined the saggy club, along with her biceps, her ass, and her thighs. They were a stubborn bunch.

Anne wrapped a robe around herself and made her way into her bedroom. She slid into a forgiving black dress and popped on simple pearl earrings. It didn't matter what she wore, seeing as she'd be alone tonight, but if she didn't make half an effort, Olivia wouldn't be convinced.

Anne sat on the edge of her bed and reached for the box of heels she kept stashed underneath. They were a new purchase, one her husband hadn't—and wouldn't—find out about. He'd go berserk if he found out she'd spent $250 on a pair of high heels when he'd worked overtime for a week to pay Gretchen's ballet camp fee.

That's what the private cash stash is for, she reminded herself.

Random birthday money she received, cash back from store returns, the hundred dollars her friend had given her to house-sit all those years ago. Anne had earned those shoes.

Standing, Anne took one last look at herself in the full-length mirror. The shoes were worth every penny of the $250 she'd spent. They made her legs look more goddess-like than human. They even gave her butt a few extra inches of lift, making the excess weight look something close to attractive.

At the last second, she slipped off her heels and tucked them neatly into their box. She covered them with tissue paper and pressed them back where they belonged. Under the bed. Then, she slipped into comfortable flats and grabbed a purse. There was no need for heels. Not where Anne was going.

Jogging downstairs, Anne tossed keys into her bag and let herself out into the cool night air. She paused, inhaled deeply. The guilt hit when she exhaled.

With a flutter of panic, she turned back inside and sprinted up the steps to Gretchen's room. She stood in the doorway, breathless, before the babysitter and a pile of children.

"Anne, are you okay?" Olivia asked. "You look flushed."

Anne raised a hand to her forehead and felt sweat beaded there. She shuffled into the room and planted kisses on her children's foreheads. She muttered half-hearted instructions to her children to obey the babysitter. When she let herself out of the room, her babies hardly seemed to notice.

Anne took the stairs two at a time. She wondered curiously if her family would notice if she disappeared. Stepped through the front door and never returned. Would Gretchen be relieved to see her meanie mom gone for good? Would Samuel even look up from his tablet? The twins…they wouldn't know. They'd be fine. They'd all be fine.

Once situated inside her minivan, Anne wiped the beaded sweat away again.

"I'm okay," she breathed to herself. "It's fine. Plenty of moms forget to say goodbye to their children."

She sat there for a minute, convincing herself it was true. When she didn't like any of the thoughts dancing through her brain, she switched to safer thinking: her evening agenda.

Anne could go walk around Target for an hour, and it'd be nothing short of heavenly. She could push a cart without kids hanging off the sides or draping their bendy bodies across the underbelly. She wouldn't have to play hide-and-seek across the clearance racks of clothes.

She could take a snippet of quiet time and read. There was a self-help book from her old friend Eliza that she'd been meaning to dive into for ages. She could grab a coffee at the all-night diner down the road and read, undisturbed. It would be a small slice of paradise.

Or she could do neither of the sensible options. The second the latter thought tiptoed into Anne's brain, she knew there was no turning back. She was going to find answers. Answers she'd been seeking for weeks. Easing her key into the ignition, she cranked the car's engine until it turned over and prayed their battery that needed replacing would last the night.

Mark, Mark, Mark, she thought as she pulled onto the streets. *It's time to find out where you've been going, oh husband of mine.*

TRANSCRIPT

Prosecution: Ms. Sands, how long have you been living in Los Angeles?

Penny Sands: A little over a year. I moved here in May 2018, and it's July now, so…thirteen months?

Prosecution: Fourteen.

Penny Sands: Whatever you say. I've never been great at math.

Prosecution: What brought you to Los Angeles?

Penny Sands: What brings anyone to Los Angeles? Lies, I guess.

Prosecution: Lies?

Penny Sands: You grow up thinking you can be anyone or do anything, but none of that's true. Everyone moves here to be a movie star, and where do most of us end up? Well, I ended up in court, so there's that.

Prosecution: When did you first meet Eliza Tate?

Penny Sands: During one of her book events. She was throwing a launch party for Marguerite Hill's second book, *Be Free*, and I had an invitation.

Prosecution: Where did you get your invitation to Mrs. Tate's event?

Penny Sands: From Roman.

Prosecution: Roman Tate—Eliza's husband—invited you to the party?

Penny Sands: That's what I said.

Prosecution: So you met Eliza Tate via her husband?

Defense: Objection. Already stated.

Prosecution: I'll move on, Your Honor.

The Court: Very well.

Prosecution: Ms. Sands, when did you know that you were in love with Roman Tate?

TWO

Nine Months Before
May 2018

P enny Sands sat on the bus, eyes peeled wide, feeling much smaller than her 124 pounds. At five feet six inches tall, she was taller than the average woman and quite pretty, if she said so herself.

She felt much younger than her twenty-six years of age as the bus rolled its way into Los Angeles. She tried to take in everything—every honk from angry cars as they cruised in and out of traffic lanes, every closed-down, boarded-up, and graffitied shop, every overflowing garbage can.

The slightest bit of confusion flooded through her. A hint of panic. Barely discernible but definitely there. Surely, the Hollywood sign was hiding out of sight, just waiting to peep over the next overpriced gas station.

The beautiful people and movie stars, they'd be just around the next corner. On Rodeo Drive, probably. The bus just hadn't made the correct turns yet. The glitz and glamour and hopefulness were tucked out of sight, waiting to be discovered by eager new hands. *They must be.*

"First time here?" The man in front of Penny turned and gave her a lopsided smile. "I can tell by that starry look in your eyes that you're new to the area. By the way, name's Kurt."

"Oh." Penny stifled a laugh. "Hi, Kurt. I'm Penny. And I didn't realize I was that obvious."

"Where you from?"

"A small town in Iowa. I'm sure you don't know it."

"Des Moines?"

She gave a faint smile. "Close enough. What about you? Are you from the area?"

"Nobody's from LA originally." Kurt smiled again, though it looked strange. It didn't reach his eyes. "We're all a mix from everywhere else. But I'm considered as much of a local as anyone now, been here twenty years. You moving here to be an actress?"

"Is it that obvious?"

"You look like an actress."

"Well, thanks...I guess. But I also like to write. I thought about screenwriting while I'm out here or even producing. One day, I'd love to direct. Actually, back home, I worked for the local paper," Penny said proudly. She'd graduated summa cum laude with an English degree from Iowa State and had nabbed one of the few writerly jobs available in her town. "In fact, the reason I'm here at all is because of a book."

"How's that?"

"Well, it sounds stupid when I say it out loud."

"Why would it sound stupid?"

"It's sort of self-helpy," she said. "Anyhow, the author got me thinking, and I realized that I wanted more. I wanted something big, something huge. And I couldn't have that in Boone, Iowa."

"No, you most certainly couldn't," Kurt said. "Where will you be living?"

Penny frowned, glanced down at the slip of paper that had grown somewhat sweaty in her palm. "An apartment near...this street?"

She held it up so he could read the address. Kurt's eyebrows twitched slightly, but Penny couldn't interpret what the movement meant.

"Do you know it?" she continued. "Is the area safe? I tried to

Google it, but it's so hard to tell online. Not that I had many options. I mean, housing prices are so high out here, and I can't afford a car just yet."

"It's right near me, actually," Kurt said. "I live a few blocks away, down on Western. Want a lift home? It's probably a twenty-minute walk from the bus station."

"Oh, no. That's fine," she said. "I like to exercise."

Kurt glanced out the window. "You're gonna walk in the dark?"

He had a point; it was darker than Penny had anticipated. Her stomach clutched at the thought of picking her way through the dark streets of Hollywood all alone on her first night. Her stomach clutched tighter at the idea of accepting help from a stranger. She knew better than to get in a car with him, but he seemed harmless enough, and the offer was tempting...

"Well, I'm getting off at this stop," he said. "I reckon you are, too, if that's your address. It was nice to meet you. Hope you enjoy your time here."

Kurt stood, then paraded down the aisle and climbed off the bus. Penny followed behind, clumsily hauling her oversize suitcase and one backpack through the narrow opening, muttering apologies as she rolled over feet and bumped into elbows.

When she reached the stairs, her suitcase went ass over teakettle down the steps and landed in a heap on the ground. Penny glanced at it in dismay, waiting for a moment as if someone might magically appear to help with her supersize load.

"Off you go, lady," the bus driver barked. "We've got a schedule to keep."

With tears pricking her eyes, Penny hustled down and retrieved her muddied suitcase from the grimy gutter. It took every ounce of her piddly bicep muscles to haul it onto the curb. Her shoulders ached, and her back was drenched with sweat. She'd worn her nicest casual dress for the occasion, along with a set of cute wedge sandals, and both were practically melting after the long bus ride.

"Kurt," she called on a desperate impulse.

She was just too exhausted to walk another step. But heaven forbid she tell her mother she'd accepted a ride from a stranger. *Just this once.* It would be a secret she'd haul to her grave.

"Are you sure it wouldn't be a hassle to give me a ride to my apartment?"

That lopsided smile reappeared. "Sure thing, honey. Hop in. It's no trouble at all."

"This is it," Penny said. "You can stop here."

As Kurt had promised, the car ride was a short one. Penny glanced over at her driver, whose chatter had slowed once they'd gotten into the car, and waited for his reaction.

She ignored the creeping feeling of discomfort in her stomach. Penny had learned not to take rides from strangers like every good little girl. And like every good little girl, she hated breaking the rules.

Penny had the manners of a Midwesterner—a comfortable, steady politeness ingrained so deeply in her that it had become part of her very marrow. She never caused unnecessary waves. She apologized when things weren't her fault. She didn't have an ounce of confrontation in her DNA.

That's why, when Kurt didn't pull over immediately, Penny merely cleared her throat, content to give him the benefit of the doubt until the first stoplight. The first stoplight came and went, however, and the piece of paper in Penny's hands grew soaked with sweat. It tore into shreds, and Penny realized it was very lucky she'd had thirty hours on a bus to memorize the street address. The print had become illegible.

"I think you missed the turn," she said, struggling to balance firmness and politeness in her tone. "I know it's nothing to look at from the outside, but the address—"

"I thought you might like to come by my place for a cup of coffee?"

Kurt slowed the car, pulling into a dark parking lot a few blocks from her apartment. "I live around here."

"It's late." Penny thumbed apologetically toward the setting sun. Twilight was rapidly becoming night, especially here, where the last fingers of sunlight were blocked by sloped, peeling rooftops. The apartment complexes around the lot rose to cocoon the car in a nest of darkness. "I texted my landlord from the bus that we'd be running late, and he said he'd wait up for me. He's being really nice letting me check in after hours, and I don't want to push my luck. Plus, I promised I'd call my mother as soon as I arrived."

Penny patted herself on the back for the last addition. If he knew that her mother was expecting a call, he'd leave her alone. *Isn't that how it always works in the movies?* This was Hollywood, after all. Men and women were supposed to be glamorous and charming and larger than life. Not fat, sweaty, and a little bit creepy.

Kurt threw the car into Park and sat back in his seat. He paused there for a mere second before reaching over to rest a hand lightly on her thigh. "Just one cup of coffee."

Penny struggled to swallow. How had she ever assumed this man was a Good Samaritan? She'd heard horror stories. They just weren't supposed to happen to her.

"I'm sorry, but I'm not interested. Like I said, my mother's waiting for me to call. My boyfriend will be worried if I don't let him know I made it."

"Uh-huh," Kurt grunted, clearly not falling for Penny's shtick. "Your boyfriend in Illinois? You need someone here, someone who can show you the ropes, teach you the tricks. Give you the connections you need."

"I'm really not interested, thank you."

Penny slipped one hand against the door handle and discreetly tried to pull. It had gotten locked somewhere along their drive. Her heart rate rose, pumping in her throat as panic set in. It was happening to her.

All those movies she'd seen where pretty young girls got kidnapped. All the awful newspaper clippings her friends had taped to her notebooks to scare her into staying put. She was going to die, here in Hollywood, as an unknown. At the hands of a man who smelled like stale Doritos.

"I think I'll walk from here," Penny said. "If you could let me out—"

He leaned over, aimed his sticky lips at Penny's. She managed to dodge the worst of it, but still his mouth pressed against her neck, and she felt the disgusting heat of him as it played over her skin in a filthy little orchestra of sweat and shock.

She gasped, unable to scream. Penny knew she should scream, knew she should pull out the pepper spray her mother had fastened to her backpack, but she was too startled. Frozen.

Finally, her brain clicked back on, and she fumbled for the door handle, her fingers toying with the lock. They shook so thoroughly she'd never understand how she managed to depress the button, but eventually, she fell through the doorway and piled in a heap on the pavement. Her backpack landed on top of her, though the larger suitcase remained captive in the trunk, put there by Kurt himself in what Penny had wrongfully assumed was a display of gentlemanly manners.

"Don't you dare come near me." Penny crab-walked backward, not caring that her pale-pink panties with hopeful little sunflowers embroidered on them were exposed to the world. She was oblivious to the fact that gravel had dug into her hands and knees, leaving tiny trails of blood as she scraped herself away from him. "I'm calling the police! *Help!*" Finally, Penny found her voice and screamed again. "Someone help!"

"Whatever, you fat fuck." Kurt merely shrugged, reached over, and shut the door. He rolled down the window, stared at her with vacant eyes that told Penny he'd done this before. "You're all the same, you know. You come here with big dreams, but none of you make it. You just take the shit jobs nobody else wants, thinking one day it'll pay off and you'll be famous."

Penny scrambled to her feet, her hand finding the pepper spray and pulling it out. She aimed it at him but couldn't bring herself to press the trigger. A part of Penny still couldn't believe this was happening.

"None of this will pay off, honey," he said. "You're not pretty enough, not talented enough, not lucky enough—none of you are. Y'all come in here by the busload with big shiny eyes. Some of you last longer than others. You?" He scanned Penny from head to toe. "You won't last longer'n a week."

Penny depressed the trigger. The pepper spray shot forward, but Kurt was already screeching out of the parking lot, leaving Penny to cough, tear up, and hunch in pain from her own defense.

She crumbled then, right there on the ground. Bloody knees, broken spirit. She pulled out her phone, intent to call the cops. She wouldn't be weak! She was strong, confident, beautiful—despite what he'd said. She was different. She refused to fade into obscurity like the others.

But as she typed the numbers 911 into her phone, her eyes blurred. What would she tell the cops when they arrived? That a man named Kurt had attacked her? Kurt probably wasn't his real name. The best description she had of him was that he smelled of Doritos and had sweat on his brow.

Dark hair, average build, a standard face. She had no clue of his license plate, and the best she could do on the car make and model was that it was a maroonish sedan and wasn't brand new. She'd never been one to have a knowledge of cars or to care, and tonight was no different.

As for the attack—*what* attack? Penny thought back, her face flushing with embarrassment. He'd rested a hand on her leg and tried to kiss her. She'd gone berserk. What woman hadn't had a man do something of the sort? It happened all the time. Every day.

Her mind went through all the scenarios, and eventually, they all circled back to the same thing. The police wouldn't lift a finger. This was Los Angeles. There were television shows made about the LAPD and their wild cases. A young woman who was brand new to town and offended because a man had tried to invite her up to his apartment for a cup of coffee? Not even a blip on their radar.

Her suitcase was the biggest issue. The bastard had taken nearly everything she owned. He'd cleaned her right out. Her clothes, her pajamas, her underwear. The pillowcase she'd brought to remind her of home. Her little diaries filled with musings about what it would be like moving across the country—alone. Her diary hadn't included anything like this.

Penny's hands dampened with perspiration from anger and frustration. It wasn't as if she could just replace everything she owned with the snap of her fingers. While some things were priceless, others cost money. Thankfully, Penny had smartly stashed her valuables—keys, wallet, phone—in her backpack to keep them close. But that wouldn't help her get dressed in the morning. The only article of clothing she had left was the dress on her back.

She'd need to replace her lost items with *something*, and at the moment, that task felt impossible. Penny would have about $52 to her name after paying the deposit, along with the first and last month's rent, on her apartment. She'd have to choose between restocking her closet and eating food until she could find a job. Not exactly the warm welcome to the city that she'd anticipated.

Why was it? Penny mused. Why was it that mothers spouted such nice, pretty phrases to their little girls about having big ambitions and bigger dreams? They were conditioned to plump their daughters full of confidence and excitement and then set them free in the world. But they forgot to warn their baby girls about men like Kurt.

Why bother carefully crafting Jenga-like formations of hope in their daughters' hearts if only to have the pieces toppled by men smelling of stale chips? Penny had rolled into the City of Angels hoping to see stars in the sky, expecting to see stars beneath her feet. Stars, stars, stars.

But as Penny looked up, the sky was dusty with pollution and flooded with artificial brightness. There wasn't a glimmer of natural light. And beneath her feet were nothing but cigarette butts and discarded liquor bottles, the famed walk of stars somewhere far, far away. Penny couldn't help but feel that the very dream that had carried her here had dissipated in an instant. Vanished like the stars.

Then again, Penny was different. Kurt would find out soon enough that Penny wasn't quite as innocent as she looked. With a twinge of guilt, she reached into the pocket of her dress—a nifty little feature for Penny's nifty little hobby—and pulled out an expensive watch. She raised it to her nose and took a sniff. The faint scent of Doritos lingered, though it was nothing a little polishing couldn't take care of.

She wiped the clock face against the fabric of her clothes and wondered how a man as awful as Kurt had secured an authentic Rolex. Another familiar twinge of guilt nudged Penny into remembering that she had a conscience. But Penny wasn't in the mood to deal with her conscience, so she talked back.

Kurt was the one to blame in this mess. He'd all but attacked her. Penny had only nicked the watch from his cup holder as a reminder. A reminder that she could look at whenever she was feeling down—a reminder that she had survived worse.

Was it really a crime to steal from a thief? Kurt had taken everything from her. Her suitcase, her excitement, her hope. He'd even tried to take her body and make it his. Kurt was a bad man. He didn't deserve nice things.

And it was with a feeling of quiet justification that Penny tucked the watch back into her pocket and felt her lips turn into a slight smile. *All's fair in love and war.* Penny might have lost the battle, but she wasn't a victim. She had taken her own little prisoner of war, and she had earned it. If she pawned it, maybe it'd feed her for the next few weeks. Or she could keep it, like she kept all her other precious trinkets...

Penny found her apartment eventually. It took twenty minutes to wake the landlord, a man who looked like an extra out of *The Sopranos*. He held a cat in his arms and a cigarette perched between his lips, his dark hair combed back in greasy little rows.

"I thought this was a no-smoking building," Penny said. "I just assumed... Maybe you have a lease I could read over or something?"

"Why?" he grunted, stepping out of his ground-floor apartment. "You pay me, and I leave you alone. We don't need a lease. You're just lucky I let you check in late. If we had a lease, you'd see the office hours stopped at 6:00 p.m., and I'd have to kick you out until morning."

Penny didn't have the funds or energy to be tossed out on the street for the rest of the night, so she stifled a sigh and gave a shrug of her shoulders. Looking satisfied, the man introduced himself as Lucky and left his door open behind him as he made his way upstairs. A loud TV blasted from inside, and the smell of animals and old smoke was enough to make Penny gag.

She climbed behind him to the second-level apartment. He let her in, handed over a key while she traded him for the check she'd kept safely stashed in her bra. The last of her money. Her final crumbs of financial security.

Penny cleared her throat as she stepped into a bare room. "I thought the ad said that the apartment was furnished."

The screen on the window was torn. Old wooden floorboards creaked even before she stepped on them, and the kitchen counter—a white, cracked lacquered surface—was stained with an unidentifiable substance. A bed frame sat in the corner, but there was no mattress. A dresser missing three of its drawers was pushed against one wall. It was painfully obvious the carpeting in the sad excuse for a living room hadn't been vacuumed.

Penny turned to look for Lucky's response, but he was already gone. A door on the first floor slammed shut, and the television cranked up a few notches. Someone yelled for a glass of water above her. Moans filtered through the open window, dreadfully loud as two voices—one male, one female—rose in an excitable crescendo toward an inevitable finish.

Penny's very heart sagged. She sat on the floor of a studio apartment that was costing her over $1,300 a month. Penny didn't swear (good Midwestern Catholic girl that she was), but this place was a piece of shit.

Her phone rang. She took it out, saw her mother's number, and pushed back the tears threatening to fall.

"Mama?" Penny answered. "How are you?"

"I've been worried! You were supposed to call me the second you arrived. According to the bus schedule, you should've been there forty minutes ago."

"I'm just getting to my apartment. Sorry to worry you."

"So?" Her mother's voice hinged on the brink of terror and excitement. "Tell me all about it. Can you see the Hollywood sign from your apartment? Did you meet anyone famous yet?"

"It's amazing. Just magnificent." Penny pulled herself to her feet, made her way to the window, and glanced out at her view of a dumpster where a woman was currently tugging her skirt down and pocketing money in her bra. A man climbed into a car and reversed down the alley.

Penny bit her lip and stifled a sob. Then she glanced at the Rolex sitting on her cracked countertop and took a deep, steadying breath as she reached for it. She clutched it in her fingers so hard her hand knotted in a fist.

"Just wait until you hear all about it, Mama," she said, releasing her grip on the watch and draping it over her wrist, admiring the look of her dirty, dirty secret. "You won't believe the people I've met."

TRANSCRIPT

Prosecution: Mrs. Tate, how long have you worked in the publishing industry?

Eliza Tate: This is the only job I've ever had.

Prosecution: How many years? Ballpark is fine.

Eliza Tate: Over a decade.

Prosecution: I'm assuming you consider yourself a professional, then, after ten-plus years in the business. You've thrown launch parties, organized readings and signings, facilitated book club discussions.

Defense: Your Honor, is there a question here?

Prosecution: Mrs. Tate, have you ever facilitated a literary event before?

Eliza Tate: Of course. Plenty of them.

Prosecution: And in your extensive experience,

have you ever had a book club discussion turn to a plot for murder?

Eliza Tate: No.

Prosecution: Are you telling me, Mrs. Tate, that you didn't discuss the subject of murder on the afternoon of February 13, 2019, with Anne Wilkes, Penny Sands, and Marguerite Hill?

Eliza Tate: I don't remember everything we talked about. We had a lot of wine. We discussed a lot of things. Do you remember everything you talked about on February 13?

Prosecution: I don't. But I would certainly remember if I'd made plans to murder a man.

THREE

Nine Months Before
May 2018

Carpe diem, Eliza," Harold droned. "This really is an opportunity for you."

Eliza folded her hands in front of her stiff posture. Her nails, carefully manicured, were painted bone white. She'd dressed to impress for what she'd thought would be the announcing of her (well-deserved) promotion. Eliza smoothed down her custom-cut pantsuit, then touched her hair, which she'd had done in an elegant blowout especially for the occasion.

"Eliza?" Harold pressed. "Say something, doll. I know this is a shock, but I need you to tell me you understand. Please don't stand there in silence."

"Very well, then." Eliza cleared her throat, smiled sweetly at her boss. "Fuck you, Harold."

"Come on now. Don't do me like this. You and I have been friends for ages."

"You know as well as I do that I deserve that promotion."

"We're cutting costs. The publishing industry isn't what it used to be. You've seen the changes coming. We have to survive."

"The publishing industry is thriving," Eliza said through gritted teeth. "You still have your job, don't you?"

"Doll—"

"Don't try to sweet-talk me, Harold." Eliza's entire body shook, but she took a deep breath and moved her hands behind her back to cover the tremble. "You could have saved my job if you wanted, but you didn't. At least have the balls to be honest."

"Now, Eliza—"

She was already gone. Eliza had turned on her shiny new heels and stomped down the hall. She didn't bother to clear out her office. Her assistant could do that for her later and ship her any personal items left behind.

Eliza frowned at the thought. She wasn't big on personal items. That was for the other 98 percent of women who bought books like Marguerite Hill's *Take Charge*. Books that Eliza helped shepherd into the world, books she helped shove down consumers' throats with their messages of *Happy, happy, happy!* and *You can do this!*

It was all bullshit. Bullshit on a silver platter that she expertly placed on airport bookshelves so that working moms and jet-setting women could select a feel-good read to display proudly on their tray tables during flight. She sold a promise.

A promise, Eliza thought as she pounded her finger against the elevator button, *that will always end up crushed beneath the feet of someone bigger, bolder, richer, stronger*. All these women would ever gain from buying self-help crap were fragments of hope.

Eliza hopped into her convertible, a luxurious white thing that the bonus from her last promotion had bought her, before pulling out of the parking lot and easing onto the streets of Beverly Hills. Flicking down her mirror, she swiped on an extra smudge of blood-red lipstick to fortify her defiance.

Let them fire me, she raged internally. *They don't know what they're missing*. To hell with Harold, to hell with her assistant, to hell with them all.

She would show them. Not in the *rah-rah-rah* ways of Marguerite's book but in the ways of Eliza Tate. Let the battle begin, and let it be raw, bloody, and brutal.

She smiled at herself in the rearview mirror, her lips bleeding bright, and settled a pair of oversize sunglasses over her eyes.

Yes, she thought. *This is only the beginning.*

Eliza noted the absence of her husband's vehicle when she arrived home. She wasn't surprised to find she'd arrived first, seeing as he taught acting classes at his studio several nights a week.

The Tate house was located in a rich development not a mile north of Beverly Hills. Eliza could have easily walked to her office, but that would have defeated the purpose of her expensive car. She glanced over her shoulder but couldn't see the road through a tall fence that blocked most of the tourists from peeping into the sweeping, open windows that lined the front of their home.

Once inside, Eliza kicked off a pair of gorgeous shoes that Roman had given her to celebrate something or other. She basked in peaceful silence for a long moment before climbing the stairs to her bedroom. She changed out of her pantsuit and hung it carefully, like a thin piece of tissue paper, to preserve for another day.

After changing into a set of yoga pants and a tank top she'd picked up at T.J. Maxx, she headed back downstairs. Grabbing a bucket, mop, and gloves, Eliza armed herself for a whole new battle as she set to work scrubbing the floor of her shiny, mostly stainless-steel kitchen.

It was fascinating, even to Eliza, how quickly she could shed one layer of herself and slip into another. Work Eliza and Home Eliza were two very different people, and she kept both personas on tap, ready to dispense either when necessary.

In the professional environment, Eliza naturally excelled. She'd always been good at work, work, work. Rules, rules, rules. Things that made sense. She'd grown up as the straight-A, extra-credit-obsessed, quietly serious student. Those skills had helped her develop into a no-nonsense, capable employee all bosses loved. Eliza thrived on friendly competition and fat, twinkly gold stars.

When evenings rolled around, Eliza would slink home and, like a chameleon, peel off her first skin and sink into her second. She admired those individuals who could be themselves all the time, regardless of their audience. Genuine people—that's what they were called. That wasn't possible for Eliza, not if she wanted to survive.

"Honey!" The front door opened in sync with Roman's greeting, startling Eliza from her spot on the floor. He came around the corner, his face changing to an expression of surprise. "Did Andrea forget her cleaning day again?"

Eliza directed a weak smile toward her husband. Her darling, naive husband. She'd been bewitched with the stunning Roman Tate the first time she laid eyes on him. Football star, theater major, well-dressed man in her English class—Roman had been an anomaly. One flash of his charming smile and Eliza had fallen head over heels for her husband before she'd even known his name.

The man still had a presence. Tall and broad-shouldered, Roman had the windswept, dark hair of a movie star. His skin was a glorious shade of tan. Roman liked to let people think he was Italian, but Eliza knew the only genuine Italian flare Roman had in him was the hint of fresh basil she had added to the previous night's pasta dish.

"No, Andrea didn't forget to come," Eliza said. "I thought I told you—I had to fire the cleaning lady."

"Are we talking about the same girl?" Roman frowned. "Curly hair? I liked her. What happened?"

"My grandmother's china disappeared."

"Ah, well." Roman flashed a quick smile. "We never used that china anyway. Would you like me to hire someone else?"

"No, no," Eliza said. "Don't waste your time. I've already taken care of it."

"Very good." Roman gave a happy nod. "Where did you get that shirt? Is it...new?"

"Oh God. How embarrassing." With a flushed face, Eliza looked down and noted her shirt had a stain above one breast, and worse, her pants had a hole in them. She'd have to be more careful. "I didn't expect you home so soon, or I'd have changed into something nicer."

Roman moved into the kitchen and set his briefcase on the counter. His hands reached for Eliza and pulled her to her feet, then spun her around. They began to work their magic on Eliza's shoulders. She rolled her neck back and forth, closed her eyes. She could almost pretend that life was perfect in moments like this.

"It doesn't matter what you're wearing," Roman whispered in her ear. "You're still gorgeous. I've been thinking of you all day."

Eliza squirmed out of his grasp, giving a reluctant giggle against the tickle of his breath on her skin. "I'm in the middle of tidying up. We have the neighbors coming by for dinner tomorrow, remember?"

Eliza inched her way to the sink and busied herself washing dishes left over from breakfast. She paused when she came to a knife covered in peanut butter. It was a beautiful knife that had come as a special gift from a special friend. Anne Wilkes, Eliza's college roommate and current best friend, had given her the knife, along with a matching cake server and two spoons, on her wedding day. Each had Eliza's and Roman's names carved into the handle along with their anniversary.

"I thought we agreed to save these utensils for special occasions," Eliza said, not quite meeting Roman's eyes. "They're so beautiful; it's a shame to get them caked with peanut butter."

"Why have beautiful things if you don't use them?"

Roman stepped behind Eliza and inched closer still, sliding his arms over her belly. His legs were clad in dark jeans, and he wore a white V-neck shirt underneath a zip-up black sweater. He smelled familiar, sweet, expensive. She closed her eyes and took a breath.

As if sensing the change in Eliza's demeanor, her husband reached for her rubber gloves and peeled them from her arms. Tossed them into the sink. Spun her around, pressed his lips to hers.

Eliza felt her breath sigh out as he molded his body to hers and deepened the kiss, settling into a lovely, familiar rhythm. When his fingers hooked over the edge of her yoga pants, her entire body sizzled.

He teased her with his fingers through the soft fabric, dipped his head as his tongue flicked against her skin and sent shivers racing across her body. Then he pressed into her, took her against the kitchen counter, and sent Eliza's mind into a black spiral as they moved together until finally, she called his name as they collapsed into one another.

Roman winked, then backed away. He broke into a low whistle as he turned on a heel and sauntered out of the kitchen. With flushed cheeks, Eliza looked and saw the window open. *The neighbors*, she thought briefly before she adjusted her bra strap and set the coffee maker to brew.

When it was done and she had two cups in hand, she followed Roman's path from the kitchen and found him in his office. He closed his laptop when he heard her enter, slamming it shut a bit too swiftly before swiveling to face her.

"What is it?" Roman accepted a mug of coffee from Eliza. "When you look at me like that, I know you've got something on your mind."

"I quit my job today." Eliza leaned against the wall, feigning nonchalance.

"Why?"

"I've decided to start my own company."

"I thought you liked your job?"

Eliza ran a finger around the rim of her mug. "If I'd stayed where I was, I would always be second to Harold. It's time I started something of my own."

"Well, you know I support you." Roman paused to consider, then shook his head in time with a deep chuckle. "If anyone can succeed at starting their own company, it's you."

"Thank you," she said briskly. "I hoped you'd see things that way."

Roman turned back to his computer, signaling the conversation was complete. Trembling from the anxiety of it all, Eliza dragged herself upstairs into their bedroom, straight into their beautifully remodeled shower. She studied the eye-wateringly expensive bottles of soaps and shampoos from high-end boutiques, knowing that she'd filled them with knockoff replacements from Target. It was all a façade. Everything was a façade.

Flicking the shower on, Eliza climbed under the stream of hot, hot water. She scrubbed and scrubbed, her fingernails raking angry paths down her arms. She washed herself until her skin was red and raw and she was cleansed of the lies. Then she climbed out of the shower and studied her bedraggled, bare face in the mirror.

Sick with the weight of secrets, Eliza plodded barefoot and naked into her walk-in closet. She selected the fluffiest robe in her collection and wrapped it around her body. Then she knelt and very carefully pulled out a box.

She fingered her grandmother's fine china. One of the teacups was broken, chipped. She'd dropped it in her haste to hide the collection from Roman just before she'd fired Andrea.

Eliza ran a hand over the sharp edge, let it prick at her skin. And she wondered with a heavy heart when the rest of her life would shatter into pieces and the lies behind the curtain would pour forth into the world.

TRANSCRIPT

Prosecution: Ms. Sands, when did Eliza Tate discover that you were having an affair with her husband?

Penny Sands: I'm not sure. You'll have to ask her.

Prosecution: What if you had to guess?

Penny Sands: I suppose she probably knew the night I met her at the Pelican Hotel.

Prosecution: Did you and Eliza become friends at any point over the past year?

Penny Sands: I thought so.

Prosecution: And you didn't think that was odd? That Mrs. Tate would befriend her husband's mistress?

Penny Sands: Maybe a little. I just assumed she didn't know about me and Roman.

Prosecution: But you just stated for the court that you suspected Eliza Tate knew about you and Roman at the Pelican Hotel.

Penny Sands: I said I didn't know for certain, but you made me guess. In retrospect, I think Eliza knew a lot more than she let on. Eliza always knows more than she lets on.

Prosecution: What makes you say that?

Penny Sands: When Eliza Tate invited me into her home, I suspect she knew exactly what she was doing.

Prosecution: Why did you go?

Penny Sands: Because I was curious. Curiosity killed the cat, I guess.

Prosecution: Interesting choice of words, Ms. Sands. On February 13, whose idea was it to discuss murder at book club?

FOUR

Eight Months Before
June 2018

Penny hunched forward in her seat, scribbling notes in cramped handwriting to preserve the pages of the notebook her mother had sent to celebrate her twenty-seventh birthday. As an actress, a creator, a writer, an artist, there was nothing Penny loved more than the sight of a fresh notebook or the accompanying gleam of ink when pen touched virgin paper. The options were endless in that split second before ideas were ruined by reality.

The gift was more cherished by Penny than ever because she no longer had the luxury of purchasing a new notebook every time the whim struck. She couldn't run to the local art store and browse the rainbow selection of pens. She couldn't choose several at random and add them to her credit card tab, knowing it would be paid off at the end of the month by a steady salary.

Over the past month, Penny's credit card had become a revolving door, never quite in the black, her bank account never quite plump enough to provide any sort of cushion. Everything Penny made, she scrimped and saved and spent on her education. Writing courses—everything from stand-up comedy to TV pilots to a Second City sketch class—acting workshops, directing classes, any and all free seminars she could find.

Meanwhile, her cupboard was thinly stocked with a bag of dry white rice. She'd learned the hard way that it took ages and ages to boil the cheap bag of red kidney beans from the store. She'd also learned that beans gave her awful heartburn, a symptom she'd grown intimate with because Tums were alarmingly expensive and didn't fit into her new budget.

"Stop." A hand reached down, fingertips coming to rest on her notebook.

Penny vaguely became aware that the voice washed over her from above. The voice of her favorite instructor. He spoke with a staccato, slightly accented tone that lilted with passion and had become comfortingly familiar over the past six weeks.

When Penny had found this class amid a sea of others, she'd glommed on to it, immediately knowing that this time, it was different. He was different. She was different because of him. She couldn't hand over her credit card fast enough to pay for more sessions from the marvelous Roman Tate.

She glanced at the male hand that covered her paper, noted the sturdiness of it. The dark hair that crept up his arm, slid under his shirt, and peeped out the collar of his V-neck.

"S-sorry," Penny stuttered. "I didn't realize—"

"You're missing everything." Roman didn't seem to be chastising. Merely disappointed by her lack of understanding. "Come."

"Where?"

"With me." He beckoned for Penny to follow him onstage. "You won't learn anything by scratching notes on that pad of yours. You learn by doing."

Penny felt the eyes of twenty-plus students watching as one foot moved forward. Nerves flicked around her peripheral, but she battled them back. She raised her chin higher. It was now or never. She hadn't moved out to Los Angeles to soak in a tub of mediocrity.

"What now?" Penny asked once onstage.

Roman's face melted into a smile as if he sensed there'd been a change in Penny's attitude. He seemed to like it.

"Good girl," he murmured, but only for her ears. Before turning to face the class, he gave her a private wink. "I'd like everyone to learn a valuable lesson from Ms. Sands. Taking notes, reading from a book, watching films—while these practices are essential to becoming a strong actor, they are just the beginning."

He strode with long legs over to the side of the stage and flipped a switch. The theater went dark, and the stage gleamed under the spotlights. Penny couldn't see anything but stars. *Stars, stars, stars*, she thought. Not the sort she'd been hoping to find.

"Take a look at this scene." Roman approached her, gave her a short page. "Get the gist of it."

"I can't memorize anything that fast."

"Aha. I don't want you to memorize. I want you to take what's written and make it your own."

Penny's heart pulsed against those thin little seedlings growing in her chest. "I'm not good at improv. I prefer to get comfortable with a script before I act."

Roman contemplated this, resting his hands behind his back as he faced the class. "Tell me, Penny, have you ever experienced a time while acting onstage, writing in your journal, or simply daydreaming where you completely and utterly lost yourself in the moment?"

She cleared her throat. "Um—"

"Where the world blacked out around you? Maybe you had the music turned up so that it pulsed through your veins. Your eyes might have closed, your breathing stopped, your heart raced."

He paused, letting the words soak in as Penny shivered in anticipation. His voice was like liquid sex. Smooth and sultry, mesmerizing. She'd never met a man quite like him, and as he continued to speak, she found her eyes closing, her core pulsing, as she drifted away on the silky river of Roman Tate's words.

"Close your eyes," Roman instructed. "Everyone."

Penny's eyes were already closed. She didn't care if anyone else listened; all that mattered was this experience. It felt revolutionary, as if she'd taken some drug, fallen down a transcendent, *Alice in Wonderland*–type hole. She needed Roman to continue more than she needed her next breath.

"Maybe it was an action scene, the thirst for blood so strong, you could taste it. The soundtrack beating through your skull, taking you onto a battlefield during the Second World War." Roman stilled, the room halted. Not a soul breathed. "Or maybe it was a scene of passion, a moment of lust."

Penny couldn't tell if she was imagining it or if the feel of a man's breath on her neck was real. Her eyes closed tighter. Her hands balled into fists. She heated from the inside, filled with a rampant surge of want teased from the depths of her spirit.

"A moment of untamed desire," Roman said as if reading Penny's thoughts. "Of the desperate coupling of two souls in wild, manic love."

Penny wasn't imagining it. She could smell his cologne now, feel his breath on her exposed shoulder. She wondered if it was his finger tracing down the bare skin of her back or if she was imagining that, too.

"Sweaty sheets, tangled limbs, moans that start slowly, involuntarily." Roman's voice was a mere whisper, yet it boomed throughout the studio and kept his audience transfixed. His words grew louder, louder, as he continued. "Until together, with the dark desires of forbidden lovers, the two shout each other's names into the ether…"

The silence was intense.

"And then break into pieces."

Roman's footsteps carried him away from Penny, leaving her to wonder if she'd imagined his breath, his touch. If she'd begun to fall under the spell of Roman Tate.

"Let's try this again." Flipping another switch, Roman brought the studio back under harsh spotlight. "Tell me, Penny, have you ever experienced a moment while acting that took you to another place entirely?"

She began to speak, but her voice didn't work. It felt broken, out of practice, hoarse. When she cleared her throat, Roman smiled as if he knew the charm he'd cast over her.

"Yes," she said finally. "At times, I suppose I get carried away."

"Indeed." Roman's lips twitched in her direction. "See me after class, will you, Penny?"

"But—" She glanced listlessly at the script in her hand. Her shoulders sagged, and she felt drained of energy. Exhausted, like she might after a particularly intense round of lovemaking. Her creativity had sizzled and then fizzled in the time she'd been onstage. "I thought you wanted me to do a scene?"

"I think my point has been made." Roman easily turned toward the sea of students. "That will be all for now, Ms. Sands. Please take your seat."

Penny returned to the torn fabric on her chair and slid her notebook in front of her. She was so distracted, so hot and bothered, that she didn't notice what happened onstage for the rest of the hour.

It was as if she'd turned a new leaf. Something in Roman's words had stirred a new longing in her, bringing about a transformation that was all too welcome. She no longer felt broken by her lackluster experiences in a new city. She no longer felt vulnerable and weary, out of control. Instead, she felt empowered. Somehow, she'd experienced a patch of greatness, of genius, in a dingy theater off Sunset Boulevard, surrounded by aspiring actors.

They don't understand, she thought dully, gazing around at her classmates. *They want the fame, the glory, the prestige.*

Penny wanted to be an artist. Her very spirit craved it, desired the freedom of expression, the life-changing, soul-twisting call for something greater.

It suddenly seemed that only one man in the entire city—maybe the entire world—understood her. The need to create, to bring to life scenes of blood and death so realistic, an audience could taste the filmy copper on their tongues as they watched life seep away on a screen. Or to bring a burning desire to the audience, spurring racing heartbeats as two forbidden lovers came together on the pages of a screenplay in a sweeping culmination of lust and denial.

Yes, Penny thought. Only one man understood her, and that man stood tall and stately onstage, an undiscovered gem of talent in a sea of shiny stars.

That was when it hit her.

Somehow, over the course of a month and a half, Penny Sands had fallen madly, hopelessly, desperately in love with Roman Tate. And he wanted to see her after class—alone.

TRANSCRIPT

Defense: Ms. Moore, how long have you been babysitting for the Wilkes family?

Olivia Moore: On and off for the last three years. I found the job listing on a corkboard at UCLA when I was a freshman.

Defense: How often would you say you babysit for the Wilkes family?

Olivia Moore: It goes in spurts. Sometimes, it's every other week. Other times, we go a few months without touching base.

Defense: And what's the typical length of time you watch the Wilkes children?

Olivia Moore: Under normal circumstances, oh, I'd say anywhere between two and six hours depending on the evening.

Defense: Have there ever been extenuating circumstances?

Olivia Moore: Excuse me?

Defense: You said under normal circumstances. I'm wondering why you said that, if circumstances have been anything other than what you'd classify as normal.

Olivia Moore: Well, there was one time that I watched the kids for a little while longer. That was just because Mark needed help, and it was the right thing to do.

Defense: Mark—you mean, Detective Wilkes?

Olivia Moore: Yes.

Defense: Where was his wife?

Olivia Moore: We didn't know. That was the problem.

Defense: How long was Anne Wilkes gone?

Olivia Moore: Three days.

Defense: Where did she go?

Olivia Moore: I don't know the answer to that.

Defense: She didn't tell you where she was going?

Olivia Moore: Not exactly. She just walked out one night…and didn't come back.

FIVE

Eight Months Before
June 2018

One month after Anne followed her husband for the first time, she was ready to go again. It had taken her several weeks to build up the confidence to return to the chase. But now that her confidence was raring to go, Anne could hardly wait to get answers. In a twisted way, she was almost looking forward to it.

Anne hadn't taken control of her life in far too long. She'd let herself become complacent, a victim to motherhood, mediocrity, and busyness. In taking charge of her situation—by demanding answers— Anne had awakened a layer of defiance in herself that she hadn't exposed to oxygen in years.

For the past fourteen years, she'd been Mark Wilkes's wife. A devoted wife to a decorated cop, second only to her title of loving mother of four rambunctious children. She was homemaker, support system, chef, maid, and shoulder to cry on. But that was about to change.

"I'll be back in a few hours," Anne told her mother. "I was supposed to meet Mark for dinner, but he's working late. I'm meeting a mother from playgroup instead."

Beatrice Harper had flown in two days before, and Anne was deviously planning to use the built-in childcare to fuel her new amateur detective hobby. It was fair, really. Payback for her mother's visit.

Beatrice only came to visit her daughter at Christmas and at

Easter. This special trip was disguised as a checkup for Anne, and Anne didn't appreciate it. She was fine. *Fine, fine, fine.* She wouldn't be surprised if her mother and husband had colluded to babysit Anne, and that was ridiculous.

As Anne bid goodbye to her mother, she donned her trusty purse and scooped up the car keys to her old soccer-mom van. Glancing back at the house she and Mark had scrambled so desperately to afford, she wondered if it had all been worth it. They'd saved and saved, cut corners and budgeted. Worked overtime and begged loan officers for better news.

When they'd finally purchased the house, it hadn't had a lick of furniture for a month. Anne and Mark had wanted to buy everything new, everything together—start their married lives with bright, fresh furniture.

They'd made love on the floor the first night in their house. They'd moved from the living room to the kitchen counter to the carpet in the walk-in bedroom closet. They'd giggled, dreaming of the furniture they'd someday buy. And when they'd bought the bed and the couch and the kitchen table, they'd made love on all of them, too.

With four kids, it was expected that the romance would eventually slide. But Anne hadn't lost the gut-twisting love she had for Mark; it just came out in different ways. When he brought home sunflowers—her favorite—from the farmer's market, it gave her butterflies. When he held the twins on his lap and read them silly books in silly voices, her heart melted. So why was he throwing it all away?

Tonight was the last night she'd wonder. Unbeknownst to her husband, she'd installed a tracking app on his phone. This whole evening had been planned, step by step. Anne would know her husband's secrets no matter the cost.

This is it, Anne told herself. She could feel it in her bones. Call it motherly intuition or a wife's instinct, but Anne was convinced she'd found the root cause of her husband's disappearing act.

The dot on the map that signified the location of her husband's phone had left work an hour ago, then beeped in a line across Los Angeles to a small nook in Culver City where it had come to a stop.

Anne had plugged the coordinates into her own GPS and followed the directions across the city. She passed bustling Culver City, a quaint little town complete with cutesy book shops and newfangled Mexican fusion restaurants. A Trader Joe's had recently popped up, and a Whole Foods was rumored to be moving in across the road.

The street where Anne found her husband's car was not part of this up-and-coming neighborhood. It was part of a neighborhood riddled with overflowing trash cans and vehicles parked every which way, making two-lane streets a one-lane obstacle course. Police didn't bother handing out parking tickets around here. They had bigger problems.

Anne watched a possum crawl out of a garbage can and skitter through the darkness into overgrown bushes that had made the walkway to one apartment complex all but impossible to navigate. It was with a jolt of surprise that she spotted Mark approaching that very building. He strolled to a stop and perched against the gate to wait.

Tucking her minivan behind a moving truck a few blocks back, Anne settled in to watch. She could see Mark clearly (the binoculars helped with that), but unless Mark was really looking, he wouldn't see her in return. Anne's theory was tested as Mark ran a hand through his hair and cast a quick glance toward the road. His attention was focused back on the apartment complex before Anne could blink.

Even from her hiding spot, she could tell he was wearing his favorite pair of jeans—the ones stained by jelly from when Gretchen had thrown a fit a few months back and slapped her toast on her father's lap. Anne had worked on the stain for hours. Nothing had helped, and still, Mark had refused to throw them out. He said the stain was a badge of honor, and Anne had found that adorable.

Anne's patience was finally rewarded when a woman appeared at the gate to let Mark inside. The woman was...not a woman. She was a girl. Maybe eighteen? Definitely not older than twenty-two. Anne's insides blistered with betrayal.

The woman—*girl*—wore loose-fitting cotton sleep shorts and a sweater that hung off one shoulder to reveal a swatch of pale skin around her collarbone. The sort of outfit that looked casually sexy on today's youths with their pert little bodies and big, bright eyes. On Anne, the outfit would look laughable.

The girl unlatched the gate, then looked up at Mark with a smile. There was definite familiarity in her gaze. The two knew each other, a fact that was only confirmed when they embraced. She moved away first, a bounce to her step as she opened the gate farther and gestured for Mark to follow behind her. Anne watched, her throat growing dry, as her husband followed another woman into an unfamiliar apartment.

It was only when the door marked by a crooked number nine closed that the finality of the situation hit Anne. She expected to be hurt, devastated, appalled at the confirmation of her worst fears. Her husband was dating a child!

As Anne picked up one of her daughter's water bottles and slurped wine from the straw, it dawned on her that the emotions she was experiencing were faulty. Instead of the hurt she had prepared to feel, the only thing in her chest was the pilot light of rage that had been simmering for the past several weeks.

As Anne plunked the Mickey Mouse wine bottle back into the cup holder and pulled away from the curb, she knew... That pilot light would burst into an inferno if she wasn't careful.

TRANSCRIPT

Defense: Mrs. Wilkes, please describe your relationship with Eliza Tate. How did you meet?

Anne Wilkes: We were roommates in college. We've been good friends for a long, long time.

Defense: Are you still friends?

Anne Wilkes: As far as I know.

Defense: Were you being blackmailed, Mrs. Wilkes?

Anne Wilkes: Not exactly.

Defense: What if I told you we had evidence to the contrary?

Anne Wilkes: I'd ask who's the son of a bitch that spilled the beans.

Defense: So you were being blackmailed?

Anne Wilkes: If we're being honest here—

Defense: We are being honest. You've sworn to tell the truth.

Anne Wilkes: The truth is that I'm not the one on trial here. And apparently, motives are easy to come by in this case. Eliza's not the only one who wanted him dead, okay? That doesn't mean I killed him.

SIX

E liza hated asking for anything.

She stared into the water glass as she waited for the rest of her party to arrive, watching as sweat beaded on the outside and slipped down like raindrops on a window. A pool of water gathered on the table beneath her cup. She extended a hand and swiped listlessly at the dampness.

An attentive server jumped to attention, moving quickly to Eliza's side. He lifted her water glass without speaking, patted it down with a towel, then added a napkin beneath it. The whole thing was over and done within a matter of seconds.

Eliza hadn't always dined at expensive country clubs, worn sky-high heels, or splurged on weekly blowouts from the best salons in Beverly Hills. She'd grown up in Beijing under the watchful eyes of two incredibly strict parents. Eliza's mother and father had expected nothing but greatness from her, and when she inevitably achieved it, there was no reward. No pat on the back. To say they had been pleased with her accomplishments was a stretch.

Eliza had moved to the States just before college. She had enrolled at UCLA where she blew through an undergrad degree in three years, then rolled straight into a master's program. After graduation (and a quickie wedding), she'd gone on to secure a prestigious job at Thompson Public Relations along with a fat salary. She had risen rapidly through the ranks until she'd obtained a position second only to Harold. *Fucking Harold.*

Eliza had no plans to tell her parents she'd been laid off; they just might die from the shock of it. Her parents hadn't visited America in well over five years, and the last time they'd come, they'd spent the entire visit prodding her about the possibility of children. Before they'd left, her mother had said the next time they visited would be for the birth of Eliza's first child.

Eliza wondered if she'd ever see her family again.

Two beautiful figures arrived at the restaurant then, drawing Eliza from her daydreams as she pulled herself to her feet. She fought hard against the bile rising in her throat, biting down on her lip at the thought of the task that lay ahead of her.

"Good evening, Mr. and Mrs. Tate." Eliza stood, brushed her hands over the trim skirt covering her thighs, and smiled at her husband's parents. "I'm so pleased you could join me for dinner."

"We're very glad you reached out to us," Mrs. Tate said. "And for the millionth time, Eliza, call us Todd and Jocelyn."

Eliza smiled politely as she did every time her mother-in-law insisted Eliza call her by her first name. Not only would Eliza's upbringing not allow for such informalities, but deep down, she suspected both Todd and Jocelyn preferred the demure image of the daughter-in-law that Eliza had presented from the very start. Todd especially.

Eliza watched the handsome older man as he slid off a suit jacket and looked over his shoulder impatiently for a waiter to take it off his hands. Eliza had chosen Todd's country club as the location for their meeting because she'd known that making him comfortable, letting him feel superior and powerful, would give her the best chance of getting what she wanted. It didn't matter what Todd thought at the end of the day; Eliza held the reins. She didn't need to be bold and brash if she could daintily pluck each string just the way she wanted.

Todd had the chiseled look of a Hollywood star and often turned heads whenever they were out as a group. However, Todd Tate had no interest in the arts whatsoever and had made his money as some sort of financier. His lack of interest in creative pursuits made for dull discussions of Eliza's and Roman's careers at the Christmas dinner table.

Jocelyn Tate, however, was more interesting to Eliza. A small woman nearing seventy, she appeared outwardly to be in her early fifties. Her blond hair was kept up at the same expensive salon where Eliza received her weekly blowouts, and her figure remained trim through rigorous exercise routines and strict diets. She looked the part of a rich man's wife, but Eliza suspected that a peek below Jocelyn's veneered surface would lead to some peculiar secrets.

"It's lovely to see you, darling." Jocelyn sat first, gesturing for her daughter-in-law to follow suit. "We're sorry to hear Roman couldn't make it, but—"

"Is he still teaching those ridiculous classes?" Todd sat next, his legs spread wide, one arm sprawled over his wife's chair as if he owned the world. "The ones at that decrepit studio? Can't believe anyone buys into his nonsense."

Eliza gritted her teeth. Todd's habit of cutting his wife off every time she spoke had always grated on her. As her marriage progressed and the years ticked by, Eliza was finding it more and more difficult to keep her tongue in check.

"Roman loves his work." Eliza measured her words, feeling Jocelyn's eyes fix on her. "It's what initially drew us together, actually, but you've heard that story."

"Yeah, yeah. You met in one of those hippie classes," Todd muttered. "A theater degree. I still can't believe I paid fifty grand a year for my son to chase women and dance around onstage."

"Todd." Jocelyn's fingers trembled. "Eliza and I would like to enjoy our dinner without your colorful commentary."

Eliza looked down at her fork, studied it like it was a piece of art.

She'd never been under the illusion that Roman's parents' relationship was perfect, but recently she'd been seeing more and more cracks appear.

"Eliza knows I didn't mean anything by it." Todd eased back in his chair, daring his daughter-in-law to make a peep. "I've got nothing against the…" He hesitated and glanced at his wife. "I mean, those kinds of people. Hell, I just didn't think I'd ever see my son wearing tights."

"I apologize, Eliza." Jocelyn's fingers twisted her linen napkin before she seemed to realize her nervous tic was on full display. She spread the cloth in her lap, smoothed it before turning a pleasant expression back to the table. "Where were we?"

"Actually, I think we can probably order." Eliza gestured to the hovering server. "We can chat once the food has arrived. I'm sure everyone's hungry."

Jocelyn shot her a look that was torn in two—part relief, part something else. Almost as if she had been hankering for an argument. But the server arrived then, the Tate family ordered, and topical conversation ensued, pushing aside all threat of a full-on dinner disaster.

Eliza waited until halfway through dinner to engage the next steps of her plan. It was a delicate thing, and she couldn't rush it. Before she'd picked up the phone and dialed Jocelyn Tate to invite her to dinner, she'd thought long and hard about whether she wanted to do this. Whether she could do this.

Once her decision was made, Eliza set to finessing the details with the same level of painstaking accuracy that she put into her work. Eventually, the plan rolled into motion when Todd spotted one of his friends at a nearby table.

"It's Nathan!" Todd pushed his chair back and heaved himself to his feet. "I haven't seen the bastard in over a year. Traveling with his wife on a big European tour if I remember right. You ladies mind if I catch up with him? Don't wait on me to finish eating."

Todd didn't pretend to wait for a response before tossing his napkin on the chair and pushing his near-empty plate toward the center of the table. Jocelyn had barely touched her Niçoise salad while Eliza had made a valiant effort to nibble at the edges of her ahi tuna, but neither of the expensive platters was even halfway finished. Eliza's stomach churned, and she, too, pushed her plate away.

"Mrs. Tate," she began, then stopped when her mother-in-law put down her fork and stared intently back at Eliza.

"Yes?" Jocelyn pressed. "What do you need?"

"It's not..." Eliza swallowed, glancing at the napkin in her lap. "It's not like that."

Jocelyn lifted one petite shoulder in a shrug. "I'm not silly enough to believe you invited us here because you enjoy our company."

Eliza's lips parted in surprise. This was not going the way she'd intended. Usually, Eliza was the overprepared one in a room. She excelled at planning; she was known for obtaining fantastic results during work negotiations, even when the tables were turned against her. That wasn't the case this evening.

"That's not true," Eliza said weakly. "It's not that I don't enjoy your company."

"It's quite all right," Jocelyn said. "I believe you enjoy my company fine enough, but my husband can be quite intolerable."

Eliza's surprise morphed into shock.

Jocelyn sighed, then peered over her shoulder. Todd and Nathan had moved onto the ruddy, red-faced, too-loud-laughter portion of their discussion. "You'd better speak quickly if you'd like to discuss business before my husband returns."

Eliza tipped her chin upward and fought back the pink blush of embarrassment. "I did come here to ask a favor of you and your husband. And I'm afraid it's quite a large favor."

"I didn't imagine you'd call for something trivial."

"It's money. I've recently quit my job, and I'm branching out to start my own public relations company. I need more funding than what Roman and I have in our bank account."

A shrewd look twinkled in Jocelyn's eye, as if she knew something wasn't right. "Does Roman know you're meeting with us?"

"Mrs. Tate, I really don't want to bring my marriage into my business. As I stated earlier, the reason I asked you here on my own terms is because I don't want Roman's name dragged into our arrangement."

"It might be your business, but he's also your husband."

"And it's my personal promise that I'll pay you back," Eliza insisted. "I always make good on my promises."

"Yes, your vows mean something to you." Jocelyn again frowned at her lap. "I only wish I could say the same about my son."

"You warned me," Eliza blurted.

Even before the words came out of her mouth, she wished she could take them back. There'd been an unspoken agreement between Eliza and Jocelyn that they'd never speak of the moment in question ever again. The moment on her wedding day when, dressed in a beautiful white gown—paid for by the Tates, of course—Eliza had been warned by Jocelyn Tate that she was making a mistake.

The wedding had been in Vegas, much to the Tate family's dismay. For their only son, they'd envisioned a grand country-club wedding. A big to-do with a guest list ten pages long and a bill to match. Eliza's family had wanted the same for their daughter—or they would have if Eliza had taken the time to tell them she was getting married.

Everyone had assumed the whirlwind romance was due to an unfortunate accidental pregnancy. That Roman had knocked up Eliza, forcing the two to marry in a shotgun ceremony. However, when no baby came nine months later, a year later, ten years later, people stopped speculating and chalked up the union to a bizarre blip of fate.

Despite the clandestine nature of their elopement, Roman had decided to invite his parents along, never expecting they'd come. However, they had arrived toting a beautiful wedding dress in hand, a bouquet, a cake. Eliza had felt like a real bride. Until Jocelyn Tate approached as the wedding bells began to chime in the sticky-hot chapel and handed over a set of keys without speaking.

Eliza looked at them, confused.

"It's not too late," Mrs. Tate said. "I've only met you a handful of times, but I feel as if I know you. I know you'll be faithful. You're a hard worker. You will provide the lifestyle that Roman is looking for. That's probably why he's asked you to marry him."

"That's not true," Eliza said. "I don't have any money to my name. He's marrying me because he loves me."

"You might not be wealthy yet, but you recently landed a big job. What's your starting salary?" Mrs. Tate formed the question as if she wasn't really looking for an answer. "We both know you'll do quite well. So does Roman."

"But—"

"Do you think the timing is coincidental?" Mrs. Tate licked her lower lip, stalling. "Roman asked you to marry him days after you secured one of the most coveted jobs in the industry. There was an article on you in the *Hollywood News*—one of the women under thirty to watch."

The cold, hard metal keys landed in Eliza's hand. She could only stare at them.

"But I also know my son," Jocelyn continued. "I know my husband, and in a way, Roman and Todd aren't so very different."

Eliza had been bewildered by her comment. Todd was a close-minded, rich, often cruel man. Her husband-to-be had an artist's soul and a soft heart. He was marrying an immigrant, he loved the theater, he read poetry by night and played football by day. Roman was beautifully complex and wonderful and cared nothing for worldly things or money or fame. Eliza told Jocelyn all of it, that she was wrong.

"Things change," Jocelyn said with a weak smile. "You deserve to be happy."

"I am happy," Eliza whispered. "I love Roman. More than anything."

At the time, Eliza had meant it. Her mother-in-law seemed to understand. As soon as Eliza said those words, a light extinguished in Jocelyn's eyes as she reached for the keys and plucked them from Eliza's palm.

"Ah," she said briskly. "I was afraid of that."

Then she leaned forward and pressed a kiss to Eliza's forehead before leaving the back room and disappearing into the chapel to take a seat beside her husband.

Still reeling with confusion, Eliza had slipped the veil over her eyes and walked, unaccompanied, down the aisle to meet her husband. She and Jocelyn had never spoken of the moment again.

Until now.

Jocelyn's eyes flashed. "Do you still love him?"

"I don't see how that's relevant to our business."

"How much money do you need?"

"Sixty thousand dollars."

The sum sat there on the table like a stack of dirty laundry. Eliza had done it. She'd said it. She'd voiced her needs, and now all she could do was let the chips fall where they may.

Jocelyn pursed her lips. "I assume you have a business plan?"

"As a matter of fact, I do. I'm currently in the process of securing my first large client. Have you heard of Marguerite Hill? She writes popular women's self-help books. *Take Charge* swept the bestseller lists last year. She's got a new book coming out next year—*Be Free*—and I've presented a proposal for what my company could do for her. I suspect we'll win her business."

"What's the name of your company?"

Eliza's mouth went dry. "Eliza Tate Public Relations."

Jocelyn smiled as if she suspected Eliza had made the name up on the spot. "So you had a business plan in place before you quit your job, but you are only just now realizing you need additional funding?"

"It was a gross miscalculation on my part," Eliza said, feeling her cheeks heat with shame. "I'm sorry it's so last minute."

"You are the most detail-oriented young woman I've ever met."

Jocelyn raised her water glass to her lips and crooked an eyebrow. "Were you fired?"

"Laid off."

"Does Roman know?"

"Enough."

Jocelyn nodded, unperturbed. "Does Roman still..." She frowned, looked down. Her fingers brushed gently over a bruise on her wrist that looked suspiciously like a thumbprint.

"Roman has his flaws." Eliza watched her mother-in-law tug her sleeve down to cover the mark. "But he's my husband. I'm sure you understand."

Jocelyn studied Eliza more closely. Eliza couldn't tell whether the tint in her eyes was one of crushing disappointment or grudging respect.

"Well, then, consider your request done. It's the least I can do. I imagine you want the funds transferred to a personal account? Or actually, I'll just have Todd write a check in your name."

Eliza swallowed as Todd wrapped up his conversation across the room and sauntered back toward their table.

"Thank you, Jocelyn," Eliza whispered. "For everything."

TRANSCRIPT

Defense: Four months ago, the victim filed for a restraining order on you. Why?

Penny Sands: You'll have to ask him.

Defense: It's impossible to ask the victim, seeing as he's dead.

Penny Sands: Right. What's your point? I didn't kill him. I wasn't allowed to be within one hundred feet of him, remember?

SEVEN

C ome in."

With trembling fingers, Penny twisted the doorknob and let herself inside the office at the back of the acting studio. She found the room dimly lit, a bit musty due to the age of the building, but neat. Movie posters dripped down the walls while spines of brightly colored books winked out from dusty shelves.

Most of the books were on the craft of writing screenplays, acting, or navigating the shark-infested waters of Hollywood. Surprisingly, one shelf was dedicated to a selection of self-help books. Yet another thing they had in common. Yet another reason fate had brought them together.

"Thank you for sending this along." Roman wore a pair of glasses that Penny had never seen on him before. They were thick-rimmed and made him look studious in addition to striking. He gestured to his computer where, presumably, he was studying Penny's screenplay. "I always knew you'd be a talented actress, but I hadn't suspected your writing would be incredible as well."

"You like my work?" Penny twisted her hands before her body. "Are you just saying that?"

Roman gestured toward the chair. "Take a seat."

She exhaled a breath through pursed lips. It was working. Her plan would be worth every moment of careful preparation. All Roman had needed was a gentle touch in the right direction to get the wheels spinning. And that light touch had been a teensy white lie about a screenplay.

"Your writing is good," Roman said finally, pulling his glasses from his face and setting them gently on the desk. "Very promising work, Penny. I'm impressed."

Her heart leaped like a jackrabbit. "You're just saying that!"

"Why would I lie to you?" He spread his hands wide. "I promised you honest feedback. Now, there are plenty of things to improve—"

"Oh, I know it's not perfect."

Roman smiled patiently at Penny's interruption, then picked up his glasses and slid them back onto his nose. "I hope you don't mind, but I printed out the first half and redlined some of it for you. In terms of the bigger, global changes, I thought it might be best if we covered those with a conversation. The red pen is so impersonal."

Penny nodded, holding her breath.

"Now, Penny, *now* is the time for you to take out that dreaded notebook and begin scribbling away."

She spent the next half hour, right up until the start of class, scribbling nonsensical notes into said notebook. Roman offered her candid suggestions to improve pacing and structure. He broached the idea of a big cut at the beginning and a bigger twist at the end. Penny nodded along like she knew exactly what he was talking about.

"I've got to get class started," he said. "However, if you'd like to revise and send it back to me, I'd be happy to take another look."

"I would be honored," Penny said and then realized she sounded stupid. "I mean, that'd be awesome."

Not that it mattered what Penny said, because she wouldn't be revising anything. It wasn't exactly her script to revise. She didn't know what the hell Roman was talking about when he told her to cut the second scene or add suspense leading up to the first twist. Because she hadn't written a word of it.

But none of that mattered. Some things were more important than the truth. And what really mattered was that her borrowed piece of art had gotten Penny face time with the elusive Roman Tate.

"It's my pleasure. Moments like this are what roped me into teaching in the first place." Roman leaned back in his chair and crossed his arms over his chest. "Finding inspired students, helping them to discover their creative paths. This industry is bloated with actors, writers, producers who are so focused on the money, the fame, the *business*. It's a breath of fresh air to meet someone like you."

"That's how I feel! And it's why I love your class."

"It's a challenge to find someone who values the artistic aspects as much as I do. I think we have a lot in common."

"Oh my God, yes. You know, we even have the same taste in books. I actually own half that shelf there." Penny waved a hand toward his wall. "The one by Marguerite Hill was a game changer for me. It's actually the straw that broke the camel's back."

"How do you mean?"

"It's the very thing that prompted me to move out to Los Angeles and"—Penny paused for a dry titter—"you know, *Take Charge* of my career."

"Ah, then what I'm about to say next will come as an even better stroke of luck." Roman stood and shifted his long legs before turning to stare at the book Penny had referenced. "My wife is a publicist. She's worked with a lot of these authors you see here, including Marguerite Hill."

"Seriously? That's amazing. Your wife sounds awesome."

Roman exhaled, a complex look crossing through his eyes. "That would be one way to describe her."

The complex look passed, to Penny's annoyance, as Roman continued listing off his wife's impressive accolades.

"In fact, my wife is starting her own company and is looking for new clients," Roman said. "I won't make any promises, but if you carry on with your work, maybe I can tempt her into taking a look at your portfolio."

"That would be incredible."

Penny's curiosity was piqued. She wanted to know more about Roman Tate's wife. The woman who had taken Penny's unsung hero off the market. And if it led to more face time with Roman, so be it.

A mere second later, Roman's hand landed on Penny's shoulder and brought her soaring mind back to earth. She was trapped somewhere between head and heart, feeling lost in the messy swirl of it all as Roman leaned close to her.

A funny thought crept into her mind as Roman pushed the script back to her. *Poor, poor Ryan Anderson.* Maybe Penny should pass along the notes on his script. It was the least she could do for taking creative license and pretending Ryan's work was her own.

"There's one more thing I wanted to discuss with you," Roman said. "I know you're new to the city, and sometimes it can be hard to get on your feet."

"Ain't that the truth."

"If you're looking for a little extra cash, I might have a proposition for you."

Penny's pulse pounded. This wasn't where she'd expected the conversation to go. She wasn't ready for...*that*. She just wanted alone time with Roman to see if they were compatible. To see what she was missing out on in this life. She wasn't really trying to ruin a marriage; these were all just dreams. Bad, bad dreams.

"My wife's friend is looking for a babysitter." Roman interrupted her thoughts with yet another surprising twist to the conversation. "Do you have experience with kids?"

"Yes," Penny lied. "I love kids," she lied again. "I'm available most evenings, except when I'm here, of course."

"Wonderful. I'll pass your information along if that's all right?"

"Absolutely. Thank you for thinking of me."

"It's my pleasure." Roman's fingers lingered a second longer than necessary. Eventually, he gave a final squeeze and pulled his hand away. "I look forward to seeing more of you, Penny Sands," Roman said softly. At the last second, he added, "And your work."

"I can't tell you how much this means to me." Penny stood, smoothed her skirt over her backside. *Had she done it on purpose?* she wondered, feeling a glow of satisfaction as Roman's eyes followed her move. *Maybe, maybe.*

Roman walked Penny to the door. She hesitated, feeling the distance between them shrinking, the air ballooning out of the room and leaving her breathless. Penny didn't need to look up to see Roman's hand as he raised it over her shoulder and rested it against the doorframe. She didn't need to breathe to inhale his scent.

Then Roman's hand snaked out, his fingers grasping Penny's jaw. He hovered over her, his touch both commanding and gentle in one gift-wrapped package. His breath was spiced with mint, his cologne an expensive, exotic cocktail.

He waited just long enough for Penny to say no. To shut him down and back away. To strike him across the face. To demand an explanation. To press herself against him.

Penny did nothing but close her eyes. An electric fire burned at her, clawing its way across her skin. Raking hot with intensity, flush with shame. Burning brilliant with passion and flaming into ashes with horror as their lips touched.

TRANSCRIPT

Defense: Mrs. Wilkes, when did you find out your husband was being investigated by Luke Hamilton?

Anne Wilkes: The night of Eliza's event at the Pelican Hotel.

Defense: When you first heard the accusations, did you think your husband was guilty?

Anne Wilkes: Of course not.

Defense: You already suspected your husband was having an affair. What happened to your relationship when you found out there was more to the story?

Anne Wilkes: Nothing. I didn't tell him anything. Sometimes, it's safer to lie. In fact, if more people lied, maybe someone wouldn't have ended up dead.

EIGHT

Seven Months Before
July 2018

Secrets were heavy.

Heavy, living, breathing things that grew and morphed, changed and mutated over time. They suffocated and drowned their keepers; they blistered with anger and deepened with depression.

Having never known the true weight of a secret before, Anne wondered if this one would be the death of her. It had grown inside her soul, taken root, and bloomed, pregnant and swollen, until it threatened to burst at the softest breeze.

It consumed her mind, day and night. Her interactions with her children had grown listless. She'd started skipping playdates because she couldn't fathom the idea of making conversation with happy little mothers when she was weighed down by an anchor. She could barely sustain her daily routine, clinging with a desperate greediness to the last dregs of normalcy.

As she loaded Gretchen's sandwich with potato chips between slices of whole wheat bread (God forbid the school find out she'd packed chips—full fat!), she was suddenly struck by the ridiculousness of it all.

Here she was, the doting mother and wife. Playing the role of hostess and cook and maid, but why? Had one single person noticed the barbell chained to her ankle over the last several weeks? Who among her darling family had asked what was on her mind as she drifted, distracted, through life?

No one.

Anne slammed the top slice of bread onto the sandwich and heard the *crunch* of chips as she stared at it, bile rising in her throat. She'd told no one about Mark's visits to a young woman living in a suspect neighborhood. Only she and the possum knew about their dalliances on Tuesday nights.

When she could, Anne still made the trek over to the offending apartment. Tuesday nights on repeat. For some reason, that was the day they'd chosen for their weekly rendezvous. Anne wondered why not Monday, when the week was fresh? Or Friday, when the weekend was their oyster? Or Wednesday, as a halfway point?

Not that it mattered. Anne should have forsaken her weekly jaunt altogether and pushed it out of her mind, but the problem was, she couldn't. There was something addictive, something tantalizingly awful about watching her husband derail their neat little life.

Week after week, Anne's heart hardened, her gut tightened, and when she finally drove home, she became a tight ball of fury as she collapsed into bed riddled with guilt and shame. The heaviness that accompanied such secrecy threatened to drown her in her sleep.

Through it all, Anne couldn't bear to confront her husband. Her mind danced a deadly duet between the logistics of the fallout a divorce would cause (insurance, a steady salary, a father figure for the kids) and the emotional turmoil the secret gave her (anger, flashes of an anger so murderous she startled herself). Together, everything was wrapped in a tender layer of sadness.

Anne finished making Gretchen's sandwich and threw some carrot sticks into Samuel's paper bag. The babysitter would arrive in under ten minutes. It was, once again, Tuesday night.

Instead of letting the anger consume her, Anne was pleased to find a calmness descending over her shoulders as she climbed up the stairs and checked on the kids. All were sleeping by some miraculous turn of events. Gretchen's angelic little lashes dusted posy-pink cheeks. Samuel's thumb was stuck in his mouth, despite his recent birthday when he'd promised to give up the habit. The twins lay sprawled, hands in the air, curled into their side-by-side cribs. In sleep, they were perfect.

Anne went to her room, sat before the small mirror perched on the old dresser that she'd made into a piecemeal sort of vanity. When they'd first been married, she'd installed Hollywood-style bulbs while Mark added a large mirror. She'd found a refurbished stool at a garage sale for five bucks to add to the display. Mark had sanded and painted it for her, along with the dresser.

It'd been quaint, years ago. Anne remembered their honeymoon days, specifically the year after they'd been married. She would don her best robe, whip her hair into a loose updo, and preen before the vanity as she gazed lovingly at her new, precious diamond wedding band.

Mark would come into their room, find her there, and whisk her onto the bed where, shrieking, they'd make love until gasping and spent. It had been a time of easy euphoria. She'd felt rich, full of life, satisfied beyond belief with the hand fate had dealt her.

Now, the dresser looked cheap and dingy. Gretchen had smeared blue nail polish along one side, and a chunk of mirror had cracked off in the top right-hand corner. Two of the drawers didn't fully shut, and the one that did squeaked like the dickens, so Anne ended up leaving it open so as not to wake the twins when she reached for her deodorant.

Anne glanced into the cracked mirror and swiped on the same shade of lipstick she'd been wearing since they'd gotten engaged. It was a bit crusty, and Anne had been meaning to pick up a new tube when she was at the store. But in addition to being distracted with her shiny new secret and forgetting about her shopping list, Anne had also found herself being inordinately frugal.

Just in case, she told herself. Just in case she had to get used to managing four children on a single mother's (lack of) income. She'd begun putting the extra pastries back during grocery store runs, buying on-sale grapes instead of the organic apples her children loved. Anne's running shoes had developed a hole in the bottom that she was staunchly ignoring.

Anne rose, dressed in jeans and a T-shirt. She'd given up the pretense of wearing her evening best to spy on her husband. It made her feel even more pathetic that she had to lie to a twenty-something babysitter. There were plenty of lies swirling through the atmosphere already without Anne adding to the problem.

Tonight is it, she decided.

The babysitter was ringing the doorbell when Anne reached the landing. Anne had asked Eliza if she knew anyone who would babysit on short notice, because Anne had been forced to let Olivia go for personal reasons. Shame Olivia was so nosy.

Thankfully, Eliza's husband had been able to recommend a young girl from his acting class who was looking for work. After a quick interview and an hour trial run with the kids the previous weekend, both women agreed to move forward with their working relationship.

"Hi there, Penny," Anne said. "Thanks so much for coming by tonight."

"Oh, thank you! I'm so glad you're trusting me to be here with your kids," Penny said. "I was really looking forward to spending more time with them. They're just adorable."

Anne nodded along, thinking the kids would be better in Penny's hands than her own. She wasn't sure if that was devastating or a relief, so she ignored it. Instead, she let the young woman in, gave her instructions, and paid her cash up front.

"I usually don't collect money until the end..." Penny looked at the wad of bills in her hand. "I mean, whatever you prefer."

"My husband might beat me home, and I don't want things to be awkward. He doesn't know the going rate." Anne scrounged up a wink. "This way, we're all square."

"Okay, well, have a wonderful time," Penny said. "We'll be fine here. Well, duh. We're not going anywhere—sorry, bad joke. Call if you need anything at all."

Anne was barely listening as she shrugged on her coat. As she grabbed her keys, she idly wondered if Penny would ever disappear for three days and leave her children behind. Probably not. Women like Penny lived pretty, perfect little lives.

Anne arrived outside the apartment complex a few minutes later than she'd intended. She'd stopped to get a coffee from the gas station, a funny little splurge she allowed herself despite her new penny-pinching ways. Though the real splurge was the Bailey's liqueur that she tipped into the cup in place of creamer.

Hunkering down in her seat, Anne settled in to watch. Mark arrived, and the same old routine began again. As Anne drank more of her coffee, she stopped tasting the Bailey's. She added a little whiskey from the flask in her purse to spice things up.

It wasn't enough for her to just watch anymore. She needed to do something, and the alcohol helped her think. It gave her confidence. Armed her with numbness and rage instead of the delicate hurt that plucked at her like vicious paper cuts, she could formulate a plan of attack.

Setting her coffee into the cup holder, she reached for the handle of her car door. Her dismally unpainted nails rested against it, frozen there as she watched the same song and dance continue outside the gate—the hug, the brief kiss on the forehead, the disappearing act behind the overgrown shrubs.

Before she knew it, they were gone, and it was too late. The gate was locked. Anne's self-esteem might have been at an all-time low, but she wasn't climbing over a fence to knock on the door. She'd wait, wait, wait some more. She'd gotten good at waiting.

But an hour into waiting, Anne grew restless. She'd tried to pep herself up with the self-help book Eliza had given her a while back, but that was equally depressing. Marguerite Hill, the author, was all about seizing control of one's life, and Anne had never felt less in control. So she dialed the one woman she knew who could take charge better than anyone else.

"Eliza," Anne said once her friend answered. "Are you free tonight by chance?"

On the other end of the line, Eliza hesitated. A low chatter sounded in the background, along with the clinking of dinnerware.

"Oh, are you out with Roman?" Anne asked. "We can meet a different—"

"No, I'm just finishing up dinner at the country club with my in-laws," Eliza said. "I can meet you after. Same place, thirty minutes?"

"I need an hour," Anne said. "I have to clear my head."

Anne hung up with Eliza, then stepped outside the car and into the fresh night air. It had an instantly sobering effect. She walked toward the apartment complex, surprising herself, no doubt buoyed by the booze. Then she stopped. Turned around. Climbed back into the car and waited some more. Even whiskey from a flask didn't make her invincible.

Finally, once she was confident she was under the legal limit, Anne pulled away from the curb and pointed her mom van filled with empty car seats and the carcasses of juice boxes toward the usual place. A place she hadn't gone for years.

The usual place was a local dive bar just off Wilshire. Anne and Eliza had discovered it during their younger years when they'd shared an apartment down the block. The two girls had met during their freshman year of college when they'd been paired together as random roommates. It took one semester of bonding before they agreed to ditch campus, find part-time jobs, and get a regular apartment.

At the time, Eliza had been a fresh-faced, hopeful grad. Anne had been focused on her relationship with Mark, planning their upcoming nuptials, anticipating children and a full life together. Their friendship had blossomed over the trials and tribulations of an otherwise happy, uneventful college career.

Garbanzo's Bar and Grill had been the only digs close enough to walk to from their pinprick of an apartment. As neither college student could afford the cost of a cab, the dive bar had been the logical option for all their moaning and complaining needs.

They'd met at Garbanzo's when Anne's brother had died and again when Eliza's family had come over from Beijing, leaving her battered and hurt after their visit. They'd met there after Eliza's shotgun wedding, and they'd planned Anne's extravagant nuptials over glasses of cheap red wine. Though both women had long since outgrown the dismal charm of sticky floors and slimy tables, neither could give up the dirty, trusted locale that housed their deepest secrets and grandest desires.

Anne pushed open the door, pleased to see that nothing had changed in her long absence. The same tarnished gold bell tinkled lightly as she entered, a necessity, since most of the time, the bartender, Joe, sat on a stool in the back, smoking with the chefs. Health department be damned.

This evening, however, Joe was out front, his focus on the television where he was screaming obscenities at a wrestling match. A few figures sat hunched over the bar, two men, one woman. It smelled like flat beer and grease. The biggest difference Anne noted was the bald spot on Joe's head that had increased in circumference over the last few years.

"Annie!" Joe called as she entered. "Long time, no see. I thought you forgot about Uncle Joe!"

Joe Garbanzo was the only person in the world allowed to call her Annie. Mostly because Anne had been too timid to correct the oversize man the first time he'd nicknamed her. Decades later, and it just seemed rude to mention it. He'd also deemed himself an honorary uncle to the girls, though why, Anne could only guess. The only words they usually exchanged were a greeting by name and then, "The usual?"

Joe winked at her. "The usual?"

"That would be fantastic. Same table," Anne said. "Eliza should be here any moment."

Anne slid into a booth tucked along the back corner, as far away from the television screens, the restrooms, and the kitchen doors (from which the faint scent of cigarette smoke was never quite extinguished) as she could manage. She tried to unfold the paper napkin over her lap and simultaneously peel her jeans from the upholstery. Neither worked, and she forfeited the napkin on the table in a pile of something she hoped was ketchup.

Five minutes later, the cheese curds and beers arrived—tap Coors Light with four olives each. Anne wrinkled her nose, wondering how old the olives were and if Joe had scooped them into the glasses with his bare hands. It was funny, the things she noticed now that she was nearing forty. Things she hadn't thought twice about when she'd been twenty-three and invincible.

Eliza arrived a few minutes later, looking wildly out of place in the dive bar. She wore a trim, professional skirt, stockings, and a blouse that buttoned up to her neck. Her thin legs rose out of cute pumps that clicked across the floor. Eliza was forced to stop once en route to unstick her heel from a particularly grimy patch on the floor.

"Sorry about that," Uncle Joe called from behind the bar. "Had a fight in here earlier and beer went everywhere. Haven't had a chance to clean it up yet."

Joe went back to lounging against the counter, thick arms folded across a protruding belly, and studied the match on television. He'd never clean it up, and everyone knew it.

"I'm so sorry to make you drive all the way over," Anne said as Eliza slid into the booth, her eyebrows knitting as she tried to scoot along the vinyl fabric and found herself stuck in place. "You look like you've just come from, well, I dunno—the Ritz. Some huge business meeting or something."

Eliza waved a hand, a caginess evident in her movements. "Let's talk about you. By the way, did that girl work out? The babysitter? Roman said he emailed you some names."

"She's wonderful. Penny's with the kids now actually," Anne said. "Lifesaver."

"What happened to Olivia?"

"She got too nosy."

Eliza looked at Anne's purse with a calculated stare. As Anne glanced down, she saw the flash of metal from the flask that she'd forgotten to tuck underneath her scarf.

"Ah," Eliza said. "Is everything okay?"

Anne's face heated as she shoved her purse to the end of the bench. "I'm fine. It's fine."

"Well, my ass is not stuck to this seat for the fun of it," Eliza said sweetly. "Something's not fine, and I need a distraction. I had the night from hell, so distract me already and spill. Something. Anything. Except beer," she added, giving a dark glance at Joe before studying the damage to her shoes in depth.

"It's about Mark."

Eliza narrowed her eyes. She had dark, shiny hair wrapped in a chignon at the nape of her neck and eyelashes that extended for miles. Her skin was perfect. Anne suspected that Eliza was immune even to the inevitable layer of grease that descended on patrons of Garbanzo's. Anne would be breaking out in acne for a week thanks to one lonely plate of cheese curds.

Eliza reached for a curd, took a sip of beer. "Well? Don't just stare. Distract me already."

"It's embarrassing," Anne admitted. "But I suppose since I took you away from your fancy dinner, I owe you an explanation. I think Mark is having an affair."

"You think? Or you know?"

Anne breathed a sigh of relief. Eliza had barely flinched at the mention of the affair. Anne knew she'd called Eliza for a reason, and this was it. She'd know exactly what to do.

"Some combination of the two. It all started a few months ago."

The story poured forth then, every last detail—from the first time Anne had left the children to spy on her husband to a few weeks back when she'd toted the twins with her on a stakeout after firing nosy, nosy Olivia. Anne mentioned her crumbling resolve and the way she'd failed to confront her husband when the opportunity had been within reach.

"You've got to stop doing this to yourself." Eliza shook her head, and her eyes filled with sympathy despite words that were clipped and even. "You can't go to that apartment anymore."

"I know."

"Your brain knows, but your heart doesn't. You will ruin yourself if you keep doing this. You have to let it go."

"Let it go?"

"Men." Eliza dunked a cheese curd in ketchup. "It's wrong, but they stray. Women do it too. I'm not saying our gender is never at fault. But for now, let's focus on men."

"I don't understand. It's not..." Anne shook her head, bewildered. "It's not acceptable."

"No, it's not. So you need to decide your tolerance level. You're going to have to confront Mark sooner or later, and you have to be ready for all the scenarios."

"That's so...cold."

"It's how I work." Eliza's posture gave off an easygoing, laissez-faire demeanor. Her eyes, however, glittered. "How do you think I made my money? Not by asking politely. Especially when men are involved."

Anne felt sudden moisture in the corners of her eyes. The first tears she'd cried (aside from the torrents of them on her bed pillows) since she'd discovered Mark's extracurricular activities.

"Sweetie..." Eliza reached across the table and rested her hand on Anne's.

She let it sit there without speaking. It was just what Anne needed.

After a few minutes and several curious looks from Joe, Anne sniffed and wiped her eyes. No sooner had she tossed the napkin into the growing pile in the corner of the table than Uncle Joe appeared with two shots of vodka.

He plunked them down, grunted "On the house," and left.

He'd been doing that for years, every time the girls had one of *those* nights at the bar. Some things never changed, and in a sea of change, the steadfastness of Uncle Joe struck Anne as an incredible relief. She dissolved into tears all over again.

Eliza tugged both shots toward herself. "I don't think—"

"It's fine," Anne repeated. "I'm fine. One shot won't kill me."

"Anne—"

"It's no big deal," Anne said, reaching for the shot. "I need to relax."

"If you say so."

Both women downed their drinks.

"Feel better?" Eliza asked.

Anne licked her lips, reached for a fork, and stabbed an olive from her beer. "A lot better."

"You're just trying to be strong for your kids and your family," Eliza said. "You and Mark have four children. That makes things complicated. Have you thought about how you'll talk to Mark about everything?"

"I don't know what good it would do, honestly. I can't leave him."

Eliza nodded along. "Would you leave him if you could?"

Anne considered. She gave the only answer she could. "I don't know. I love him."

"If you want my advice, talk to Mark. This is eating you alive, and if you don't do something about it..." Eliza's eyes flitted toward Anne's purse like it was a sordid little goody bag. "Things won't end well."

"What do I say?"

"That's why you need a plan," Eliza said. "I suggest you talk to him sooner rather than later, but you need to be prepared. What if he tells you he's in love with this woman, and he's planning to leave you and the kids and shack up with her?"

Anne felt her body go rigid. Her veins prickled with ice, and her legs felt shackled to the sticky surface of the booth. She'd never considered the fact that it might not be her choice. It might be Mark's choice to leave, and in that case, she wouldn't be able to do a thing about it.

"You never considered that aspect," Eliza murmured. "I'm sorry to be crass. I just think you need to be prepared for whatever the outcome when you do confront him."

Anne nodded dully. "I never truly thought it might be serious between them."

"I'm sure it's not, which is why you need to talk to him before you drive yourself insane." Eliza shrugged. "Whenever I have doubts about Roman, I meet them head-on."

"How?"

"I—" Eliza stopped, took a swig of her drink, then ran French-tipped nails across her bottom lip to wipe away a stray bead of beer. "Well, I hired a private investigator. Roman still doesn't know that part."

"I want his name," Anne said quickly.

"He's expensive."

"I've saved up some money."

"Are you sure you want to go down that route?" Eliza asked delicately. "I'm not claiming it's admirable."

"You did it."

"You shouldn't live your life like me. It will only get you in trouble."

"I want to be sure. I don't want any gory pics of them doing the deed or anything, just a name on the apartment. Maybe some background on the girl. How soon can we meet with him?"

Eliza pulled her clutch toward her, opened it, removed thirty bucks, and tossed them on the table. It covered their nine-dollar bill and then some. "I'll take care of it."

TRANSCRIPT

Prosecution: Mrs. Tate, please describe your relationship with your husband and how it's been over the past year.

Eliza Tate: It was a typical marriage. We had good times and bad.

Prosecution: Did you love him?

Eliza Tate: He was my husband.

Prosecution: Noting for the jury that Mrs. Tate hasn't answered the question, though I think it says enough. How did you feel when you discovered that Roman had a mistress?

Eliza Tate: If you're talking about his relationship with Penny, that was hardly his first affair.

Prosecution: Your husband's affairs don't bother you?

Eliza Tate: You can't possibly understand our

relationship. I knew Roman was flawed when we married, but our love goes deeper than that.

Prosecution: Are you saying you'd do anything for your husband?

Eliza Tate: I didn't murder anyone, if that's what you're asking. And if you actually wanted to find out who did, then I'd look to someone with real motive. The woman he knocked up and left for broke has a pretty good reason to want him dead.

NINE

What a night, Eliza thought, reminiscing first about her evening at the country club with the Tates, then her impromptu nightcap with Anne as she pulled her convertible into the driveway. Eliza parked, frowning at the blue vintage Corvette taking up her spot. She was too tired to entertain. All she wanted to do was climb in bed and sleep and then hope tomorrow dawned sunny.

"There's my sweetheart." Roman sounded chipper as he greeted Eliza in the entryway. Too chipper. "I got the message you'd be late."

"Sorry for the short notice," Eliza said. "I hadn't planned on meeting Anne tonight, but she said it was urgent. By the way, Anne was thrilled with the babysitter you sent her way."

"No problem. Penny's a nice girl, and she needed the work."

"Win-win."

"Certainly is," Roman said. "Anyway, I have a little something for you."

Roman changed the subject, dipping out of sight and retrieving something from the kitchen. When he returned, he had a bouquet of flowers in hand.

Eliza looked down, bewildered. "What are these for?"

Roman slid an arm around Eliza's waist and drew her close. He placed a kiss on her forehead, then inched his way down until his lips were on her neck and Eliza's body was seamlessly pressed against his. "I wanted to apologize for last night. I don't know why we always get so heated talking about money. I'm sorry we argued."

Eliza untangled herself. "You know I hate flowers," she said, mentally adding the cost of the lush bouquet of Stargazer lilies in his hands and tacking it on to their mounting bills. "They'll just die in a week."

"Eliza." Roman gave a playful *tsk*. "You're worth it. You're my wife."

"Well, thank you." She plucked the flowers from his hands and desperately tried to ignore her aching head. She hadn't had hard liquor in ages. "Do you have company?"

"No, why?"

"There's a car in the driveway."

"The car's mine."

"You bought…" She cleared her throat. "A car? Without talking to me first?"

"It's an investment. The value will only go up over time." When Eliza still didn't seem convinced, Roman's eyes shifted from the flowers and back to her. "It's just money. We discussed this last night. I need to have some freedom and not feel like you're breathing down my neck with every expense."

"How much was it?"

"I paid fifty, but it's easily worth seventy-five."

"Grand?"

"Of course grand."

"Does it even run?"

"I drove it home."

Eliza leveled her chin, looked into her husband's eyes. "You have your G-Class, and now you have your Corvette. Pick one, please, and sell the other. There's no sense in you having two cars."

"I can't use the Corvette as my daily driver."

"Then sell it," she said abruptly, feeling edgy, pushing the needle. He'd chosen the wrong day to be impulsive.

"No."

"You must." Eliza's fists clenched as she stared down her husband. "We can't afford it."

"We just fought about this last night, Eliza. You've got to stop nagging me about money."

"This isn't nagging; this is *it*, Roman. Our bank accounts are dangerously close to empty." Eliza let the flowers fall from her grasp as she balled her hands into fists. Immediately, she wished she'd kept her mouth shut, but she'd spoken the truth, and she could no longer ignore it. "We are broke."

Roman's gaze settled on her. A new expression appeared on his face, a satisfaction that caught Eliza off guard. Almost victorious.

"I know," he said.

"You know what?"

"I know everything."

"I don't understand."

"I know you've been funneling money into my checking account," Roman said. "Quietly, as if I'm stupid enough to ignore the fact that the numbers on our bank account are dwindling."

"This was a test?" Eliza's lips parted as she sucked in a sharp breath. "You knew this whole time, yet you went and bought a car?"

"There was money in my checking account," he said pointedly, a righteous anger sizzling below his brown eyes. "Why were you trying to keep our finances from me?"

"I—I wasn't."

"Honey." Roman's voice took on a sweet, soft tone. "I've asked you not to lie to me."

"I tried to tell you that we didn't have much—"

"You didn't try hard enough," Roman said. "You wanted me to think we were doing just fine. Why was that, Eliza? Why didn't you tell me sooner?"

Eliza froze and found herself wondering that very same thing. But she knew why. She hadn't told him sooner because money was the one aspect of their marriage that she could control. She brought home the cash. Roman didn't make diddly-squat teaching acting classes. It was Eliza who kept him fueled, made this lifestyle possible.

It was the one thing she brought to the table in their relationship. Eliza owed Roman a good life after what he'd done for her, and she could no longer deliver it. And that broke her heart.

"I understand if you're upset," Eliza said. "But I will fix this. I've already started."

Roman seemed to sense he was being led into a trap, and he didn't know the way out. "You've started to fix it? How?"

"I asked your parents for a loan."

"You did what?"

"Tonight, before I met with Anne, I had dinner with your parents at the country club and asked them for money. It's a business investment."

"Without telling me."

"It is my problem, my loan, my favor to ask of them."

Roman shook his head. "You shouldn't have done that."

"Roman—"

"I mean it." He backed away, his eyes taking on a new look that Eliza had never seen before. "You shouldn't have done that, Eliza."

TRANSCRIPT

Defense: We've been talking about motive, Ms. Sands, so I'd like to further discuss the restraining order the victim took out on you a few months before his death. What pushed him to do that?

Penny Sands: I don't know. He was a psychopath. Why did he do any of it?

Defense: If I recall, that's what he said about you when he spoke with the police.

Penny Sands: Then it's my word against his, and he's dead. I guess that means I win by default.

Defense: He stated that you continually tried to contact him, even after he asked you to stay away. Is that true?

Penny Sands: I had a pretty good reason to want to talk to him.

Defense: It's noted here from the victim's personal files that you had begun taking things that belonged to him. He recorded in a journal that you stole several items. Is this also true?

Penny Sands: I borrowed, like, a pen. It wasn't a big deal.

Defense: Why did you take it at all?

Penny Sands: It was an accident. It's not like he deserved any of his nice things.

Defense: Did he deserve to die?

Penny Sands: Someone thought so. Why don't you ask the *other* woman he was sleeping with? I don't think she was happy when she found out about me.

TEN

Six Months Before
August 2018

God, baby—*yes!*"

Penny winced as he pounded into her, rattling the bed frame. Her hands reached up, clasped the rails as the headboard banged against the wall.

"You are so damn beautiful." He lowered his head to her neck, hot breath tickling the skin beneath her chin. "I've had my eye on you since the first day you walked into class. I saw you, and I thought to myself—"

"How about we *don't* talk?" Penny murmured. Then she added quickly, "It's sexier when you leave a little to the imagination."

"Ah." He grinned, then resumed the stupid thrusting motion he'd been doing with his hips for the last two minutes. "I see. So you like it when—"

Penny pressed her lips to his in a sloppy kiss. It was her last resort, but she was willing to try anything for a moment of silence. Her efforts were rewarded for a few precious seconds before the blissful silence was shattered by a deep groan. He leaned against her, panting.

"Do you have a condom?" he murmured. "I think I forgot mine in the car. I should have—"

"It's fine," Penny mumbled. "I'm on birth control. Let's just—"

She stopped herself before she added *get this over with*.

Even Ryan Anderson, idiot that he was, would recognize that for an insult. Poor Ryan whose script Penny had borrowed. He'd then bought her dinner three nights running in a series of lackluster dates. Finally, Penny had allowed him into her apartment and beneath her sheets out of sheer sympathy.

Ever since the day Roman had kissed Penny, she'd been unable to banish him from her thoughts, though she'd tried. She'd tried and she'd tried and she'd tried every trick in the book to rid her mind of him, but she'd failed.

Roman was there—always there, front and center, every waking moment. He hovered in her thoughts when she ate and exercised and watched television. When she showered, shopped, walked the streets. She woke up drenched in sweat, sheets twisted around her in a dramatic mess after explicit dreams that were ten times more erotic than whatever Ryan was doing down below.

Penny closed her eyes, wishing for her mistake to finish so she could go back to her lonely existence. This was all her fault, not Ryan's. She'd accepted not one but three dates with him. Even after the first had been beyond boring and the second not much better, she'd agreed to a third. Not because the third time was a charm but because she was desperate to fill her mind with anything—anyone— that wasn't Roman Tate.

Ryan was everything Roman wasn't. A struggling actor in his late twenties, Ryan had booked one national commercial three years back, and he clung to those fifteen seconds of fame like a lifeboat.

Where Roman was quietly confident, Ryan was uncertain and timid. Where Roman was darkly alluring and dangerously out of reach, Ryan was delightfully boring and a little too available. Ryan was her age. He was appropriate to date. He was safe.

In falling for Roman, Penny had set herself up for failure. She reckoned he knew how to listen and when to speak. He sure as hell wouldn't forget her name. Penny was also willing to bet that Roman Tate could make Penny forget her own name with one kiss, one touch, one stroke of a finger.

As Ryan rolled onto her, Lucky banged on the ceiling from his apartment downstairs. Ryan grinned as Lucky shouted something about there being kids in the house.

"That was amazing," Ryan mumbled. "How'd you like it?"

Penny stared blankly at him. She wondered what he'd say if she announced that the experience had been *somewhat endurable*.

"It was..." She hesitated. "Yeah."

"Glad to hear it." Ryan grinned, stroked a thumb down her cheek. "I was wondering if I could make you breakfast in the morning?"

"Actually..."

"Sorry, I get it. Too forward." Ryan flashed her a quick smile. "My bad. I'll get out of your hair."

Penny merely raised her eyebrows as Ryan skedaddled out of bed. She studied him as he moved, thinking that most women would find him attractive—striking even—with his dirty-blond hair and piercing blue eyes. Yet Penny couldn't muster any enthusiasm for Ryan Anderson whatsoever.

Eventually, Ryan let himself out of the apartment with a wink. Penny gave a half-hearted wave, not bothering to get up and lock the door after him. She lay in bed until his footsteps faded. Then she sat up and thrust the window open in hopes the fresh air would wipe away the stench of sex.

Penny stared outside at nothing in particular, frustrated that even her evening with Ryan hadn't taken her mind off the one man she couldn't have. She'd come so close, and yet her kiss with Roman had made him seem that much more unavailable.

There was an ache inside Penny that longed to pick up her phone and call Roman for no reason at all. She wanted to tell him all the little things about her day, to share the simple things that wound up being the foundation of a real, true relationship.

Penny longed for those moments, for the teensy moments that created dazzling memories. She wanted to whisper her brilliant new ideas for a television pilot late at night as she lay next to Roman in bed. To send him the stupid memes that reminded her of him when she listlessly browsed online. To go grocery shopping with him in sweatpants before retiring to the couch with a bottle of inexpensive wine. She wanted it all. And couldn't have any of it.

Another same-but-different niggle of guilt crept down Penny's spine as she closed her eyes and relived the moment in Roman's office when they'd kissed. It'd been soft, sweet. Short. Almost a mirage, and on some days, Penny found herself doubting it'd ever happened.

They'd never spoken of it again. Roman and Penny simply existed together, floating through the same plane, catching each other's eyes now and again as a shared memory flitted between them, fleeting as a firefly, before it disappeared again. In those brief moments, the guilt vanished.

And then there were moments like these. Moments where Penny's palms grew clammy and her stomach wriggled with disappointment. *What had she done?* To herself? To Roman? To his wife? The only saving grace was that Penny already had a relationship with guilt; she was no stranger to it.

In fact, Penny had all but accepted guilt—distantly, like an annoying second cousin she saw at holidays. A nuisance she'd gotten used to, acknowledged, and then dutifully ignored time and time again because if she didn't, she'd fall apart.

Penny knew, too, that if she pushed the incident in Roman's office out of her mind, the guilt would eventually tamp down to a manageable size. When she'd started taking other people's things in high school, guilt had come around then, too.

But with time, patience, and a good bit of stubbornness (along with a long thread of rationalization), that guilt had subsided. It had gone from crashing ocean waves to the faint whisper of the ocean one hears when holding a seashell to their ear. And with time, their kiss would be nothing but a distant tremor, the seashell that housed it long since forgotten on a faraway beach.

For now, however, the waves raged strong and hard, fast and

overwhelming. Penny gulped, found it hard to breathe. She picked up her phone and scrolled until she found her mother's number—the one person who could center her and help plant her feet on firm ground instead of the ever-shifting sand on which Penny stood.

Curling around herself, Penny hit Dial. The evening breeze was warm, tasted of desert air and dust, stilted by floral tones from the blooming bush that insisted on surviving in the alleyway beneath her window. Penny studied it, feeling a bit like the plant herself. Left alone without much in the way of sustenance, expected to thrive amid rocky darkness. If only she were strong enough to bloom.

Amy Sands cut to the chase after a quick greeting. "What's wrong, honey? You sound upset."

Penny flipped a pen between her fingers. The pen didn't technically belong to her—it was a little trinket she'd adopted from Roman's desk. She might not be able to have him, but she had something *of* his. A small reminder that there was a chance. A teensy, tiny chance they'd met for some cosmic reason.

"There's this guy," Penny said with a sigh. "I think I'm in love, but I can't be. He's married."

"Oh, honey."

Penny felt her throat closing at the stroke of kindness in her mother's voice. Amy Sands was a heavyset woman, each of her two hundred pounds packed with love and warmth and hominess. Suddenly, Penny felt herself crumbling toward tears, wishing her mother's soft arms could wrap around her, protect her from the mess her life had become.

Penny had moved to Hollywood to make a name for herself. Yet here she was, toiling away at a job that barely classified as legal. She showed up to work at a casting company every day and sat behind a miniscule desk in a grody room with carpet that looked as if it'd been molding since the eighties.

The man in charge—Jack Hardy—hadn't bothered to learn her name. On her first day of work, Jack had listed her duties (check people in and ignore phone calls), then punctuated it with a grunt and a tilt of his chin. His partner, a petite woman who probably weighed eighty pounds soaking wet—with about twelve of those pounds being foundation and mascara—had introduced herself as the casting director. Together, they cast extras for obscure reality TV shows that nobody had heard of. It was an ugly business.

"If you're not happy out there," Amy Sands said after a pause, "then why don't you move home?"

Penny warmed with the idea of her old job, her old life. Her cozy little existence in a cozy little town. She missed every inch of it. She missed the smell of the small local newspaper office where she worked. She missed her daily lavender latte from the café down the street, a place where she didn't need to order because they knew her by her approaching footsteps.

She missed the short drive home to be with her family for every little holiday. She even missed the sporadic blind dates her friends would set her up on—dates with insanely average men whose biggest crime was that they still called their mothers once a day for advice on clothing choices.

A huge part of her, most of her, in fact, wanted to turn tail and return to Iowa. Pretend the last month or two of her life had never happened and start fresh. There, she knew which way was up and which was down. Out here, there was no road map. Her life was an unfinished script waiting to be finalized. The possibilities were both equally thrilling and terrifying. Would she fly? Or would she fall?

"I miss home," Penny admitted. "But I can't come back."

"Why?"

Penny tapped the pen harder and harder against her leg in agitation. The question was a simple one, but her mother's tone was layered and complex, a kaleidoscope of questions all balled into one. Penny tried to put her feelings into words, but for someone who claimed to be creative, she hopelessly failed.

Finally, she whispered, "I don't know."

Her mother heaved a guttural breath, and Penny could practically see her nodding in their tiny little kitchen in their tiny little house in their tiny little town. Amy would be sitting at the table with her hands wrapped around a cup of peppermint tea, staring at the dusty pink curtains draped across the window over the sink.

There would be clutter from a day's worth of homemade cooking, the smell of something sweet hanging in the air from her latest bake. The linoleum floor would be cracked with age but tidy and swept, the dishes put away, and the herb pots near the sink freshly watered. Penny longed for home so much that it hurt.

She wouldn't mind heading back for a visit, but her bank account couldn't handle a foot-long sub for lunch, let alone the cost of a cross-country plane ticket. Not to mention if she went home, there was the legitimate fear that she'd never leave again. She'd stick there, like a fruit fly to a trap, dying a slow death because she'd chosen a life that wasn't hers to live.

Somewhere, deep down, Penny believed she was different. She had to believe it, or there'd be no reason for her to suffer in an apartment complex that served as home to more rats than humans or to work a crappy job when she'd held a perfectly respectable position at a perfectly respectable newspaper in a perfectly respectable town.

Penny vaguely wondered if it was all an illusion. If she was as deluded as Ryan, claiming his way to fame from a dandruff commercial. Did he feel the same way, that he was special? Did everyone? Or was there a reason behind Penny's belief? It was imperative she believe that she was one in a million or nothing else made sense. But what if she was wrong?

"I'll be home for Christmas," Penny said. "Anyway, I should let you go. I just wanted to hear your voice."

As Penny lay on her secondhand mattress, she stared up at the stars through her window. If she couldn't have Roman Tate, she'd have to start taking drastic measures to forget about him, at least until she could swim. As it was, the cloudy waters soared around her, roared in her ears, blurred her vision. It was with a touch of anger that Penny realized the situation was anything but fair to her.

She had been ready to give Roman everything. And he'd led her to believe it might be possible. With that kiss, he'd crossed a line—a line that had sent Penny's heart into tachyarrhythmia with the thought that they might be possible. *Together* might be possible. Then Roman had all but ignored her in the following weeks, sending Penny into a dangerous spiral that left her motivation weak and her heart frayed.

Penny was anything but weak. When people stole from Penny, she stole back. Next week, she would take a stand. She'd go into Roman's office after class and cancel her remaining sessions. See what he had to say about that. If he let her go, then her answer would be sparkling clear, and she would be free to lick her wounds, regroup, and focus on Penny Sands.

She perused her emails, stopping when one caught her eye.

TheRomanTate@gmail.com glared at her from the screen, the simple subject line taunting her as if he'd somehow read her mind: Class Next Week.

Her finger hovered over the Delete button. It would be so easy to say she hadn't gotten it. That the message had been trapped in her spam filters, and she'd missed it completely.

But Penny knew from the moment she laid eyes on the name that she was weak. Her finger twitched, clicked. Her resolve to be rid of Roman—so strong just seconds before—crumbled like dust.

TRANSCRIPT

Defense: Why did you fire Olivia Moore as your babysitter?

Anne Wilkes: I, er, I didn't fire her.

Defense: Ms. Moore testified yesterday that you fired her in June 2018.

Anne Wilkes: Okay, well, I did fire her. But I later apologized. She's not…fired. She just didn't want to come back after I accidentally fired her.

Defense: Why did you fire her in the first place?

Anne Wilkes: She overstepped her bounds. She and Mark were ganging up on me, and I didn't like it.

Defense: Ganging up on you?

Anne Wilkes: There was an incident a while back that my husband can't get over. I thought we'd moved on, but he still doesn't trust me. I found texts on Mark's phone from Olivia. He'd obviously asked her to report back about me. I hired a babysitter for the kids, not for myself.

Defense: Mrs. Wilkes, I'm sorry to be blunt, but I have to admit, your husband's concern for you seems legitimate. After all, what sort of mother disappears for three days without a word?

ELEVEN

Hello, there. I'm looking for Mr. Hamilton." Anne approached a young woman with curly dark hair seated behind a standard metal desk littered with file folders. "I'm sorry, I'm a little late for my eleven o'clock appointment. I had to pick up my son from daycare last minute. He wasn't feeling well."

"Mr. Hamilton is expecting you," the woman announced cheerfully. "Feel free to take a seat. He's just on a phone call now. Can I get you something to drink?"

"No, I'm fine."

Luke Hamilton—Eliza's private investigator—was headquartered in one of a million Los Angeles strip malls, the small suite flanked by a Zankou Chicken on one side and a Laundromat on the other. There was no indication whatsoever on the outside that Suite 101 would hold the answers to Anne's biggest questions.

Anne sat, bouncing Harry on her lap. His face was flushed, and she put her cheek to his forehead to check his temperature. Her daycare provider had called an hour earlier and informed Anne that her son had been sick and needed to be picked up immediately.

Dragging Harry along to this meeting was the absolute last thing Anne wanted to do, but what choice did she have? She couldn't reschedule—she'd never get the opportunity to be alone again. Plus, she couldn't wait one more damn second.

Clutching her baby to her chest, Anne rocked him until he got bored of the sticky closeness and wiggled backward. He clapped his hands, and Anne reached for her purse and pulled out a baggie of Goldfish. She fed him one after another, continuously checking his forehead, until the curly haired receptionist announced that Mr. Hamilton would see her.

She really should have turned around and walked away then. She should've taken Harry home, measured his temperature, and cuddled him until he felt better. It was time for the madness to stop. If only Anne could confront her husband and get to the meaning of his evenings away, her life could return to normal. Or whatever the new normal would look like.

But she couldn't risk it. What if Mark gave her an answer that she wasn't ready to hear?

Anne stood, stretched her legs, and wobbled on low heels as she followed the young woman down a short hallway and into a private room. She'd dressed up for the occasion, a thought that struck her as quite sad. The last time she'd worn pantyhose and a black skirt had been before she'd gotten pregnant with Gretchen.

"Good afternoon." Luke Hamilton greeted her once his receptionist had left the room. His eyes shifted toward Harry, though he didn't offer commentary. "Thank you for taking the time to come see me."

"I'm so sorry I was late. My son got sick at daycare this morning. He's not *sick* sick, nothing contagious, just something he ate. My husband couldn't pick him up because he's a cop and, well, I'm sure you know that." Anne stopped. "I'm sorry. I'm a bit flustered."

"That's natural." Luke gave a kind smile. "As you can imagine, I don't have loads of happy clients considering my field. I'm used to a bit of nerves."

"Of course," Anne gushed. "Thank you."

Luke cleared his throat and pulled a stack of papers toward himself.

He appeared to be nearing his late fifties, a trim, dark-skinned man who was handsome in a stately sort of way. His hair was cut short, his clothes well fitted though casual. Wire-framed glasses covered his eyes.

"You said you had news for me?" Anne pressed when Luke didn't look up from the pages on his desk. "I guess I should start by saying thank you for taking my...er, my case. Eliza speaks very highly of you."

Luke gave a faint smile, his eyes flicking up for a brief second, then back down at the file before him.

"Right, I should probably keep my lips zipped about your other clients," Anne said quickly. "Privacy, top-secret stuff, and all that."

Luke glanced once more toward Harry. "I do have some updates for you. Are you sure now is a good time?"

"It's best if I know sooner rather than later."

Luke ran a hand over the top page of the report, seeming to consider his words carefully. "I was able to look into your husband's Tuesday evening activities, and I believe I can shed some light on the situation."

Anne's heart pounded.

"The apartment where he spends his time..." Luke looked at Harry yet again, then finally brought his gaze to rest on Anne's. "The lease is in his name."

"What do you mean, *in his name?*"

"Mark has rented the apartment for the last five months," Luke clarified. "He's been paying for it."

"How has he been paying for it?" Anne massaged her forehead with one hand. "I mean, I understand he's using money—our money—but we have bills! We have—" Anne stopped herself. She scooted Harry closer, smoothed the thin tufts of hair back as he pounded a fist against her shoulder. "Forget it. Was there anything else?"

Luke looked truly sorry as he glanced down at those dreaded pages on his desk. He seemed to hate what he had to say next.

"If you'd like to continue a different time—"

"Do you know who she is?" Anne asked.

"The young woman occupying the apartment recently turned eighteen, recently graduated."

"Graduated…" Anne blinked. "*High* school?"

He nodded.

She blinked again, then let out a derisive snort.

"Her name is Harmony Feliz."

Anne took the news with as stoic of an expression as she could muster. When Luke looked at her as if wondering if he should continue, Anne nodded.

"She was raised by her mother and father in Silver Lake. Attended public grade school, high school, and recently graduated."

"Did you find out how she met my husband?"

"Not yet. I could look into it, but I've…" The private investigator studied the back of his hands. "There wasn't much left of Eliza's retainer."

"The money is gone," Anne puzzled out. "I have a little bit more in my savings, but I'm afraid I don't know your hourly rate or how much you'd need in order to keep digging on this woman."

"May I make a recommendation, Mrs. Wilkes?"

Anne tilted her chin upward. "I suppose."

"This is not my place, and I understand that I am overstepping my bounds in saying so, but it wouldn't be right for me to accept your money without cautioning you first." He paused for a breath. "You seem like a nice woman. Obviously, you have a family to care for, and I feel for your situation. But I don't believe there's much more I can do for you. The only person who can provide the answers you're seeking is your husband."

Anne sat rigid in her seat, waiting a long beat. "Thank you, then. I suppose that'll be all. Am I supposed to tip you? I don't understand how this industry works."

Luke rose, his eyes dimmed with sadness. "We're all settled, Mrs. Wilkes. Would you like to take the files with you?"

"No," Anne said. "I've heard enough."

TRANSCRIPT

Prosecution: As a professional publicist, would you say you can put a spin on just about anything?

Eliza Tate: That's pretty much a requirement in the industry.

Prosecution: Yet you say that you were not responsible for any part of the murder that took place on the evening of February 13?

Eliza Tate: Correct. Which I've stated several times.

Prosecution: It's interesting, then, that the police found your fingerprints on the murder weapon. How would you spin that story?

TWELVE

Six Months Before
August 2018

Eliza checked in with the maître d' of Beverly Hills' hottest new restaurant, taking care to select a small table near the window that would fit her prospective client's taste. This lunch had to be perfect, and Eliza was prepared to cater to every strange whim and quirky desire.

She knew Marguerite Hill hated to sit outside (too sunny) and hated to sit in a booth (too sticky) and hated to sit near the restrooms (for obvious reasons). Finally, Eliza located a table that seemed to fit the bill all around and promptly sat, ordering a bottle of Marguerite's favorite white wine to be waiting, chilled.

With a minute to spare, Eliza daintily touched up her hair and makeup. She sped through a few emails on her phone, forcing herself to stay *busy, busy, busy* so her mind didn't wander to less-than-pleasant topics. Such as the state of her relationship with her husband.

Eliza put her phone down when she caught sight of the familiar, frizzled hairstyle signaling Marguerite Hill's arrival. Marguerite, bestselling self-help author of the past year, was a hot commodity in the publishing industry. And if Eliza's luck held, today would be the day she swooped Ms. Hill out from under Harold's nose and secured her as a client. It would put Eliza Tate PR on the map with a sparkling splash and the pop of a champagne cork.

The server showed Marguerite to her seat. Eliza stood, taking in the woman's aura—the entire charade that had become famous along with Marguerite herself. The author was young, in her early forties, but she kept up a carefully groomed image that gave her the impression of being much wiser than her years.

Her blond hair was dyed with streaks of silvery-gray—a strange style that interns assured Eliza was completely *en vogue*. The spiral curls had been teased into a frizzy mane that appeared to bloom from the very roots of Marguerite's scalp, twisting away like blackberry vines, barely contained with a floral scarf in bright shades of pinks and greens and blues.

Marguerite wore a bright-orange sheer kimono draped over her shoulders. Beneath, a simple white bodysuit disappeared into high-waisted jeans that exposed a trim figure, one kept in great shape thanks to a diet of earthy greens, plant-based proteins, and weeklong fasts. The whole outfit was topped by a pair of god-awful sandals wedged onto bare feet.

Ironically, this version of Marguerite Hill was not the one Eliza had first met several years before. That Marguerite Hill had flaunted her slim figure in tight designer dresses and sky-high heels. Her hair had been dyed jet-black and straightened until it shone like a glittering veil. Her eye makeup had been heavy and dark, her mascara thick and voluminous. She had been picture-perfect.

Then her book had skyrocketed to success. Her Instagram account had gained hundreds of thousands of followers overnight. She'd begun posting inspirational quotes from her first book, *Take Charge*, followed by images of her new, raw-food diet. She'd steadily begun to post photos of herself and her new look.

Soon enough, she'd secured a slew of sponsors—everyone from natural makeup companies to organic clothing lines to free-range chicken farms wanted to be linked to success. Everyone wanted to hitch their wagon to Marguerite's. The smell of money burned strong in the air.

Eliza had watched, amused, as the author traded cute pumps for leather sandals and tight dresses for baggy overalls. Her smoky eye shadow had evaporated, only to be replaced by expensive (and invisible) antiaging creams and lotions. Her hair had gone from black to gray in the snap of a finger. Overnight, Marguerite Hill had become the most popular guru in America with the bohemian lifestyle to prove it.

Marguerite's fans loved her new vibe. A vibe that, as Eliza well knew, was the result of a carefully curated collection of social media photos. It was all bullshit. But to Eliza's great surprise, Marguerite's fans gobbled the bullshit out of her (expensively moisturized) palm.

"Hello, darling," Marguerite said in a slightly clipped, almost-accented voice. "Thank you so much for agreeing to meet me for tea."

Eliza didn't bother to correct her about the fact that this wasn't a tea party. Marguerite had been born in Louisiana and was about as British as Tony Soprano, but that hadn't stopped her from perfecting a lilt to her speech that was faintly reminiscent of an obscure European country.

As an immigrant who had spent endless hours trying to eradicate any trace of accent from her speech, Eliza found this practice baffling. Then again, Roman let people think he was as Italian as his name, which was a total fabrication of his true heritage. Apparently, Eliza surrounded herself with people who preferred to be anyone other than themselves.

"Absolutely," Eliza said. "I hope this restaurant will suffice. They have the sashimi platter that we both adore."

Marguerite winced. "Actually, dear, I've gone vegan."

"I hadn't seen the news."

"I decided to go completely vegan about two hours ago." Marguerite put a hand over her heart and let out a tinkling laugh. "But as I always say, one must seize the day! Why wait until tomorrow when we can start today?"

"Take charge!" Eliza echoed weakly, wondering why Marguerite couldn't have waited until tomorrow to go vegan. The sashimi platter at this place was worth breaking a fast over. Wasn't pescatarian in these days?

"Surely you haven't given up wine," Eliza said quickly. "I have a bottle of your favorite chilling."

Marguerite made a sucking sound through her teeth. "As a matter of fact, I've been thinking about it. I sort of like the idea of being a complete teetotaler."

"I've always thought there was something a bit romantic about authors and alcohol," Eliza said, grasping at straws. "Having a glass of sparkling wine late at night, sitting at the computer, tap-tap-tapping away at your next piece of genius."

Marguerite rested a pale, manicured fingernail to her lips. "You know, I think you're right. Fuck, I'm glad I didn't post that I'd given up alcohol online, or I'd have to turn down this glorious bottle of wine! Screw it. I can always be booze-free tomorrow."

"Absolutely." Eliza hurriedly gestured for the server, announcing as he arrived, "We're ready for the wine. And a bit of the complimentary bread whenever you're ready."

"Bread is *out*," Marguerite said when the basket arrived on the table. "I've always loved a good hunk of warm gluten, but I'm thinking I might have to abstain soon. Gluten-free is big. What a drag."

"Tell me about it," Eliza said, grabbing her newly filled glass of wine and taking a swig, forcing herself not to touch the delicious, steaming basket of bread on the table or the artisan garlic butter. "Speaking of, I have some ideas that I think could be fabulous for your image."

"Is that so?"

"I have an entire proposal if you'd like to see it." Eliza removed a binder, placed it tantalizingly on the table. "But I think we should order first. If, of course, there's something here that works for you?"

Marguerite crooked her eyebrow, leaned forward. "Let's cut to the chase, Eliza. You and I both know I'd really love to have the rack of ribs, but just in case someone's watching, I've got to stick to my vegan shtick." She flicked the menu open and scanned it with a frown. "Which of these would look best in a photo?"

Eliza forced a smile, then perused the menu. She pointed out some sort of eggplant parmesan dish that the server assured them was served on a beautiful platter.

"Why don't I get the zucchini blossom?" Eliza said. "Then you can take a picture with whichever looks better."

"I like the way you think," Marguerite said. "Do you like zucchini?"

"Does anyone?"

A gleam entered Marguerite's eyes. "Color me interested. You know, I was quite shocked when I got the email that you and Harold were parting ways. The rumors are that you were let go."

"I'm going the road alone." Eliza dodged the question.

"How does Roman feel about that?"

"He's supportive."

"Is he, then?" Marguerite's eye flicked over to Eliza's with a deliberate pause. "That's good."

"It's not exactly his choice, seeing as it's my career."

"I agree it shouldn't be his choice. I just wondered how he took the news."

"I don't really understand why you seem to dislike Roman so much."

Eliza's bluntness surprised even her, but it was a thought that had pricked at her mind for months. Ever since the author had started infusing little comments about Roman into the conversation every chance she could get. While she was embarrassed for blurting it out, Eliza wanted to hear the answer.

"I don't trust him," Marguerite said. "I think he's holding you back."

"Holding me back from what?"

"Are you happy in your relationship?" Marguerite's cool blue eyes met Eliza's. "Is Roman everything to you? Because that's what you deserve. If he's not, you have options."

"Options," Eliza echoed.

"I can help," Marguerite said. "After all you've done for me, it's the least I could do in return."

"No, I—" Eliza shook her head, but her nerves were jangling. What had Marguerite seen in Roman to set her so off-kilter around Eliza's husband? "Let's forget about Roman for now."

"Doll—"

"He's not my biggest concern—that's you. I'm opening the doors to Eliza Tate PR, and I'd like you to be my first client. I can assure you that with your next book, we can shoot you higher in ranks than ever before. The *New York Times* list. The *Wall Street Journal*."

"Can you get *Be Free* on Oprah's book club?"

"Better," Eliza gushed, leaning forward. "Reese Witherspoon is in."

"Tell me more about your proposal. And take the book off the table. Reading makes my eyes ache."

Eliza removed the binder and stashed it in her bag. "Let me start by saying that you've got a great platform, and I'm going to make it better. You've roped in the mommy crowd, but I think we can do more. Let's focus on the younger readers—those twenty-somethings who are perpetually scrolling through Instagram, sharing posts, shouting about their favorite authors, taking pretty photos of books and socks and—"

"Yes." Marguerite pointed a finger at Eliza. "I love it. You understand me. And I understand you, Eliza. Better than you know."

"I think I do," Eliza said diplomatically. "And I'm ready to get started now. Let's kick off your next project with a launch party."

As she spoke, Eliza kept a constant watch on Marguerite's wineglass to ensure it never got too empty. She herself hadn't had more than a sip—she needed to stay sharp—but Marguerite was two and some glasses in and going steady. A greedy gleam had appeared in Marguerite's eyes.

"A launch party? When?" Marguerite murmured. "*Be Free* doesn't come out for another year."

Eliza watched with pleasure as Marguerite reached for a hunk of warm bread and buttered it up, popping a slice in her mouth, too distracted by the images of success and fame to care about calories from gluten.

"Eliza Tate PR doesn't do things like everyone else. We'll have the social sites buzzing early," Eliza said. "That's one of the perks of signing with me. As my first client, you'll be my absolute top priority. I am throwing all my eggs in your basket, Marguerite."

"Go on."

"I believe in you so much that I'm willing to gamble my career on it. I want to help you further your dreams of helping others."

"How do you plan on helping me help others?"

Eliza cleared her throat, took a delicate sip of wine. Then looked Marguerite in the eye. "By selling a shitload of your books."

Marguerite sat back in her seat and raised her glass. "Show me where to sign."

Eliza grinned.

Marguerite tipped her wineglass toward Eliza. "No time to waste. Get out that binder, will you? Take notes. I want to get started. This launch party must be *the* place to be. I want paparazzi. Influencers. Can we get Reese there? Maybe one of her producers?"

"I'll take care of it."

Eliza pulled out her binder as instructed, brazenly opening the cover to reveal a sheaf of blank pages three-hole punched and shoved inside. She watched with pleasure as understanding clicked in Marguerite's eyes.

"Oh, you cocky little bitch." Marguerite drained her glass. "You didn't have a plan at all."

"No, but I have this." Eliza slipped a single-page document from the back folder of the binder. She slid it over, waiting while Marguerite skimmed the contract that would exclusively hitch Marguerite's wagon to Eliza's for the next year. Unabashed, Eliza slid a pen across the table.

Marguerite reached for it. Toying with the pen, she took the cover off and, with a faint click, clipped it on the back end. She eyed Eliza carefully.

"We're going to do great things together, you and I," Eliza said. "I can promise—nobody can stop us."

TRANSCRIPT

Defense: Detective Wilkes, how well do you know Penny Sands?

Mark Wilkes: Well enough, I suppose. She babysat the kids for a while. She got to be good friends with Anne through the babysitting gig. They hung around these last few months. Sometimes Penny would have dinner at our house or whatever.

Defense: Do you have Ms. Sands's number on your phone?

Mark Wilkes: I do.

Defense: Have you ever texted her?

Mark Wilkes: Sure. To set up babysitting times, check in on the kids when we were out, that sort of thing. She'd send pictures when Anne and I were at dinner of the kids in their jammies. Cute stuff like that.

Defense: What about texting conversations that weren't about the children?

Mark Wilkes: I was only friends with Penny through Anne. We never hung out without my wife. Unless I drove her home or something.

Defense: But did you ever send a text message that wasn't a logistical babysitting question?

Mark Wilkes: I guess, maybe a few times.

Defense: What sorts of things would you text about?

Mark Wilkes: I don't know. We weren't… It wasn't inappropriate if that's what you're asking. You can check my phone records. I'm sure you have already, so you should know.

Defense: Did you ever discuss your wife in these messages?

Mark Wilkes: Sure, but just to check on her.

Defense: Were you concerned about Mrs. Wilkes?

Mark Wilkes: Look, I know what you're getting at, and it's not like that. Anne's not the one on trial here. My wife is in a different place than she was three years ago.

Defense: She was diagnosed with postpartum depression after Samuel, yes? She started drinking to cope, according to medical records. Then she left the kids with the babysitter, without notice, and didn't turn up for three days?

Mark Wilkes: I told you, she was going through a hard time. She wasn't sleeping and was barely eating. She'd sometimes have a bit too much wine. She'd get a little paranoid, a little nervous that she wasn't a good mother. When she left, she was trying to do what was best for the kids. She's not the first woman to go through something like this.

Defense: I understand. Was your wife diagnosed with postpartum depression after the twins' birth?

Mark Wilkes: Not yet. Er—no. I mean no.

Defense: But you said specifically "not yet." Is it possible your wife's symptoms are returning? Is that why you've been checking in with Ms. Sands? Is that why your wife fired Ms. Moore, because the babysitter saw too much?

Mark Wilkes: That's none of your business.

Defense: Can you tell me where your wife was the night of February 13?

Mark Wilkes: Out with her girlfriends. I didn't know where. I don't track my wife's movements, because I trust her.

Defense: Maybe you don't track her movements…but did you find out that she was tracking yours? How did that make you feel, Detective Wilkes?

THIRTEEN

Six Months Before
August 2018

Headlights flashed through the window of the Wilkes residence, startling Penny from her perch on the couch. She scanned the baby monitor, saw the little monsters were peacefully sleeping, and hurried into the kitchen.

The adults were home thirty minutes earlier than expected, and Penny hadn't cleaned up her mess. Hastily, she tossed a sandwich into some plastic wrap and shoved the whole thing into her purse, along with a few granola bars from the pantry and a bag of chips that were nearing their expiration date. They probably wouldn't be missed.

Flicking on the faucet, Penny held the Wilkeses' bottle of vodka underneath, letting water cascade over the lip until it refilled to where it was when she'd started. Not that anyone would notice the missing Grey Goose, either, seeing as Penny had found it tucked in a shoebox in the back of Anne's closet.

Which was a bonus because there'd be no danger of the water substitute freezing and giving away her tried-and-true high-school trick. And even if it did, Penny didn't think that Anne would be publicly wondering about her private stash. Most women didn't keep their liquor in a shoebox.

If Penny had learned one thing from her little hobby, it was to steal from people with secrets. People with secrets rarely reported a thief. It was too dangerous.

Breathing heavily, Penny jogged downstairs after sliding the vodka back into its safe cardboard house. Oddly enough, the front door still hadn't opened, and Mark and Anne were nowhere in sight. Penny let out a sigh of relief, then frowned. Had she imagined the whole thing? They couldn't have gotten lost from their driveway to their front door.

Feeling annoyed that she'd rushed for no reason, Penny peeped through the curtains and found her answer. Mark and Anne were twined around one another in plain sight. The floodlights from their driveway illuminated the sickly sweet couple as Mark—handsome, handsome Mark—pressed Anne against the minivan and slid a hand over her ass.

Penny should have given them privacy, but she couldn't stop watching. How could such an average, normal couple be so in love after all those years? Anne and Mark had kids, responsibilities, an average home. Anne wasn't gorgeous. Mark wasn't sexy, but he was a cop, and that gave him immediate attractive points. They sizzled together like teenagers. Why couldn't Penny find someone to look at her like that?

Without warning, Mark suddenly turned his head, scrunching his face to peer against the light at the windows. Penny dropped the blinds, holding her breath and hoping desperately that he hadn't seen the twitch of the curtains. Stupid, stupid. She knew better than to push her boundaries.

A minute later, the front door opened. Both Anne's and Mark's faces were flushed, and private smiles fluttered just beyond reach. Penny wondered if they'd really eaten dinner at all or if they'd just gone straight to a motel. Not that Penny cared. If the love of her life ever noticed her, she would be doing the same thing. *All in time*, she told herself as she pasted a smile on her face.

"Your angels are sleeping," Penny said. "They were just dolls tonight."

Penny rattled off a list of bogus activities they'd accomplished, along with a few snacks she thought they'd eaten. She left out the part about how she'd yelled at Gretchen when the little beast wouldn't put on her pajamas or how she'd hidden Samuel's tablet in her backpack when he refused to take his eyes from the screen. Penny wasn't a saint.

"Wonderful," Anne said, forking over a fistful of cash. "Thank you so much, again, for being here. We really appreciate you helping us out lately."

"Anytime," Penny said. "I hope you two had a nice night. Couple of cocktails, little bit of romance? Just what the doctor ordered. You're both glowing."

"Yes on the romance," Mark agreed. "But we're not big drinkers."

Ah, Penny thought. Hence his wife's vodka in the shoebox. She'd tuck that little nugget away in case she ever needed it. Penny liked to have a pocketful of surprises at the ready. One never knew when they'd come in handy.

"Can Mark give you a ride home?" Anne asked. "I'd offer to do it myself, but I have to check on the kids."

"Oh, I don't want to be a bother. I can catch the bus."

"It's not a problem." Mark flicked his keys around his palm. "I didn't even pull the car into the garage."

"Actually, I was going to meet a friend for a drink near Beverly Hills. If it's not too much trouble, I would really appreciate a lift."

"Gah, to be young and single again!" Anne gave a tittering laugh, then winked at her husband. "I'm kidding of course. Have a great time. Are we still on for Saturday, Penny?"

"Saturday it is," Penny said. "Do you want me to bring anything?"

Anne waved a hand. "Just come over for breakfast, and if you don't mind sitting outside, you and I can chat while the kids play at the park across the street."

"It's a date," Penny said.

Mark gave a peck on the cheek to Anne, then gestured for Penny to follow him outside.

Penny hugged her purse against her side, wincing when the bag of chips crinkled audibly. Luckily, Anne was halfway up the stairs and Mark had one foot out the door, so neither of them noticed. She had to be more careful. She was slipping in her old age.

Once in the car, Penny and Mark managed polite small talk until halfway through the drive. Penny was content to stare out the window and let her thoughts on the evening percolate, but Mark wouldn't leave well enough alone.

"I'm a little worried about Anne."

"Oh?" Penny murmured.

"I know you've been spending some time with her and the kids lately, and I was wondering if you noticed anything different about her."

"Noticed what exactly?"

"Oh, I don't know. She just seems a little nervous or on edge. Maybe something's bothering her? I thought maybe she'd confide in a girlfriend."

"I'm honestly surprised to hear that. The two of you seemed pretty cozy tonight."

"I love her more than anything," Mark said. "She's just a tricky one to pin down."

Penny was again thrown for a loop by Mark's comments. Anne seemed as easy to pin down as anyone. She was a mom to four kids with a squeaky-clean police officer husband. What possible skeletons could be in her closet? Besides the odd bottle of Grey Goose.

"She seems okay," Penny said. "I guess she hasn't told me anything to raise my hackles."

"I'm sure I'm imagining it," Mark said hastily. "Sorry to have asked."

"No, it's fine. Actually, this is good right here."

Penny gestured to a random street corner in the heart of Beverly Hills. There were a few restaurants winking at her with their lights despite the lateness of the hour. Any one of them would do.

"Anne's got friends who live over here," Mark said easily. "I suppose you know them? Roman and Eliza?"

"They referred me to you," Penny said. "Are you good friends with them?"

"Anne and Eliza are the real friends. I just tag along."

"Do you know Roman?"

"Just peripherally. Interesting fellow. Why?"

"No reason. Anyway, thanks for the ride."

"Sure," Mark said. "Is your friend here? I can wait until you find him. Or her."

"I see her inside," Penny said. "Drive home safely. Good night to you and Anne."

"Hey, Penny…" Mark cleared his throat. "Maybe don't tell Anne I asked about her? She gets a little touchy if she thinks I'm digging into her space."

Vodka, vodka, vodka, Penny thought again. "No problem."

Humming a ditty, sweet, naive Mark smiled and rolled up the window as Penny waved goodbye. She let herself into the first restaurant she passed and lied to the clerk about meeting someone so she could use the restroom. Once inside the bathroom, she bolted herself into a stall and pulled out her purse. She shuffled the pilfered food aside until she found the one souvenir that meant something to her.

It was a photo of Anne and Eliza together that she'd lifted from an album in Anne's dresser drawer. But that wasn't the important part. On either side of the women stood their husbands. Penny had been caught off guard when she'd seen Roman's face this evening. She clutched the picture closer and studied him in painstaking detail.

Penny's fingers trembled. If only he weren't married. If only they'd met sooner. If only he were single…

Finally, Penny exited the restaurant and escaped into the fresh night air. It was cool enough that she hugged her sweater closer as she made her way down the block. She crossed the bustling Wilshire Boulevard and strolled up a gorgeous, palm tree–lined street that split, zippering into a residential neighborhood. Penny took the path on the right.

She'd memorized his address. How she'd gotten it wasn't important, but if someone needed to know, she might tell them it was from the little address book in Anne's vanity under the entry of Eliza Tate.

Penny's feet slowed as she neared the house that belonged to him. The first pass, she sauntered by casually, hands shoved in her pockets as she pretended to be soaking in the picturesque scenery. She stole a glance down the driveway and caught sight of a few cars parked there. The lights were blazing from every orifice of the skeletal house, taunting Penny as she huddled deeper against her sweater as a brisk wind teased hair across her face.

The second time, Penny moved even slower as she passed his residence. She just wanted a glimpse. To see how the other side lived. To see what sort of woman made Roman Tate tick. What sort of woman had intrigued him enough to give up all others for a lifetime. Penny wondered what it would take to get him to notice her.

There was movement behind the window. A slim figure carried a tray of food into another room. The rustle of stolen chips triggered Penny's annoyance as she watched the rich, the wealthy, as they chowed down on gourmet meals while she was stuck sneaking scraps from her employers.

Penny's head ached. She'd had too much vodka. The kids had been so loud. She needed to go home, to get some rest. The last thing she wanted was to be caught standing outside the Tate residence. That would be one surefire way to get Roman thinking she was nutty. And Penny wasn't nutty; she was dedicated.

"What are you doing here?"

Penny swiveled toward the voice. "Roman. You scared me."

Roman stood sheathed in shadow by the front gate. In his hand, he carried a garbage bag that was only a quarter full. He tossed the bag into the trash can waiting at the end of the drive for the next morning's maintenance. *Probably his excuse for creeping out mid-dinner party*, Penny surmised as Roman slid his hands into his pockets, looking almost mystical as the streetlamp kissed his high cheekbones. With his dark turtleneck and black jeans, he looked practically draconian in nature.

When it was clear Roman wasn't going to speak (and really, why should he when it was Penny who needed to explain?), she cleared her throat. Raised her eyes to his.

"I, uh, was in the neighborhood," Penny said. "Had a drink with a friend at a bar and went for a walk to clear my head after."

"Lies." Roman took one step closer to her.

"I did have a drink," Penny revised. "And I was in the neighborhood."

"Lies," Roman said, taking another step.

"Not the drink."

"No, not that." Roman took a third step. He was near enough for Penny to smell the whiskey on his breath.

"Not that," Penny chimed in a whisper.

"Why are you here?" he repeated finally. His eyes flicked toward the window as a wave of laughter sounded from inside. "This is my house."

"I just—" Penny swallowed hard. "I don't know."

Roman's eyebrow raised. More laughter from the inside. *Ha-ha-ha*, Penny thought, the sound getting on her nerves. Suddenly, nothing was funny. That hint of anger returned, her guilt at being outside Roman's house taking a back seat to the injustice of it all. If anyone could rationalize their way out of a sticky situation, it was Penny Sands.

"Damn it, Roman." She took a jagged breath. "What the hell is going on here? You kissed me in your office, and then..."

Roman raised a hand, pressed it over Penny's mouth. "They'll hear you."

She smacked it away. "I don't care! It's the truth, isn't it?"

"It's complicated." Another flick of his eyes. *Flick, flick, flick.*

"Then you shouldn't have kissed me. I deserve better. Your wife deserves better."

"You don't understand."

"Then explain."

"Roman, did you get lost out there?" Another titter of laughter followed as a woman's voice trickled through a rectangle of light splicing the otherwise dark driveway. Roman must have left the door cracked.

"Be right in," he called over his shoulder, keeping his gaze firmly moored on Penny's. "I can't talk now. Soon, I promise. I'll explain everything."

"But—"

Then, like the very ocean itself, Roman tugged Penny below the surface as his lips crashed against hers, and together, they swirled, topsy-turvy through uncharted waters. Her hands dug into his hair, and though she tried to stop, she couldn't. When Roman finally released her from the kiss, Penny was left standing speechless on the sidewalk outside the Tate house, watching the man she loved return to his pretty little life.

TRANSCRIPT

Defense: When's the last time you had a glass of wine, Mrs. Wilkes?

Anne Wilkes: A few days ago. I don't know. I don't keep track.

Defense: That's interesting, isn't it? Many recovering alcoholics know the date of their last drink.

Anne Wilkes: I'm not a recovering alcoholic.

Defense: Did you or did you not check yourself into a rehab facility three years ago? Your son Samuel would have been about a year old at the time.

Anne Wilkes: I checked myself in, and I checked myself right back out. I'm fine. Going to that center was a mistake. I had everything under control then, and I still do now.

Defense: Your husband testified yesterday that he's been concerned about you. That you're drinking again. Have you seen a doctor recently, Mrs. Wilkes?

Anne Wilkes: I'm sorry, how is this relevant to the case?

Defense: Your Honor, Mrs. Wilkes has a history of making rash, unstable, and downright danger-ous decisions. She also had a reason to want the victim dead. I think Mrs. Wilkes's precarious mental state is completely relevant to the case at hand.

The Court: Please answer the question, Mrs. Wilkes.

Anne Wilkes: My mental state isn't precarious. It's fine. I'm fine. I walked away from my kids once, and I don't plan on doing it ever again. Not for him, at least. If I had killed him, I would have made damn sure I wasn't caught. Whoever killed him was sloppy. That's not how I work.

FOURTEEN

Six Months Before
August 2018

T
he launch party for *Be Free* is tonight, and I kept your name on the guest list in case you changed your mind about attending," Eliza said. "You really should come. You'll love Marguerite. Plus, you need to get out and talk with other adults. Keep your mind off things at home."

"I don't know."

"Well, you know where to find me. It's not every day you're invited to the Pelican Hotel."

Anne considered Eliza's invitation. "I'd love to come, but the kids…"

"What about that new sitter Roman sent your way?"

"Penny? She's great. But I had her over twice last week to help, and we saw each other on the weekend… I can't spring this on her short notice."

"You have a husband, don't you?"

"Mark? You think he'd offer to watch all four kids at bedtime?"

The pause told Anne that Eliza was having a hard time understanding the monumental task she'd be asking of her husband.

"Whatever. That's not important," Anne said on a sigh. "Tonight is about you. *Your* company is throwing a launch party for Marguerite Hill! How awesome is that? I have her book in my van."

"The first one? I gave that to you ages ago. Have you finished it yet?"

"I've made good progress," Anne hedged. "The kids have been sick for the last few weeks."

"And the weeks before that?"

"I'm working on it!" Anne grinned across the phone line. "It's not my fault. If you'd made it mandatory reading for a book club or something, maybe I would have finished it on time. You know I need deadlines, or I'll procrastinate forever."

"A book club." Eliza sounded genuinely intrigued. "Not a bad idea actually. Anyway, I'll see you tonight. I know you'll make the right choice."

The door opened downstairs, and Anne sighed yet again. "Speak of the devil, I've got to go. Time to feed the vultures."

"We're having catered appetizers tonight." Eliza needled Anne with a tantalizing lilt to her voice. "Bacon-wrapped scallops for starters. There will be a nice bubbly champagne, chilled of course, and an ice wine tasting. And don't forget the best part of all…"

"I'm already drooling. Don't torture me."

"You don't have to cook, wash, or clean a single dish."

"I think I just had an orgasm."

"See you soon."

Eliza hung up first, leaving Anne to stare at the silent phone. She blinked, considering the invitation while stifling the longing rising with it. Did she want to go? The answer was an easy, resounding yes. Should she go? That answer was a bit murkier. She had kids to feed, a husband to look after, a house to clean…

Anne sighed, returning to fiddle with her dresser some more. She was determined to fix it so the damn drawers didn't squeak. For some reason, the state of the vanity had become an obsession for her in recent weeks. What had been a minor inconvenience for more than a decade had suddenly become a major headache. She couldn't stop fixating on the stupid thing.

Wiping sweating palms on yoga pants that hadn't seen the inside of a washer in far too long, Anne set to work. She'd been picking away at this project for days, but the Wilkes household had been more chaotic than normal as of late.

Harry had picked up a nasty bug at daycare that had been transferred from one child to the next until the rotation was complete. Anne had been up to her elbows in sick children for weeks, so much so that she'd barely had time to think about Mark.

And when she did finally focus on her husband, he pretended everything was hunky-dory. The last time they'd gone out to dinner while Penny watched the children, they'd skipped all four courses and had spent the night making out in the van and ordering McDonald's drive-thru sundaes. Was it any wonder Anne was baffled?

It was only when she stopped to think that she found herself in trouble. Anne still hadn't decided what to do with the information she'd gleaned from the private investigator. It seemed too crass and trashy to confront Mark head-on with it. But she couldn't go on ignoring the fact that he was lying to her. And on the path to trading her in for a busty little coed.

"Damn it!" Anne raised one leg and propped her foot against the dresser as she yanked against the stuck top drawer. "Stupid piece of junk! Let go—"

Anne yelped as the drawer squeaked loose with a grating cry of wood on wood. She flew back, plopping harshly on her tailbone as the contents of the drawer flew everywhere. Underwear landed on the floor, and the small tub of makeup she kept stashed out of sight from her children clattered away, tubes of lipstick and mascara rolling under the bed.

Mark found her like that. Sitting on the floor, a comatose mess, staring blankly at the rubble scattered around their bedroom. The drawer hung open, leaning precariously from its perch like a wiggly tooth not quite ready to fall out. Anne didn't notice any of it.

She didn't move the first time Mark called her name, nor did she move the second. The third time, she twitched to attention. Without responding, she rose to her feet, wincing as her heel came to land on a set of tweezers that would no doubt be bent out of shape. The only nice pair she had left, gone for good.

She blinked and instructed herself not to cry. It worked, but only just.

"What are you doing here, honey?" Mark asked, the original smile on his face melting away as he caught sight of the look on Anne's. "Is everything okay? Are you... Should I call the doctor?"

"Stop it! Just fucking *stop it*!" Anne swiveled to face him. "Don't you trust me?"

"Anne, please."

"I'm telling you everything is fine," Anne insisted. "Just peachy."

"Did I do something?" Mark raised his hands in surrender. "Is it the kids? Long day?"

"Long day?" Anne raised one of her eyebrows, her voice taking on a high-pitched whine that rivaled the screech of the broken drawer. "Try a long couple of weeks. Are you aware it's been a game of whack-a-mole around here? One kid pukes, and I clean it up. Before I throw out the trash, the next turns around and gets sick all over everything. It's been weeks, Mark!"

"I know, and I'm sorry. I'm sorry so much of the burden around here has fallen on your shoulders lately. But they've all been through it now, and we're on the tail end of the bug—"

"We?" she blurted. "*We?*"

"I mean..." Mark studied Anne as if the right answer was elusive. "I know I've been working a lot—too much, probably. But we've had some big cases come in, and I couldn't pass up the overtime."

"Right. Well, thank you for your sacrifice."

"I took you out to dinner. It's not like we haven't spent any time together."

"I appreciate that. I do. But what I really need is about a week of sleep."

"You're not thinking…"

"Yes, Mark." Anne wheeled to face her husband. "I'm thinking about running away for a week and leaving the kids with the babysitter. Again. Is that what you wanted me to say?"

Mark's eyes narrowed. "That is not funny."

"I'm not laughing."

"Sweetheart, I understand you are stressed and tired and exhausted and sick of the kids being sick. But you're taking this out on me. Can we just talk about it? Maybe make an appointment with Dr. Olsen?"

"I don't feel like talking, and I especially don't feel like talking to a shrink."

"Come here. I think you need a back rub and a nice bath. Take a little time to cool down, collect yourself, and this will pass."

"What exactly will pass?"

"This…the rough patch. Whatever it is. The kids are growing up so fast. The twins will be out of diapers soon enough. Car seats will be next. Before you know it, you'll be wondering where your babies went."

"That's not what this is about. This is about my life falling to pieces, Mark." Anne waved her arms toward the dresser. "Look at the stupid vanity. The drawers don't work. My things are ruined. I wake up the entire house every time I need to grab a bra. And for crying out loud, it's not even a real vanity! It's a set of drawers playing dress-up."

Mark stilled. "I never knew that bothered you. I thought it was sentimental. We made it, you and me. It was one of the first pieces of furniture we owned together."

"Yes. We still own it almost twenty years later, and it's a piece of crap."

Mark looked at the tipsy drawer, the clothes scattered on the floor. Then he quietly began to pick everything up and pile it into haphazard stacks on the bed. Underwear. Makeup. A few bras that had toppled out.

When he finished, he gently slid the drawer back into place, tested it a few times. Aside from the errant squeak that had been there for years and never bothered Anne before, it worked perfectly. Then he went through and checked every other drawer. They all worked just fine. Once he finished, he turned and left the room.

Anne sank back to the floor. Tears were stuck somewhere deep in her psyche, not interested in leaving. She felt stuck. *Stuck, stuck, stuck.* She couldn't cry; she couldn't calm. All she could do was stare at the dresser, every chip and flaw on display, formerly charming, now a nuisance.

When the sun went down outside her bedroom window, Anne finally pulled herself together. She stepped into her closet and stared at the racks of clothing there. Nothing would work.

She reached down, fumbled through her shoeboxes, and found the lucky winner. Sitting on the floor of her closet, shrouded by old dresses and jeans hanging over her shoulders, Anne released the emergency bottle of vodka from her stash and tipped its contents into her mouth. She frowned, smacked her lips. God, her tolerance was getting strong. Since when had Grey Goose started tasting like water?

Anne took one more swig and then tucked her darling bottle back into the box where it belonged. She kicked it against the wall and then stood, waiting for the alcohol to kick in. It did but just barely as she thumbed through her dreary old selection of clothes.

Everything Anne owned screamed "mom" across it in bold, invisible letters. Yoga pants. Button-down shirts. Sweatshirts that boasted the name of Gretchen's dance studio or Samuel's soccer team. Even her jeans were high-waisted and unattractive.

It wasn't until Anne really got creative digging around in the back of her closet and unearthed the few things she'd hoarded from her pre-baby days that she found a winner. A bright wrap dress in a shade of blood red that Anne had purchased some ten years back on a shopping date with Eliza. She'd never worn it.

Anne pulled it out and held it against her body. Because the fabric was flowy and the style a wrap, it was forgiving enough to slide easily around Anne's four-babies-later physique.

After thirty minutes of preparations, Anne paraded downstairs, expecting everyone's heads to turn. Unfortunately, she had overestimated her family's observation skills.

When she reached the landing, she found Gretchen sitting on the couch with a bowl of ice cream in her lap and a can of whipped cream next to her. Samuel was perched like a cat on the high back of an armchair where, like the cat, he wasn't allowed to climb.

The twins were fussing with one another on the floor in front of the TV, alternating between staring at the screen and whacking one another with a toothbrush in the shape of a banana. Mark had put on a ball game and kicked his feet up on the ottoman.

As Anne watched, Mark leaned over and swiped the whipped cream from his daughter. He encased the entire tip in his mouth and depressed the nozzle until it hissed with the blissful sound of ejaculating whipped cream. Then he shot a cheesy smile at Gretchen before swallowing.

She burst into giggles at the sight of her father's antics until she toppled over sideways, tucking her head on his lap and curling her legs up next to him on the couch. Mark laid a tender hand on her forehead and playfully tugged his fingers through her hair. Gretchen pointed at the TV and asked a question about the game, and Samuel hurried to give his input, looking quite pleased when Mark praised his answer.

Anne inhaled sharply at the sight of her neat little family enjoying life without her. They hadn't noticed her absence nor her presence. Gretchen took pride in sassing back to her mother, but the second Mark came home, she perked right up into a sweet little girl. Samuel selectively couldn't hear when Anne spoke directly into his ear, but when Mark whispered a question from ten miles away, Samuel rushed to answer. Anne had never felt more invisible.

A spurt of jealousy streaked through her. Why did Mark commandeer such love and attention when he didn't deserve it? The children were oblivious to Mark's lies. All they saw was the wonderful man, the caring, devoted father Anne thought she'd married.

With a whisper of shame, Anne reminded herself that they didn't need to know any of it. Mark could be a bad husband and a good father all at once. That was what made the inner workings of her heart so sticky to maneuver. She didn't love the husband he was becoming, but she still admired the father he was to their children. What did that mean for their marriage? For their family?

"Mark," Anne said sharply, the jealousy eating away at her tone. "We don't stick the can directly into our mouths in this house. That is how we pass around sicknesses in one continual cycle."

Before Mark could respond, Gretchen reached for the can and tipped it upside down. She made a tower of whipped cream straight on her tongue before lazily handing the can back to her dad. Anne wasn't sure whether Gretchen had simply perfected the art of tuning Anne out or if she'd heard her mother and staunchly ignored her.

"Gretchen!" Anne snapped. "What did I *just* say?"

"What?" Gretchen said, turning to face her mother with a defiant look. "Dad did it. If Dad does it, why can't I?"

"Gretchen," Mark began uncertainly. His eyes flicked toward Anne with a look that said he knew he should be punishing Gretchen but that he really didn't want to follow through. "Listen to your mother."

"Actually, listen to your father," Anne corrected. "I'm going out tonight."

Mark's eyes landed more solidly on Anne, and he gave a low whistle. "You look amazing."

"Thank you," Anne said stiffly. "I don't know exactly when I'll be back, so don't wait up."

The words took a while to sink in. Between the ball game in the background and Anne's red dress, Mark was clearly struggling to line up the puzzle pieces. He tilted an ear toward the TV as if listening to the game while his eyes fixed on Anne's cleavage. In his defense, her cleavage hadn't been visible to the public eye since sometime circa 2013.

"Sorry, what did you say?"

Anne felt weak with frustration. Her daughter didn't listen, and neither did her husband. Samuel might as well *be* the cat for how much attention he paid anyone else. The twins were excused from Anne's wrath, but they had spent the last hour entertained by a single banana toothbrush, so that wasn't saying much.

"I said I'm going out," Anne said calmly. "I figure since you're home, you can put the kids to bed."

"All of them?"

Anne merely blinked. "Unless you'd like to pick and choose your favorites."

Mark shot to his feet. "I'm just surprised. Er, I was hoping to watch the game, and…" His eyebrows knitted together. "You didn't say where you're going, did you?"

"Eliza's new company is throwing a book launch party. I think it would be good for me to get out for the night."

Anne could see Mark racking his brain for the mention of any such party. A tiny part of Anne would normally have felt bad for misleading her husband, but she didn't have room for an extra dollop of guilt this evening.

"Be careful with the twins. If they chew on that toothbrush too much, the bristles come off. Samuel is not allowed on the back of the chair like that. I suggest you get him down before he hits his head trying to leap off the back like Tarzan again. And Gretchen will try to tell you her new bedtime is eleven thirty. It's not. Lights out by nine. That means books, teeth, bath, everything else." Anne glanced at her watch. "That doesn't leave you much time, and the twins both need a bath. Samuel will need a snack."

"A snack?" Mark echoed, as if that were the deal breaker. "What sort of snack?"

"Not ice cream," Anne said, "since it looks like that's what you let them eat for dinner."

Mark ran a sheepish hand through his hair. "I just… We kept

waiting for you to come down and say dinner was ready, and then they got hungry, so I let them have a little snack."

"It sounds like you have everything taken care of." Anne checked her watch again. "I really should be going."

A panicked look appeared in Mark's eyes. "You're really going? I thought—wasn't I invited? Maybe we could get the babysitter to come by..."

Anne let Mark flounder for a few moments. When he petered out, she smiled.

"I'm sure you have everything under control," she reiterated. "Don't worry about waiting up for me. I don't know when I'll be home."

"Anne—"

"I already told you," she said calmly, leveling her gaze on Mark's and daring him to bring up *the unmentionable incident*. "I am leaving, and I don't know when I'll be home."

TRANSCRIPT

Prosecution: How often did you see Roman Tate while in a relationship with him?

Penny Sands: I didn't keep track. There's no journal with a tally or something. Why does it matter?

Prosecution: Weekly, biweekly, daily?

Penny Sands: I don't know. I suppose a couple of times a week.

Prosecution: Where would you meet?

Penny Sands: Mostly where it all started. The Pelican Hotel.

Prosecution: Why there?

Penny Sands: Well, my apartment is a dump, and Roman was still living with his wife. I'm sure you can understand why that would've been awkward.

Prosecution: Then how did you end up in Eliza Tate's living room on the afternoon of February 13?

FIFTEEN

Six Months Before
August 2018

P enny gasped at the price. *Three dollars for a stupid can of beans?* She stood there, blocking the aisle as she hugged a plastic basket to her chest, gazing at the can in her hands like it was a brick of solid gold. At the Mexican supermarket down the street from her apartment, she could buy a bag of dried beans for eighty-nine cents that would last her a week. This was highway robbery.

Still, Penny plunked the damn beans in her basket with a frustrated flourish before stomping toward the front of the store. Swinging by the cold case, she nabbed a stupid Fiji water and added that to her tab, too. When she reached the meat section, however, she lost her nerve. The price stamped across the chicken breasts was just too much. Instead, she reached for a head of lettuce that was two shocking dollars more expensive than it needed to be.

Then again, that was the price tag of her field trip to the ritzy grocery stores near Beverly Hills. Heading over to the sample cart, Penny snagged two chunks of cheese instead of the customary one. If she was going to donate half her savings to this stupid store, they could at least feed her lunch.

She was halfway into the cheesecake sample at the bakery when she felt the hand on her arm. Choking down a bite of buttery crust, she turned and pasted a look of surprise on her face.

"Penny?" Roman's voice asked a question, but the look in his eyes said he wasn't fooled. "What are you doing in my neck of the woods?"

"Oh, hi." The cheesecake was suddenly sticky. Penny swallowed. Again. "Just doing the weekly grocery shopping."

Roman's eyes flicked to her dismal basket. In his arms, Penny noted, was a spread of delicacies. Fresh produce, beautiful fruits, packages of meats and cheese, and even a bottle of champagne. *What's he celebrating?* she wondered aimlessly.

"I see," Roman said. "That looks like some diet."

"Just the essentials today. How about you?"

"Same," he said. "Just on my way out."

"Me too."

Penny scurried toward the register first, as if that would make her cover story hold water. She wasn't convinced Roman believed her. She wasn't convinced she cared.

"We're together." Roman's voice rolled warmly over Penny's shoulder as she set her basket next to the clerk. "Please ring these up together."

Penny's shoulders went rigid. "You don't have to—"

"You've barely got anything." Roman waved her arguments away. "It's not worth the paper of two receipts. You're saving the world, Penny Sands, one receipt at a time. You can't say no to that, can you?"

"I couldn't possibly."

She played along, wondering how on earth they'd gone from their awkward last encounter to this playful, exciting one. And just like that, like the snap of a breadstick, Penny thought they were back on track.

Once they'd checked out and each held her bag—one significantly more full than the other—Penny and Roman walked side by side out the sliding doors. She glanced sideways at him and wondered if this was what it would feel like. Their life, if they were ever allowed to live it together. Grocery shopping, cracking jokes, smiling beneath a sunny day.

"Where's your car?" Roman asked. "I can walk you to it."

"I took the bus."

"The bus?"

"You know, the big thing with wheels that carts people around town."

"I'll give you a ride home," Roman said. "Where do you live?"

"That's really not—"

"Hollywood?"

Penny wondered if Roman had checked her files or if it was a lucky guess. Maybe it didn't make a difference.

"Hollywood," she confirmed. Then, on a whim, "I guess if you're not busy..."

The car ride to Penny's apartment started out quiet. They passed the first few minutes listening to easy jazz, staring out the windows. There were a million questions Penny wanted to ask, but to do so would ruin the day. After two city blocks in tense silence, Penny made the snap decision to relax and enjoy. To let Roman make the first move this time around. Penny had cued him up. It was time to let him take the reins.

Twenty minutes later, and Roman hadn't taken a swing. The two had managed bits of small talk as they cruised through the palm tree–lined streets but had avoided anything of substance. In a sense, it was almost a relief—the normalcy of it all.

"I'm right here," Penny said finally, gesturing toward her building. "Thank you so much for the ride."

"You're not going to invite me up?"

Penny wiped her sweaty palms on her lap. When she glanced over at Roman, she saw him give her a teasing smile, but a sparkling challenge glistened in his eyes. She wasn't sure what to make of it.

"I don't have a great place," she said. "Sadly, the inside's not much better than the outside."

They both stared at the outside for a moment.

"I think that's a wise decision," Roman said, his lips flickering in another quick smile as he turned back. "It was nice seeing you today."

"Roman..." Penny heaved a breath.

She wanted to ask what they were doing. Why he was so kind and friendly to her sometimes, and why, other times, he was cold and distant. But she couldn't vocalize those questions, because they might ruin everything. She'd learned from Ryan Anderson that sometimes, less was more. More could quickly become too much. And too much was...suffocating.

"It was nice to see you, too." Penny climbed out of the car, ripping her gaze from Roman's before they broke their peaceful moment. "I guess I'll see you around."

She rushed inside, hoofed it upstairs. She was just putting away her paltry items when there was a knock on the door. Penny just about fainted onto her can of beautiful, overpriced beans. Three dollars was a small price to pay for the day she'd had. Especially if it involved Roman coming upstairs because he'd found he just couldn't stay away.

Rushing to the door, Penny pulled it open, her heart sinking as she found Lucky standing there instead. He wore a stained wifebeater and pinched a cigarette between his lips. He held a grocery bag in his hands.

"Some asshole left this outside my door with your name on it," Lucky said. "Is it the same asshole who keeps sending you flowers?"

"I—" Penny didn't think Ryan's incessant flower sending was a particularly asshole-ish move, but apparently it annoyed her landlord. "Sorry."

"Tell your suitor that deliveries need to be left outside your door," Lucky said. "Next time they leave something outside my door...it's mine."

"Understood."

Penny reached for the bag of groceries and drew it to her. She kicked the door shut behind her and immediately went to the couch and deposited it on the cushion next to her. On top, there was a note: *Enjoy. —Roman*

Penny pressed the note to her chest. It was written in pencil on the back of a receipt for gas—something that had probably been sitting in Roman's glove compartment. Then she set it down and reached for the bag.

She spent the next half hour carefully unpacking the gorgeous, gorgeous supplies that would feed a king for a month. As she delicately washed raspberries and daintily plucked grapes off their vines, she felt optimistic for the first time in weeks. He cared for her. He must, or else why would he have left her a bag of groceries that had cost well over a hundred dollars?

There was the small chance Roman would have done the same thing for anyone—offered a ride, gifted groceries, made light banter in the car. But was that actually true? If it were Ryan Anderson he'd run into in the store, would Roman have offered him a ride home and teased him about being invited upstairs?

Penny popped a grape into her mouth and chewed.

She thought not.

TRANSCRIPT

Prosecution: Mr. Anderson, please tell us about your relationship with Penny Sands.

Ryan Anderson: Well, I noticed Penny the day she walked into class. I don't think she noticed me, though. Not that I was surprised. I mean, she's gorgeous, and I'm just…well, me.

Prosecution: What made her start noticing you?

Ryan Anderson: I asked her on a date a few weeks into class.

Prosecution: And she accepted?

Ryan Anderson: She sure did. We went out a few times.

Prosecution: Did you ever have sex with Ms. Sands?

Ryan Anderson: Do I have to answer that?

The Court: Yes.

Ryan Anderson: We slept together a couple of times. It was great. Penny's great. We were starting to care about one another, so don't get any ideas about her being easy.

Prosecution: You started to care for Ms. Sands?

Ryan Anderson: Yeah, I did. I really liked her. What's not to like? She's cute, sweet, fun. Not enough of that out here in Hollywood.

Prosecution: Did Penny reciprocate your feelings?

Ryan Anderson: I think so.

Prosecution: Why did the two of you stop seeing each other?

Ryan Anderson: It was her choice. She started dating someone else.

Prosecution: Did you know who?

Ryan Anderson: Not at the time. I obviously know now.

Prosecution: Were there any hard feelings between the two of you?

Ryan Anderson: Nope. There weren't then, and there aren't now. At least as far as I know.

Prosecution: You studied under Roman Tate as well, didn't you?

Ryan Anderson: That's where we met.

Prosecution: What did you think of him?

Ryan Anderson: I thought he was talented. But apparently the real talent was his wife.

Prosecution: What makes you say that?

Ryan Anderson: Eliza Tate killed her husband and almost got away with it. I mean, that's rule number one in Hollywood, right? It's always the wife.

SIXTEEN

Six Months Before
August 2018

Skulking into the familiar studio off Sunset Boulevard, Penny smoothed the flirty ruffles fringing the bottom of her skirt and wondered if this would be the night. The night Roman finally explained everything.

The thing that had been bothering Penny about their relationship was that she'd never set out to destroy a marriage. As a rule, she only stole things that wouldn't be missed. She didn't steal *husbands*. Penny had never desired complicated, and she was entering the definition of complicated—especially after their pleasant pseudo-date at the grocery store. So what if Penny had orchestrated it? Roman was the one who'd offered her a ride home.

Three strikes and he's out, Penny reminded herself. Roman had been promising to explain himself for some time now, and he'd had plenty of opportunities. If he couldn't make good on his word to come clean to Penny, there would be no more chances. As difficult as it would be, she would walk away.

Sliding like an eel into her auditorium seat, Penny made a show of adjusting her headphones to avoid conversation with her peers. She doodled on the notebook in front of her, so lost in her thoughts, she didn't bat an eye when Ryan Anderson took the chair next to her.

"Hey, Penny," he said, flicking his pretty hair off his pretty forehead. "You look nice."

Penny gave a tight smile, a flimsy nod.

"Say, I was wondering," Ryan continued, oblivious to her sour mood, "if I could buy you a drink tonight?"

Penny looked over at Ryan. He flinched under her scathing stare. A wiggle of guilt tripped into Penny's stomach, but she pushed it away and relented slightly, softening her glare around the edges.

"I'm not sure that's a good idea."

"But—I thought—" Ryan frowned. "I'm sorry, I guess I got the wrong impression. Did I say something wrong? I thought we had a nice time?"

"No, we did… It's not you. I'm not in a great place right now."

"Ah."

The wiggle of guilt returned. Ryan had been nothing but sweet and interested in the weeks following their last date, texting her occasionally and sending flowers to her apartment once a week. But Penny couldn't find it in herself to muster any sort of enthusiasm in return. A fact that was more than a little concerning if she thought about it. So most days, Penny avoided thinking about it.

Roman entered the room then, looking like a man against Ryan's boyish, hopeful expression. A sigh fell from Penny's lips as she watched him, unable to ignore the fact that Roman refused to make eye contact with her. She looked down and scratched at her notebook. Debated. Got an idea.

"Actually…" She spun back to face Ryan and encouraged her lips to wear a smile. "Let's get a drink," Penny amended. "It'll be good for me to get out."

"Great! I'll pick you up at your place around ten."

As Penny nodded in confirmation, she felt the first pricks of satisfaction trickling down her spine. Penny had learned the hard way that people liked to take from her. They took, and they took, and they took…until she took back. Currently, Roman was taking everything from her. In order to regain a tiny bit of control, it was time for Penny to act. Even if the only thing she could take was her willingness to wait.

Penny's false smile flickered into one of genuine interest as she felt a figure approach her seat. Without glancing that way, she knew it was Roman. She could sense his presence by the flash of hot breath against her neck. But instead of feeling hopeful and uneasy, she felt calm and collected. That was what taking did for Penny—it balanced her.

"Could I speak to you for a moment, Ms. Sands?" Roman's voice rolled like a thundercloud over her shoulder. "In private."

Ryan gave Penny a knowing smile. *If only he knew*, Penny thought dryly, pulling herself from her seat and stalking backstage after her instructor. It was abandoned since most students either hadn't yet arrived or were filing into their seats.

"I'm sorry," Roman said abruptly, whirling to face Penny in a darkened corner of the room.

He caught Penny off guard, both with the intensity of his stare and the apology. "For?"

"Let's not play this game." Roman's lips twitched into a ghost of a smile. "I don't think it's a good idea for you to go out with Ryan Anderson."

"What's it to you?" she said in shocked disbelief that her plan had worked so quickly. "You're married. Remember?"

"I know boys like Ryan, and I know women like you." Roman inched closer to Penny. His hand came up as if he wanted to touch her, but he refrained. "You deserve better."

"The man I want isn't available."

"What if he is?"

Her throat dried. "He's not—"

"Would an unavailable man kiss you like this?" Roman backed Penny against the wall, pressed her hard against it. He dipped his head to hers, tasted her. Lingered.

His touch made Penny shiver; his words made her blush. Her

head knocked against the wall. She liked it, the raw intensity of it all. She'd never felt more wanted, more needed. It was her weakness, to be wanted, her kryptonite. And either Roman Tate had fallen right back in love with Penny Sands, or he was even better at playing the game than she.

But as Penny knew, all good things came to an end. This time, the end came in a rush as Penny's wits flooded back to her. She stepped back, hugging her arms around her body. "You promised! You promised me you'd explain."

"Penny—"

"That's the last time you'll kiss me." Penny felt tears sting her eyes. "I don't know why, but I care too much about you to have half of you. And if you aren't ready to give me everything, then this is where we end."

Penny waited, watching Roman's face for a sign he would relent, silently wishing the hopeful part of her would die so she could walk away unscathed. But emotions were stubborn things, and Penny's refused to let go without a cost.

When Roman couldn't do more than shake his head, Penny blinked and gave a nod of finality. She turned, striding away from him even as he started to speak. She never heard what he had to say, because she was already gone.

Karma, karma. Penny had taken from many, and now the thing she wanted most was being taken from her. Not that it had ever been hers to have—a small fact that had never stopped her before.

As she stalked out of the studio, she ignored Ryan's confused wave. She ignored his text, too, and burst out the doorway through the throng of students trying to weave their way inside. Penny got an elbow to the ribs while another student stepped on her foot. She didn't stop until she was outside, sucking fresh air like her life depended on it.

She didn't look at her phone until she made it home. A text message was waiting for her.

Four words.

Can I come over?

Penny's phone beeped.

She cracked one eye open and was rewarded by a shard of sunlight piercing her bedroom window. The shades were pulled, but as most of them were broken or dented, they failed to block the morning's rays.

The figure next to her shifted, groaned. "Can you do something about the brightness? I'm going blind."

Penny was too busy reaching for her phone to respond. After one look at the screen, she sat up in bed, pulling the sheets tight to her chest. Another email. Another message from Roman.

"Did you hear me?" Ryan mumbled. "Put your phone down, babe. What's so important this early in the morning? Don't tell me it's him."

"Him?" Penny froze. *Was she that obvious?* If Ryan Anderson had noticed that Penny had been obsessing over Roman, who else had noticed? "What are you talking about?"

"I don't know. You tell me."

Penny was too distracted by her phone to worry about Ryan's somewhat cryptic answer. Maybe Ryan had just made a lucky guess, and it was Penny who was driving herself wild with paranoia. Musing over the idea, she hauled herself out of bed and slipped her robe over naked shoulders. Tightening the strap around her waist, she grabbed one of three towels she owned and threw it over the curtain rod to block the light.

"You look nice." Ryan peeked out from under his arm. "Come back to bed. I didn't mean anything by it."

"Let me put on some coffee first."

Ryan made a playful, half-hearted swipe for Penny's robe, but she ducked out of the way and scurried toward the kitchen. Instead of feeling playful back, she felt annoyed. Not that Ryan had done anything wrong. To be fair, he'd been quite generous the previous evening... starting with the big bouquet of beautiful roses and ending with her first orgasm in months. His persistence had to count for something.

Unfortunately for Penny, his persistence was a bit smothering. She found his lavish gifts too forward. His thoughtful, frequent texts annoying. She hated the way he called her on the phone *just to talk*. She shrugged off his advances every time they were in public and he tried to kiss her or, God forbid, hold her hand.

She was being ridiculous. Other women would kill for the attention Ryan was trying to shower on her. But Penny's logic had broken somewhere along the line, and as her thoughts of Ryan coincided with her memory from the previous evening, a rush of warmth climbed Penny's spine, followed by a slow drip of guilt into her belly.

She'd kissed Roman. Slept with Ryan. And the fact that she'd done both in one day meant she'd probably been trying to scrub Roman's kiss from her mind by sliding between the sheets with Ryan.

Penny shoved the carafe a bit too hard into the coffee maker, rattling the glass walls. She scrunched her eyes shut to prevent the nausea from overtaking her. Penny's mother had warned her about men like Roman, but she hadn't listened; she'd thought she could handle him. But Penny Sands was no match for Roman Tate.

Penny leaned a hip against the counter. At the same time, she wasn't interested in a man like Ryan. She had simply latched on to him like a lifeboat in a raging ocean, hoping for a splash of warmth in a dark and frigid storm.

Roman, on the other hand, was a yacht—a magnificent, elusive boat far superior to all the rest. Ryan Anderson would never be a yacht. But what good was a yacht if it was always out of reach? Shouldn't she choose the lifeboat if the alternative was drowning?

As the coffee gurgled to life, she glanced again at her phone before flipping it upside down and leaving it on the counter. She made her way back to her lifeboat and perched on the bed. Ryan's fingers stroked her knee, and the simple movement weakened her resolve. But it didn't eradicate it.

"Ryan, I'm going to be honest with you."

He ran a hand through his hair, his gym-toned muscles flexing as he gave her a curious look. "Okay."

"Like I told you last night, I'm not in the best place right now. Emotionally, I mean. I'm trying to get over someone."

"I was right." Ryan winked. "It was him that texted you this morning. I know the signs."

Penny sighed. "I don't want you to feel like I'm using you."

"You can use me all you want. I don't mind."

"Just so long as we're clear, this isn't..." Penny hesitated. "We're not, like, an item or anything."

His grin faded to a more neutral expression, and he shrugged. "Don't overthink it. We're just having some fun. Isn't that what life is all about?"

Penny gave him a ghost of a smile. She wasn't sure she knew what life was about anymore. Chasing dreams? Finding a soul mate? Living by the rules...or breaking them all?

She shrugged. "I suppose a little fun wouldn't kill me."

"Damn right," Ryan said. "And if it does, isn't that the way to go?"

Still wondering if Ryan might be onto something, Penny shuffled into the kitchen and hunted for breakfast. She scrounged up a Pop-Tart from the embarrassingly bare pantry and plunked it into the microwave. Penny didn't own a toaster.

While the sprinkled slab of sugar spun around and around on a paper napkin, Penny's finger got twitchy. She reached for her phone. Toyed with the lock screen. Eventually, she slid it open.

She pretended that she wasn't going to read Roman's email—especially not with Ryan waiting for her one room over—but she didn't fool herself. Her thumb pulled the notifications bar down to reveal an intriguing subject line. Penny couldn't resist. She never could when it came to Roman.

Subject: Invitation
From: TheRomanTate@gmail.com
Message:

Dear Penny,

I can explain—tonight, I promise.
    7:00 p.m. at the Pelican Hotel. Cocktail attire.

                                        Yours truly,
                                        Roman

TRANSCRIPT

Prosecution: Who was invited to the book club event on February 13, 2019?

Eliza Tate: Well, we had two events that day. The main one—book club—had an invitation list of about twenty industry guests. I'm not sure I remember the entire list off the top of my head, but I'm sure you've been given a copy of it.

Prosecution: What was the other event on that date?

Eliza Tate: It was a mock book club. A practice run for later that evening.

Prosecution: Why did you need a trial run for a book club?

Eliza Tate: It wasn't any old book club in the evening. We had several popular bloggers, Instagrammers, and journalists attending the evening's event. Being that it was Marguerite's first appearance for her newest work, I wasn't going to throw her to the wolves. Especially when the media was involved. Everything needed to go perfectly.

Prosecution: Who was at the trial run?

Eliza Tate: Me, obviously. Marguerite Hill. Anne Wilkes. Penny Sands.

Prosecution: It has been noted that you served wine at this event?

Eliza Tate: Is it really book club without wine?

Prosecution: At three p.m.?

Eliza Tate: It was happy hour.

Prosecution: Did Mrs. Wilkes have a glass of wine?

Eliza Tate: She might have. I don't remember. I don't police my guests.

Prosecution: Did you have wine?

Eliza Tate: I did. Several glasses. Probably why I don't remember if Anne was drinking.

Prosecution: Were you aware that Mrs. Wilkes checked herself into rehab a few years back?

Eliza Tate: Yes.

Prosecution: And are you aware that she checked herself out?

Eliza Tate: I picked her up myself.

Prosecution: Why didn't her husband pick her up?

Eliza Tate: He thought she needed to stay, so he refused to pick her up.

Prosecution: Was there tension between you and Detective Wilkes after that?

Eliza Tate: I don't know. I'm best friends with Anne, not Mark. I don't really care what he thinks of me.

Prosecution: So if Mrs. Wilkes needed help, she could count on you?

Eliza Tate: Yes.

Prosecution: Mrs. Tate, did Mrs. Wilkes ask you for help on the night of February 13? Help with anything at all? A favor? Perhaps a big favor?

Eliza Tate: If you're asking whether I'm taking the fall for Anne murdering my husband, then no. I love Anne, but I don't love her that much.

SEVENTEEN

Six Months Before
August 2018

Eliza watched her husband over the dinner table.

She sat back and fiddled with the stem of her champagne glass, sending bubbles skittering across the surface like water bugs. Roman slung his arm over another woman's chair. Eliza frowned at her tuna tartare. For some reason, the stupid loan from Jocelyn and Todd had pushed Roman over the edge.

Running a finger around the rim of her champagne glass, Eliza drew out a nervous, high-pitched note. When several pointed gazes landed on her finger, she retracted it sharply, watching as Roman put his hand on Marguerite's shoulder.

Eliza watched her husband whisper into the ear of her prize client, wondering what he could possibly be telling her. In the other woman's defense, Marguerite had looked quite uncomfortable with Roman's advances at the beginning of the night. She'd continuously glanced over at Eliza to gauge her reaction as Roman took care to refill her wineglass or brushed his elbow against hers.

At first, Eliza had gotten a laugh out of it. Roman had chosen the wrong woman to seduce. Marguerite disliked every fiber of Roman— who he was, what he stood for, how he walked, talked, spoke. But as the night went on, Eliza's internal laughter died down. She hadn't given her husband enough credit.

Marguerite eventually softened under the charms of Roman Tate. Eliza had seen the exact moment when it had clicked—during the dessert course when Roman had offered Marguerite a bite of his tiramisu. She'd given one last look at Eliza, but when Eliza didn't react, everything changed. Instead of dubiously fending off Roman's advances, Marguerite leaned into them, eager and intrigued.

Her soft laughter at his words grew a bit louder. Their eye contact lingered boldly. It wasn't Marguerite's fault the way this twisted fairy tale was unfolding; she was just a pawn. The poor woman was being played by Roman, and that annoyed Eliza.

Standing, Eliza pushed in her chair and flashed a demure smile around the table. "If you'll just excuse me, I have to go check on the caterer and make sure everything's ready next door. Please finish your dessert and join me when you're ready."

"See you over there, dear," Roman said with a flash of a smile. "I'll stay back and make sure the guest of honor finds her way."

Marguerite met Eliza's gaze dead-on. "How kind of your husband."

Eliza sucked in a breath. "I'm a lucky woman."

Leaving her husband to cuddle up with her star client, Eliza wobbled her away across the street, unsure what to make of the events from dinner. Roman's behavior made her uneasy for more than one reason, and she wasn't quite sure what to do about it. She needed time to think. She needed a rebuttal, but what? How could she fix this?

Eliza made her way from the dinner restaurant to the event venue. She tottered into the Pelican Hotel on ridiculously high heels, smoothing her skirt as she bypassed the front desk and made her way straight to the ballroom. Once inside, she hesitated, leaning over a cocktail table for support. She'd just closed her eyes when a voice startled her from behind.

"Oh God. I'm ridiculously early, aren't I?"

Eliza straightened, turning at the unfamiliar voice. She peered through the beautiful centerpiece—a stunning bouquet of lilies—toward the young woman standing in the doorway.

The first guest looked supremely nervous, her eyes rapidly flicking one way then another as if hunting for the quickest exit from the room. She wore a poppy-red, one-piece jumper with teeny, tiny straps across bare shoulders. The pantsuit swished around trim legs, and the buttons on her chest, as delicate as flowers, hid an impressive display of cleavage.

This woman didn't have the haunted, half-starved look of many aspiring models or actresses in this city. She had the fresh-faced, healthy glow of a woman brimming with hope and ambition. When she walked, it was on a set of chunky heels that wobbled slightly, and as Eliza looked closer, she realized the shoes were held together with a swatch of duct tape.

Eliza hid a smile. The jumper wasn't from anywhere fancy. A department store maybe. A secondhand boutique at best. The fabric had pilled slightly and was of dubious quality, details Eliza noticed as she moved closer. Not that it mattered, since the woman had a stunning figure and the benefit of youth. With her smile, nobody would notice her clothes.

"I'm sorry to bother you," the guest said, twisting the toe of one shoe into the ground. "But do you know if this is the launch party for Marguerite Hill's new book?"

"It is. Come in and make yourself comfortable."

"I'm Penny." The girl threw a hand over her face and cringed. "This is so embarrassing. I should have known when they said the party was at seven, they meant *seven*—not six thirty."

Eliza smiled. "Someone has to be first. May I ask how you heard about the event?"

The woman's face paled at the question. "Holy moly, you're Eliza Tate, aren't you?"

"Guilty."

"I...er...I recognize you from pictures in your husband's office. I'm one of his students."

"Penny—oh, you're *the* Penny! You babysit for the Wilkeses. Anne is a close friend of mine. She raves about you all the time. It's so nice to finally put a face to a name."

"You're telling me." Penny scoffed, her cheeks blooming to a rosy shade of pink. "Well, I'm a huge fan of Marguerite Hill, so I'm thrilled to be here. *Take Charge* was actually the book that gave me the courage to move to LA. I can't wait to get my hands on *Be Free.*"

"You're new here, then?" Eliza thought that explained quite a lot about Penny.

"I've only been living here a couple of months. I'm from a small town in Iowa. I'm sure you've never heard of it."

That explains even more, Eliza thought. "Well, welcome. Marguerite will be so glad to hear about your experience with her book. I'll introduce you when she arrives. It should be any second now."

"You'd really introduce me?"

"She'd love it."

"I would…" Penny cleared her throat. "Never mind. It's stupid."

Eliza caught a fleeting glimpse of uncertainty in Penny's eyes. "What is it?"

Penny shrugged out of a small shoulder bag patterned with bright florals. It didn't match a thing she was wearing, nor could it be described as cocktail-hour elegant. Instead, it was just plain fun. Eliza wondered when she'd last bought something just because it was *fun*.

From her bag, Penny withdrew a dog-eared copy of *Take Charge.* "Would it be totally rude to ask her to sign my copy?"

"She'd love it," Eliza confirmed. "In the meantime, help yourself to something to drink. It's an open bar."

Leaving Penny to fend for herself, Eliza strolled to the kitchen attached to the ballroom with thoughts of Penny on her mind. Anne would have to be careful keeping a beauty like Penny around the house, as sweet as she seemed. If Mark had already strayed once, as Anne feared, was there a chance he'd run off with the nanny?

Mark's indiscretion was more unfortunate than most of its kind. If anyone had asked Eliza years ago if Anne and Mark would last, she'd have given a hearty nod. They were perfect together. They made sense as a couple. If they couldn't make it work, Eliza was leery anyone could.

Eliza quietly sized up the catering staff as they moved like a well-oiled machine, bustling teensy plates topped with bacon-wrapped scallops to the earliest guests and ushering finely sliced strawberries and bananas and pineapples onto skewers at the chocolate fountain.

Satisfied, Eliza returned to the party room, realizing she'd never gotten an answer from Penny as to how she'd secured an invitation. She wondered if it hadn't come offhandedly from Roman or Anne. Not that it mattered, seeing as Penny was another warm body to add to the evening's head count, and a bigger party made for a bigger impression on Marguerite. A bigger impression on Marguerite meant a bigger paycheck for Eliza. A bigger paycheck for Eliza meant she could get her family out of financial hot water and back to the way things were before.

At that moment, Roman Tate strolled arm in arm into the ballroom with Marguerite Hill. Her face tilted toward his as she dedicated her full attention to his words. The lines around the author's mouth crinkled into a smile as she laughed at whatever he'd said.

In response, he reached out and rested a palm on her wrist. Marguerite tugged her fingers through her hair, tucking a stray piece of curl behind her ear, then licked her lower lip. Eliza wondered if it was on purpose or if it was a subconscious touch. They'd launched into a sort of dance, a seductive ritual. Objectively, it was fascinating to watch. If only it weren't Eliza's husband on one side and her best chance at success on the other.

Eliza made her way to the pair, coming to a stop before them. Marguerite boldly pulled her hand away, though her face didn't hold the slightest hint of an apology. If anything, her eyes held a dare. Eliza did a double take, wondering what had changed since the beginning of the evening when the author had so carefully fended off Roman's advances. But the curious moment had passed, leaving Eliza to wonder if she'd imagined the whole thing.

"Marguerite, may I have a word with you?" Eliza murmured. "There's somebody I'm dying to have you meet."

TRANSCRIPT

Defense: You've been in Penny Sands's apartment, yes?

Anne Wilkes: Yes, several times.

Defense: What was it like?

Anne Wilkes: Simple. She's young. It's easy to forget what it's like to move to a new city and have no money. She did the best she could. I helped her out when I was able.

Defense: Do you think Ms. Sands needed money?

Anne Wilkes: Who couldn't use a little extra money?

Defense: How far do you think Ms. Sands would have gone to procure additional funds?

Anne Wilkes: Roman's murder wasn't about money. That was personal.

EIGHTEEN

Six Months Before
August 2018

Anne felt wildly out of place as she headed toward Beverly Hills and her best friend's book launch party. A pinch of annoyance sat with her at the sheer fact that she was driving a minivan to the big event. Eliza and her husband would no doubt be showing up in some trendy new ride. She had no clue what the rest of the guests would be driving, but it certainly wasn't a minivan. Especially not one that ran on a prayer and crossed fingers.

Anne drove past the entrance twice, the first time because she missed it, the second time because she couldn't believe the valet rates posted out front. Fuming at the injustice of a twenty-four-dollar fee, Anne parked blocks away from the venue and vented some of her frustration by stomping the half mile back to the hotel gates.

"Twenty-four dollars," she huffed, swinging her purse onto her shoulder as she continued to stomp inside. "When's the last time I spent twenty-four dollars on myself?"

Anne curbed her stomping at the entrance to the banquet room at the hotel. She paused, taking in the stunning expanse before her. Eliza had orchestrated a brilliant display of elegance intertwined with glamour.

The demure, pearly tablecloths were offset by sparkling centerpieces. The simple uniforms of the waitstaff contrasted with the tiny elegance of the appetizers they carried on crystal trays. Champagne flutes filled with glittery shades of pink and gold complemented the bronze molding around the edges of the room.

"Anne, sweetie, you made it!"

Anne looked up to find Eliza rushing toward her. She inched her purse higher on her shoulder, sliding it behind her body to mask the obscure logo.

"So glad you came." Eliza took Anne by the shoulders. "And don't you look marvelous! When's the last time these ladies have seen the light of day?"

Weak with relief, Anne laughed when Eliza winked at her chest. "Are you sure I look okay?"

"Don't be ridiculous. You look amazing. Nobody would ever guess you had four kids in that little number." Eliza gave her a stare that told her she wasn't joking. "Did you find the food?"

As soon as Eliza mentioned food, Anne realized she was starving. "As a matter of fact, I came ready to eat. To hell with my diet. I'll start tomorrow."

"That's what I always say," Eliza agreed.

"That's not what I say, though." A new voice joined the conversation. "I always say why start tomorrow when you can start today?"

Anne turned toward the woman at Eliza's elbow, a striking figure who appeared just a few years older than Anne but in dramatically better shape. It took a moment for Anne to place the woman, and only when Eliza gave a hefty clear of her throat did she put it together.

"Marguerite Hill?" Anne managed. "I recognize you from the picture on the back of your book. *Take Charge* has been in my van forever, and I can't wait to get my hands on your newest one. Eliza's been telling us all about it."

"I guess you haven't gotten to the chapter about starting today instead of tomorrow?" Marguerite gave a sly smile, then leaned in and raised a hand conspiratorially toward Anne. "I'm just joking, love. Easier said than done, yeah?"

Anne gave a nervous chuckle at the strange accent in the author's voice. Anne could've sworn Eliza had said that Marguerite was from somewhere like Montana, but her words had an oddly European note to them. "You can say that again."

"Anne, help yourself to the appetizers," Eliza said. "If I could just have a moment alone with Marguerite, that would be lovely."

Anne left the two women to chat and strode over to a table filled with dainty trays of finger foods. En route, she realized she was holding her head higher. Tipping her shoulders back. Adding a sway to her hips. Almost as if she was on her way to recovering some old relic of herself that she'd forgotten existed, a woman who met interesting people and wore intriguing clothes and tasted exotic foods. A woman who did more than clean up vomit and wipe snotty noses.

Anne glanced around the room, a beautifully adorned space, noting additional details as she sashayed from one food platter to the next. Elegant candlesticks fitted with regal purple candles cast a dim glimmer to offset the chandelier hanging low in the center of the room. The smart-looking waiters bustled around, whisking champagne glasses from cocktail tables mere seconds after they'd been set down by wandering guests.

And the guests! Anne noted. Thin, gorgeous women, some of them in downright stunning gowns, others in flirty party dresses. Still others paraded around in power suits like important executives. The handful of men mingling at the tables were even more impressive in their expensive suits, sipping bourbon or whiskey on the rocks like the lead in an action flick.

Anne was willing to bet these men didn't go home and turn on the ball game and suck down a Budweiser. They were here to discuss literary fiction; they were cultured and attentive and good listeners and...

Anne felt her neck grow hot as she caught the eye of one such man. He was tall and broad-shouldered, his muscles neatly defined beneath his suit. He wore wire-rimmed glasses that enhanced the salt-and-pepper spattering in his hair. Through them, he looked at her, raised a glass. His lips pursed as their gaze lingered for a second too long.

Flustered, Anne turned away, skimming her heel on the ground and nearly falling face-first into a chocolate fountain as she struggled to regain her balance. She wasn't like Mark. She was loyal. Dedicated to her family. And before she could decide otherwise, she stabbed a strawberry and stuck the spear under the flow of chocolate, shoving the whole thing in her mouth.

She'd just reached for a second helping of the bacon-wrapped scallops when a low male voice rumbled over her shoulder.

"I hoped I'd see you here."

Anne spun around, her mouth still awkwardly full. "Roman! God, wow. It's been so long. You look great."

A shadow flickered over his face. "Thank you. Say, do you have a minute to chat? You look beautiful by the way. I hope Mark's here. If you came alone, you'll be swamped with suitors."

Anne's cheeks warmed. "Mark's home with the kids."

"Ah, unfortunate. Anyway, I was hoping we could chat for a minute."

"Sure. Would you like to sit down?"

Roman didn't seem satisfied with any of the nearby seating options when Anne pointed them out, claiming they were too loud for conversation. Ever the dutiful friend, Anne followed Roman to the back of the ballroom where he pushed through one of the curtains to reveal a small roped-off area.

"I see you have access to the VIP lounge," Anne joked as they entered. "I suppose you'd be considered a guest of honor."

Roman's smile was a patient flicker. "One would think."

He gestured to one of the couches, and Anne sat there while he chose a maroon armchair that resembled a throne. They were seated in a private lounge decked out in dark reds and seductive blacks. A gorgeous display of Stargazer lilies and birds of paradise sat on a coffee table, poking their heads out from an exotic compilation of greens and pinks and oranges. The room held a highly perfumed floral aroma from the bouquet that was almost intoxicating.

Anne wished she'd brought a plate of appetizers to the room to give her hands something to do. She'd never felt quite comfortable around Eliza's husband. She couldn't exactly say why. Partly because of his demeanor, partly because of his looks. The dark hair, a strong jawline, the almost-black eyes and deeply penetrating gaze that seemed to pierce right through her.

Anne had always figured that someone so good looking had something to hide. A ridiculous notion probably, but the lingering feeling had never dissipated. It was only exacerbated as Roman shifted in his seat and studied her, letting her sit in unease. The only way to make it through Roman's awkward silences was to wait them out. She'd learned that years ago.

"This is a great party," Anne finally offered. "You must be super proud of Eliza for starting her own company. I know I am."

Roman gave a soft snort. "I'm not sure she had a choice. She was fired from her last job."

"I didn't realize that."

"I'm surprised she didn't tell you. It seems she shares the rest of her secrets with you."

"What are you talking about?"

"Eliza must have told you about the private investigator she hired to follow me around. You didn't find Luke on your own."

"N-no." Anne choked on the lie. "Roman, it's not—"

Roman pressed a finger to his lips to shush her. "I don't care about all that. And before you ask, don't worry. I haven't mentioned a word to Mark, though I did consider it. I think a husband has a right to know when he's being followed. From experience."

Anne felt the color drain from her face. Her fingers trembled. She had blown everything. The only scenario worse than Anne confronting her husband about the affair, about the PI and the stalking and everything else, was someone else beating her to the punch. Especially someone like Roman.

It was with a slow dawning of realization that Anne saw there was more to Roman than she had anticipated. His silences weren't accidentally awkward—they were planned, manipulative devices. He had a way with words, the ability to twist them, stretching and expanding and shrinking them until they were mere remnants of their former selves, like a stretched-out rubber band left to curl in on itself after the elasticity had tired.

Anne was also certain that Roman was aware of his looks and the effect they had on women. However, this evening, Roman didn't need to use his looks or his cunning or his twisted silences to spark fear in Anne. He was using pure, old-fashioned techniques. Blackmail.

"What do you want me to say?" Anne's body quivered as she hovered in the chasm between anger and terror. "Whatever Mark and I discuss—or don't discuss—is our personal business."

"Fair enough, but I've gone and made it my business." Roman eased back in his seat. "But this doesn't need to be difficult, Anne. I need something, and you can get it. Look at it like a business arrangement."

Anne glanced down at her feet. The urge to leave the room built up, bubbling just beneath the surface. She had half a mind to swing her purse over her shoulder and stomp the half mile back to her car. But Roman had her pinned to the chair, and he knew it.

"I *knew* when Eliza fired the maid, even though she tried to keep the place clean herself. I knew she funneled chunks of money into my account every month like an allowance. It's like she thinks I'm her little puppy dog on a leash—cute, playful, but too stupid to manage my own life. Do you know how humiliating that is for a man?"

"I swear I didn't know any of that."

"You didn't, but I did," Roman said. "That's the thing, Anne. I know everything."

"I don't see how this has anything to do with Mark or me."

"We can make this quick." Roman was watching her with pity in his gaze. "Luke is a buddy of mine. We didn't start out that way, but when I suspected he was following me, I turned the tables on Eliza. It's sad, really. Our marriage wasn't always doomed. I loved her. Still do, even."

"I think you should talk to Eliza. You guys can sort it out, I'm sure. Eliza is crazy about you."

"She was, maybe still is in her own strange way. But I can't trust her anymore."

"She only hired a PI because she thought you were having an affair."

"After all we've been through, she should trust me. I married her so she could stay in the country."

"You married her because you knew she'd provide a comfy, cozy life for you," Anne retorted, unable to help herself. "You're no saint, Roman."

"No, I don't think I am," Roman said. "In fact, that's why we're here tonight."

"Where exactly is here?"

"I know your secrets. Better yet, I know Mark's. And you'll do everything in your power to protect him, which is where I come in. That's the beauty of a marriage like yours, Anne—it's not over yet. You two can make things work."

"What do you mean?"

"I paid Luke Hamilton more than Eliza was offering." Roman gave a thin smile. "I bought the information your private investigator was supposed to be providing to you."

Anne felt her stomach sink. "That's not ethical of Luke."

"Is having your husband followed without his knowledge ethical?" Roman let the question hang between them for a long moment. "Like I said, I did love Eliza. Still do. But I don't like when people underestimate me. My father's been doing that for years, and I don't need it from anyone else."

"I'm sure that's not true."

"Oh, Anne. You know it, I know it, Eliza knows it," Roman said. "Unless I turn into Tom Cruise overnight, my own father will always be disappointed in me. And my mother… I think she's afraid of me."

"Why would that be?" Anne managed.

"I think she's afraid I'll turn out like my father." Roman gave Anne a darkly thin smile. "And we wouldn't want that."

"Why are you telling me this?"

"Feels good to get it off my chest," Roman said easily. "It's nice to talk to someone who won't report my father to the police because I shared his dirty little secret. He hits her, you know. But my mother will never leave him. I called the cops once when I was seven. When they showed up, she denied everything, told them I made it up for attention. How do you think that made me feel?"

"That's awful, Roman. I am so sorry."

"Do you know what I just can't figure?" Roman sat back in his seat, looking deep in thought. "They love each other. Really, truly, in some twisted way. Isn't that fucked up?"

"Are you like him?" Anne asked quietly. "Have you ever—"

"Don't play the saint, Anne. I'm not the one who left my kids for three days without a word. You're just as fucked up as I am. We all are."

Anne's throat began to close. "You still haven't told me why I'm here."

"I want money. I thought that'd be obvious."

"From me?" Anne gaped. "I don't have money. Plus, you and Eliza are loaded."

"*Were* loaded," Roman said. "Past tense. And I don't like to give up pretty things. That's where you'll help me out."

"How'd you get the money for Luke, then? He's not cheap."

"No, but like I said, we used to have money. Those morsels Eliza doled into my account bit by bit—she thought I squandered the money on stupid, frivolous things. On women, fancy dinners, hotels, the like. Paranoid, that one. It's a miracle she hasn't had *you* followed after your little incident."

Anne swallowed hard. "You saved the money, I'm guessing?"

"Tucked it safely away." Roman leaned forward, his elbows coming to rest on his knees, his eyes gleaming with confidence. "The truth is, Anne, if I want a woman, I don't pay for her company."

Anne felt her cheeks heating.

"Don't worry. It's not you I want." Roman's eyes flicked over her. "If I was looking for a woman's company, I could do better than a housewife who spends her free time spying on her husband."

Anne flew to her feet. "What the hell is wrong with you, Roman?"

"Luke Hamilton belongs to me. Do you understand what I'm saying?"

Anne hadn't yet fully connected the dots, but lines were starting to be sketched. She could see where he was going with everything, but she hadn't fitted together how Roman planned to emerge victorious.

She toyed with the frayed edge of her purse. "Are you going to tell me why you haven't talked to Mark yet? Told him you know about the affair?"

Roman looked annoyed. "It's no wonder you and Eliza are friends. You both don't get it, do you? This is so much bigger than Mark and some stupid woman."

"What do you mean, it's bigger than that?"

"Luke didn't give you every last detail that he dug up on your husband."

"I still don't understand why Luke would tell you anything about our private life. He has no right."

"It was Eliza's money paying your bill," Roman said pointedly. "Eliza paid Luke for you. See, Luke and I have an arrangement, and when anything with Eliza's name on it crosses his desk, he brings it to me. Let the highest bidder win. The check was in her name, so he came to me looking for an auction, and I gave him one."

"I don't believe you."

"That doesn't matter. We all know how this works. Money makes the world go 'round. I've got a secret. If you've got money, that secret stays quiet."

"I don't have any money. I already told you that," Anne said bitterly. "Like you said, I'm nothing but a housewife. I haven't worked in nearly a decade. We have four children and live in Los Angeles. Our savings account is abysmal. If Mark got laid off, we wouldn't be able to pay the mortgage on our house for three months without filing for bankruptcy."

"Right," Roman said. "But Luke helped me out with that little... kerfuffle. As it turns out, your mother is one rich bitch. I met her once at your house, never liked her."

Anne's mind went immediately to Beatrice Harper. The woman who vacationed on Martha's Vineyard. The woman who lived in a pristine, hundred-year-old Victorian house that qualified as a historical landmark. The woman who could afford to send her grandchildren to college without batting an eye. And the very woman who had never given her daughter a dime.

"I have no way to access that money," Anne said. "Most of it is tied up in funds for the kids' college tuitions, and we can't touch it until they're eighteen."

"I don't care about college funds. I care about cash. I don't care if you get the money from your parents or if you whore yourself out to pay for it. I just want fifty thousand dollars by next month."

"Or what?"

"Or I let Mark's little secret slip to the police. Or better yet, a journalist. The DA. Someone who won't find Mark's little *whoopsies* quite so amusing."

"They can't fire him over an affair." Anne's lips felt dry. She still wasn't used to the word *affair*.

"I'm not talking about that. I'm talking about Mark's integrity." Roman studied Anne carefully. "It might seem as if Mark is a hero, a real stand-up officer. But what if I told you he wasn't as squeaky clean as he's led everyone to believe?"

"Are you insinuating that my husband is a dirty cop?" Anne scoffed. "Don't be ridiculous."

"Are you willing to take the risk that I'm wrong?" Roman shrugged one shoulder. "Fifty grand will keep me—and any evidence to the contrary—quiet. That way, you won't have to run the risk that I am very, very right."

Anne paused. Did she believe that her husband was a crooked cop? A year ago, she would have bet her life that her husband didn't have a lying bone in his body. Now, Anne wondered how much more there was to Mark Wilkes.

Still, she trembled. *Fifty thousand dollars?* There was no way she could get that sort of money. From anywhere. She and Mark didn't have anything near that in savings. They'd have to sell the house, and that would defeat the purpose of keeping this mess a secret.

Briefly, Anne flirted with the idea of phoning her mother. She pictured the call and snorted right there in front of Roman. There was even less chance of Beatrice giving her the money than of Anne being able to sell the house and keep the secret from Mark.

At this point, Anne's best option would be to go on a crash diet, pick up a pair of stripper boots, and head down to the local club. And that was preposterous. Nobody wanted to see Anne naked.

Unfortunately, Anne knew how this worked. She read books, watched movies. This was just the beginning. Fifty thousand dollars was the start of a journey that would never end. She and Roman were entering a dangerous game of chicken that would go on until one of them flinched. Or ended up dead.

With a shudder, Anne suddenly understood the word *motive* in a new light. She'd always thought that mystery plots were too far-fetched, too unrealistic to ever exist in this world, especially not in Anne's modest little life dedicated to raising four decent human beings while keeping her sanity intact. Her biggest problems were supposed to be keeping her children fed and bathed and the numbers on her bathroom scale at a reasonable level. And, of course, not running away from her family—again.

"If I'm going to get you that much money," Anne said finally, "I deserve to know what you think my husband has done."

"I figured you'd ask." Roman tipped forward in his chair. He beckoned with his finger for Anne to lean closer. "Don't worry. I've got nothing to hide from you."

Then Roman told her. Every last detail.

Anne had always said she'd never be able to kill anyone. That murder wasn't in the cards for her. But as Roman whispered in her ear, she felt nothing. She felt neither sick nor angry, desperate nor frightened. She merely wondered what it would be like if Roman ended up dead.

TRANSCRIPT

Defense: Ms. Hill, you were at both book club events on February 13, correct?

Marguerite Hill: I'm the author. The whole point was my being there.

Defense: It's been established that the subject of murder arose on the afternoon of the thirteenth. Would you say that it was the content of your book that spurred the group's discussion toward murder?

Marguerite Hill: I'd say that's ridiculous. My book discusses women—our power, our rights, and the ability to take control of our lives. There's nothing about murder.

Defense: I read your book, Ms. Hill. Impressive. You're a talented author.

Marguerite Hill: Thank you.

Defense: But I found it interesting, reading your work under the current circumstances—specifically, the murder trial happening as we speak. Are there not several themes in your work about women taking what's theirs, especially when it comes to men in a position of power?

Marguerite Hill: I suppose. But how does that relate to killing someone?

Defense: Let me read an excerpt to you, Ms. Hill. This comes from page 48 of *Take Charge*: "Ladies, I urge you to take what is yours, no matter the cost. It's your right—your duty—to stand up for yourselves. By whatever means necessary."

Marguerite Hill: So? I stand by my words.

Defense: So what if a woman read this and took it a little too literally? What if she thought that when you said "by whatever means necessary," it included murder?

Marguerite Hill: That's her problem, because that's preposterous. That's not how I intended it in the slightest. I don't even have a clue how one might interpret it in that light.

Defense: What if that is what you meant, Ms. Hill? I'm not convinced you're telling us the truth. Is your name Marguerite Hill?

Marguerite Hill: Of course it is.

Defense: Has it always been Marguerite Hill?

Marguerite Hill: I changed my last name to Hill when I got married. I kept the name after we divorced because I'd already used it on my work. My ex-husband and I are on friendly terms, so I didn't care about changing it back.

Defense: What about before that?

Marguerite Hill: Before what?

Defense: Ms. Hill, as it turns out, your name was Katherine Bonaparte on your birth certificate.

Marguerite Hill: But how did you…

Defense: Look, Ms. Hill. I'm sorry for what happened to you as a child. The crimes against you were unspeakable and awful. But it's time to be honest with the court. Please explain to the jury who you are, where you come from, and why you changed your name.

NINETEEN

Six Months Before
August 2018

Penny watched as Marguerite Hill flitted around the elaborate ballroom, a small posse flocking along beside her. Among her troupe walked Roman Tate.

It hadn't been difficult to Google the event list for the Pelican Hotel and find out that Roman's wife was throwing a party for Marguerite's new book. Penny was still trying to puzzle out Roman's reason for inviting her here. If he'd wanted to explain why he'd kissed her—among other things—wouldn't it have been more prudent to go somewhere alone, just the two of them? Somewhere—anywhere—his wife wasn't?

To Penny, it felt like she was a carrot being dangled just under Eliza's nose. Was this all a big game to Roman? Was Penny his midlife crisis—a back-alley affair that would flash-bang bright, then fizzle to blackness when he returned to his wife and groveled for an apology?

Penny wasn't going to stick around for any of that. She refused to be the other woman. So why had she come at all? Why hadn't she ignored Roman's email or sent him a giant fuck-you message back?

Because she was curious, and everyone knew that curiosity killed the cat. Penny wanted to know more; she wanted to know everything. She wanted to see Eliza with her own eyes, know the woman whose husband she had kissed. She wanted to see Marguerite Hill in person, her beloved guru, and hear from her lips that everything would be okay. That Penny's life wasn't over, that she could still take charge and move on from the messy trails she'd left behind.

And lastly, she was curious to hear Roman's explanation. Would he be up-front with her? Would he lie? Would he tell her it had all been a mistake, and could she please keep their little interludes secret?

Nursing a vodka martini and chomping on one of the blue cheese–stuffed olives that came speared as decorative flair, Penny watched the smartly dressed group arrive at the party and slowly disperse. A few members of the group made their way over to the bar while others spread throughout the room in search of conversation with other attendees.

Penny fingered her H&M steal, biting her lip as Roman helped Marguerite out of her coat. The jacket was a shimmery pink thing that was entirely unnecessary in southern California temperatures, but it was stylish nonetheless and likely expensive. The guest of honor deserved to dress with a little pizzazz.

Penny was fascinated by Marguerite Hill and everything she stood for. Her last book had hit the *New York Times* list at number ten. She'd been a nobody before her unexpected success, much like Penny herself. Almost overnight, Marguerite had become the newest self-help guru on the continent. And now Penny was standing a stone's throw from her idol.

There was something about Marguerite—something about the look in her eyes or the way she spoke. Maybe the way she moved or the way her words galloped across the page. Something about her that made Penny shiver. The woman was not to be taken lightly.

As Penny continued to stare over her martini glass, she couldn't help but observe Roman as he inched closer to Marguerite. Was it Penny's imagination, or were the two positioned a hair too close together? Maybe it was the little touches that threw Penny off or the way Roman tossed Marguerite's jacket over his shoulder after she'd shrugged it off.

Maybe Penny wasn't the only one Roman had his eye on. Penny wasn't sure whether that made her feel better or worse, but she knew it made her feel something. And that something quickly became jealousy, an emotion that pinged around her chest like a ball in a pinball machine. Penny fought it back with every fiber of her moral compass, but it was a futile effort.

Trying to ignore her rattling nerves, Penny turned her attention to someone more interesting than either Roman or Marguerite. She watched Eliza Tate with mounting curiosity, wondering what she knew. Was it possible that Roman had confessed everything and she knew about their secret interludes?

When Penny entered the room, she'd seen a beautiful, forlorn-looking woman draped over a cocktail table, looking like a broken-hearted Disney princess waiting for a prince who would never come. Eliza's long, shiny dark hair had been pulled over one shoulder, and her dress—sleek and short—was made from a crisp black fabric that made Penny feel like a starry-eyed teenager in her clearance-rack jumpsuit.

Penny might as well have worn sparkly eye shadow and chomped on bubble gum. It would have matched the duct tape slapped on the bottom of her shoe because she hadn't wanted to shell out for a pair of new heels.

Turning to the bar, Penny slipped another olive between her lips. She was being stupid all over again, pining for a partner she couldn't have when there was a real, tangible man bringing her flowers. Ryan Anderson might never be a yacht. But he made for a damn good dinghy.

"I'm glad you made it." Roman's voice clapped over Penny's shoulder, prickling her skin in anticipation of a coming storm. "I worried you wouldn't want to see me."

"I'm still waiting to hear one good reason why I shouldn't walk out the door right now." Penny stared into her martini as she tasted the sour words. "You're married."

"You knew that from the day you met me."

Penny's face heated.

Roman leaned inward. "Yet you still wanted me."

"I'm leaving—"

"Penny," he chided gently with a matching shake of his head. "I'm sorry. That came out wrong. What I meant to say was that there's a greater force pulling us together. I can feel it, and I think you can, too."

Penny's throat went dry. "What's gone on between us should never have happened. It's not fair to anyone."

"You're wrong."

Roman looked so convinced, it gave Penny pause as she stared into her drink. Somehow, most of her cocktail had already disappeared. She hadn't eaten much all day, considering she'd picked her way around suspect beans for lunch.

"You're an asshole." The alcohol must have hit her harder than expected, which explained her newfound backbone. "I can't believe I fell for your whole..." Penny waved her hand over Roman, head to toe. "All of it. I have half a mind to tell your wife everything."

"Go ahead," Roman said. "But first, take a breath and have another drink. I promised you there's an explanation, and I'm getting to it. Once you hear me out, you can do whatever you like, and I won't try to stop you."

Penny gave a shrug of disbelief. She'd committed this far.

Roman eased closer, gestured for the bartender. "Another martini for her, a whiskey neat for me."

"I'm okay." Penny drained her drink and waved off the bartender. She ignored Roman's gaze as it fell on her profile. "I haven't eaten dinner. The alcohol's gone straight to my head."

"We'll take that martini," Roman assured the bartender. Turning to Penny, he gave her a generous smile. "Best to loosen up. Events like this are always a bit...stuffy. If you need food, there will be appetizers floating around."

Penny made a noncommittal noise in her throat.

"Have you had the opportunity to meet anyone yet?" Roman gestured toward the party, dodging any real conversation in lieu of light banter. "Lots of industry folks in attendance. It'd be good for you to mingle."

"As a matter of fact, I did meet your wife." The vodka in Penny's system simmered under the surface, mixing with an infusion of latent anger. "She seems very nice."

"She can be." Roman didn't take the combative bait. "Though she won't be my wife for much longer."

Penny choked on an olive. "What?"

"We're separating. All we're waiting on is the divorce paperwork."

"I-I'm...sorry to hear the news?" Penny didn't mean for it to come out sounding like a question. "When did this happen?"

"Months ago," Roman said, "but it should have been years."

"For crying out loud. Why didn't you say something sooner?" Penny fanned at her face, feeling an even bigger burst of relief than she'd anticipated. "I've been losing hair thinking that I'd ruined your marriage."

Roman's face softened. "I'm sorry. I didn't want to assume."

"Can I ask why you're separating?"

"We've been growing apart for a long time. We aren't in love anymore. Like I said, it's been years coming. I'm not sure we were ever truly in love."

Penny remembered the forlorn look in Eliza's eyes and knew that wasn't true. At least, not for Eliza. Penny recognized a woman who couldn't have what she most desired.

"Who decided it was time to get divorced?"

"It was a mutual decision. We have an amicable relationship. Hence the reason I'm here this evening. At my soon-to-be ex-wife's party."

The bartender returned with fresh drinks. Penny greedily speared another olive and chewed, hoping it would give her stomach a base coat and help to diminish the light-headedness that had her floating on a cloud of confidence. A cloud that looked bright and shiny in the moment but would no doubt appear dark and stormy and rimmed with regret in the morning.

Penny waved a hand at one of the servers toting a tray of crackers with delicate cheeses smeared on top, but a hand rested on her wrist and stopped her halfway through.

"I don't think you understand what I'm trying to tell you." Roman leaned in, raised a hand to gently touch the back of her neck. "I've been thinking about you, Penny. Unable to get you off my mind. I shouldn't have kissed you like that without telling you the truth first, but I couldn't help myself."

Penny closed her eyes, took a deep breath. She felt sick with relief and wondered what that said about her. Did she still have a conscience after all? All those years of hoarding others' things and instructing her guilt-ridden thoughts to take a hike... She thought she'd just about worn the bitch down.

But every once in a while, that voice returned—the little angel on her shoulder who hadn't completely been eradicated by the devil on the other side. Penny couldn't decide if this was good news or troublesome.

At the end of the day, Penny hadn't ruined a marriage after all. She sat, basking in the relief for a moment, wondering if that very relief was what made her human. Then, almost immediately, the relief slipped away, and a feeling of ecstasy crept into its place. Penny was left to wonder all over again if that made her an awful person. Not that she needed an answer. She'd been granted the lesser of two evils, and that was the best she could do.

As Roman's declaration truly sank in, Penny let the little sprouts of guilt that'd plagued her for months seep into the recesses of her brain as she finally, finally allowed other senses to take the wheel. Roman's breath smelled familiar now, of spicy mint and expensive whiskey. A light, appealing cologne clung to his fine suit. The touch of his hand against her wrist felt like ice cubes melting against hot asphalt—jarring cold and shocking heat.

"I hope you know my intentions were good from the start," Roman said. "I'm hoping you can carve out a few minutes of time tonight to talk more—in private."

Penny opened her eyes before glancing over her shoulder. She squinted as Eliza and Marguerite made their way across the room, stopped every few feet by eager guests as the party grew in number and volume. Their trajectory, however, couldn't be clearer.

Eliza's eyes rose to meet Penny's for the briefest of seconds. Penny's neck prickled. She poured herself over the bar, hugging a martini toward her chest in an effort to shrug Roman's hand off her neck.

"I would like that," Penny said. "But give me a minute to breathe. And I really do need to eat something."

"Of course." Roman's words were amiable, but his tone was edgy.

Penny saw a peculiar look appear in Roman's eyes as he glanced at his soon-to-be ex-wife. Roman gave her a smile, but Eliza didn't return it. Penny vaguely wondered if the divorce was as amiable as he claimed.

She didn't have time to dwell on the layers of the Tate family, however, because Eliza had finally completed her trajectory toward the bar with Marguerite in tow. Penny's throat went dry. She was so absorbed in the approaching guests that she didn't notice Roman disappearing from her side.

"Marguerite," Eliza said as she came to a stop, "this is the woman I was telling you about. Penny, meet Marguerite Hill."

"Oh my God!" Penny reached for the woman's outstretched hand and clasped it in a shake. "I loved your book. It literally changed my life."

"Is that right?" Marguerite stepped forward, eyes twinkling. "Tell me more."

For the next few minutes, Penny floated on cloud nine as she explained her journey from Iowa to California, eventually concluding her gushing praise by dragging her tattered copy of *Take Charge* from her bag.

"Would you mind signing my copy?" Penny asked. "It would mean so much to me. I can't wait to get my hands on *Be Free*. I'll have to have you sign that one, too."

As Marguerite signed the book, Penny found herself feeling truly elated for the first time in weeks. She was still flying high when Eliza and Marguerite moved on to enchant the rest of the guests and left her alone. Penny fanned herself and dropped her toothpick, depleted of olives, into her empty martini glass.

Roman was single. Penny had met her idol. Could the night get any better?

Wandering to the dessert table in a dreamlike state, Penny speared strawberries and pineapples in no particular order, barely aware of her own movements. She'd just dipped her confection under the chocolate fountain when she felt a presence next to her.

"Come with me, somewhere quiet. Just for a bit." Roman's voice startled Penny out of her happy haze. "I think it'd do us good to talk."

"I'm not sure that's a great idea," Penny said, swallowing hard. "Technically, you're still married."

"I'll answer all your questions about my relationship once we're somewhere private. But I can guarantee you that my marriage is over."

Penny's heart thumped against her chest, banged on her rib cage like a drum circle. As much as she didn't want to feel anything toward Roman, she was drawn to him like a magnet. A relentless, natural pull.

"I do have some questions," she admitted finally. "But I'd just like to talk. Nothing…else."

"I have a room upstairs." Roman reached into his pocket, pulled out a key card. "409."

TRANSCRIPT

Defense: Did you ever speak with Ms. Hill about your husband?

Eliza Tate: I'm sure he came up in our conversations. As husbands do. Marguerite and I have been friends for years, and she's met Roman on numerous occasions. It would only have been polite for her to ask about him.

Defense: How long would you say you've known Ms. Hill?

Eliza Tate: A handful of years. She was my largest client at my previous job. We worked together at the start of her first book.

Defense: Over the course of those years, did Marguerite Hill ever seem interested in your husband? Romantically?

Eliza Tate: I would have said no, up until a few months ago.

Defense: Then what happened?

Eliza Tate: The night of her *Be Free* launch party at the Pelican Hotel, I did notice that she seemed a little bit too cozy with Roman.

Defense: Were you upset with your client?

Eliza Tate: I was upset with my husband. I assumed Marguerite was just the pawn.

Defense: How do you mean?

Eliza Tate: Roman was upset with me about the loan I'd gotten from his parents. I thought he was trying to punish me by showing me that he could have other women if he really wanted. He flirted with Marguerite right in front of my eyes; he knew exactly what he was doing. Or so I thought. Now, I'm not so sure.

Defense: Why is that?

Eliza Tate: I'm beginning to think none of that was Roman's fault at all. I think Marguerite was the one trying to seduce my husband. I think *she* knew exactly what she was doing, and he was the fool. She just let him think he was in charge. It's amazing what men will do if you stroke their ego just right.

Defense: And why would Ms. Hill try to seduce your husband?

Eliza Tate: Marguerite hated Roman. She wanted me to leave him.

Defense: Ms. Hill hated your husband? Did she say so outright?

Eliza Tate: She didn't need to. Like I said, I've known Marguerite for years. Over the past few months especially, she's been prodding me to leave him. To *Take Charge* if you will and get rid of him.

Defense: And you didn't want to leave him?

Eliza Tate: It didn't matter what I wanted. I wasn't moving fast enough for Marguerite and what *she* wanted.

Defense: Why do you think Ms. Hill hated your husband?

Eliza Tate: She thought he was controlling. That he didn't deserve me. Now that I know her history, it makes more sense why she had it out for him from the start.

Defense: What does Ms. Hill's past have to do with her disliking your husband?

Eliza Tate: Marguerite's got a bit of a vendetta against men in power. Men who abuse power, I should say. After reading the stories that have come out about what her father did to her as a child, I can hardly blame her. Honestly, I think she believed she was trying to do a good thing. I think she wanted to help me.

Defense: But?

Eliza Tate: But I didn't need help. I've always taken care of myself. I knew what I was doing.

Defense: Did you tell her that?

Eliza Tate: I didn't get the chance. Because somewhere along the line, feelings got involved, and that never ends well.

TWENTY

Six Months Before
August 2018

I have to tell you, Marguerite, I am so looking forward to your next project." A man stuffed into a boring black suit extended a meaty hand toward Marguerite. "I'm Henry David, editor for the *Los Angeles Literary Magazine*. It's a small, independent, digital-only magazine I run from my blog. Any chance I could steal a few moments of your time?"

Eliza tuned out the mundane conversation, sweeping her gaze across the rest of the partygoers. The attendance was quite impressive. The food was perfection. The ambiance was on point. So why were Eliza's nerves ragged?

"That's a brilliant idea," Marguerite said, digging an elbow into Eliza's side. "Don't you agree?"

Eliza forced a smile onto her face, trying to rack her brain for remnants of a conversation she'd actively tuned out. "Sorry, which idea?"

"Book clubs." Marguerite's annoyance was thinly disguised. "What if we provided advanced copies of my book to book clubs across the country? We could get them to tweet and post about it on Instagram. Better yet, it would help get some early reviews up."

"Absolutely," Eliza said. "I've already got that covered."

"You do?"

"Of course. The first book club event is slotted for February. We should have advance copies of *Be Free* printed by then. It will be a great opportunity to snap some photos of the book in the wild."

Marguerite noticeably cheered, looking intrigued at the mention of a photo op. "Is it local? I'd love to swing by in person. Sign some copies, hear how the book was received."

Get your picture taken, Eliza thought harshly.

"It's local," Eliza confirmed. "I'll update your calendar with the details."

"Very good." Marguerite turned, satisfied, back to the blogger. "Stay tuned for photos. You can run them in your magazine with the article."

Eliza raised a hand, biting her nail as she contemplated the logistics of throwing together a book club event that would impress Marguerite Hill. She'd lied about the whole thing—there was no local book club. There was no book club at all.

"I'd love to attend, too." The reporter turned his gaze on Eliza. "Snap a few photos of my own."

"Great idea," Marguerite said. "Eliza? Where is it being held?"

"It's...uh...it's actually at my house," Eliza said, shooting the reporter an apologetic smile. "Sorry, closed to the public."

"Good idea," Marguerite muttered. "Good idea."

It was a stroke of good fortune that Eliza's good friend Dominic Schroeder strolled by at that moment. Eliza grabbed his elbow, thrust him toward Marguerite, and threw introductions at them to avoid any more questions about this nonexistent book club. Marguerite raised her eyebrow curiously at the well-groomed, handsome gentleman.

"This is Dominic, film and television agent," Eliza rushed. "He's the best of the best. Sold the latest Annie Shefflin books to Warner Bros."

"Annie Shefflin?" Marguerite raised her eyebrows. "Very impressive. I'm—"

"I know who you are," Dominic interrupted. "It's a pleasure to meet you, Marguerite. Are you at liberty to share some details about *Be Free*? I'm wondering if there's any hope of adapting it for the big screen. With the success of *Take Charge*, I'm sure the studios would be hankering for a look at a pitch."

Eliza smiled to herself and ducked out of the conversation. The two would occupy one another for the next half hour easily. The slightest mention about film rights to Marguerite, and she melted into a sugary-sweet mess. Likewise, whenever Eliza dangled a *New York Times* bestseller in front of Dominic Schroeder, his mind rang up dollar signs like an ATM.

Still beaming from her matchmaking efforts, Eliza meandered through the guests. She paused when she spotted Roman and Penny nose-to-nose in the center of the ballroom, speaking in low tones while the chandelier dripped sparkles of light over them. Eliza's throat went dry as Roman handed Penny something that resembled a credit card. *A room key.*

Penny seemed to be in shock as Roman turned on a heel and disappeared from the ballroom. She stood stock-still, alone in a sea of people, her eyes wide and unblinking as she stared down at the key. Her cheeks grew progressively pinker. Eliza could see her expression change as she digested the meaning of the plastic slip in her hand.

Grabbing a glass of champagne from a passing waiter, Eliza held it to her lips and sipped. She watched, waited. Penny's eyes flicked toward the door, then down to the key card. Then across the room and then back to the key card. It was clear she was torn.

Then, like a swift streak of lightning, a sheet of steel seemed to descend over the young woman's features. Her neck snapped high to attention. Her shoulders jerked with rigidity. Her tentative smile evened to a thin line. And like that, her decision had been made. Eliza watched, her heart sinking, as Penny made her exit from the ballroom.

Eliza reached the hall just in time to see the elevator doors slide shut. The arrow pointing upward had been selected. Closing her eyes,

Eliza let her body sag against the wall, just out of sight. She pressed a hand to her forehead.

For a moment, she debated following Penny. Eliza could storm in like a battering ram and rain fury upon both of them, but what good would that accomplish? If Roman and Penny wanted to be together, a few biting words from Eliza wouldn't stop them.

So Eliza straightened her dress and marched back to the bar. Once there, she secured two more glasses of white wine and returned to Marguerite's side.

"Has Roman left the party?" Marguerite asked as Eliza handed her one of the two wineglasses. She quickly tacked on an explanation. "He put my jacket somewhere, and I was looking for it."

"I'm sure you were," Eliza said sweetly. "But that darling husband of mine is otherwise occupied at the moment. If you wait, I'm sure he'll come back for you."

TRANSCRIPT

Prosecution: Did Roman Tate ever talk about his wife to you?

Penny Sands: A little bit.

Prosecution: Did he ever talk about their wedding?

Penny Sands: Their Vegas elopement, you mean? Sure. He mentioned it.

Prosecution: Did he explain why it was urgent they get married so quickly?

Penny Sands: I'm assuming they were in love. That's what people do sometimes. They fall in love and get married.

Prosecution: Did he ever tell you that Eliza Tate had an expiring visa?

Penny Sands: I don't remember.

Prosecution: The way I see it, Mr. Tate did his wife a favor by marrying her. For a while, Mrs.

Tate felt indebted to him. She earned a lot of money and gave her husband a nice life. But how long was she supposed to pay her debt to him while he spent her money and had affairs with younger women?

Penny Sands: I'm not sure what you mean.

Prosecution: I'm wondering if it's possible that Eliza Tate didn't want to deal with her husband—and his mistresses—any longer.

Penny Sands: I wouldn't know the answer to that. You'll have to ask Eliza.

Prosecution: It's no secret that there's bad blood between you and Mr. Tate. Ms. Sands, did Mrs. Tate ask for your help in murdering her husband?

TWENTY-ONE

Five Months Before
September 2018

The gauzy curtains twitched in the breeze, the air breathing life into the nearly translucent fabric. Penny lay curled on the plush comforter with crisp, white sheets draped just so over her naked figure. She watched the curtains dance with whimsy, the doors beyond thrown open to the morning sunlight as another Los Angeles heat wave sent warm whispers down her bare legs.

The door to the bathroom opened with a click. Penny didn't need to look back to see the striking figure cross the room. She waited until he slid under the covers to join her. Roman slipped his tanned arm over Penny's shoulders and let his index finger and thumb trace circles on her exposed belly.

"God, I could get used to this." Penny cuddled against him, basking in the sunlight and the tickle of a long, slow kiss at the nape of her neck. "It's magic. Pure magic."

Roman murmured an unintelligible agreement. *It's sort of his thing*, Penny thought, rolling to face him. She traced his jawline, thinking when a man looked like Roman, he didn't need to use English words. His nonsensical *mmm*s and *aah*s were enough. And what he didn't say aloud, she could read in the depths of his gorgeous eyes.

"I love you," Penny blurted.

A silence followed, and though it was somewhat long, it wasn't awkward. Roman leaned forward and touched a kiss to her forehead.

"You don't have to say it back," Penny added quickly. "I completely understand if you're not ready for that. But…it's how I feel. I didn't plan to say it, but the damn thing came out anyway."

"I'm getting there." Roman's kisses worked their way down to Penny's lips. "Have patience, sweetheart."

"I waited a long time for this, for us," Penny said. "I can wait a little longer for you to catch up."

Roman just smiled and nuzzled against her.

"Tell me about Eliza," Penny said.

Roman propped himself up on his elbow, his hand stilling on Penny's belly. "What do you mean?"

"I'm curious," Penny said. "You were married for a long time."

"Yes," Roman said. "We fell in love in college. Or whatever you want to call it. I always thought the two of us had more of a business arrangement than anything. Eliza is…exceptional in the workforce. It didn't translate to home life."

"Why'd you marry her?"

Roman's eyes flickered toward Penny. "I wish you wouldn't—"

"Indulge me," Penny said. "I'm not jealous. I just want to understand."

"We were dating," Roman said. "We got married fast. Eliza was up for a huge job, but her visa was about to expire. If I didn't marry her…"

"That's so romantic!"

"It was borderline illegal."

"Romantic," Penny insisted. "You took a risk for a woman you loved. Even if it didn't work out. I think that's admirable."

"Even though we failed."

"Even though it failed."

"Yes, well…" Roman winked. "I can be unadmirable, too, if you'd like to see that."

Penny giggled, wriggling against him. "I saw plenty of that last night."

"There's more where that came from."

"I want to talk," Penny said. "I want to get to know you. More, I mean. Every inch of you."

"The past is the past. I don't want to sit around discussing my ex-wife when we have this beautiful morning ahead of us. Let's order room service."

"Sure," Penny agreed as Roman extended an arm and pulled the menu toward him. He slipped on a pair of thick glasses that she thought made him look exceptionally cute. "Then let's talk about the future. Our future."

Roman placed a call to room service, ignoring Penny's request. He ordered a lavish breakfast spread from the staff at the Pelican Hotel and spared no expense. They'd returned to the scene of their first night spent together time and time again. It'd been weeks since that evening, the evening of the book launch party, and they'd spent many a night together since, each better than the last. Call it nostalgia, call it routine—Penny didn't care. She loved it. She loved him.

Roman continued his order: sliced grapefruit, full omelet, toast with rose petal jam, fresh figs and dates, and two black coffees with cream on the side for Penny. When she spent the night with Roman, she never went hungry. One of the million perks to dating a man with money.

"Two sugars," Roman added. "And extra packets of butter for the toast."

When he hung up, Penny rested her hand on his thigh. He wore nothing but black boxers, and her hand stroked through the dark hair on his leg. "I love that," she whispered. "This. Us. It's just so…easy."

"What's easy?"

"Us," Penny repeated. "You know what I like to eat and how I like my coffee. That I need extra butter for my toast."

"I know the extra butter is so you can stash it in your purse for later."

Penny laughed. "And you know that, too. I always thought this was what love would be like. Sunny mornings, lazy days, good food, and…yes, great sex," Penny added when Roman started dancing his fingers down her torso. She smacked his hand away. "Is this what you thought it would be like? Are we different than you were with Eliza?"

Roman withdrew his hand. "Why are you so intent on analyzing my ex-wife? We're no longer together for a reason. It's over."

"I know, I'm sorry. Forget I said anything. I'm just so excited about us, how far we've come even though it's only been a few months since we met. It's amazing, isn't it?"

"You're amazing."

The cross look on Roman's face dissipated, to Penny's relief. She'd have to tone down her mentions of Eliza, curious or not. Understandably so, seeing as she wouldn't love Roman digging into her past relationships, either.

Almost as if he'd read her mind, Roman winked at her. "I'm sure you have a past, too."

Penny nodded.

"Did you fuck Ryan Anderson?"

"Excuse me?" Penny recoiled. "What are you talking about?"

"Ryan Anderson," Roman said. "He's been ogling you since the day you walked into class. Did you sleep with him?"

"God, Roman. That's so rude."

"Well?"

Penny stood. "I don't want to talk about it."

"I meant it when I said you should stay away from him."

"I know," Penny said, hugging her arms around her as the warm breeze suddenly felt cool on her body. "You were jealous, even then?"

"He's a strange guy."

"He's boring is all. I went out with him a few times because I thought you were *married*. What was I supposed to do, be celibate for the rest of my life because you were in love with someone else?"

"I was trying to watch out for you," Roman said, reaching out to grab Penny's wrist. He tugged at her gently. "I don't like the way he looks at you. Maybe I am jealous. Maybe it was my only way of keeping tabs on you before I was ready to take the next step."

"That's almost sweet."

"I just know he's done it before, dated girls from class."

"He's allowed to date. I told him I wasn't interested. I don't expect him to wait around for me, nor would I want him to."

"Oh?"

"C'mon, I'm interested in *you*," Penny said, twirling to face Roman. "You idiot. It's always been you. I only went out with Ryan because I was trying to get you out of my mind."

"Come here." Roman's voice was a quiet instruction. "I'm yours, baby."

"I know." Penny let herself be pulled toward him, let their lips meet in a tangle of familiar angst that grew whenever they were apart and calmed the second they were together. "I love you. I'm sorry about Ryan. I'm sorry we argued."

"That wasn't an argument." Roman pulled Penny onto his lap. "But I'll make it up to you anyway."

TRANSCRIPT

Prosecution: When did you suspect your husband was having an affair with Penny Sands?

Eliza Tate: I saw my husband give Penny a key to his room the night of Marguerite's book launch party.

Prosecution: Why did you marry your husband?

Eliza Tate: Because I loved him.

Prosecution: Why did you kill him?

TWENTY-TWO

Five Months Before
September 2018

You owe me," Anne said as she plunked herself down at the table across from Eliza. "I had to pay the valet fee today because I was running so late. Their rates are pure theft."

"No, it's the Pelican Hotel," Eliza said. "Your coffee's on me. Will that help you to stop whining?"

"Damn right it is." Anne shifted her glasses lower. "I want the biggest, most expensive coffee that's legal, and then I'll consider us even."

Eliza repeated the order verbatim to a waiting server, studying Anne as she wiggled into her seat. Anne's gaze flicked toward the doors of the hotel almost uncomfortably, and Eliza wondered if the location held bad memories for her, too. Anne *had* argued against meeting at the hotel's lobby café, but Eliza had assumed the argument had more to do with the financial end of the spectrum than anything else.

"What'd you want to talk about?" Anne asked, sounding agitated. As if she were ready to get the check before her beverage had even arrived.

"I just thought it'd be good to catch up," Eliza said. "What with me venturing out on my own at the company and you…well, having four children, it's been ages since we got together without a specific reason."

"Well, I have to pay a sitter every time I leave the house these days since Mark is hardly around, and I can't afford that, so… I suppose you could swing by for coffee if you're bored, but you'll have to take an aspirin to avoid a headache with how screechy the twins have been lately."

"Sounds relaxing," Eliza said. "Maybe you should hire a babysitter more. You liked that Penny, didn't you?"

"Yes, thanks again," Anne said, warming to the topic as Eliza had hoped she would. "That woman has been a lifesaver. But she still costs money."

"What do you think about her?" Eliza asked. "As a person?"

"Who, Penny?"

Eliza nodded.

"I don't know. She seems great with the kids. She doesn't pry, doesn't ask too many questions. I think she steals some of our food, but hey, better she eat our old Doritos than me. My ass doesn't need the carbs."

"She steals food? Isn't that"—Eliza hesitated—"wrong?"

"I dunno," Anne said. "I tell her to help herself to anything in the fridge or pantry. I just figured, you know, she probably didn't mow through an entire family-sized pack of chips at once, which means she probably shoved the bag in her purse or something. Who cares? She's broke."

"Most people in Roman's classes are," Eliza said dryly. "Nature of the business."

"Why do you ask?" Anne pressed. "I'm not mad at you or anything for the referral. I'll sacrifice a bag of chips any day for a woman who's good with the kids and doesn't charge an arm and a leg to watch them."

"No reason."

"Bullshit," Anne called. "You always have a reason. Did Penny say something to Roman about us? For Pete's sake, did Mark try to get her to tattle on me, too?"

"Tattle on you?"

"Forget it," Anne said. "Why do you care about Penny?"

Eliza glanced upward at the hotel, noting the open balconies, the couples lounging on their private terraces, the soft clink of silverware from overhead as hotel guests enjoyed their breakfasts. *Is my husband one of them?* Eliza wondered. *Is Penny?*

"I've found some receipts," Eliza admitted. "Receipts for rooms at the Pelican Hotel."

"You're kidding me." Anne tipped her glasses all the way off her face and squinted upward.

For a moment, Eliza wondered if her friend would shout out Roman's name to the rooftop. Eliza wasn't sure she'd have stopped her if she did, but eventually, Anne turned her attention back to earth as the server appeared with two large lattes frothed to perfection.

"I hate to say I'm not surprised," Anne said with extra snap to her voice. "But frankly, I wouldn't put it past Roman."

"You've never liked him," Eliza said. "You didn't give him a chance."

"Did he deserve one?" Anne asked pointedly, then reached for her coffee and took a big sip.

Eliza knew Anne had never been the biggest fan of Roman's, but it'd always been sort of a passive thing before. An echo in the dark. A subtle comment here or there. Much slyer than Marguerite Hill's more overwhelming jabs to get rid of her husband, stat. But this morning, Anne had no shame as she spoke ill of Roman. Eliza only wondered if it was because of the potential affair or something else.

"I won't argue with you on that," Eliza said. "But I have to wonder if it's one of his students."

"You think it's Penny?" Anne considered, then frowned and shook her head. "No way. The girl's way too innocent."

"You said she steals your food."

"She took a bag of chips," Anne said. "Honestly, the valet prices here are worse theft than whatever Penny's capable of."

"It's a slippery slope," Eliza said.

"Do you have any reason to suspect it's Penny?"

Eliza thought back to the night of the book launch party for Marguerite Hill. The key card, the quiet looks, the elevator. The fact that Roman had been late coming home—if he came home at all—over the last few weeks. Ever since the stupid loan from his parents.

"Besides the fact that she's sweet, pretty, and, you know, otherwise adorable?" Anne prompted. "I don't think it's Penny. Could it be someone else?"

"It could be," Eliza murmured.

It's not, she thought, looking up again. A charge was pending from the Pelican Hotel from last night on Roman's credit card. Eliza wondered if he was trying to hide it at all anymore or if he just didn't care.

"I know this sucks," Anne said. "Believe me, I know how you're feeling right now. But it's just an affair."

"Just an affair? You almost died when you found out Mark was having an affair—not that I blame you. But what changed?"

"There are things worse than affairs," Anne said cryptically. "I got over it. Whatever. And I hate to break it to you, but I think this was a long time coming. Roman only married you for your money."

"He married me because he loved me." Eliza lowered her voice.

"Sure, sure," Anne said with a roll of her eyes. "He likes to play the hero and say he married you so you could stay in the country, but that's all an act. You were set up to make one of the fattest salaries out of your graduating class. You don't think Roman could see the writing on the wall? He knew his parents were cutting him off financially after college. He knew you'd be able to pick up the torch and carry on providing for him."

"That's ridiculous," Eliza said, though she'd wondered the same thing a million times. She just hadn't wondered it aloud.

"He's smart—when he wants to be," Anne said. "He knew you'd

feel indebted to him after the quickie ceremony. He made himself out to be a martyr, but it was all an act so you'd put up with him acting like a jerk for the rest of your life."

"And how do you know this?"

"Because I'm on the outside looking in," Anne said. "Don't tell me I'm the only person who doesn't like your husband."

Eliza thought back to her wedding day. The very day Roman's own mother had warned her about him. She thought to Marguerite and how the bestselling author seemed to have a vendetta against him, too. Eliza had always explained away the latter by blaming Marguerite's concerns on her overall attitude about men: one of skepticism and distrust. But maybe she'd been wrong.

"It's not your fault." Anne melted, letting down her victorious front in exchange for a more sympathetic one. "I'm sorry. I didn't mean it to come off that way. I'm sorry this happened to you. But honestly, I wouldn't put anything past Roman."

"What'd he do to you?" Eliza retorted, somewhat annoyed that Anne suddenly seemed to think she knew more about Roman than Eliza herself. "When have you ever initiated a conversation with Roman outside of a dinner party where I made the two of you talk?"

"This isn't a competition," Anne said. "You invited me here. You asked for my opinion. Roman's the bad guy here, not me."

"I'm not sure that he is. Maybe there's an explanation for everything."

"Maybe. Or maybe the explanation is exactly what you think it is. The question is what you're going to do about it." Anne pushed her sunglasses back up her nose. "Let me know if you need ideas, because I have a few."

"I feel like your ideas would scare me."

Anne shrugged one shoulder. "That's what happens when you've got nothing to lose."

TRANSCRIPT

Defense: When did your relationship with Roman Tate turn sour, Ms. Sands?

Penny Sands: A few weeks after it turned great.

Defense: And what was the turning point of your short-lived relationship?

Penny Sands: That damn pink line.

Defense: Please be more specific.

Penny Sands: I took a pregnancy test, and it turned out positive. Specific enough?

TWENTY-THREE

Five Months Before
September 2018

D amn it!" Penny chirped happily as one of many millions of Angeleno drivers swooped in front of her to steal the only parking space left on the block. "Idiot! Asshole!"

Whistling a cheerful tune, Penny pulled around the offending vehicle, offering an altogether pleasant middle finger as she sailed around the idiot driver in search of a new spot. Penny doubted anyone had ever been as happy as she to be shouting obscenities at random strangers. But her upbeat outbursts could mean only one thing: she'd bought herself a car.

It had been a few weeks since she'd first gone to bed with Roman Tate. Ever since that evening, they'd been spending several nights a week together back where it'd all started. Picturing her life together with Roman once he was truly free was Penny's new favorite pastime.

She dreamed about spending every evening twined around him. Lounging in bed on weekend mornings together as they sipped steaming coffee and basked under fresh sunlight. Their midnights would be filled with joyful whispers. Maybe one day, they'd even start a family.

In addition to her blossoming relationship with Roman, Penny's job at the casting company had held steady. A small miracle. Between that and the cash she'd squirreled away babysitting the Wilkes children, tacked on top of the paltry savings from her bank account, she'd managed to procure a Cadillac from the seventies that had more yacht in its DNA than car.

But Penny didn't care that it was next to impossible to park her new ride with a less-than-thirteen-point turn or that she needed to start right-hand turns a block early. Nor did she care that the paint was peeling and patches of rust tore at its skin with sharp, invasive fingernails. She definitely ignored the untalented patch job done over blemishes that suspiciously resembled bullet holes.

Penny Sands was damn proud of her car.

It represented her freedom in a whole new city. She'd moved with nothing across the country, and now she had something. She had an apartment, a job, a car…a sort of a boyfriend. Or a man-friend, really. Roman was mature and established. He knew what he was doing; he'd proved that and then some.

Whistling, Penny cruised around the block several times, earning side-eye glances from several passersby about the state of her car. She smiled brightly back. When she finally found an open slot, she eased into it with the grace of a buffalo, overly cautious not to add another dent to her precious vehicle. As she fed quarters to a hungry meter, she studied her car with the adoration of a new mother.

Nobody could ruin her bliss this evening. She had class under Roman's tutelage, and they were going out for drinks after—alone. Penny was sure they'd retire to her apartment once drinks had been drunk. Just the thought sent a thrill through her bones.

But Penny's luck seemed to be running out. As she locked her car door manually, she looked up to find Ryan Anderson climbing out of his vehicle just across the street. He raised a hand and waved. It was too late to pretend she hadn't seen him, though she flirted with the idea of feigning she'd forgotten something in her car. Instead, she waved back.

"Hey, Ryan," she said after he'd dodged traffic and joined her on the sidewalk. "How's it going?"

"I see you got a car." He nodded at her beast of a vehicle. "Congrats. The babysitting gig working out for you?"

"Babysitting?" Penny fell into step beside Ryan as they moved toward the acting studio. "How'd you know I took a babysitting job?"

"I don't remember." Ryan scratched at his forehead. "Didn't you tell me?"

Penny racked her brain but couldn't possibly remember when she'd have told Ryan, but he'd obviously found out somehow. "Well, it's paying the bills, and the kids are cute. What about you? Any new gigs lately?"

Now that Penny had a real man by her side, she felt a bit bad about dropping Ryan so quickly. Her thoughts were much kinder about him than they'd been before. Then again, everything seemed a little brighter now that she had Roman.

"Bit parts here and there, nothing to write home about." He gave her a faint smile. "Say, I know you've been busy these last few weeks, but I was thinking, maybe if you're available..." Ryan trailed off, his eyes calculating as he looked at Penny.

She returned his gaze with a sad smile. "I'm sorry," Penny muttered. "I should have told you sooner. I met someone."

"Ah. It's serious?"

"It's getting there. I'd like to see where it goes."

"Hey, that's fine. I'm just glad you told me before I made an idiot of myself."

"I'm really sorry."

"You warned me." Ryan touched her shoulder gently. "It's all good."

Penny gave a wry smile. "For what it's worth, I did have fun."

"Me too." Ryan returned her smile, added a pinch of lightheartedness to it. "I never told you—I had just gotten out of a relationship when we met. I probably shouldn't have gotten involved with you so fast, either."

"Was it serious?"

Ryan shrugged. But the cloud that drifted over his features told Penny everything she needed to know. She felt worse.

"Don't worry about it," he said, watching her face closely. "Maybe we were just meant to be each other's rebound."

"We can still be friends if you'd like."

"Ah, the old *friends* line." Ryan's voice was softer. He didn't sound convinced. "Is it him?"

"Who?" As soon as Penny echoed his question, she remembered the morning in her apartment when Ryan had guessed the text message on Penny's phone had been from another man. She squeezed out a dry smile. "Yeah, it's him. I'm sorry."

"I figured."

Penny hadn't thought Ryan had paid attention when they talked, but he was turning out to be a lot more perceptive than she'd thought. He paid more attention to Penny than any other boyfriend she'd ever dated. It almost made Penny wonder if she'd made the wrong choice, turning him away in hopes that her complicated relationship with Roman would blossom into something more.

Despite Ryan's somewhat dull nature, Penny suspected he would be the sort of man to dote on her. Buy her flowers. Hang on to her every word. Love her like she deserved to be loved. So why the hell hadn't she taken the leap with him? The tiniest pinch of guilt tugged at her as she looked over to where Ryan's lips were tipped into a frown.

"I'm sorry." Penny reached out without thinking and gave his hand a squeeze. "I sort of wish things were different."

"I'm patient." Ryan squeezed her hand back, his frown turning into a lopsided smile.

Penny laughed. "What's that supposed to mean?"

"When you need another rebound, I'm your guy." Ryan winked. "I'll be waiting for you, Penny Sands. You'll come around to me, I'm sure of it."

Still grinning, Penny gave a shake of her head. "Okay, then. I'll hold you to that."

As Ryan walked into the theater, she paused in the lobby. Penny was still smiling when she turned and found her lover—such a romantic, dramatic word—leaning against his office door.

Penny's thoughts of Ryan extinguished like a wisp of smoke as she looked into Roman's dark eyes. An intensity burned beneath, and she was reminded of the way he'd looked at her the night of the book launch party.

Her breath hitched in her throat as she stepped across the room. "Why are you looking at me like that when you've got students one room over?"

"You're the only student I care about." Roman's eyes flitted toward the entrance to the theater, then back to Penny's cleavage. "Why don't you join me inside my office?"

He hooked his finger inside the V-neck of her shirt and helped her along. He slammed the door behind her, flicked the lock shut. With a grasp of his hand, he swung Penny around like a rag doll, pinning her back against the door.

She writhed against him, her feeble, half-hearted protests lost as their lips tangled together. She was powerless against Roman's sexuality; she craved him, needed him, though she'd had him innumerable times already. He filled some deep, primal void for her, and they both felt it. He would always have his way with her, and there was nothing Penny could do about it. Nothing she *wanted* to do about it.

"Roman," she gasped. "What are you thinking? Someone could walk in here any second."

"Let them," he growled against her neck.

"What's gotten into you?" Penny threw her head back, then locked one leg around Roman's waist and dragged him toward her. "I'm not complaining, but..."

"Good."

Penny raised her other leg with the help of Roman's sturdy arms. She curled around him as he released himself from his jeans and let his pants drop to his knees. Then he moved his fingers under Penny's skirt, his eyes darkening when he felt the barely-there thong.

She groaned when his fingers touched her most sensitive spot. "I don't... I can't..."

Roman pressed into her with his full force, sending Penny's breath hissing out as his lips glanced across her neck. Her fingernails dug into his back, surely leaving marks. Her eyes snapped shut, her mind splintering into fractures of color and light and stars.

A knock on the door interrupted them. Immediately, Penny felt her face go flush, both with regret at the interruption and shame at their brazen risk. Roman all but dropped Penny, then leaned forward and pulled up his pants. He zipped and fastened his button with all-too-practiced ease.

"Get dressed," he said. "I have to take this meeting."

"But you don't know who it is," Penny mumbled dumbly, feeling idiotic as she knelt to retrieve her torn panties. "What if they heard us?"

"Straighten your skirt."

"Relax. It's not like we're doing anything wrong," Penny said, then blushed. "I mean, it's embarrassing, but it's not the end of the world. We're both adults, both single. I love you, Roman."

"Now is really not the time to have that discussion."

"I'm not pushing you to say it back to me. I'm just being honest with you."

"Oh, Penny." Roman shook his head. "Try to be realistic. It's too soon for that. I can't exactly marry you; I'm not even divorced yet." The knock on the door sounded again, more persistently. Roman's gaze flicked over her shoulder. "We'll talk about this later. I have an important meeting."

"We'll talk about *us* later." Penny didn't mean to ask the question, but her voice lilted at the last moment, giving away her insecurities. "Are we still on for drinks—"

"Tonight won't work. I'm sorry. This might take a while."

"Call me then, when you decide what you want."

Roman gave a quick smile. "Of course."

Head down, Penny shoved the carcass of her torn panties out of sight. She'd skipped lunch earlier in the week and had spent the saved money on special undies to surprise Roman. Now, they were a mangled mess, tucked into the elastic band of her skirt. Much like Penny's feelings.

Her cheeks warmed as she yanked the door to Roman's office open, wondering if his next visitor would be able to smell sex clinging to the air. She was so painfully self-conscious that she could hardly glance at the middle-aged woman waiting on the other side. But the tapping of the woman's toe against tile drew her gaze as Penny wondered with an air of annoyance what was so important it hadn't been able to wait.

Penny stilled, however, as she caught sight of the woman's face. "Anne?"

"Penny?" Anne Wilkes hesitated. "What are you doing here? God, you're a student. I completely forgot."

"Taking classes?" Penny joked, her palms clammy as her mind worked in overdrive. "I didn't know you were an actress in your spare time."

Anne. Eliza. Eliza's husband. There was no way word of Penny's dalliance with Roman wasn't getting back to Eliza. Big mistake. Even if the two were separated, Roman was still married. It wasn't right what Penny was doing; she just couldn't seem to stop herself.

"Not me. I don't act." Anne was so distracted, she'd missed the joke, her cheeks a ghostly pale. "I was just dropping something off... er...for Eliza."

"Ah, of course," Penny said. "Well, I'll see you this weekend."

"This weekend?"

"Brunch. Saturday, your place? I'm bringing fruit?"

"Yeah, yes. I mean, of course. See you."

"Anne, come in," Roman called casually from his office. "Sorry about the wait."

Blindsided by both Roman and Anne, Penny wheeled away from

the acting studio and shuffled back toward her car. There was no way she would sit through class tonight. She couldn't stare at Roman all evening and wonder what the hell they were doing together for the zillionth time. Some days, he was so sweet with her, and other days, it was like he wanted to pretend she didn't exist.

When Penny returned to her car, her night progressively got worse. A thoughtful cop had slipped a dismal parking ticket under her wiper. She plucked it off and noted the expired meter.

"Fuck!" she snarled.

Her phone beeped. She looked down, hoping against hope it was Roman, apologizing for his stupid attitude and asking her to come back.

She blew out a disappointed breath to discover it wasn't him.

Ryan Anderson: Hey, you ok? Where'd you go?

Then she got into her car, hating the peeling paint and rundown interior, and sped toward home. Once there, she found another message from Ryan waiting on her phone.

Ryan Anderson: Hope you're ok. Give me a holler sometime.

Penny threw her phone across the room and watched as it bounced once on the couch, then landed on the floor. When her mother called at their scheduled time several hours later, she curled tighter under her blanket and watched as it went to voicemail. Her mother called a second time an hour later, and Penny shut her eyes as the phone beeped, signaling a message.

Penny dragged herself off the couch around midnight. It was only once she'd showered, brushed her teeth, and made a cup of chamomile tea that she finally picked up her phone. On it, aside from the missed messages from Ryan and the mystified voicemails from her mother, was an email notification.

Penny blinked, then blinked again when she read the name in the address bar. Surely, it couldn't be. It made no sense. Unless...

No. That was impossible.

As her stomach cramped with dread, Penny touched the Delete button on the screen of her phone. Two minutes later, she pulled up the Trash folder and retrieved the message.

Finally, she couldn't take the suspense a second longer. The message would haunt her every waking moment until she bit the bullet, faced the music, paid the piper. It was time.

Address: eliza.tate@gmail.com
Subject: Urgent Request

TRANSCRIPT

Prosecution: Mrs. Tate, you say you have no idea how your fingerprints got on the knife?

Eliza Tate: No. I mean yes, I have no idea.

Prosecution: Are you implying that you were somehow framed for murder?

Eliza Tate: I'm not implying anything. I'm saying I have no clue how my fingerprints ended up on the weapon.

Prosecution: The knife was from your kitchen. Who else had access to it?

Eliza Tate: Any number of people. I've hosted plenty of parties, and I couldn't tell you when it went missing.

Prosecution: Did Anne Wilkes have access to your home?

Eliza Tate: Anne is a good friend of mine. She's been in my home many times. Are you suggesting

that Anne and I worked together to get rid of my
husband?

Prosecution: Isn't it possible? You both had a
reason to want the victim dead.

Eliza Tate: Well, I suppose anything's possible.
But if you can't prove it, does it matter?

TWENTY-FOUR

Four Months Before
October 2018

Eliza ran a duster over the living room bookshelf one last time. The house was already spotless. *This is what happens when a woman's life is falling apart*, she thought dryly. She had nowhere to release her tension except on the poor dust bunnies cowering beneath her overpriced couch. She was really beginning to hate that couch.

Roman had picked it out, along with most of the overpriced furniture in the place. Years ago, Eliza had said he'd had an eye for interior design, but now she found herself wondering if he'd just had an eye for the interior designer—a leggy blond who, in retrospect, had spent a lot more time than was necessary sizing up their house for furniture.

Her life was beginning to spiral. She wasn't sure where she stood in her marriage. Her husband was likely having an affair. Her only client was falling for her husband. Her company hadn't earned a dime. She still owed a sizeable sum of money to her in-laws.

Not knowing what else to do, Eliza pressed on, forcing herself to go about her business as usual. September melted into October, the last of the fall heat wave rearing its scorching head as the palm trees waved, oblivious to the change in seasons. Eliza wiped her brow with her sleeve and took one last look at the living room. It was good enough. Clean enough. Practically sterile.

The last thing Eliza wanted to do these days was entertain, but she'd offered to start a book club for Marguerite's work, and she refused to renege on her promises. She'd scheduled the first official meeting for one afternoon in October, a small get-together to kick things off. She'd follow it up with a larger event early in the new year once early copies of *Be Free* were available.

With an hour to spare before her friends arrived, Eliza opted for a quick shower and a change of clothes. The simple routine made her feel much better, much closer to her former self, though at this point, Eliza wasn't sure that was a good thing. She wasn't sure she remembered how to *be* her former self. Everything—and nothing—had changed.

She puttered around in the kitchen, fiddling with the canapés as she waited for her guests. A crystal decanter held a lush red wine that would accompany the appetizers. Bottles of water, cans of Diet Coke, and pitchers of lemonade sat chilling in a quaint galvanized metal tub propped against one end of the long counter. Her clean copy of Marguerite's book sat waiting to be opened.

The doorbell rang, spurring Eliza into action. She made her way to the front entrance and glued on her best welcoming expression. She opened the door to reveal her first guest waiting on the steps.

"Hello," Penny said after a slight hesitation. "I realize I'm early, once again. Ridiculously early. It's a bad habit of mine. Shall I come back in twenty minutes?"

"Don't be ridiculous. Everything's ready, and the wine won't drink itself."

Eliza ushered the young woman inside, hiding an amused twitch of her lips as she noted the car parked out front. Penny drove a beat-up Cadillac that looked like it belonged in Compton, not the upper end of Beverly Hills. Eliza admired the girl for driving it anyway.

Penny practically tiptoed into the kitchen. Eliza watched the young woman's careful movements with curiosity and wondered again why she'd accepted the invitation. Then again, Eliza herself wasn't innocent in the matter. One of the reasons she'd extended the book club invitation to Penny in the first place was because she'd wanted to get closer to the woman sleeping with her husband.

"What a beautiful house!" Penny gaped at the long marble island. "Oh my stars. It is just gorgeous. I thought this sort of place only existed in movies."

I'll bet you did, Eliza thought wryly. Judging by the piece of junk parked at her curb, Eliza suspected the young woman's apartment wasn't much better than her vehicle. She briefly wondered if Roman took her to nice places—fancy hotels, spas, fine dining—or if they screwed in back alleys and dirty motels because it upped the stakes. Then she brushed the thought away and went for the canapés.

"Can I tempt you into a glass of wine?" Eliza raised the decanter.

"Oh, no." Penny rested a hand on her stomach and made a face. "I'm feeling a little under the weather. Not, you know, contagious or anything. Bit of an upset stomach."

"This is very good wine," Eliza encouraged. "Plus, alcohol kills the bad bacteria. It's actually good for you."

"I shouldn't really."

"It's just not book club without wine." Eliza pulled down two glasses. "I hope you don't mind if I pour some for myself."

"Please, go ahead."

Eliza went ahead and took a sip. "How are you adjusting to life in the city? You said you're from the Midwest?"

"I'm adjusting." Penny's affirmative words were belittled by the furrowing of her brow. "It can be hard some days. Are you from the area?"

"I came over from Beijing to study at UCLA, so I understand what you're going through. It's lonely without family. Especially out here. Something about this city wrings it out of you."

"Yes!" Penny's eyes widened with agreement. "You just can't understand unless you've been through it. Sometimes I feel so stupid for giving up my life back home—where I had everything—to come out here where I have nothing."

Against all the odds, Eliza found herself softening further toward this young woman. Two lost souls felled before the same dark knight. Was Penny really all that different than Eliza had been when she'd first arrived in Los Angeles? Innocent, hopeful, a promising transplant to a starry-eyed city who had fallen in love with Roman's charms?

"I don't think you're stupid," Eliza said. "If you don't try, you'll never know if you could have succeeded. I'd rather die trying."

"Me too. I can't imagine how it feels to be at the top. I mean, look at you. It's all worth it, huh? All the hard work?"

Eliza pressed the wineglass hard against her bottom lip to keep from giving her honest answer. Because the honest answer wasn't pretty, just like her life. Her hard work had earned her a husband who strayed and finances that were in ruins. It had earned her a constant state of anxiety that droned endlessly in the background, the *buzz*, *buzz*, *buzz* of a persistent bee.

But she couldn't say any of that. Penny was so desperately starved for hope that it was almost pathetic. She'd opened to Eliza like a flower to the sun, leaning hungrily toward her in search of friendship. Eliza couldn't destroy the last vestiges of naive hope. If Penny wilted, it would be of her own doing.

"Everything in life comes at a cost." Eliza compromised with the gray line between truth and lies. "There are always consequences."

Blinking, Penny leaned against the counter. Eliza wondered if she was thinking of her affair with Roman and sizing up what Eliza knew. *Consequences, consequences.*

Not for the first time, Eliza wondered why she had invited Penny into her home. The emailed invitation had been crafted late at night and accompanied by a heady dose of wine-fueled confidence. The next morning, when Eliza had woken up with a headache and a response in her inbox, it had been too late to back out.

She'd spent days trying to justify her actions. The saintly side of Eliza chirped that the spontaneous invite had been an act of kindness, a way of looking out for the young girl who'd been swooped under her husband's dark wing. She was keeping an eye on Penny, watching to see how the fallout would go.

The ambivalent side of Eliza barked that it was curiosity—and nothing more—that had prompted the invitation. Who was *the other woman*? The younger, prettier, sweeter, kinder woman who'd stolen her husband's eye. Had it been Penny who'd gone after Roman, or had it been the other way around?

But the truly honest part of Eliza wondered if it was from a place of hurt. If the tiny vestiges of vulnerability that were left of Eliza, the part buried so deep, it took half a bottle of red to tease them out, had spurred her to act. In a way, Eliza was proud that a sensitive part of her still existed, proud that Roman hadn't taken that, too. Beneath Eliza's hardened, calloused outer layers, there was still a rawness left inside her—deep down maybe, but it was there. And that raw, hopeful young woman had once loved Roman Tate.

Fortunately for Penny, she was saved from an awkward conversation by another knock. Eliza excused herself and made her way to the front entrance. She opened the door to find a familiar face smiling back at her. Familiar but different.

Speaking of wilted, Eliza thought with one glance at her friend. *Poor Anne.*

"Sorry I'm late," Anne said robotically. "Kids."

"We haven't started yet. Are you feeling okay? You look a little peaked."

"Lots going on," Anne said with the glimmer of a long-lost smile. "I don't want to talk about it. I'd just ruin the night for everyone. Do you have wine?"

"I do…if you're sure that will help?" Eliza led Anne through the hallway and into the kitchen.

In answer, Anne reached for the bottle of wine and poured herself a glass. To the tippy, tippy top.

"Well, book club is a safe space to discuss your problems," Eliza said. "Especially since we're among friends. Obviously, no introductions are needed, since the two of you already know each other, so let's get started."

Penny already had a canapé in her mouth. "It's good to see you, Anne. How'd Gretchen do on her history test this week?"

"Aced it," Anne said with a weak smile. "Thanks to you of course."

Penny waved Anne off like it was nothing.

"Are you sure I can't get you wine, Penny?" Eliza asked, politely ignoring Anne's empty glass. "We have a little left."

"I'll take her portion if she's abstaining." Anne extended her glass. "I guess I was thirsty."

"It's yours." Penny nodded toward Anne. "I'm not feeling well. Bit of a stomach bug."

Anne's eyes followed Penny's hand as it went to her belly. "Are you pregnant?"

Penny's mouth popped open in shock.

"Oh God!" Anne's face went red with embarrassment. "That's the wine talking. I'm such an idiot, and it's none of my business. Forget I said anything. It's just…you told me you were seeing that guy, and—"

"You're seeing someone?" Eliza's grip tightened. "Is it new? How exciting. Come on, spill. We need the details."

"Oh, it's nothing," Penny said. "Really, it's stupid."

"I'm the stupid one," Anne said. "I can't believe I said that. Seriously, it's the wine. I haven't had a drink in ages."

Eliza knew that to be a lie. She wondered if Penny was lying, too. Were they all lying?

"No, you're right," Penny said. "I was seeing a guy, but things sort of petered out."

"Then it's a good thing you aren't pregnant, isn't it?" Anne chuckled nervously and sipped more wine. "Anyhoo, enough of that. Take it away, Eliza. How does book club work?"

"Well, as you know, I invited you all here to discuss Marguerite's *New York Times* bestseller, *Take Charge*. Her next book is coming out in a few months, so I thought we could have that be our second read."

"Works for me," Anne said, her words beginning to slur ever so slightly. "Even though I only read the first half of the book. Okay, that's a lie. I skimmed it. Nope, I read the chapter headings. I have four kids. I don't have time to read!"

"Just read the next one," Eliza said. "That's the important bit anyway. Now bring your glasses and follow me."

The three women took their books into the sitting room. Eliza and Anne carried their wineglasses with them. Penny asked for a coaster for her sparkling water. Each of them pulled out her book; Penny's was worn and ragged, Anne's was unopened but had a splatter of something that looked like ketchup on the outside, and Eliza's looked brand new.

"Thanks for coming, ladies," Eliza said. "Let's start by—"

"I'm pregnant," Penny blurted. "Anne was right. I *am* pregnant."

As silence swayed over the room like a dandelion gone to seed, drifting into oblivion piece by fluffy piece, Eliza's throat went dry. The meaning of Penny's words took some time to register, as if the connections between her brain synapses had slowed to a crawl. Once Eliza digested the information, it took her a moment longer to realize the implication of it.

She expected to feel horror. Dread. A sense of betrayal that cut beyond anything she'd ever felt. But as Eliza waited, took another sip of her wine, none of it set in. At best, she could muster a mild tingling in her extremities. Apparently her heart and head had already gone completely numb, leaving only her fingers and toes to react to the news.

"Congratulations!" Anne finally offered with a confused look at Eliza. "When are you due?"

"I—I haven't even been to the doctor to confirm it's real." Penny sank back against the couch cushions. She stared at a pair of knobby knees. "I just took the test this morning, which is why it's on my mind. I'm sorry to have blurted it out."

"That's what book club is for," Anne said. "To discuss. So long as we leave my problems off the table. Is this good news?"

Penny heaved a breath. "It's a surprise. I don't know how far along I am. I didn't suspect until…well, today."

"Plenty of people don't know they're pregnant early on," Anne said. "I wasn't expecting to get pregnant with my twins, and I didn't find out until I was eight weeks. And I'd been through two children prior and should have known the signs. I just thought I'd eaten too many cookies."

Penny raised one slim shoulder and let it fall as if that were the most excitement she could muster. "I feel awful."

"Why?" Anne asked.

Eliza was all but paralyzed on her stupid, overpriced sofa.

"This poor little human…" Mystified, Penny slid her hand over her stomach, looking shocked that life existed inside her. "He or she deserves to be loved. And I do love him or her! I mean, I think I do. But when I found out, I cried."

Eliza forced herself to make a sound. It came out like a grunt. "That's understandable. It's a life-changing event."

"Not tears of happiness," Penny clarified. "I was devastated. I didn't want to be pregnant."

Anne reached forward, the gaunt, anemic glow to her skin brightening to a healthier shade of peach. The awkwardness between the two women evaporated like a droplet of water sizzling on a scorching pan. Anne obviously understood what Penny was going through, while Eliza felt lost.

"It's very normal to have conflicting emotions." Anne's face was devoid of judgment. "Trust me."

"But you have a husband, I imagine," Penny said, not meeting Anne's eyes. "A house, stable finances, friends."

"Yes," Anne said softly, "but I promise you, my life is not perfect. It is okay to feel whatever it is that you're feeling. It's probably a mix, and that's natural."

"This baby should be celebrated." Penny looked hopefully at Anne as if wanting her to confirm or deny. "It's an innocent little person and deserves love."

"Bonding isn't always natural or easy," Anne said. "Even when the baby arrives. The love we have for our children grows with time. And even then, even with time...things happen."

"But—" Penny cut herself off with a sip of her water. "I always wanted to be a mom. It just wasn't supposed to happen this way."

"As women, we find it shameful to admit the truth about motherhood—that it's hard and confusing. Not every moment is a joyous occasion. Pregnancy isn't necessarily a glowing, wonderful time in our lives. I was not a glowing, happy pregnant woman." Anne gave a cough, then a laugh. "I had acne, my feet went up two sizes, and my stretch marks still haven't faded."

"But you wanted your children."

"I've been through three pregnancies and had three entirely different experiences. With the twins, I have to admit—" Anne stopped abruptly, blinked her eyes furiously. "I've never told anyone this before."

"I understand," Penny whispered. "But if you don't want to say it, that's okay."

"When I took that test, love was not the first emotion I felt. Let's put it that way." Anne considered, but then something in her face changed when she glanced at Penny. "If the doctor had told me I'd had a miscarriage early on, a part of me would have felt..."

"Relieved?" Penny suggested in a tiny voice.

Anne swallowed. Eliza could see the lump in her throat, so obviously painful.

"I thought the same thing," Penny said. "At this point in my life, a baby will make everything so complicated. But I could never..."

"You don't have to explain," Anne said, her face paling once more. "I know. You're not alone. I have to believe *we're* not alone. My husband and I hadn't planned to have any more children. We thought we were done. Then, I found out I was pregnant—not with one but with two babies."

"I can't imagine."

"I couldn't, either. I couldn't fathom bringing one more life into this world, let alone a second. Two more mouths to feed, two more college tuitions, two more little people to fit into my heart. My heart was already full. How could I possibly find enough love for everyone?"

"And?" Penny held her breath.

"And I guarantee you'll be a better mother than me." Anne gave a weak smile. "I left my family, Penny. Samuel was barely one year old when I left him alone."

Penny just blinked. Eliza knew the story, but she was surprised Anne was sharing it so readily. Maybe Anne and Penny were better friends than Anne had let on. Eliza wondered if that was purposeful on Anne's part or a simple fact she'd forgotten to mention.

"I walked out my front door and didn't come back," Anne said. "They found me in Palm Springs at a motel. Just sitting outside, sipping a margarita by the pool. Not rejoicing, mind you. Just sitting. Staring. Devastated. How could I go back after what I'd done? I knew it was wrong. But I didn't know how to fix it."

Penny inhaled sharply. "But you came back?"

"I left in the first place because the voices in my head were telling me I was a bad mother," Anne said. "I never felt good enough. I didn't feel bonded with my baby. I missed picture day at Gretchen's school. I stopped breastfeeding Sammy at three weeks because it fucking hurt. Everything felt wrong. I thought that my leaving would be the best thing for my kids."

"I'm so sorry," Penny said. "That sounds awful to go through. How did you..."

"Get better?" Anne scoffed. "Mark thought rehab would fix me. It didn't."

"Why not?"

"Because that wasn't the problem," Anne said. "Sure, I did drink to cope from time to time, but I was never a true alcoholic. I could have stopped, and I did. I checked myself into rehab, but that was to make

Mark happy—not me. Once I figured that out, I left. Alcohol wasn't the root of my problem."

"What was?"

"I had postpartum depression—that was a big part of it. It lingered for a long while, undiagnosed," Anne said. "I ignored it. But once I let myself get treated for it, things got better. Slowly. But not a day goes by I don't feel guilty about my choices."

"Anne, that's not—"

"I'm not telling you this story to get sympathy. I'm telling it to you so that you know you're not alone," Anne said. "Can you imagine how terrified I felt when I found out two more children were on the way? I had already left my family once. Abandoned them. How could I possibly survive the hormones, the trauma of childbirth, the intensity of newborn life all over again?"

"How did you do it?" Penny's voice was small.

"I still don't know if I am doing it," Anne said. "My point is that we're all dealt a shitty hand of cards sometimes. But things changed for me when I realized that I'm the only mother these kids will ever have. I am their best shot. I make mistakes, huge ones, but at the end of the day, I love them, and they love me. Some days, I won't lie, I still want to disappear. But guess what? I haven't yet, and you won't either. Because you can do this, Penny. If you want to."

Penny looked on the verge of tears. Anne had already gone there and back again emotionally. Meanwhile, Eliza found herself stiffly watching from the couch. For her, motherhood was a road not traveled.

"Maybe this is too personal," Anne said, "but have you considered your options?"

"I never thought of *not* keeping the baby." Penny shrugged, trying for matter-of-fact and falling short. "I've always wanted to be a mom. But I haven't had time to process everything. I haven't even told the baby's father yet. We're not...together."

Eliza hadn't realized she'd been holding her breath. Was it her imagination, or had Penny's eyes flicked over at hers for the briefest of seconds?

"I met him at one of my acting classes," Penny said. "We only slept together a few times. We weren't even in a proper relationship."

"You will tell him, though, won't you?" Anne asked. "If he's any sort of man, he'll be there to support you—one way or another."

"Telling him is the right thing to do," Penny said, though she sounded as if she wanted to be convinced otherwise. "But I'd hate to ruin his life, too. The father, he's…young and sort of stupid. We both are, I guess. I thought I was being safe on birth control, but I guess it failed."

"That happens." Anne raised her eyebrows knowingly.

"Not that there's anything I can do about it now," Penny said. "The thing is, I don't want to marry this guy just because we're having a baby together. And it's not as if he has any money. I wouldn't expect him to help out in any way, but he probably deserves to know."

"I think so," Anne said. "And who knows? Maybe he'll step up to the plate and surprise you."

"Maybe," Penny said.

Eliza watched her face carefully, and Penny's expression said it all. The father of this child wasn't going to be pleased with the pregnancy. Eliza would bet money on it. But *young and stupid?* Roman was many things, but he was neither of those. Was Penny lying about the father, or had Eliza assumed wrong?

The front door opened then, interrupting the tense conversation. Roman's long legs stretched before him, carrying his trim physique around the corner where he came to an abrupt stop in the entryway to the living room. A flicker of surprise crossed his face, stamped out quickly as he crossed his arms and studied the three women before him.

Eliza cleared her throat. "Welcome home, honey."

A layer of tension as thick as butter descended over the room. Roman's gaze slid to each of the ladies in turn. When his gaze landed on Penny, Eliza watched as she returned his stare. Penny didn't look surprised but perhaps defiant. Instead, it was Anne who had gone pale. *Curious, curious.*

"Did I misplace my invitation?" Roman asked nonchalantly. "I wasn't aware we were having a dinner party."

"It's book club," Eliza finally managed. "We're just chatting. Catching up on personal news."

"I see." Roman glanced around the room. "Anything exciting in the world of books?"

"I don't know about books," Eliza said briskly, "but we've just learned Penny is pregnant. Isn't that wonderful news, darling?"

TRANSCRIPT

Defense: At the time you found out you were pregnant, were you in a relationship with the baby's father?

Penny Sands: I…er…I thought I was. But it ended shortly thereafter.

Defense: Why did the relationship end?

Penny Sands: He wanted me to get an abortion. I wanted to keep the baby.

Defense: Yesterday, Anne Wilkes testified that she drove you to a clinic on October 24, 2018. She stated that you were thinking about getting an abortion.

Penny Sands: I wasn't really considering it.

Defense: Then why did you go to the clinic?

Penny Sands: It's hard to explain.

Defense: Try.

Penny Sands: I was broke, young, in a tenuous relationship that, in retrospect, was doomed from the start. I thought the baby deserved better than me. So yes. I went to the clinic. I walked inside, made the appointment. Anne—my closest friend—came with me. But I couldn't do it.

Defense: Why not?

Penny Sands: Because I loved the baby already.

Defense: What happened when you told the father that you were planning to keep the baby?

Penny Sands: He threatened me.

Defense: Did you call the police to report it?

Penny Sands: No, I didn't.

Defense: I have here, from the victim's notes, that you were the one who threatened him. And then he took out a restraining order on you.

Penny Sands: I sure did.

Defense: Sure did what?

Penny Sands: I told him that he'd be sorry if he ever interfered with my life or my baby's again. If that's a threat, then yes. I threatened him.

TWENTY-FIVE

Four Months Before
October 2018

I'm sorry, Mom. I can't come home for the holidays. It's just not in the cards this year." Penny winced as she broke the news to her mother. "I have to work."

"I thought you didn't like your job at that casting office?"

"It's still a job, and I need the money. I knew I'd have to make sacrifices when I moved out here."

"But a girl belongs with her family during the holidays. Are these sacrifices worth it?"

"It's all part of the gamble."

Penny realized the irony of her words even as she spoke them. A gamble. Everything had been a gamble since she'd left the safety of her own little bubble. Even the wineglass before her was a gamble. Would Eliza notice it was missing? Would she care?

A hesitation spanned several long, uncomfortable seconds before Amy continued. "I say this lovingly, Penny. But you gave up a career, a family, a lovely apartment—a home. For what? A crappy apartment, a married man, and an awful job?"

"How would you know my apartment is crappy?"

"I wasn't born yesterday, Penny Sue Sands. I know how much apartment you can get for the money you're making, and it isn't much. Also, your father showed me how to use Google's street view the other day, and your place looks like a dump." She paused to catch her breath. "I don't know what's gotten into you lately, but I feel like my daughter is getting all turned around out there."

Penny's chest felt as if it were wrapping around her like a boa constrictor. Beginning to squeeze. Lose air. She couldn't breathe. "That's not fair. You don't know what it's like being in a new city all by myself, figuring everything out on my own. I was a big fish in a small pond back home, and I had to know if I could be a big fish in an ocean."

"And what if you're not cut out for that sort of life?" Amy asked. "Big fish in the ocean are mean. They eat the pretty, nice little fishies."

"I can handle it." Penny reached for the borrowed wineglass and twisted it around, swirling the sparkling water she'd poured inside. She watched as the little bubbles gulped for air against the surface. "I'm not as naive as you think."

"Oh, I don't believe that."

Penny made a noncommittal noise in her throat. The wineglass was one of four items she'd taken the last time she'd been at Eliza's. The time she'd announced to the world that she was pregnant. She'd adopted two wineglasses—one she used, one that was untouched, still wrapped in a sweater and tucked in her purse.

The other two items were some of the riskiest things she'd taken yet. She'd spotted a set at Eliza's house, one both expensive and sentimental. A set that was likely to be missed, a set that went against all Penny's rules. She was getting careless.

Penny ran her thumb over the knife's handle and read the inscription. Roman's and Eliza Tate's initials, along with their anniversary date, were carved into the handle. There was a matching spoon that Penny had also taken...just because. The spoon she hadn't even bothered to unpack from her purse. The knife...she took joy in hoarding it because it wasn't deserved.

Roman and Eliza's marriage was doomed. They no longer had a

need for the knife to commemorate their union. Roman had gotten Penny pregnant. Whether he took the news well or took the news poorly, it wouldn't matter. Surely Eliza wouldn't take him back after that.

"Then tell me, is it working?" Penny's mother startled her back to reality. "Are you finding yourself out there?"

Penny fell silent. The truth was that she hadn't found herself at all. If anything, she'd lost more than she'd found. Bits of her had scattered, torn apart like wet tissue paper stomped across the city's dreary streets, shards of color left to drift in muddy gutters.

She wondered if she could ever be whole again. If someone could scoop up all those scattered bits of tissue and papier-mâché her back together into something bigger, stronger, bolder, more colorful than ever before. It had to be possible. Otherwise, how could she support herself, let alone a child?

It is possible, Penny determined, reminding herself that life hadn't been entirely awful since she'd arrived. She pictured bits of beauty that belonged exclusively to her: a bouquet of fresh flowers from Anne, a thoughtful text from Ryan, the wonder and awe over the whisper of new life growing inside her.

Penny could recover. She could gather the broken pieces, the torn shreds. With a bit of glue and patience and support, she could be beautiful again. The ripped and torn pieces wouldn't be discarded; they'd be woven into the person she would become.

"I think I'm on the right track," Penny said softly. "But to find myself, I think I have to lose myself first. And I don't know how to manage that."

"Oh, honey." Her mother's voice broke.

"I can't explain everything just yet," Penny said, barely holding it together. "Trust me for a little while longer. I have to go now. I'll talk to you later."

Penny hung up, emotionally drained from the conversation. She glanced at the time. Nearly 10:00 p.m., which meant class would be letting out shortly. Obviously, Penny wasn't in attendance. She hadn't seen Roman since she'd been inside his house two days before.

She hadn't known what to expect after Eliza broke the baby news inside the Tate residence. The home Eliza still apparently shared with Roman. Penny had known the two were living together, and while she'd thought it was odd, she had tried to understand. Or she had pretended to at least.

But then Eliza had called Roman *honey* and *darling* that afternoon, and ever since, Penny had been unable to shake the feeling that she was missing something. That her world wasn't quite right.

What the hell did I expect from Roman after Eliza's bombshell? Penny thought caustically. A phone call? A visit? A card? Roman knew where she lived. He had her phone number programmed into his device—or he had, once upon a time. Eerily enough, she hadn't heard a peep. She'd tentatively reached out to him with a text, asking if they could meet, which he had ignored.

She couldn't entirely blame him. Roman should have been the first person to know about the baby, but Penny hadn't gotten the chance to tell him. She'd barely come to terms with the little pink line herself. Later that day, she'd found herself at an event inside her baby daddy's ex-wife's house—an event that had triggered catastrophic consequences. Judging by the silent treatment, Penny surmised that Roman wasn't pleased with the news.

Still, Penny's heart lurched every time her email notification dinged. Her breath stuttered at the jingle of her ringtone. Latent, desperate hope lived inside her, a hope that Roman would show up at her door with a bouquet of roses and demand they be a family.

Yeah, right, Penny scoffed. *A family.* She let out a harsh laugh. There was no such thing. Roman already had a family with his wife. The only family Penny's child would ever know was a broken one. Her son or daughter deserved a father, and her baby wouldn't have one by no fault of his own.

Penny had inherited all the burdens of being a wife without the benefits of having a husband. She had the child, the responsibilities. She'd need to cook and clean and secure a stable job. She'd need to provide insurance and childcare and love for this baby, yet she had nobody to turn to for support. *A single wife*, she thought caustically. That was exactly what she was.

But was it really all Roman's fault? Was the baby his? According to Penny's calculations, she'd slept with Ryan during the start of her fertile window. By the end of it, she'd fallen into bed with Roman. Still, the baby must belong to Roman by sheer sperm volume. They'd slept together more times than Penny could count. It had to be his.

That didn't stop Penny from wondering if she owed Ryan a heads-up about her pregnancy. There wasn't exactly a handbook that laid out right and wrong for this situation. Penny was so far in the wrong that right was a distant shooting star.

And even if she did tell him, what would she say? *There is a tiny chance this baby is yours, but I also had loads of sex with our acting instructor, so statistically, it's probably his.*

Penny harrumphed at her own idiocy and stomped past Lucky smoking on the front steps. *A baby doesn't belong here*—the mantra repeated in Penny's head.

"That's unhealthy," she snapped at her landlord. "You're going to die of cancer."

The parking meters shut off promptly at 10:00 p.m. on the street outside Roman's studio. Penny arrived at 9:52 and sat diligently in her car, waiting with the engine running, until 10:01. Now that she had a baby on the way, she had to conserve every cent. She owed it to her child.

Once the meter winked to sleep, Penny slid from behind the wheel and picked her way toward Roman's studio. Armed only with desperation, she strode in, hands balled into fists. Most of the students had already left, giving the studio a ghostly, disconcerting feel.

Roman was still inside. Penny had hunted until she'd spotted his car parked on the street—the vintage one he'd been driving as of late—because she'd needed to be sure. She'd come this far and had let herself get this riled up. There was no way she was bowing out now. As she hauled herself into the lobby, she noted Roman's office door was closed.

Penny inched toward it, pausing as she rested a hand against the wood. A hot sizzle flashed down her spine as she remembered being pressed against the other side in a whirlwind of lust. Back when she believed her life with Roman was going somewhere, somewhere beautiful. Now, everything felt hollow—preemptively so maybe, but she couldn't shake the foreboding feeling that the end was near.

She raised a fist and knocked on the door. When Roman didn't answer immediately, she impatiently twisted the knob, pushed it open, and stepped into the room. Penny let the moment wash over her fully, taking a second to digest it all as she stood before him.

For the first time in a long while, Penny felt calm and in control. When she rested her hand over her belly, her confidence grew bolder. She was no longer fighting for herself and her stupid dreams. She was fighting for the innocent babe that would be born to a young, broke, unwed mother. He or she deserved better.

"Penny." Roman leaned back in his chair. "I expected you'd come."

He wore those studious glasses that made him look like a smart, creative, empathetic professor. The same glasses that had made Penny fall deeper in lust with him the first time she'd stepped into his office. Now, she wondered if it was all a ruse.

"I should have told you sooner," she whispered. "I'm sorry."

"About what?"

Penny's lips parted in surprise. "The baby."

Roman sighed as if disappointed in his pupil. "Are you sure the baby is mine?"

"Chances are pretty damn good. I'll let you do the math."

"You told me you were on birth control."

She sucked in a breath. She'd prepared for all sorts of responses from Roman, but the one thing she hadn't anticipated was blame. "Look, I apologize for the way you found out. That was wrong. I hadn't planned on saying anything to Eliza and the other girls, but it just came out. I was in shock."

"*You* were in shock?"

"It doesn't sound like you believe me," Penny said. "And if you're insinuating that I was trying to trick you into getting me pregnant, you're very, very wrong. I might have loved you, but I'm not *that* stupid."

"You're either very, very smart or very, very stupid. Otherwise, how do you explain showing up at my house, for my wife's book club, to look me in the eye while she announces your pregnancy?" Roman pursed his lips. "What do you want from me?"

"You don't get it, do you? I don't want anything at all. I'm just here, informing you about the baby. I should have done it sooner, but this is the hand we have been dealt. I'm sorry. The ball is now in your court."

Roman spun a pencil between two fingers. "You're not seriously thinking about keeping it?"

Penny felt herself visibly blanch. "Thinking about it? I've already decided—I'm having the baby. Period. *Fin*. End of story."

Roman stood, snapped the pencil against his desk with a delicate *click*. He strode across the room, closed the door behind Penny, and lowered his voice to a soft hum. "I would strongly suggest you reconsider. I've already offered to give you whatever you want. That offer expires the second you leave this room."

"Are you threatening me?" Penny didn't back away as he brushed against her.

The physical contact wasn't subtle. It was meant to intimidate. Penny held on to her confidence, grasping at it with slippery fingers.

She shivered. Roman moved so he stood between Penny and the exit, blocking any easy escape. She held her ground as the scent of his spicy cologne, the one that had previously driven her wild, now churned her stomach. How had she been so blindly in love with this man?

Her mother had been right. It had been a mistake to chase after Roman Tate. Penny had fallen for his brilliant sparkle. Roman was a disco ball of glittering silver dots dancing across a dark ceiling. Penny had chased the glimmer, chased and chased and chased until she realized it was all an illusion. As she'd reached out, clinging to her naive beliefs that he was the answer to all her problems, she'd grasped at air. Roman wasn't the disco ball. He was the darkness around it.

"I would never threaten you," Roman said. "I'm just trying to talk sense into you. It's obvious you're not thinking straight. Use your head, Penny."

"Don't talk to me like I'm a child. I'm a grown woman, a mother now."

"You don't have to be."

"I'm not giving up this child."

"If you *were* on birth control, then you wouldn't have to make that choice." Roman's eyes hinted that he didn't believe it. "If you had been taking birth control, then you were already trying to prevent the conception of a child. You have options."

"*One* option. Nonnegotiable."

"I'll pay for the abortion if that's the issue."

Penny felt as if she'd been gutted. "I can't believe I loved you. Tell me the truth, Roman. Are you and Eliza even separated?"

"I'm trying to talk sense into you. Penny, you're practically a child yourself. Can you afford the hospital bills? A crib? Diapers? A car seat? Going solely off the state of your car and apartment, the answer is no."

Penny shook with anger. Her fists tightened into balls. It took everything in her power to stand in silence and look at him. When Roman extended a hand and rested it on her shoulder, Penny flinched.

"Think about the bigger picture," he implored. "You moved

here—what, six months ago?—to make something of yourself. You're talented, Penny. You could go far in this business, and I mean that."

She closed her eyes. His fingers on her shoulder singed through her dress.

"A baby changes everything," he continued. "How do you expect to star in a movie when you're struggling to lose the baby weight? How will you be creative with your screenplay when you're up with a child every hour of the night? How will you pay for health insurance?"

Penny wanted to interrupt but couldn't. Roman was siphoning the very fears from her own mind and spitting them back at her. These ideas were nothing she hadn't considered, but somehow, hearing them from his mouth made them polluted.

"Your dreams are over, Penny. But it doesn't have to be this way."

Penny forced her eyes open but left her fists clenched. "It was a mistake to come here. I should have seen the writing on the wall."

"Make this simple on all of us, please."

"Did you ever love me at all?" Penny ducked out from under his grasp. "Were you ever going to leave your wife?"

Roman sucked in a breath. "For Christ's sake, Penny. Don't do this."

Penny swallowed hard. She hurried to the door, her heart pounding. One glance over her shoulder told her Roman hadn't moved.

"I'm keeping the baby," she said hoarsely. "Just leave me alone."

"This is a mistake, Penny," Roman warned. "You're not thinking straight."

"I know exactly what I want, Roman. And if you ever try to interfere in my life or the baby's, you will be sorry."

TRANSCRIPT

Defense: What would you say your relationship with Penny Sands was over the last year?

Anne Wilkes: At first, it was professional. She babysat for us. Actually, she was referred to us by Roman and Eliza Tate. I now realize the irony of that.

Defense: You said at first it was professional. What about after that?

Anne Wilkes: We became friends. It was a natural sort of thing. I'd come home and chat with Penny for a bit. Once or twice, we had a drink together or took the kids to the park.

Defense: What sorts of things would you discuss?

Anne Wilkes: Whatever friends talk about. Where we came from, where we're going. Who we love, who we hate. You know the drill.

Defense: Was there anyone Ms. Sands mentioned hating?

Anne Wilkes: I don't think Penny is capable of hate. She's a nice young woman.

Defense: So you didn't notice anything strange about Ms. Sands?

Anne Wilkes: You're talking about her little hobby, aren't you? Yes, I know about it. That doesn't mean Penny is a bad person. She's just flawed like the rest of us.

Defense: Please clarify for the court what you mean about Ms. Sands's little hobby.

Anne Wilkes: She collects things. Little trinkets.

Defense: By collects, do you mean steal?

Anne Wilkes: Sure.

Defense: Did she tell you this?

Anne Wilkes: Of course not. She took things from me, too. It seemed like some sort of odd compulsion. But it never hurt anyone. It wasn't anything important.

Defense: How did you discover this compulsion of Ms. Sands's?

Anne Wilkes: I found a photo that belonged to me in her apartment. She'd obviously taken it without asking. And then there were the things she'd taken from Eliza…

Defense: What had she taken from Mrs. Tate?

Anne Wilkes: A serving set I'd given Eliza for her wedding. There was a knife, a little spoon.

Defense: This knife—it had Mr. and Mrs. Tate's initials engraved on it?

Anne Wilkes: Yes. And their anniversary date.

Defense: Did you confront Ms. Sands when you found it?

Anne Wilkes: No. I didn't really think twice about it, to be completely honest. I happened to see it when I was moving a bunch of baby things into her apartment. We were reorganizing, and I shuffled some things around.

Defense: You didn't think it was odd?

Anne Wilkes: I just didn't connect the dots. The picture I chalked up to an accident. Maybe a copy had gotten tucked in a book I'd loaned her or something. As for the utensils, I assumed…I don't know, that she'd borrowed them from Eliza for a special dinner or something. We were all friends; we did things like that.

Defense: Did she ever return the knife to Mrs. Tate?

Anne Wilkes: I don't know.

Defense: I don't think she did, Mrs. Wilkes. Do you know how I know?

Anne Wilkes: No clue.

Defense: Because that's the very knife that killed Roman Tate. Mrs. Tate's fingerprints might've been on the weapon, but the knife was in Ms. Sands's possession. Now tell me, do you still think it's a harmless little hobby, Mrs. Wilkes?

TWENTY-SIX

Two Months Before
December 2018

C all if you need anything." Anne faced her husband on a clear Saturday morning as she finished detailing her keep-the-kids-alive instructions. "The twins are fed. Gretchen is planning to make a list of presents she wants for her birthday, so I left supplies on the counter. Samuel needs to be read to for half an hour before he gets screen time."

"I've got it under control," Mark said with a smile that stopped Anne in her tracks. "Go on. Have a good time with your friends."

Anne stood stock-still while her husband leaned forward and pecked a sweet kiss on her forehead. She could only give him a baffled look as she wrapped her cardigan tighter around her body and spun off toward the car.

As she drove toward Hollywood, Anne let her brain wander over the uneventfulness of the past few months. She had delivered a check to Roman for the full amount he'd requested the night she'd met him at his studio. The night she'd run into Penny. Anne had wondered if Penny would mention the event to Eliza, but thankfully, it didn't seem to have come up. Thank God for small miracles.

Thank God for big miracles, too. It hadn't been easy, but Anne had managed to get Roman his money, thanks to a career before children and an unattended 401k. In another lifetime, Anne had held a full-time job for almost a decade. She'd spent that time funneling money into her retirement account, and thanks to a healthy employer match program and impressive growth due to a booming stock market, she'd had enough money to cover Roman's demands.

There'd been a steep penalty to withdraw the money from her retirement account, but Anne wasn't going to split hairs over tax laws. She'd made a few phone calls when Mark had been at work to secure the money, funneling it into a new bank account that her husband knew nothing about. She'd proceeded to write Roman a big, fat check that he'd promptly cashed. As far as Anne knew, they were even.

But what was to stop Roman from turning Mark in to the police now, short of more money? Surely the fifty grand she'd paid him wasn't enough to support Roman Tate's fast and furious lifestyle for very long.

Anne stopped on a side street that, even in Hollywood, was too unfavorable to require metered parking. Climbing out, she made her way to the trunk where she had two laundry baskets full of the kids' old stuff. She paused there, one basket in her arm, glancing toward the apartment complex. She wondered sadly if this was as good as it would get for Penny.

Striding through the doorway, Anne washed the thought away and scoped out the entrance for a dial-in panel. It took a good few minutes before Anne realized there was no code...or security features whatsoever. The door was unlocked.

Anne hesitated in the lobby, but it was only a second before Penny's head popped over the second-floor railing. Her face lit into a smile.

"Come on up," Penny called, shuffling her rapidly expanding frame to the top of the stairs. "Better yet, I'll come down."

"Don't be ridiculous. I'm not letting you lift a finger." Anne shook her head at Penny. "I'm here to help. With how much you've helped me out these last few months with the kids, it's the least I could do."

Anne began to climb, her shoes making loud, echoing noises. The steps hadn't been swept in what appeared to be months, and several of the boards were creaky and lopsided. The whole apartment had a slightly unsanitary feel, and Anne couldn't help but think it was no place for a young woman to live alone, let alone with a baby. Anne had the guilty thought that she should have paid Penny a higher hourly wage.

After summiting the staircase, Anne deposited the first laundry basket inside Penny's apartment. When she straightened, she studied the studio space and hoped her face reflected a pleasant expression. In reality, Anne was surprised. She hadn't expected to find a luxurious condo tucked inside the unsavory building, but she also hadn't expected…*this*.

The apartment was the size of a shoebox. And not a nice shoebox belonging to a fine pair of high heels but a teensy little thing from the corner discount rack, dusty and crumpled and missing one flip-flop. The kitchen was cordoned off by a small counter. One person could fit inside it at a time—cooking dinner as a couple would be impossible. The living room blurred into the bedroom without any real separation. If it could be called a bedroom.

Penny's bed consisted of a mattress and box spring set on the floor. Her dresser was a scratched-up mess that suddenly made Anne's refurbished, makeshift vanity look as if it'd been salvaged from a royal palace. Her closet door was the accordion type that folded in on both sides, except one side was completely missing, and the other looked permanently jimmied open.

A pleasant breeze sailed in through the window, but upon closer inspection, Anne realized it wasn't by choice. The window was propped up with a sturdy wooden ruler, and the screen had a huge rip down the center.

"It's not much," Penny said sheepishly. "But it's the best I can do."

Anne caught herself staring. It had been so long since she'd been a broke student that she'd forgotten what it was like to pull herself up by the bootstraps and make ends meet.

"When I was first pregnant, I was terrified," Anne reassured Penny. "I was afraid I didn't have enough—enough finances, enough stability, enough *stuff*. I told Mark, and he told me the stupidest thing, but I thought it was adorable at the time. And it was actually quite helpful."

"What's that?"

"People have been raising babies since the days of cavemen. And all they had was a rock for a bed and a stick," Anne said with a thin smile. "They'd look at this place and find it luxurious. You're doing fine, Penny. The baby doesn't care what your apartment looks like. He just wants to be loved."

"I have love," Penny said softly. "I really do. It's starting to become real."

"Becoming a mother is an experience you can't quite put into words," Anne said. "You'll find out soon enough. It gets better, I promise."

Penny wrung her hands together. "I hope so. At the moment, it's more overwhelming than exciting. I'm realizing how expensive babies can be. I can't thank you enough for giving us your extra stuff."

"It's been my pleasure," Anne said. "And such perfect timing that it must be fate. The twins are just growing out of their baby things, and I would be donating them anyway. I'd rather know they're going to a good family."

"A family," Penny echoed. "Right."

Anne felt her lips press together. "Your family will be whole, just the way it is. But out of sheer nosiness, have you heard from the father?"

Penny's shoulders straightened. "He doesn't want to be involved with the baby."

"I'm sorry. He should still—"

"I don't want anything from him," Penny said sharply. "It's much better this way. Trust me. Oh, look at this adorable onesie."

Anne could read the unspoken words behind Penny's change of

subject. Penny was done discussing the father. Muttering an excuse, Anne dipped out to her car to retrieve another load.

"Here you go." Anne perched the second laundry basket on the end of Penny's ramshackle couch. "I do have two car seats in perfectly good condition, too, if you'd like. They've never been in an accident. I know most people prefer to buy new, but…"

"I'd love to buy one from you."

"It's yours, and I'm not taking any money for it," Anne said. "Now, before I leave, let me show you how to set up this baby monitor. We're not using it anymore, so it's yours. One of those newfangled ones that streams straight to your phone. I'll show you… I think I still have the app on my phone."

Penny took a deep breath. "Thank you, Anne."

Anne ducked her head and began unloading the laundry bins. What she didn't tell Penny was that the feeling was mutual. Where Penny's needs in this season of life were physical, financial needs, Anne's were emotional. She needed a distraction from everything at home, and Penny was just that.

Anne had guided Penny through her journey into motherhood with a gentle hand. She'd helped secure everything from prenatal vitamins to a closet filled with maternity clothes. In a world where Anne had lost control of everything—her home life, her husband, her marriage, her finances—she wanted to excel at something. To be good at one wholesome thing. When Penny looked up at her with appreciation, it fed something in Anne that had been deprived of sustenance.

The two women worked together for several hours, rearranging furniture, setting up sleeping spaces and makeshift changing tables, hanging tiny clothes on tinier hangers in a tiny closet with big, broken doors. By the time they finished, the place had been transformed.

"Come with me," Anne said. "Is there a grocery store near here?"

"There's a Trader Joe's down the street," Penny said. "But I was planning to order a pizza if that sounds okay."

"I have a better idea." Anne slipped on her shoes and pulled open the door. "Let's go for a walk. It's nice outside."

Penny's lips twitched into a curious smile, but Anne didn't offer any further explanation. Before Anne knew what was happening, Penny playfully looped her arm through Anne's and guided her outside. They strolled to the shop on the corner, and when they returned an hour later, their arms were laden with goodies.

"I wish you'd let me pay for this," Penny said, eyeing the bags as she unlocked her door. "This is ridiculous. It's too much."

"This is all part of the Anne Wilkes makeover package," Anne teased, following Penny into the apartment. "Give me five minutes, and you'll see why this step is crucial."

Penny sealed her lips into a thin line, though the discomfort didn't entirely disappear from her eyes. Anne set to work pulling materials out of the paper bag. She unearthed several small tropical houseplants. A bouquet of fresh flowers. An array of pleasantly scented candles.

She carefully arranged each around the room, nudging them this way, then that way, on the newly dusted furniture. When Anne completed the finishing touches, she and Penny stepped back to survey the transformed studio.

Penny's hand came up to her throat. She toyed with a necklace there, fumbling with the charm on it as Anne watched her, pleased with the reaction. The space wasn't exactly gorgeous, but for Penny, it was perfect.

The bright-yellow bedspread shone under the afternoon sunlight. The mopped floor and dusted wood gleamed, their sheen bright and crisp, a faint lemon scent covering the hint of secondhand smoke in the air.

Baby paraphernalia had been placed thoughtfully around the room, bringing in a lightness, an airiness that highlighted hopeful signs of new life. The flowers and plants added pops of greenery—along with bursts of deep purples and bright pinks and splashes of orange—and the pretty, flickering candles smelled of pecan pie.

Penny swallowed hard. She cleared her throat, but the words didn't come. Anne put a hand on Penny's shoulder and squeezed.

"I really wish I had vases," Penny said finally.

Anne glanced at the makeshift Coke bottle they'd used to contain a fresh flower bouquet. "I think it's vintage."

Both women looked at one another and burst into laughter. They laughed, and they laughed. They laughed until they found themselves teetering onto the ragged old couch and clutching at their stomachs. Then they laughed some more.

When they gathered themselves, Penny popped a frozen pizza they'd picked up into the oven, and the apartment burst into hominess with the scent of cheap marinara and gooey mozzarella.

"Paper plate?" Anne asked. "Pizza cutter?"

Penny pointed to a cupboard for the plates, then unearthed a knife and gave a wry smile. "Pizza cutter."

Anne grinned and grabbed plates along with some sodas they'd also grabbed on their walk. They carried their plates to the middle of the apartment and plopped back onto the couch, crossing their legs and gossiping as they munched through soft dough and greasy pepperoni.

Hours later, Anne stood at the door. She felt a genuine burst of regret that she had to leave, and to stall, she cast a glance around the room as if there were one surface she'd missed in her polishing, one table she'd forgotten to dust.

When it all came back squeaky clean, Anne sighed. Her cheeks hurt from smiling, and her abs were sore from laughing. She couldn't remember the last time she'd had such a wonderful day.

"I had a really nice time." The simplicity of Anne's words felt empty against the bloom of emotion in her chest. "Thanks for adopting my babies' stuff."

"I appreciate it more than you know."

Both women studied each other. An understanding floated between them, and Anne was grateful she didn't have to rely on the flimsiness of the English language to express her true sentiment. Gratitude, hope, friendship. Such little words for such big feelings.

Anne reached out a hand and gently rested it on the light bulge of Penny's stomach. "Thank *you*, little guy."

Before Penny could respond, Anne's phone burst to life with her ringtone.

"It's probably Mark," Anne mumbled. "I'm sure he's trying to figure out what to feed the kids or something. I told him I'd be gone all day, but…you know…" Anne's face turned red as she realized that maybe Penny didn't know all about husbands. "I'm sorry. I shouldn't—"

"It's fine," Penny said. "You don't have to watch what you say around me."

Anne didn't hear Penny's response, however, because she was too busy staring at a name on her phone. A name that sent fear arcing through her stomach. A name she'd hoped to never see again.

"I'm sorry," she muttered to Penny. "I have to get going."

"Is everything okay?"

Anne waved a hand and forced a smile over her shoulder as she launched herself down the stairs two at a time. "I'll be fine."

"Wait—your laundry baskets!"

Anne had already reached the landing. "I'll grab them later."

"Wait a second, Anne!"

Something about Penny's tone stopped Anne in her tracks. She turned and looked back, expecting to find a fresh, youthful smile. To see eyes that were bright and shining, focused on the joy that so often accompanied new motherhood.

Instead, Anne found a stare from eyes that burned cold and hard. A smile tinged with grit and determination. Anne's breath caught in her throat as she wondered if behind the lip gloss and easy topknot, Penny was not the innocent girl she'd suspected but a woman not to be underestimated.

"If you need anything," Penny said, her voice slicing the air like a knife, "anything at all, don't hesitate to call."

"I won't."

"Anne," she repeated firmly. "*Anything.*"

Anne nodded, then ducked out the front door. As she made her way to the waiting van, a message blinking on her phone, she wondered how she could have pegged Penny so incorrectly. Despite their giddy day spent together, Anne wondered how much she didn't know about her newest friend.

But even curious thoughts about the peculiar Penny Sands were pushed to the back of Anne's mind as she redialed the number without listening to the message. Her hand shook as she held the phone to her ear.

"What do you want?" she rasped into the phone. "I thought we were done."

"Oh, Anne," Roman said quietly. "You've got one month."

TRANSCRIPT

Defense: Detective Wilkes, how long have you been a cop?

Mark Wilkes: Almost twenty-one years with the LAPD.

Defense: Thank you for your service.

Mark Wilkes: It's the only thing I've ever wanted to do. It's a pleasure to serve our city.

Defense: Before you became a detective, what did you do for the LAPD?

Mark Wilkes: I worked in the GND.

Defense: The Gang and Narcotics Division?

Mark Wilkes: That's correct. I was there a decade. Started as a beat cop before that. Worked my way up.

Defense: Would you say you've dealt with your fair share of bad men?

Mark Wilkes: That's part of the job description. Yeah, I'd say I've seen a few bad guys.

Defense: Do the bad guys always get justice?

Mark Wilkes: That's our goal. Of course, sometimes, they get away.

Defense: What if you know someone is guilty of a crime but you can't prove it?

Mark Wilkes: We both know that occasionally happens. As a lawyer, I'm sure you've experienced it, too. My answer? Innocent until proven guilty.

Defense: How do you feel about vigilante justice?

Mark Wilkes: Er, I'm not sure what you mean. I am a law enforcement officer. I believe in the system. I believe in justice through the system.

Defense: What if things get personal?

Mark Wilkes: I would go to the police and follow standard procedure like anyone else.

Defense: Play along with me, Detective. Let's say you discovered that your wife was being blackmailed. Earlier this afternoon, you stated that you love your wife, yes?

Mark Wilkes: Of course I do.

Defense: You'd do anything for her?

Mark Wilkes: I suppose. Yes.

Defense: Would you kill for her?

Mark Wilkes: I see where you're going with this, and no, I'm not your man. I didn't kill anyone.

Defense: Have you ever killed someone while on duty?

Mark Wilkes: I have. I'm sure you know that as it's public record.

Defense: The truth is, Detective, that you've killed a man before. How do we know it didn't happen again?

Mark Wilkes: For starters, there's no proof. Secondly, I had no motive.

Defense: Did your wife tell you she was being blackmailed by Roman Tate?

Mark Wilkes: No, she did not.

Defense: Did your wife tell you she killed Roman Tate?

Mark Wilkes: What?

Defense: I'll rephrase. If your wife came to you

and said she'd killed a man—a man who, by all
accounts, was disliked by several individuals—
what would you do? Would you turn your wife in
and risk your children losing their mother, or
would you help her bury the body?

Mark Wilkes: The body wasn't buried.

Defense: No, it wasn't. But interesting of you
to know that detail. That's all for now, Your
Honor.

TWENTY-SEVEN

One Month Before
January 2019

Happy birthday, dear Anne. Happy birthday to you."

Eliza and Penny finished their off-key jingle with a round of applause. Anne slouched in her seat, hating the attention. She preferred her birthdays to be without fanfare these days, seeing as the only thing she was celebrating was an influx of wrinkles and a few more gray hairs.

But Eliza Tate didn't believe in letting birthdays slip by without a massive celebration, which was how Anne had ended up at this particularly expensive restaurant getting sung to by a staff of well-dressed wannabe actors. This restaurant even had a crumber—a man whose sole job was to wipe crumbs off the table. It was ironic, seeing as Anne didn't need a crumber at an elegant restaurant where she could eat her own meal in peace; she needed a crumber at home where four children liked to feed the floor with their macaroni and cheese.

"You have to let me pay," Anne said. "Or at least split the bill."

"It's on us," Penny chirped gleefully. "Eliza and I will split it."

The bill arrived, and Eliza looked at Penny with a crooked eyebrow. "It's on me. You have more important things to spend your money on."

"But—" Penny gave a feeble argument, but after one look at Eliza's credit card, she nodded. "Thank you."

"Shall we?" Eliza pushed back her chair and stood. "I'll have the valet pull the car around."

Anne watched her two friends as they shuffled about, gathering their things from the beautifully ornate chairs. They made their way out of the modern, sleek restaurant where the grill boasted an open fire behind the counter and promised the freshest of food. Anne watched Eliza hand her valet ticket over to the man waiting at the door. There was no parking lot at a place like this.

Anne reached into a bowl of colorful mints while they waited and snatched a few from the glass container. Penny caught her eye, gave a sly smile, and did the same. They turned away, stifling their giggles like sneaky children.

"I'll be right back," Penny said, tucking her assortment of mints into her coat pocket. "I left something at the table."

Anne nodded, too busy shoving her own mints into her purse to care. It would be embarrassing to be kicked out of a restaurant on her birthday because of some pilfered candies.

"Car's here," Eliza announced. "Hop in."

A light drizzle had descended over the city, giving the night a hazy, surreal sort of glow. Rain was uncommon enough in Los Angeles to still be considered a novelty. Anne vaguely remembered her days growing up on the East Coast where she'd found rain to be an utter pain in the ass. Precipitation wasn't all that special when it rained more than it shined.

But today, the rain felt romantic. For the first time in ages, Anne wasn't thinking about her husband. Or her kids. Or her finances. Or fucking Roman Tate.

Anne was thinking about the two faces grinning back at her as they all piled into Eliza's convertible. Eliza had put the top up beforehand, which didn't surprise Anne in the slightest. Eliza had probably checked the weather three days in advance and marked dainty little raindrops into her color-coded calendar.

Eliza carefully pulled out of the crowded restaurant driveway and eased onto the streets. Penny reached from the passenger's seat to crank up the music. Anne, tucked in the back with several brilliantly colored gift bags, bobbed her head along with the beat and was startled to realize that she was well and truly having a blast.

With everything that had been going on lately, Anne's promising mood was nothing short of a miracle. She blinked at the lurch of emotion. Somehow, these women had made her feel like she was in the middle of a romantic comedy—three women, giddy after a night out, a glass of wine, and a shared, devilishly good slab of cake. Anne had half a mind to ask Eliza to put the top down on the convertible so they could sing in the rain.

But like all good things, Anne's good mood had to come to an end. Her elation evaporated as police lights appeared behind Eliza's car. The cruiser had come out of nowhere. Anne should've known that a night this pleasant would come with a catch, just like everything else these days. Now, poor Eliza would be slapped with a speeding ticket on Anne's birthday, and Anne would feel obligated to pay it. *Happy birthday to me.*

Anne cursed under her breath. The siren grew louder, nearer. Eliza pulled over. Penny sighed and rubbed her forehead between two fingers.

"I'm sorry," Anne said. "I'll pay if you get a ticket. You weren't even speeding!"

Anne saw Eliza's eyes flick toward the speedometer, but she didn't comment as both cars came to a stop. A minute later, an officer approached the driver's side door. Eliza rolled her window down, her documents at the ready.

"License and registration, please."

Anne's head shot up when the cop spoke. "Mark?!"

"I hear there's a birthday girl in the car." Anne's husband grinned back at her, his once-brown hair now peppered with handsome gray. "Happy birthday, sweetheart."

"What are you doing here?" Anne blinked. "How did you know…"

"I told him," Eliza said with a quick smile in the rearview mirror. "He called me last week and asked where I'd be taking you out to dinner."

"I've never missed my wife's birthday," Mark said in explanation to Penny. Then he gave his full attention to Anne. "And I wouldn't miss this one, either. I love you, honey."

"Holy shit." Penny clasped her hands to her chest. "This is like a real, honest-to-God movie moment. I love it. You are so freaking lucky, Anne."

Anne felt torn in half. The old and the new warred within her. Their original love—a love that had started as two college students in lust—had grown into a mature, tender sort of love. The sort of hard-earned love that was forged as Anne had watched Mark play with their children. As she'd witnessed him giving up nights and weekends to work overtime and keep food on the table. That sort of love was supposed to last a lifetime.

But that old love was tarnished now, diluted by lies and half-truths. There had been so much piled on Anne in the past year that she didn't know what to believe anymore. As she watched her husband slide toward the back seat and pull the door open, extending a hand toward her like a prince pulling his bride from a chariot, she eased her hand into his and let him guide her out of the car.

There, on the shoulder of Hollywood Boulevard, Mark drew Anne into his arms. She inhaled his scent, a unique mix of woodsy cologne and simple Irish Spring soap. It never ceased to bring her comfort. His lips met hers, familiar in their touch, their softness, their care. For a moment, Anne forgot everything. She let herself sink into her husband's arms. When they parted, she had tears in her eyes. Because it was a Tuesday night, and Mark was here, with her, instead of at the god-awful apartment with that god-awful girl.

For tonight at least, Mark had chosen her. And if he could choose her once, he could choose her again. And again. And again. His affair meant nothing, Anne was sure of it. If she ignored it, there was a good chance it would fade into the background, a dirty little splotch on the otherwise happy pages of their love story. The only thing stopping them from being happy now was the miserable Roman Tate.

Mark saluted Eliza. Eliza waved and put the car in drive before carefully taking off down the street and leaving the couple alone on the side of the road.

"What is this all about?" Anne asked, suddenly feeling the dampness from the rain as it soaked through her clothes. "You're never home this early."

"I can be for you," Mark said. "I love you, Anne. It's your birthday."

Anne stared helplessly after the convertible. "But Eliza's got all my presents."

Mark laughed, his blue eyes twinkling. "I'm sure she can drop them off later. Can I tempt you into a bit of dessert?"

"Are you joking?" Anne slid her hand into Mark's. It was too easy to feel their original love rear its beautiful head. "That restaurant served me a lettuce leaf and called it the main course."

"McDonald's dollar menu work for you?"

"Is there any other place to get a sundae for a buck?"

Mark withdrew his hand from Anne's and threw it over her shoulder instead. "I hope you know how much I love you."

Anne seriously considered her answer. "I love you, too."

It was the truth. So was the fact that Mark had lied. And as he opened the passenger's side door to the police car for Anne, the tears that had pooled in her eyes began to fall.

It was such a shame that Anne's fairy tale would have to end.

TRANSCRIPT

Defense: Tell me about your friendship with Penny Sands.

Eliza Tate: I don't know, honestly.

Defense: You don't know what?

Eliza Tate: Being on trial has made me rethink all my relationships. I thought I knew my husband, my client, and my best friends. Now, I'm not sure who is my friend and who is trying to frame me for murder.

Defense: It's strange, don't you think? We've got no shortage of motive in this trial. There are plenty of people who wanted the victim dead, and I think we can all agree on that. But the curious part is the evidence. We have plenty of that, too. We've got your fingerprints on the murder weapon. The knife that killed him was a gift to you from Mrs. Wilkes, and she had access to it. Even Detective Wilkes is under suspicion because he's married to Mrs. Wilkes and could have helped her get rid of the body. But what about Ms. Sands?

Eliza Tate: What about her?

Defense: She had the biggest reason of all to want him dead, yet there's not one trace of evidence that she might have killed him. Is she really that innocent, or is she smarter than the rest of you?

TWENTY-EIGHT

One Month Before
January 2019

I'll be right back," Penny said, tucking a slew of complimentary mints into her coat pocket. "I left something at the table."

Eliza had scored the trio of women reservations at a hot new restaurant in town for Anne's birthday, and it was the first time Penny had eaten a truly gourmet meal in her life. On Hollywood Boulevard no less. Penny couldn't help but think she should be on cloud nine, savoring every moment of this surreal experience, but instead, she was shoving free mints into her pockets to savor after a midnight snack of ramen noodles.

Anne nodded at Penny's flimsy excuse to duck back to the table, but she was too busy tucking mints into her own purse to notice anything out of the ordinary. Maybe Penny and Anne weren't so different. When it came to financial matters, it seemed they were on the same page—a vastly different page from Eliza Tate's. But what would Anne think of Penny's little hobby?

A harmless little hobby, Penny reminded herself as she eased past a server and made her way to where she'd sat with Eliza and Anne mere minutes before.

"I forgot my ring here," she said to the busboy clearing the table. "It's black. Did you happen to find it when you were grabbing the dishes?"

The young man offered Penny a bright smile. "Here you go, ma'am."

Penny blanched at the word *ma'am*, but she didn't offer a correction. She supposed that according to him, she was a ma'am. He couldn't be over twenty-one. A thought that made Penny feel every one of her twenty-seven years.

If nothing else, Penny was definitely too old to be carrying on with her hobby. It was getting dangerous, becoming a compulsion. She couldn't stop. She'd see something and need it. Want it. Take it. The limits between harmless prank and full-on thievery were beginning to blur.

This is the last time, she promised herself, sliding the ring onto her finger and admiring it in its new habitat. The petite, shiny black band fit perfectly on her pointer finger. She knew from spending time with Eliza that the ring wasn't terribly expensive. She'd acquired it on one of her many trips to Italy from a street market. It was a piece of jewelry that Eliza surely wouldn't miss but would mean the world to Penny. A ring from Italy—how *exotic*.

After all, if Eliza had truly cared about this particular piece of jewelry, she wouldn't have forgotten it at the table in the first place. Penny had watched her remove the ring when the server brought around a tray of warm washcloths to wipe their hands before the meal. Before this evening, the closest Penny had ever gotten to a warm washcloth at a restaurant was the Wet-Nap Buffalo Wild Wings handed out after a meal.

Penny had watched and waited, but all meal long, Eliza hadn't seemed to remember the ring sitting right beneath her hand. It'd been tucked just out of sight beside her water glass. Penny had spent the meal debating whether to tell Eliza about her forgotten jewelry or to merely let fate play out.

She'd opted for fate, and fate had led her back to the table to adopt the ring. It was just a tiny token, a little heirloom of a woman she admired so dearly. *Imitation is the sincerest form of flattery*, Penny thought. It would round out her Eliza Tate collection. And then she'd stop.

But as Penny returned to the front of the restaurant, the familiar sensation of guilt crept slowly down her spine—this time, stronger than ever. Hadn't Penny already stolen so much from Eliza? Too much? More than any woman should ever take from another?

She slid inside the car and repeated to herself: *This is the last time.*

TRANSCRIPT

Prosecution: Ms. Hill, please tell me what you remember about the afternoon of February 13.

Marguerite Hill: I don't remember all that much. We were drinking and talking at the book club trial run. Regular chitchat. Nothing special.

Prosecution: I would think you'd remember if the subject of murder came up?

Marguerite Hill: Well, it did. But it wasn't my idea.

Prosecution: Whose idea was it?

Marguerite Hill: Anne started it.

Prosecution: Mrs. Wilkes started the discussion on murder? How did she broach such a sticky subject?

Marguerite Hill: I don't remember.

Prosecution: That's convenient, seeing as none of the other women seem to remember, either.

Marguerite Hill: I don't know why you're wasting your time looking at me. I'm not the one who said I'd kill my husband with a knife.

Prosecution: Can you please repeat that for the court? One of you stated that you'd murder your husband with a knife?

Marguerite Hill: Eliza said if push came to shove, that was how she'd do it.

Prosecution: Do what?

Marguerite Hill: Murder Roman Tate.

TWENTY-NINE

One Month Before
January 2019

Eliza watched as Anne and Mark walked, hand in hand, back to the police cruiser after a night spent celebrating Anne's birthday. She found herself idly wondering if Mark had borrowed the vehicle from a friend, seeing as he'd recently made detective. Unless the movies were lying, detectives didn't drive squad cars.

"That is so freaking romantic," Penny said, hugging herself as she watched the couple disappear in the rearview mirror. "I wish I could find the same thing Anne and Mark have, but I think all the good ones are taken."

Eliza found this ironic coming from Penny in light of her situation, but she didn't comment aloud. She was too busy calculating how far back this dinner would set her financially, considering she'd footed the entire bill. The number at the bottom of the receipt had given her heart palpitations, but she had to keep up appearances, or the other women would start asking questions. Hard questions Eliza wasn't ready to answer.

"I—That was thoughtless of me," Penny mumbled, her face brightening beneath the dim light from the streetlamps. "I'm sorry. I didn't mean...about the good men being taken..."

"It's fine," Eliza said shortly.

She didn't care to linger on the subject of men any longer. Eliza knew the heavy truth about men. All men. Mark included.

For example, Mark hadn't planned this evening as Eliza had claimed. A week ago, Eliza had called *him* at work and gently suggested he might want to make plans for Anne's birthday. Mark was a good person overall, just a little misguided when it came to his marriage. He thought everything was fine in his life. According to Anne, nothing was fine.

Together, over a series of phone chats, Eliza and Mark had cooked up the little cop car skit that would hopefully be enough to impress Anne. Eliza had lost faith in men long ago, but Anne hadn't, and she deserved better than what Mark was offering. She and Mark had four kids together—a family, a future, a life that meant something. They could overcome their hurdles.

Pulling the car away from the shoulder, Eliza pointed them in the direction of Penny's apartment. A light rain dusted her windshield, prompting her to switch on her wipers. The car fell into an easy silence. For some reason, Eliza and Penny never quite had as much to say when Anne wasn't around.

It was funny how groups of three friends worked, especially with women. Why was there always one woman who was the glue that held things together? When Anne, Penny, and Eliza were all together, they each had a great time. Separately, Anne and Penny seemed to be getting closer by the day. Eliza had spent years feeling comfortable around Anne. So why did Penny and Eliza have a harder time finding common ground?

It was with a bit of relief that Eliza finally stopped before Penny's apartment.

"Thanks for coming," Eliza said. "I know it meant a lot to Anne."

"I wouldn't have missed it. Though I really wish you would've let us split the bill."

Really? Eliza wanted to say, but she didn't. After all Penny had put her through, Eliza still had some strange form of sympathy for the girl. An odd kinship that she couldn't quite describe. She was intrigued by the young woman if nothing else.

"Don't be ridiculous," Eliza said instead. "My treat."

Penny finished her thank-you routine, then shut the car door and made her way into her apartment building. Eliza watched, lingering for a second longer than necessary at the curb as she let her mind wander. She rarely let herself think about Penny—not like this. But sometimes, she couldn't help it.

This was who her husband had chosen to be with—at least for a short time. Eliza replayed the memory of the Pelican Hotel event over and over again. She remembered Penny standing before the elevator doors as they opened, looking hopeful in her pretty red pantsuit while she clutched a card that would change the trajectory of her life.

Or had it? Penny had never opened up to Eliza or Anne about the true identity of the baby's father. She was sticking to her story about the baby daddy being a young man from her class whom she'd slept with a few times out of sympathy. She'd repeated it so many times and with such steadfast confidence that Eliza was beginning to believe her.

Roman, of course, hadn't said anything at all to Eliza. He was still distant, but that was the new normal. Ever since the night they'd argued about the loan from his parents, he'd begun to slip away, further and further away.

Eliza wondered if there was more to his change in behavior than a simple loan, but she was too afraid to ask. Their life, their relationship, was holding on by a thread already. Eliza just needed time to get on her feet and out of debt, and then she could decide what to do about her marriage.

Once again, Eliza edged her car onto the road and headed home. She made it to the first stoplight before she glanced down at her hand and cursed. Her damn ring—she must have left it at the restaurant. It wasn't monetarily important, but she had gotten it on her first trip abroad with Roman, and it meant something to her. She spun the car back in the direction from which she'd come. When she made it to the restaurant, she waved the valet over and explained the situation.

"You can leave your car here, ma'am," he said. "If someone found your ring, it will be at the front desk."

Eliza hobbled inside, her feet killing her from the expensive shoes she'd bought a few years back and never worn. Now that she was short on cash and not willing to shop for frivolous items, it was amazing the things she could find in her own closet. Things that looked brand new. Things she'd ignored for years because she had so much fucking *stuff*.

"Hello, my name is Eliza Tate. We just had dinner here tonight," she explained to the concierge. "If I could—Oh, there's our waiter. Could you flag him over? I think I left a ring on our table, and I was hoping someone turned it in."

The concierge flagged the waiter over and stepped aside to let them talk. Eliza relayed her question. A smile flooded the server's face.

"It's a black ring, right?" he said. "Yeah, the other gal you were here with came back right after dinner and took it. She said it was hers, but I'm sure she meant it was yours."

"Which gal?"

"The young, pretty one." The waiter looked immediately embarrassed. "Not that y'all aren't young and pretty, but—"

"Thanks," Eliza said. "So she definitely has the ring?"

"I watched her put it on her finger."

"Great, thanks," Eliza said. "I'll give her a call then. She's probably already left me a message, and I just didn't see it. I was in such a rush to get back here."

"Don't worry, ma'am. It's in safe hands."

Is it? Eliza wondered dryly as she returned to her vehicle. She sat in the driver's seat and pulled out her phone, looking for a message from Penny. It wasn't there. Not entirely surprising, since the two women had had an entire car ride to discuss things such as lost rings.

No matter, Eliza mused. Penny could easily have forgotten she'd grabbed the ring, considering the rigmarole with Anne and Mark. A simple misunderstanding—that was all it was.

Dialing, Eliza ignored the impatient valet as Penny answered.

"Hey, hon," Eliza said. "Any chance you found my ring at dinner?"

There was a beat of silence as Penny paused.

"I was wearing this black ring," Eliza said. "You probably didn't even notice. It wasn't expensive, just a little sentimental. Roman bought it for me in Italy is all. Anyway, I thought I'd call both you and Anne to see if it'd turned up."

"Gosh," Penny said finally. "I haven't seen it. I'd try Anne if I were you."

"Will do," Eliza said. "I'm sure she'll have it."

To the valet's relief, Eliza hung up and drove away from the restaurant for the second time that evening. She headed home, her mind occupied with intriguing new thoughts.

Had Penny stolen her ring? Eliza's knuckles gripped the steering wheel tighter. Why in the world would Penny steal her ring? It wasn't as if there was a huge diamond on it that she could pawn off for lunch money. It made no sense.

As she drove, Eliza found herself doubting everything. She'd assumed Penny had been the one taken under by Roman's charms, but what if it was the other way around? What if Penny took what she wanted, stealing freely, then played the innocent card? Was it possible she'd latched her pretty nails into Roman and gone in for the kill? Had she tried to get pregnant?

Preposterous, Eliza assured herself. That was ridiculous. No sane woman would go that far, ever. Full stop. And Penny wasn't insane. Over the last few months, as Eliza had gotten to know Penny, she'd determined that the young woman meant well; she was just a little lost. Now, she wasn't so sure.

Eliza was halfway to Beverly Hills when she reached for a water bottle and caught sight of a darkened glint against it in the cup holder.

Look at that, Eliza thought. Her ring had found its way home.

But Eliza wasn't foolish enough to think Penny had softened between her theft at dinner and her apparent change of heart on the car ride to her apartment. Why hadn't she just told Eliza about the ring? What was Eliza missing?

Feeling more befuddled than ever, Eliza decided she'd have to be a little less careless around Penny moving forward, and a little more attentive. Something about Penny Sands wasn't quite right, and Eliza wasn't going to be fooled...again.

Fool me once, shame on you.

Fool me twice...

TRANSCRIPT

Prosecution: Ms. Sands, it was established during Mrs. Wilkes's testimony that you have what you call a "little hobby" of stealing things from others.

Penny Sands: I wouldn't say it's stealing. It's… it's adopting certain items that other people no longer need.

Prosecution: That's stealing. Taking something from another without permission.

Penny Sands: Technically, that might be correct. But I never hurt anyone. And I mostly took stuff that didn't matter to other people.

Prosecution: Like an anniversary set of utensils? As previously mentioned, Mrs. Wilkes testified that she found several items in your apartment that didn't belong to you. A photo you'd taken from her house. A knife and spoon with Eliza's and Roman Tate's initials on it. How did those artifacts end up in your care?

Penny Sands: The picture was stupid. I was

babysitting Anne's kids and saw Roman, and I just… I don't know. I took it. There's no real monetary value to a photograph.

Prosecution: And the utensils? That's what we're interested in, Ms. Sands. The knife.

Penny Sands: It was the day I told Anne and Eliza that I was pregnant back in October. I was just so mad at Roman. So upset with him that I wanted to hurt him, just a little. Plus, it's not like he needed an anniversary set anymore. He had an affair and got me pregnant. Eliza would never have stayed with him once she found out.

Prosecution: When were you planning to tell Mrs. Tate that her husband was the father of your child?

Penny Sands: I wasn't.

Prosecution: Why not?

Penny Sands: Because I'm not entirely sure he is.

Prosecution: We'll come back to that later. For now, I want to focus on the knife. How did you acquire it?

Penny Sands: How does anyone acquire anything? I picked it up and put it in my purse. Not exactly rocket science. It was in their kitchen drawer, just sitting there.

Prosecution: Interesting, Ms. Sands. Interesting how the murder weapon ended up in your apartment just a few months before Mr. Tate ended up dead.

Penny Sands: I didn't have it when he was murdered.

Prosecution: Who did?

Penny Sands: I don't know, but it was stolen from me.

Prosecution: When did you realize it was stolen?

Penny Sands: When it was entered into evidence as a murder weapon.

THIRTY

The Day Of
February 14, 2019

Eliza shuffled appetizers and finger foods onto platters. For the first time in many months, she had splurged. Instead of warming frozen appetizers and pretending the food was homemade, she'd had food catered for the evening. She was expecting over twenty industry guests at the book club event, so it was easy to justify as a business expense.

While Eliza hadn't yet repaid the loan from Roman's parents, she was finally starting to see promise in her company thanks to the imminent launch of Marguerite's new book and the paychecks coming in from her client. If all continued as projected, Eliza would be free and clear of debt within six months. It wouldn't make her life perfect, but it would be a step in the right direction.

Eliza popped a delicious gruyere-and-spinach quiche into her mouth and glanced at the clock. The ambiance was set with half an hour to spare. The attendees would be here soon enough, along with Marguerite Hill—guest of honor. Eliza studied the wine, the appetizers, the hint of elegant décor and was pleased with how everything had come together.

All that was left was for Eliza to shower and change into something nicer. Marguerite was thoroughly prepared for the event, thanks to the afternoon's trial run in which Eliza, Anne, and Penny had grilled her on the content of *Be Free*. She had acceptably answered all their questions…until their discussion had turned to the subject of murder. That one had stumped the author.

It had stumped Eliza, too. And Penny and Anne. It must have been the wine Eliza had served or the fact that most of the men in their lives were acting unreasonably at the moment. Something had been in the air, and a little vent session had been in order.

That's all it was, Eliza reminded herself, shaking off the creeping feeling of guilt. It was healthy actually. Good to air out their problems in the trusted company of friends. It was only the four of them after all. Who would they tell?

Anne and Penny had long since gone home but would be back shortly. Their task for the evening ahead was to pepper Marguerite with softball questions she could hit out of the park to impress the social media influencers in the audience. Also in attendance would be several booksellers and a few librarians—whoever Eliza could lure into her home with the promise of a meet and greet with the author and a complimentary glass of wine. And a photographer of course. Marguerite's choice.

The author had left Eliza's home after their earlier session to spend her day at a nearby salon getting her hair touched up, her mani and pedi refreshed, and a facial that would leave her natural complexion glowing. It'd cost as much as the catering.

Eliza headed upstairs to shower, but when she reached the landing, she paused. Something was wrong; she just couldn't put her finger on what. A sizzle in the air? Her closed bedroom door? She couldn't remember the last time she'd closed her door. Eliza and Roman lived alone. They had no need for privacy.

She moved closer, listening. Her shoulders tensed at a shuffle from inside.

Eliza had just raised a hand to turn the knob when she heard it—distinct, this time. A low groan, then a female voice. Nothing muffled about it. There was a woman in Eliza's bedroom, and she wasn't alone.

Eliza's first inclination was to back away. She hesitated, took a quiet step toward the staircase. But she stopped as a wave of indignation crashed over her. She refused to be intimidated out of her own bedroom. With a stubborn twist of the handle, Eliza threw the door open.

Deep down, Eliza knew the gist of what she'd find. She'd been preparing for this moment for a long time, she realized as she gathered her wits in the hallway. Now that it was actually happening and she was confronted with an affair in the flesh, Eliza expected to feel many things as she stepped through the door. She just hadn't expected to be rendered speechless.

"Eliza!" Roman's voice rolled off his tongue, smooth and buttery, the moment he saw her. "We didn't expect you home so soon."

"We." Eliza coughed, struggling to recover her wits. "We?"

She gave a shake of her head, her tongue feeling heavy, leaden. Her body sank into numbness, complete from head to toe. She was a dead weight. If someone threw her into the ocean, she'd sink straight to the bottom. She'd be dead before she even thought about swimming.

"I'm surprised *we* didn't know I'd be home," Eliza said, fighting to regain some semblance of calmness, "seeing as *we* were scheduled to be downstairs in twenty minutes."

A set of long, thin legs were wrapped around her husband's bare torso, the splash of frizzy hair against the pillow all too familiar. Eliza caught sight of bare breasts and refused to avert her eyes. Spaghetti-thin straps of lace swirled around the smooth skin of the woman's stomach, a touch of expensive, classy lingerie in an unclassy setting.

"Marguerite." Eliza addressed her client crisply. "I don't think it's necessary for you to attend book club tonight. In fact, the event is canceled. Unfortunately, you came down with a nasty, nasty stomach bug."

"But—"

"Also, our contract is terminated. I won't utter a word of this little indiscretion to anyone in the industry so long as you pay me in full for the agreed-upon campaign. Our professional relationship is over."

"I'll get you your money," Marguerite said. "Give me a week."

"Fine." Eliza turned to Roman. "Honey, we're done. Marguerite's plan worked. This is it. I don't want to speak to you again. We'll let the lawyers handle our assets."

"Eliza, don't be rash—" Roman started.

"This"—Eliza waved her hand—"is you speaking to me."

The doorbell rang again.

Eliza turned, jogged downstairs to greet her guest, and didn't look back.

Eliza spun the steering wheel and made a sharp left, not bothering with a blinker. She barely bothered with the brakes.

"Are you sure everything is okay?" Anne sat in the passenger's seat, her knuckles gripping the safety handle for balance. "You can tell us—"

"I'll tell you when we get there," Eliza said shortly. "Did you finish the phone calls?"

"I sent out texts to the guest list," Anne said. "The attendees know book club is canceled."

"Thank you."

"You are aware that we have a pregnant woman in the back of the car," Anne murmured feebly. "I'm sure she would like to make it there alive. I want to make it there alive, too, so I can hear what you have to say. Where is *there* by the way? Are you sure everything's okay?"

"It's fine." Eliza's voice was a thin blade—an icicle on a cold winter's morning, reflecting a brilliant shade of sunlight. "Here is *there*."

The Garbanzo's sign flickered above the three women as they exited the car, Penny and Anne moving slowly, a bit shakily, as they tested their footing and seemed surprised to find themselves on solid ground. Eliza caught Penny glancing up and down the street as if looking for their destination.

When Eliza led them into Garbanzo's, Penny's eyebrow raised, but she didn't make a peep about their dismal surroundings.

"Eliza, Annie," Uncle Joe called from behind the bar. "You brought a friend! Pretty thing, too. How you doin', little mama?"

Penny looked at Eliza first, then Anne. Then down at her stomach as if she couldn't quite believe Uncle Joe was talking to her.

"He's an old friend," Anne muttered to Penny. "Don't mind him."

Eliza led the way across the room to the usual table. Penny scurried close behind. Once all three women had their backsides firmly stuck to the vinyl seats, Anne and Penny looked expectantly across the table. Eliza waited until Uncle Joe had deposited four shots of tequila in front of them.

"Can I get a glass of water?" Penny asked.

Anne raised a hand. "I'll take a beer. Whatever you have on tap."

Uncle Joe grunted in acknowledgment. He left the table and disappeared for a moment behind the bar. When he returned, he brought with him several glasses of water and a beer that he slid in front of Anne. He gave a nod at the women and then returned to his post, leaving the women alone in silence.

"I can't drink." Penny broke the silence with a longing gaze at the tequila.

"Those are for me." Eliza extended her arms possessively around the shot glasses before hugging them greedily toward her. "I earned them."

Anne extended a hand, plucking a shot from Eliza's arms. "Except this one. What are we drinking to?"

"Divorce." Eliza raised her tiny glass, noted Anne's surprised expression, then tossed the alcohol back. She let out a satisfying hiss of disgust. "And to book club."

Penny blinked. "I'm a little confused."

"Marguerite Hill is currently in my bed," Eliza said. When the other women didn't react, she continued, "Screwing my husband."

Penny blanched. "You mean Roman?"

"Yes, Penny, I mean Roman." Eliza pulled another round of tequila toward her but didn't lift it to her lips. "Don't act surprised that he's having an affair. I know there's a very good chance Roman is the father of your child."

Anne gasped. "Eliza! Don't be ridiculous. Penny is our friend. Don't take this out on her."

Penny played with her water glass, running her finger absently across the rivulets of condensation dripping down the outside.

"I'm not an idiot," Eliza said. "Don't worry, Penny. I don't blame you. Did Roman tell you he was separated from me, just waiting on the divorce papers?" At Penny's blank stare, Eliza continued. "He's used that line before. On your favorite author, as a matter of fact. Just think—if Marguerite Hill gets pregnant, your children would be related. You're in fine company."

Penny choked on something invisible until Anne thwacked her on the back.

Anne looked flabbergasted. "But what about the classmate you told us about? Mr. Young and Stupid?"

"That wasn't a total lie," Penny confessed, hanging her head. Her cheeks pinkened beneath the bar's dim lighting. "I'm so sorry. After all you've both done for me, I feel awful. I owe you an explanation."

"Uh…" Anne blinked. "Yeah, I'd say so."

"It's true about the classmate. I *was* dating him, but I broke up with him when I thought…" She cleared her throat. "When I thought things were getting serious with someone else."

"You fell in love," Eliza said, "with my husband."

"I can't possibly explain how very sorry I am." Penny sounded miserable. "I was so stupid."

"You weren't the first to be blinded by Roman, and you obviously aren't the last. I thought he loved me, so if you're stupid, so am I."

"It's not the same thing."

Eliza gave a cough as she swallowed the second shot of tequila. "I do feel bad for you, Penny. I don't think Roman is evil, but he sure is stupid."

"I don't know," Anne said, paling. "Maybe there's more to Roman than any of us thought."

Eliza and Penny both waited for Anne to explain.

"I mean, he cheated on you multiple times," Anne continued, looking flustered. "That's not an accident at that point."

"Maybe," Eliza agreed. "By the way, Penny, I'll make sure Roman pays his portion of child support. Just because he's an idiot doesn't mean your baby should suffer."

"I don't want anything. I couldn't possibly accept more of your help." Penny turned her attention to Anne. "You have to understand, the only reason I accepted your hand-me-downs was because this child deserves it, and I will do anything for him. Anything."

Anne took a gulp of her beer. When she set it down, her lips moved, but no sound came out. Her eyes glinted in a way that said she understood, even if a bit reluctantly. She tried again, looking to Eliza. "What does this mean for you?"

"What option do I have?" Eliza asked. "We've spiraled out of control."

"If you suspected Roman and I had been together all along, why didn't you divorce him sooner?" Penny asked quietly. "Why didn't you say something?"

Eliza glanced down to where she'd inadvertently shredded her damp napkin into hundreds of tiny pieces. "Because I loved him. And I owed him. I owed him everything. If he hadn't married me, I wouldn't be here today."

Penny blinked her eyes rapidly. "Oh."

The door to the bar opened after Eliza's admission and acted as a hard stop to the women's conversation. The entire bar froze as Eliza turned her head and spotted Marguerite Hill standing in the doorway.

Uncle Joe called out a hearty greeting that wasn't reciprocated. Marguerite only had eyes for Eliza. Her gaze was wild and sharp, and her white shirt was buttoned all sorts of wrong beneath a black blazer. Her hair was an utter mess. Marguerite Hill had never looked more of a disaster.

When Eliza blinked, the tension broke. The room resumed its normal background chatter, glassware clanked behind the bar, and cars honked and squealed on the streets beyond Garbanzo's walls. Eliza reached for another shot of tequila and tossed it back.

By the time she swallowed, Marguerite was already on her way over.

"I'm sorry," Marguerite gasped, coming to a stop beside the table. "I was only trying to help you get away from him."

Eliza managed to keep her tone steady. "Did you ever think that maybe I didn't want to get away from him?"

"Roman strayed," Marguerite said. "First Penny, then me. Probably others. I thought if I could just show you… I never intended to sleep with him. I just wanted to flirt a little. You'd get the picture."

"You think you know everything, don't you?" Eliza persisted. "You're the guru. But you made a mistake with my husband. You fell in love with Roman, didn't you?"

"I didn't mean to—"

"He didn't love you back," Eliza stated. "You tried to play him, and he played you. Well, it worked. I am done. You can have him."

"No, it was all lies…" Marguerite shook her head, frantic. "I can't—He can't get away with this."

"With what?" Eliza asked. "What do you propose we do?"

"You don't get it, do you?" Marguerite's expression hardened. "Men are rotten. They all are. My father, Roman, the whole lot of them."

"I understand you have a deep distrust of men, but I wonder if it's time—"

"What?" Marguerite interjected. "To move on? Get over it? How do you move on when your own father raped you? I was eleven years old, Eliza. Eleven fucking years old."

The table went deadly quiet. There were no right answers. Even in a room full of wrong, all the women could agree on that.

"But nobody wants to know those details," Marguerite said. "They don't want to hear the truth. That would *suck* for a PR campaign. Really muddy up my Instagram feed."

"Marguerite—"

"We need to teach Roman a lesson," Marguerite said. "He can't get away with this."

Eliza was too stumped to offer a response. The author was coming unhinged; Eliza had never seen her so crazed. The evening's events had triggered her into imploding, slowly, surely...

Turning her attention back to the women sitting across from her, Eliza spoke in a low, throaty tone, surprising herself with her agreement. "She's right, you know. He shouldn't get away with this."

THIRTY-ONE

The Morning After
February 15, 2019

E liza Tate didn't believe in hangovers.

What she was experiencing was not a hangover but a whiff of karma back to haunt her after a night of overindulgence. Whoever would have thought book club could get so out of control?

Eliza's smile widened with gratitude as a server approached her, balancing an oversize latte. It was served in a trendy little mug that was nearly the size of her head. He placed the saucer and beverage on the table before her, dropped off a platter of raw sugar cubes and organic creamer, and then hesitated politely by her side.

"Are you ready to order, ma'am?"

"I'm still waiting on two others," she said. "They should be here any second."

The server nodded and backed away. Eliza waited until he'd gone, then greedily pulled the frothy mixture toward her, studying the intricate heart detailed by the barista on the surface, the white foam freckled with flecks of black lava salt. Only in Santa Monica had coffee become a form of art. And the sort of thing one needed financing to purchase.

Eliza ignored the price tag and instead closed her eyes and savored the thick, milky flavor, the rich espresso and hints of bitter dark chocolate. Her headache temporarily eased at the first hit of caffeine.

Along with the easing headache came a surge of another emotion. Guilt, maybe? Shame? Confusion? The second half of the night had turned into a blurry, sludgy memory. Unfortunately, those memories weren't so far gone that she couldn't recall the topic of conversation.

Guilt, she thought.

The feeling in her belly was definitely guilt.

Eliza forced the sensation away, cramming a million tiny pieces of guilt into the recesses of her mind as she surveyed the café around her in search of her two friends. Book club buddies. *Partners in crime?* she wondered dubiously.

But Penny and Anne were late, late, late. They should have arrived ten minutes ago. Under normal circumstances, Eliza wouldn't have minded their tardiness. She'd have zipped through emails on her phone, arranged calls with clients, read the latest manuscript to cross her desk—but not this morning. This morning, she didn't have the energy for any of it. She wanted her damn friends to show up and reassure her that last night had been nothing short of a bad, bad dream.

Eliza studied the ambiance around her, basking in the rare seventy-degree February day in Los Angeles. Ladies balanced on pale-blue retro bicycles, pedaling down Main Street. The community garden across the way bustled with activity, the exterior fences tipped with pops of yellow sunflower leaves and fat, juicy tomatoes dripping from vines. Overgrown boys carried surfboards across their shoulders, and women with scraggly dreadlocks strolled the sidewalks in ragged-looking swimsuits and cover-ups, completing their outfits with five-hundred-dollar sandals.

The sun warmed her cheeks. The not-quite hangover lulled Eliza into a false sense of calmness as she sat back in the white wicker seat, a small umbrella shielding the worst of the rays from the outdoor patio. Her eyes closed again, and she drifted into black waters, her fingers tapping listlessly against her coffee mug.

"Eliza Tate?"

A man's low, rumbling voice pierced the thin curtain of Eliza's sleep. Her eyelids flashed open behind her sunglasses. She was grateful for the mask, even more so when she realized the man standing before her was a uniformed police officer.

"Yes, that's me," Eliza said briskly. "How can I help you?"

"Is there someplace quieter we could talk?"

Eliza's gaze wandered over his shoulder, and she caught sight of Penny making her way up the steps to the café. The young woman's eyes flicked over the patrons, brightening when she saw Eliza. Penny gave a quick wave, then froze as her eyes slid seamlessly over to the cop.

Eliza studied Penny curiously. The young woman's face had gone as white as Eliza's frothed milk, and her posture was stiff, sharply pointed, like the blade of a knife. Her hand gave a nervous twitch, and as Eliza watched, Penny's car keys clattered to the cement walkway. The sound shook Eliza back to reality.

"No, here is fine," Eliza said, trying to hurry the officer along. She gestured toward Penny. "I'm busy at the moment, meeting some friends for brunch. Is it a parking ticket?"

"I'm sorry, but I really think—"

"For God's sake, spit it out. I don't have all day."

The cop's face twitched with an unidentified emotion. *So many unidentified emotions*, Eliza thought sullenly. If people just wore their hearts on their sleeves, it would solve a lot of issues.

"I'm very sorry to have to inform you, Mrs. Tate, that we found your husband's body this morning."

Eliza felt shards of glass in her throat. Scratchy, bloody pieces.

"My husband's body?" she repeated. "His *body*?"

"Your husband passed away late last night. I'm so sorry."

Eliza pressed her hands to her forehead. It wasn't enough. She reached for the complimentary glass of ice water, pressed it against her cheek. Beads of sweat bloomed on the back of her neck, slid down her skin, and soaked into her blouse. She asked weakly, "Was it a car accident?"

"We suspect foul play," the officer said. "I'm sorry again to have to break the news to you. I hope you'll understand that we need to ask you a few questions. Mrs. Tate, where were you last night?"

"I stayed at a hotel," Eliza said. "My husband and I…"

The cop waited.

"I was out late with the girls," Eliza revised. "I got a room at the Pelican Hotel. You can check."

"I will. Now, if you wouldn't mind—"

"How did he die? I assume you're dancing around the fact that my husband was murdered."

The officer shifted his weight uncomfortably. "I'd rather discuss the details down at the station, ma'am."

"My husband is dead. I deserve to know how he died."

"I'm not arguing with you, but I do think a matter this sensitive is best discussed in private."

Eliza waited him out. While the news of her husband's death was somewhat alarming, she couldn't say she was entirely surprised, especially after her day yesterday. She just wasn't sure who'd had the guts to do it.

The officer glanced around, surveying the bustling brunch scene. He wiped his brow and glanced toward Penny's rapid approach. Still, Eliza waited. She drew her lips into the thin line she knew to be intimidating and made eye contact with the officer from behind the shield of her reflective lenses. Silence could do wonders to intimidate a man.

"He died from multiple stab wounds," the officer finally said. "At his house."

"Our house."

"What?"

"It was *our* house."

"Of course. I'm sorry."

Eliza sank back in her chair, sickened. Weak. More sweat beaded. Her head throbbed. A knife clattered against a plate, a dog barked, a baby hiccupped and gurgled. The noises of the world were magnified in Eliza's ears. They echoed like sounds shouted into a deserted tunnel, banged around inside her skull, then faded into nothingness.

The cacophony of sound from the bustling café dimmed to nothing. The air suddenly felt too stale to breathe, and the sun burned too hot on Eliza's hand. Her fingertips felt scorched as she rested them against her mug.

"Ma'am?" he asked. "Are you feeling okay?"

"Eliza?" Penny's hand clutched at Eliza's shoulder. "What's going on?"

Eliza winced. The girl's nails were digging into her, piercing at her skin. It was too tight, too forced.

The cop turned to Penny. "If I could have a moment alone with Mrs. Tate, I would appreciate it."

"She can stay," Eliza snipped. "We don't have secrets between us. Not anymore."

The officer gave a longer look at Penny, then turned back to Eliza. "Mrs. Tate, it would be beneficial for all involved if you could join me at the station to answer a few questions."

Penny's fingers dug excruciatingly deeper into Eliza's muscle. "Oh my God," she murmured. "Is it Roman?"

Eliza's gaze flicked up at the young woman before turning a deadened stare at the cop. "I'd like my lawyer."

THIRTY-TWO

The Morning After
February 15, 2019

Anne Wilkes tried hard to mask her hangover, but she was unsuccessful.

"Mom, please." Anne looked over to where her mother had begun to reorganize her cupboards at 8:00 a.m. on a Saturday morning. "That banging is driving me insane."

"It's unbecoming for a lady to drink so much." Anne's mother, Beatrice Harper, sniffed. "It lacks class. And it's not safe. For you or the kids."

"Mom. Please."

"I just wish you'd get help, Anne."

"I don't have a problem. I can stop drinking if I want, okay? I'm not going to fucking leave the kids."

"Again."

"Excuse me?"

"Leave them again," Beatrice said evenly. "You're very lucky the doctors wrote you a note the last time so you didn't get in bigger trouble."

"I had postpartum depression. It's an actual illness—not an excuse."

"Sure," Beatrice said. "Even so, a civilized book club doesn't last until three in the morning. And by the way, where was your husband last night?"

"Mark?" Anne swallowed. "He didn't come home?"

"You didn't know?" Beatrice said. "How could you not know?"

Because, Anne wanted to say, *Mark has a lot of secrets*.

"I didn't hear Mark come home," Beatrice said. "And I can't believe you didn't notice."

The reason Anne hadn't noticed was because she'd fallen asleep the second her head had hit the pillow. Anne's bedtime was 10:00 p.m. on a good night. An evening of drinking at a bar with her friends was enough to knock her out cold for a week. Anne had come home, seen the basement light on, and assumed Mark was working late out of his home office.

Not feeling particularly inclined to start a conversation with him that would likely last all night, she'd gone upstairs and fallen asleep. When he wasn't in bed when she woke up the next morning, she figured he'd gotten an early start in the office. He'd been doing that a lot lately.

Anne leaned against the doorway to her own kitchen and felt like an outsider. As always, her mother had transformed Anne's average house into something fit for a magazine spread. The dishes were put away, the counters wiped spotlessly clean. The twins were chattering away happily in their Pack 'n Play in the living room while her older children had miraculously found ways to occupy themselves. With startling clarity, Anne realized that her mother was even capable of organizing the children.

"I'll be back by noon," Anne said. "Can I bring you something from the café?"

Her mother didn't bother to look up. "I'm making breakfast for your children. Homemade, as it should be."

Anne stopped in the living room, smacked four kisses across the heads of each of her babies. They didn't bother to look up. She was running late, but she paused in the doorway and glanced back, scanning one last look over a living room with happily playing children.

With a very unladylike arsenal of curse words coupled with a lead foot, Anne managed to make it to Santa Monica only fifteen minutes after she'd agreed to meet her friends. She pulled into a parking spot half a block away and strode toward the outdoor café that would put a major dent in her very slender wallet.

She stopped at the picket fence before the restaurant. The place maintained an aura of rustic ambiance, though Anne knew for a fact that it was brand new. The materials had been roughed up to look worn, the wicker chairs supposed to look like something out of *Country Living* when really, they'd likely been purchased from an overpriced boutique catalogue.

But it wasn't the decor or the sunny day or the sight of her friends that stopped Anne in her tracks. It was the sight of a uniformed cop standing by the table. The look of horror on Penny's face. The deadened stare in Eliza's eyes as she looked at the officer and murmured four awful words.

"I'd like my lawyer."

God, no, Anne thought. *This can't be happening.*

Penny raised her gaze then and caught sight of Anne. Their eyes locked in nervous trepidation. Anne couldn't bring herself to unfreeze from her position. She merely stared back at Penny, wondering if their lives had spiraled wildly out of control.

Was it possible that their dirty little secrets were about to become very big twisted truths?

THIRTY-THREE

Two Weeks After
February 2019

Eliza blinked as she rounded a corner on the famous hike, pausing to wait for Anne to catch up. The sun beat hard on her shoulders. She'd put sunscreen on, though why she'd bothered, she wasn't sure. They were coming for her. She wouldn't see the light of day except for in the prison yard if the police had any say in the matter.

"I really…" Anne gasped. "I really…don't…think we should be doing this. You might be recognized."

"We should act exactly the same as we did before," Eliza said. "We have nothing to hide."

"Eliza—"

"We're almost there."

Eliza squinted ahead to where she could see the peak of the Runyon Canyon trail, LA's hottest hike. Celeb sightings were frequent on these trails. It was not a place to spend time if one was trying to stay out of the spotlight. But Eliza wasn't trying to stay out of the spotlight. She was trying to live her life.

"Damn it, slow down," Anne said. "I'm fat. I can't keep up with you."

"You're not fat," Eliza said, though even she knew it sounded mechanical. She was just too focused on sweating out her frustrations with the investigation to pay all that much attention to Anne's fitness complaints. "It's good for us. Plus, I'm trying to make a point. I won't swap out my friends because of a stupid rumor."

"Maybe it's not—"

"The top is just ahead. You can do it."

"For crying out loud, Eliza! Stop. Just stop." Anne threw her hands up in the air. She was sweating, her face pink, her arms glistening under the toasty afternoon temps. "Just stop."

Eliza spun around, wiping her brow with the edge of her tank top. "What?"

"I *am* hiding something."

"What?"

Eliza felt the first tingles of wariness creep down her scalp at the look in Anne's eye. Roman had been dead for two weeks. The police were in the middle of a full-fledged investigation, and it seemed their only suspect was Eliza.

It's always the wife, she thought dryly. These last few weeks, when the panic had tiptoed up Eliza's spine and grabbed hold of her consciousness, the only thing that calmed her was to remember that she was innocent. And even if she wasn't completely innocent, there was no evidence to put her in an orange jumpsuit.

"I lied to the police."

"Why would you lie?" Eliza shifted to the edge of the path to allow a young, gloriously fit couple to power by. "And why are you telling me this now?"

"I didn't know what to do. Everything happened so fast, but now... The weight of the secret has been killing me."

"What did you do, Anne?"

"I didn't do anything. But on the night Roman was murdered, Mark didn't come home."

Eliza let out a huge sigh tinged with relief and frustration. "What the hell, Anne? You scared me. Is this about Mark's affair again? I'm telling you, there's not—"

"It's not about the affair," Anne said. "It's about Roman. I told the police that Mark was home with me. As you know, they've been asking everyone for alibis."

"Right…and?"

"And that was a lie."

"He was probably with—"

"He might not have been with her," Anne said. "I don't know where he was."

"You don't think he had anything to do with Roman's death, do you?" Eliza eyed the path with skepticism, but they were alone. "Just because your husband is an adulterer doesn't mean he's a murderer. Sorry, but I think you're being paranoid. He didn't have any motive to want Roman dead."

"What if I told you it's not paranoia?" Anne swiped at her forehead with the back of her wrist. "What if I told you there was a reason?"

"Mark has only met Roman a handful of times. Why would he ever want Roman dead?"

"Trust me on this," Anne said. "He's not the only one. I wanted him dead, too."

"I don't understand."

"Eliza, your husband made some bad choices," Anne said. "I didn't kill him. But what if my husband did?"

THIRTY-FOUR

One Month After
March 2019

R oman Tate was dead. Now, Anne's marriage was dead. She couldn't take the lies anymore. She had suspected the end was coming for some time and had ignored all the signs. She hadn't wanted it to be true. But now that she had to wonder if her husband was a crooked cop, an adulterer, and a murderer all in one, she was beginning to see things in a different light.

"I'd like you to get rid of it," Anne said with a flick of her wrist at the movers. "Now, please."

"But—"

"The garbage is fine," Anne said firmly. "Even better, put it in back by the bonfire pit. We'll burn it."

The mover looked toward Anne's old, mangled vanity. A sign of everything that had gone wrong in her relationship with Mark. What had once been quaint and quirky had grown ragged and old, smudged with the fingerprints of children and the wear and tear of a busy household. While Anne had grown unhappy with the steadily deteriorating state of her vanity, her husband hadn't seemed to notice anything wrong at all.

He gave a shrug, then gestured at his colleagues and gave a low whistle. The men wrapped the vanity with a heavy cloth, then retrieved some sort of dolly to lug the thing downstairs. Anne stood out of the way and watched, her chest tense and her breathing forced.

If the affair had been the only trouble with her relationship, Anne could have moved on. She could have made things work with Mark. She could have forgiven him quickly and swiftly, and while the betrayal had hurt, she would have swallowed her pride for the sake of her family. Unfortunately, the truth—a slippery, black snake—had slithered into their lives, and it was so much more.

Mark was due back at the house today. He was scheduled to arrive at noon, and it would be the first time Anne had seen him since Roman had been found dead. *Murdered*, Anne reminded herself. The same day Anne had asked her husband to move out.

The police still hadn't arrested a suspect. They'd questioned Penny, Eliza, and Anne over and over. Anne wondered if the other women had broken, shared their secrets with the police. *Is that why the cops are hanging around?* The authorities hadn't let their suspicions of the three women drop despite a lack of evidence. Anne couldn't help but feel she'd already been condemned in the eyes of the police.

Plenty of people had motive, Anne thought wryly. And with that, Anne wondered—not for the first time—where Mark had been on the night of Roman's murder. She hadn't asked him. Instead, she'd kicked him out of the house. Had she asked him to leave because of the state of their marriage or because she was afraid of him? Of what he was capable of doing?

Anne had told Mark that she needed time to think things through, and she couldn't think with him sleeping next to her. His response had been simple. *So you know then.* Anne had pointed toward the door, and Mark hadn't argued. He hadn't even tried to offer an explanation.

Anne glanced down at her phone, debating a call to Eliza. At the last second, she dropped her cell back into her pocket. This—the vanity—wasn't Eliza's problem. The poor woman had enough to deal with already. The loss of her husband, a police investigation, a company that was a complete and utter mess…

Instead, Anne debated dialing Penny's number but quickly dismissed the thought. The poor girl was in just as deep as Eliza but for a myriad of different reasons. Compared to Penny and Eliza, Anne had limited problems.

It was better she didn't talk with her friends anyway. The more they spoke, the more Anne suspected the police would think they'd gone in on something together. Eliza had disagreed, telling Anne and Penny that she thought their caution made them look guilty and that they should continue to interact with one another as usual.

"I'm not losing my friends over this," Eliza had announced to Penny and Anne the day after Roman's death. "I'm not staying away from you because of one ridiculous rumor that I offed my husband."

A response had been on the tip of Anne's tongue. She wanted to ask *Well, did you?*

But she never asked. Neither had Penny.

Just like Eliza hadn't asked Penny or Anne if they'd done it.

None of them wanted to know the answer.

The door downstairs opened as the movers shuffled the vanity outside. Mark slipped through the door behind the movers and made his way upstairs, looking confused as he entered the bedroom. They faced one another in silence. It was Mark who spoke first.

"So this is it?" he murmured. "You haven't even asked me to explain."

"There's nothing to explain," Anne said firmly. "It's the lying that I can't handle. I could've gotten past the rest of it."

Mark looked like he wanted to say more, but at the last second, his face crumpled. He looked Anne dead in the eye. "It doesn't matter what I say, does it? You've made up your mind. It's over."

Anne closed her eyes. "Yes, Mark. It's over."

Mark made his way toward Anne and stood before her, studying her with a quiet intensity. In one swift, unexpected move, he took Anne in his arms and pressed her to his chest. Anne felt the dampness of tears on her skin.

Anne found herself hugging him back, her nails digging into his skin as she wished upon all the stars that things were different. But they weren't, and their tender embrace came to an end. Anne lifted a file that contained divorce papers from the bed and handed it to her husband. He tucked the folder under his arm and left the room without a backward glance.

Anne waited for the lump in her throat to fade. When it didn't, she ignored it instead. Picking up the phone, she dialed the one person who would know what to say.

"Eliza," Anne said, "are you free?"

There was a long hesitation from the other end of the phone. "As a matter of fact, I'm not. I can't talk now."

"It's Mark."

"I'm sorry, Anne," Eliza said briskly. "This will have to wait."

THIRTY-FIVE

One Month After
March 2019

Eliza sat in her newly leased, barren office, fingers flexed over her computer keyboard. She'd gotten the keys to her first solo office just three days after her husband's death and, simultaneously, three days after the loss of her only client. It was salt in the wound to sit behind her desk and pretend to work, but what could she do? She was on the hook for six months of rent. She might as well use it.

Humming a tuneless tune, Eliza stared listlessly at her hands. To anyone peering in from the outside, it would look as if she were deep in thought. Truth be told, she was simply killing time, musing over a chip in her nail polish and wondering when it had gotten there.

In another round of irony, in the month since her husband's death, Eliza had found herself suddenly in the black. She'd been able to pay off all her debts, including the loan to Jocelyn and Todd, in large part due to the sale of Roman's cars. All was going well in the world of Eliza Tate. Except, of course, for the fact that her husband was dead.

A knock sounded on the door, startling her from the study of her chipped nail. Eliza jerked to attention, fielding a flash of annoyance that she hadn't gone ahead and hired an assistant. The CEO of Eliza Tate PR shouldn't be opening her own damn door. Then again, the CEO of Eliza Tate PR needed to get clients in order to need an assistant.

"Good afternoon, gentlemen." Eliza opened the door to reveal two uniformed policemen standing in the hallway. "Can I help you with something?"

"Mrs. Tate?"

"That's me." She glanced pointedly at her shiny name plaque on the door.

The taller cop's gaze followed, but he didn't appear amused. He scratched at the back of his head, then glanced over Eliza's shoulder. "May we come in for a moment?"

"I'm very busy, so I hope we can make this quick."

Eliza returned to her seat. She sat, folded her hands across her desk (tucking the chipped nail out of sight), and tried to look disinterested in whatever the cops had to say.

On the inside, however, Eliza trembled with nerves. Ever since she'd come to this country, she'd felt uneasy around law enforcement, as if they would somehow sniff out the fact that she didn't belong. That she was an imposter, an intruder.

She wondered if the fear would ever leave her very marrow, despite its ridiculousness. She'd been married for ages, a working member of society for even longer. She belonged in this country as much as anyone else, but old habits died hard.

She studied the cops, wondering what had brought them crawling out of their cave. The police had bothered her plenty in the weeks after Roman's death, but she'd finally started to think they were through with her. Eliza had even started to wonder if they'd just give up on her husband's case and move on to the hot, new murder du jour.

They need evidence. She reassured herself with the familiar phrase and took a deep breath. She'd been repeating it over and over to herself in the time since Roman's murder.

"We can make this quick," the shorter cop said, flicking his gaze to Eliza. "Mrs. Tate, you're under arrest for the murder of your husband, Roman Tate."

Eliza couldn't process what they were saying. "But that's impossible."

"Mrs. Tate, you have the right—"

Eliza held up her finger as her phone rang. It sounded shrill, eerily so in the bare cement walls that formed her office. She answered, speaking evenly, barely processing Anne's sobbing voice on the other end of the line.

"I'm sorry, Anne," Eliza said briskly once Anne had mumbled on and on about her very-alive husband. Anne's problems were just not that important right now. "This will have to wait. The police have arrived to arrest me for my husband's murder."

Eliza hung up on Anne, then looked to the officers. "There must be a mistake. Your people have questioned me a hundred times. I told you I didn't do it. I am innocent. And unless you have evidence—"

"We do, Mrs. Tate."

"That's impossible. How can you have evidence if I didn't do it?"

"This will be a lot easier if you cooperate with us."

"Cooperate? You mean admit to something I didn't do?"

"Come down to the station with us. Everything will be explained."

"I want my lawyer."

"I'm sure you do."

Eliza frowned. "What's that supposed to mean?"

The taller cop stepped forward, removed a pair of handcuffs from his waist. "All I'm saying, Mrs. Tate, is that things aren't looking good for you."

The other cop shook his head, a false sadness sliding over his features. "They never do when the wife's fingerprints turn up on the murder weapon."

Eliza felt her face go numb first. Then her arms, her hands, the tips of her fingers and toes. The world seemed to halt on its axis, suspended in space and time, while the cops surrounded her.

The panic in her chest grew in its intensity as she was hauled from her office. How was this possible? She hadn't killed anyone. As Eliza climbed into the back of a cop car, her brain whirred at a million miles an hour. There had to be an explanation. How had the cops found the murder weapon? Where? And most importantly, how had her prints gotten onto it?

THIRTY-SIX

One Month After
March 2019

I s there anything we can do to make you more comfortable?" asked a detective dressed in slacks and a sky-blue button-down shirt. "Something to drink, maybe? Coffee?"

"Just so long as the bathroom is close by, I should be fine." Penny dropped herself into a chair, groaning with the effort of it. "I hope we can make this quick."

"We'll do our best." The detective sat opposite Penny at the interview table. "Ms. Sands, we've invited you here to discuss the murder of Roman Tate."

"Eliza wouldn't have killed her husband. I don't know why you've arrested her."

"Isn't that a little ironic? A defense coming from her husband's mistress?"

Penny winced, then shook her head. She rested a hand on her stomach as she met the detective's gaze. "You don't understand what you're talking about."

"You're right, I don't. That's why you're here. When did your affair with Mr. Tate begin?"

Penny's breath hitched. "I didn't realize it was an affair. He said he was separating from his wife."

"At the time of his death, Mr. Tate was still wearing his wedding ring."

"Yes."

"Was he wearing it when you started seeing him?"

Penny thought back to the day when everything had changed. The day in Roman's office when he'd promised her great things. Wild success. Then he'd turned her very dreams into the trap that broke her.

"Yes, he was wearing it when our relationship began."

"You didn't think to ask him about it?"

"I did ask him about it, and he told me he was separating from his wife."

The detective jotted down a note on a tiny piece of paper. "Did he explain the cause of the separation?"

"He only said that it was a long time in coming. There was a mention of how he was still on good terms with Eliza. That it was a mutual and amicable separation—no kids, no messy dividing of assets. They were going to split things down the middle and carry on with their lives."

"Would it surprise you to learn that Roman Tate had no real assets to split?"

Penny blinked. "Excuse me?"

"I thought you said that you and Mrs. Tate were friends."

"We are, but I'm not privy to her personal finances. What do you mean Roman had no assets to split? The Tates are loaded."

The detective ignored Penny. "When did you begin seeing Mr. Tate?"

"I met him when I signed up for his acting classes after moving to Los Angeles. I suppose that would have been sometime in June of last year. I don't remember the exact date, but I'm sure there's a confirmation email somewhere that would state when I began paying tuition."

"I'll need to see any correspondence that corroborates your testimony."

Penny gave a vague, tired wave of her hand. "Fine."

"When did your relationship go from professional to something more personal?"

She was forced to think on the question. Not because she couldn't remember but because she couldn't be sure of the correct answer. When *had* it switched over?

It might have been the day Roman had called Penny up onstage, his dark eyes fixed on hers, that musical voice lulling her into a moment of heady lust before the rest of her classmates. She could still feel the ghost of his breath on her shoulder, the whisper of his touch on her back. Skin against skin, as if he were right here in this room. But that was impossible, because Roman Tate was dead.

Penny bit her lip, studied the cop across the table.

"I'm thinking," she said at his raised eyebrows.

Maybe it wasn't the day onstage when things had changed. Maybe it was the moment she'd accepted his offer for feedback on her stolen script. She'd gone to him knowing it was a ruse, knowing she wouldn't walk away unscathed, and she'd been right.

Penny felt the familiar growl of anger rising in her gut as she remembered—all of it, every sordid detail. She rested a hand on her belly and felt movement there and, beneath it, a pit of despair.

Roman Tate had ruined her life.

"I didn't know the question was so complicated." The cop cleared his throat. "I'm looking for a date, ballpark if that's the best you can do."

"Of course it's complicated," Penny snapped.

But when had their relationship truly ramped up to new highs? Penny was beginning to think it hadn't been that day in his office after all. It had probably been the first time they'd seen each other outside the studio, a date disguised as a business dinner. They'd ordered wine, lingered. He'd picked up the check, walked her to her car. Penny closed her eyes, recalling the way his thumb had traced down her cheek in a playful, seductive goodbye.

Her skin burned. Then her eyes flashed open, her cheeks on fire.

"Are you feeling all right?" the cop asked. "Can I get you more water?"

"I'm fine," Penny said. "Give me a minute. I'm not sure on the exact date."

That wasn't entirely true, however. Penny did know the exact date. At least she knew the date of the obvious start of their personal relationship. The first time they'd had sex.

Sick with memories, Penny leaned against the desk, pushing thoughts of damp sheets and pleasured cries out of her mind. "The summer of last year. July or August. Is that good enough?"

The officer jotted another phrase onto his notepad. "When did you discover that Mr. Tate wasn't actually separated from his wife? And had no plans of doing so?"

Penny's lips thinned. "We went over this the first time you questioned me."

"At that time, we hadn't found enough evidence to arrest anyone in conjunction with Mr. Tate's death," the detective said with a coy twitch of his lips. "That has since changed."

"So you say," Penny said with a snort. "But then you tell me your best guess is Eliza. She didn't do it."

"Did Eliza love Roman?"

"Yes," Penny said. "At least at some point."

"Are you aware that we suspect Eliza and Roman's marriage was a fraud from the start?"

"What?"

"Eliza Tate's visa was due to expire three weeks after she married him. Did Roman ever mention the fact that he'd married Eliza only to grant her citizenship?"

Penny looked at her hands. "Not really."

"Did he tell you what suddenly changed in his relationship, then?" The cop clicked his pen on and off, on and off. "Why he was suddenly going to divorce his wife after all these years?"

Penny stared at him. Watched the *click click click* until finally he got the picture and stopped.

"He said he was getting older and realizing that life was too short to remain unhappy."

"Eliza made him unhappy?"

"He said he stayed with Eliza because it was easy. They were comfortable together. But he wanted to find the one true love of his life."

"And I suppose you thought he was talking about you?" The cop clicked the pen once, but at the look on Penny's face, he halted abruptly. "You being the love of his life, I mean?"

"I'm not an idiot." Penny glanced at the table, feeling the color crawl up her neck. "I know this sounds stupid to you, but it's more complicated than you can ever know."

"Did you love Roman?"

"Look, I thought I did, but I was wrong. Now, is there anything else?" Penny winced as a wayward baby heel poked her in the ribs. She carefully dug a finger into her belly, easing him into a gentler position.

"Can I get you anything else, Ms. Sands?" he asked. "If you're in need of a break, we can always pause for a moment."

"I'd rather finish up and go home."

"Then I'll make this brief." The detective bowed his head and pulled his notes closer. "I'd like to go over your timeline once more. You met Mr. Tate last summer in June. Sometime in July or August, you began to see him romantically."

Penny stared back as he looked up at her questioningly.

"When did you..." He cleared his throat. "When was your child conceived?"

"Sometime in July."

"Around the time you began seeing Mr. Tate."

"That's what I said."

"Does Mrs. Tate know you're pregnant?"

"It's pretty hard to miss, don't you think?" Penny shifted her bulk. "I've been friends with Eliza since Marguerite Hill's launch party at the Pelican Hotel."

"Tell me more about the party."

"How is that relevant to the investigation?"

"Were you there on the invitation of Eliza Tate?"

"No," Penny said. "Roman invited me."

"When did you more formally befriend Eliza?"

"A few months later, I guess. She asked me to be part of her book club."

"Let me get this straight: you agreed to be in a book club with your lover's wife?"

"I hadn't realized it was an affair. I already told you that. Roman said he was on good terms with his wife...or soon-to-be ex-wife."

"When did you find out that Mr. Tate had no intention of separating from his wife?"

"I still don't know that. Maybe he did intend to separate from Eliza. How should I know what really went on in Roman's head? I only know what he told me, and he sure as hell didn't tell me the truth."

"Do you—"

"Shit." Penny glanced down, resting a hand on her swollen belly. "I think that was a contraction."

The detective's head shot up so hard, Penny heard his neck crack. He stared at her, alarmed. "Should I call someone?"

Penny crunched forward, gripping the table until her knuckles turned a ghastly white. "I think I'm going into labor."

"Let me drive you to the hospital."

"I can drive myself, thanks."

"Ms. Sands..." The detective stood, made his way around the table, and helped Penny from her chair. "I have one last question for you. Is Mr. Tate the father of your child?"

Penny pulled her arm from the detective's grasp. "I don't know."

"What do you mean, you don't know?"

"I mean," Penny said, her voice pinched and tight, "I had sex with more than one man during my fertile window. I don't know that I can spell it out any more clearly."

"I'll need the name—"

Penny cut him off with a groan. "It doesn't matter who the father is. This baby is mine—end of story. Now, Detective, I really need to get to the hospital."

"I'll call you an ambulance. It's too dangerous for you to drive yourself."

The second the cop left her side, Penny helped herself right out of the room. She didn't look behind her as she exited the building and made her way to her car before the detective could return.

As Penny drove, she turned on the radio and hummed along. Whether the baby belonged to Ryan or Roman was irrelevant. Both were out of her life for good. Roman a little more permanently than Ryan.

Instead of heading to the hospital, Penny cruised home, parked the beat-up car that had been serving her well for the last few months at an expired meter in front of her apartment. She let herself inside, dropped her purse on the couch, and went to the cupboards. There, she found a stack of saltines and a jar of Nutella. She grabbed a butter knife and returned, taking a seat next to her purse.

Kicking her feet onto the lopsided coffee table, she balanced the jar of Nutella on her stomach. She thought back to her interview with the detective in an attempt to straighten everything out in her head. Roman wasn't the only person who could lie. Penny lied too.

She'd lied about her contractions, for starters. She wasn't in labor—not even close. She wasn't due for another month. The baby had been conceived in August, not July. She'd just wanted an excuse to end the interview early.

As she flicked the television on to an old season of *Survivor*, she casually chomped through a line of saltines, watching as a group of pretty people duked it out in bathing suits for the chance at a million dollars. *I could use a million dollars*, Penny thought lazily. And she could lie, cheat, and steal her way to the top if that was what it took.

After all, Penny had gotten very good at lying these last few months. She'd lied to her friends. She'd lied to Roman. She'd lied to her mother and to herself and to the detective at the station. There were so many lies surrounding Roman's murder, it was a wonder the detectives had been able to pin any sort of evidence on Eliza.

Which was the biggest problem of all. Penny suspected Eliza hadn't killed her husband.

So why had she been arrested for a crime she hadn't committed?

THIRTY-SEVEN

Two Months After
April 2019

Anne slipped a pair of sunglasses over her eyes and leaned against the exterior of her van, watching the youth softball game from the parking lot. As the two teams crossed paths at the switch of an inning, she let her gaze wander to the other end of the lot where Mark's car was parked. Anne had gotten quite good at avoiding her almost ex-husband in public.

Mark hadn't yet signed the papers, despite them being in his hands for several weeks. Anne's phone was loaded with messages from him. In them, he begged her to talk, to listen, to give him another chance. Anne hadn't been ready to talk. She still wasn't. What could she say?

She hadn't told her husband about the private investigator or Roman's blackmail. Mark thought the divorce was because of the affair. It wasn't, but there was no point in telling him that when the result was the same. Especially because Anne wasn't sure if she wanted to know the answers to the outstanding questions swimming around her head—questions like where he'd been on the night of Roman's death.

Anne had other things to keep her busy now—her four children, for instance. Or finding a job that could pay for her new lifestyle as a single mom. Or the fact that her best friend, Eliza Tate, had just been arrested for murder.

Thankfully, Anne's mother had agreed to help in the interim. Beatrice Harper was currently at home watching the three youngest kids while Anne forced herself to sit through Gretchen's game—not one hundred feet from her husband.

The things she did to support her kids, Anne thought dryly. She'd rather stick a pen in her eye than talk to Mark, yet here she was, hidden behind sunglasses and a hat, as if a flimsy disguise could prevent her husband from recognizing her.

Still, the sunglasses came with an added bonus. Instead of watching the dugout where her daughter was getting ready to bat, Anne's eyes flicked over to Mark. He stood against the fence, clapping and whistling. Gretchen turned a toothy grin toward her father, then gave a gigantic wave in his direction. She didn't bat an eye at her mother.

Anne's heart clutched. She'd imagined these days for years. Bright, hopeful years where she'd looked forward to having a family of her own. She'd longed to watch lovingly as her husband leaned over the fence at a softball game to cheer on his daughter. Pecked her forehead when she scored a home run. Stuck a Band-Aid on her knee when she fell.

Now here she was, complete with the kids and the husband, but it was all wrong.

Anne managed to dodge Mark's gaze as the game finished. As soon as the teams wrapped up their mandatory handshakes, Gretchen sprinted over.

"Mom, please, please, *please* can Erica take me out to get ice cream? Both her mom and dad are going, and Violet is, too. Pretty please? They said they can drop me off afterward."

Anne looked up to find Erica's parents. However, instead of locking eyes with Erica's mother, she got swept into a stare-down with Mark. Anne held his gaze for a long moment, her confidence fortified only by the fact that he couldn't see her eyes behind the shades.

She felt Mark's gaze following her as she broke eye contact with him. Anne dragged herself across the field to make plans with Erica's family and was rewarded with yips from three young girls when it was all said and done. Gretchen barely remembered to wave goodbye to her mother before racing off with her friends.

After bidding Erica's family goodbye, Anne spun around on impulse. She no longer sensed Mark's gaze on her. For some reason, that bothered her more than if he'd been watching.

Guilt wormed its way through her stomach. Was it possible she'd been too harsh on him and had finally pushed him away? For how hard she'd fought to keep their family together, in the end, she'd given up. She felt uneasy thinking of herself as a quitter, but what other choice did she have when all the evidence was stacked against Mark?

Still, she found herself moving toward her husband's car, briskly at first, then at a jog as she saw him sliding into the driver's seat. She was breathless by the time she reached his window, and she didn't know exactly why.

She raised a hand, knocked.

Mark rolled the window down, a reluctant question in his eyes. "Anne?"

Anne pushed her sunglasses onto her head as if that would reveal her true identity. "I'm ready to talk," she said finally. "Can we go somewhere private?"

Mark led the way to a small rental home he'd booked when Anne had asked him to leave. She'd been out front several times to drop off or pick up the kids, but she'd never stepped foot inside.

Her husband led the way, moving silently. Anne felt as if they were strangers navigating a somewhat awkward but not entirely horrible first date.

She kicked off her shoes in the entryway and studied the small space. It was neat, sparse. Mark had kept it clean. The only signs of someone living in the space were a single dish, a single glass, a single spoon, a single bowl on a drying rack. The very singleness of it all broke Anne's heart.

Mark grabbed two bottles of water and led the way to the back patio. Two chairs were perched around a card table. He plopped the waters down, then waited until Anne took a seat before easing into the one opposite her.

They sat in silence, sipping their waters, for a long minute.

"Do you have something stronger?" Anne muttered.

Mark sucked on his lower lip. "Are you sure..."

He trailed off. Looked into Anne's eyes.

"I'm fine," she whispered. "I promise."

Mark disappeared into the kitchen and returned carrying two beers. With a wry smile, he popped the tops off both, then leaned his bottle toward Anne's. They clinked, the chirpy sound chiming across the sunny afternoon like a bell choir at a funeral.

"To what am I cheering?" Mark asked. "Besides you speaking to me?"

Anne couldn't hide a small smile. That was the problem with talking to Mark. It was too easy to like him, to love him. They were so familiar with each other that even something as simple as sitting on the deck with a couple of beers took Anne back to better days. Days she wanted to reclaim. *Oh*, how she longed for them.

"He's dead," Anne said finally. "And I want to know the truth."

"Excuse me?"

"Roman Tate is dead," Anne repeated. "And I want the truth."

"What does Roman Tate have to do with anything?"

"Come on, Mark. We're over. We both know it. The affair—"

Mark's eyebrow shot up. "What affair?"

"The affair!" Anne waved a hand. "The reason we're getting divorced. One of the reasons, I should say."

"I'm not having an affair. I never have. Anne, I—"

"Do you think I'm stupid? Where do you go on Tuesday nights?"

Mark closed his eyes. "I thought you *knew*."

"I do know," Anne said. "I saw her. The girl you're seeing."

"You've got it all wrong. I'm not dating anyone. Harmony Feliz is my daughter."

Anne felt the bottle of beer slipping from her fingers. She steadied it, then tapped her fingers against the glass and stared at her feet. The cement was patchy and broken. Weeds crept up through the crumbled bits. One tiny flower bloomed beneath the table despite the odds stacked against it.

"Excuse me?" she finally managed.

"Harmony is eighteen years old," Mark explained. "When I met you, I was seeing her mother, Angelina. We'd been…intimate several times."

"I never knew."

"I didn't tell you because I didn't think it was relevant." Mark looked sheepish. "I mean, you and I weren't exclusive at that point, or at least I didn't think so. Angelina and I dated for a few months, but after my third date with you, I knew I had to choose one."

Anne's throat went dry.

"I was young and stupid. I'm not proud of any of this," Mark said. "I saw Angelina once or twice more. We'd been going together off and on for a while, but it was never serious. We saw each other between other relationships. We were just—"

"You were fuck buddies."

"A bit harsh, but if that's what you want to call it, I suppose I can't argue."

"Did she know the situation?" Anne asked. "Was she in it for the sex, or had she fallen in love?"

"We knew what we were. Neither one of us was pretending it was anything more than that."

"You're sure?" The knowledge of Penny's unreciprocated relationship with Roman was still fresh in Anne's mind. "Sometimes wires get crossed. It never ends well."

Mark shot her a darkly frustrated look. "After you and I went away to Morro Bay for a weekend, I made up my mind."

"So while we were cuddled up in that cute little bed-and-breakfast and you first told me that you loved me," Anne said, feeling sick to her stomach, "I wasn't the only one you were dating?"

"After that, you were. I never saw Angelina again," Mark pleaded. "I swear to you. I called her from our hotel room while you were showering and broke up with her. We never spoke again."

Anne waited patiently, her insides fluttering with anxiety. She didn't want to hear what Mark had to say next, but she needed to know. She'd gone this far. There was no turning back.

"Angelina died last year." Mark raised his beer to his lips, took a sip. "I only found out when a young woman contacted me via Facebook."

"Harmony."

"She'd done some digging into her past. Apparently, her mother had never told her that her father—the man Angelina ended up marrying—wasn't her biological father."

"If her mother never told her, how did she find out?"

Mark gave a snort. "Going through her mother's things, she found a wedding photo of her parents. She was two years old in the photo, and it got her wondering."

"They could have had her out of wedlock and got married later. Plenty of people do it."

"True, but her mother had always lauded the fact that she'd had a whirlwind romance with Angelina's father. They met and were married six months later."

"Harmony's good at math."

"I guess you could say that."

"Did she tell her father?" Anne struggled for the proper phrase. "Her...unbiological father?"

"He was the first person she told. She went to him and asked him for the truth. He gave it to her straight."

"Did he know your name?"

"No. Harmony found out who I was with a bit of investigative prowess. She picked through her mother's diaries, journals, whatever."

"Like father, like daughter," Anne said wryly. "Sounds like she'd make for a good detective."

Mark shrugged. "She's sharp. And determined."

"Maybe Angelina was sleeping with other men, too," Anne said, her mind flicking back to Penny's confusing little love triangle. "Have you considered the fact that Harmony might not be yours?"

"She is," Mark said. "I agreed to a paternity test."

Anne's blood went cold. "When?"

"Shortly after she came to me."

"And you never told me?" Anne's hands twitched around her beer bottle, then stilled. "I'm your wife, and you never once thought to mention to me that you might have another child?"

"After the twins were born, you went on and on about how we couldn't possibly have any more children. We couldn't afford it, we had no more room in our home, we had no time."

"Right. So you didn't tell me this because I didn't want to have another baby?" Anne let out an exasperated sigh. "News flash, Mark. The deed had already been done. Your logic makes no sense."

"Put yourself in my shoes."

"Believe me. I'm trying to."

"As all of this was happening, I was in shock. Complete and utter shock," Mark said. "Not only did I feel guilty about the timing of our initial relationship, but I felt guilty about Harmony. I've had a daughter walking around for eighteen years, and I never knew her. I'd never once thought about her, never attended a graduation or a ball game. Never paid a cent toward her upbringing. Never changed a diaper, kissed her forehead. All those things that we've done with Gretchen, Samuel, the twins... I missed out on that with Harmony through no fault of my own."

"Some fault of your own."

"Angelina never told me!"

"Never once?" Anne gave a skeptical frown. "She never once hinted that she was carrying your child?"

"I told you, we didn't speak after the night I told you that I loved you. I honestly didn't think about her after that weekend. She never tried to contact me."

"Ah."

"I know finances have been tight, especially paying for the twins' daycare, the sports activities, the house repairs—everything hit us at the same time. So I tried to pick up extra shifts at work. I felt obligated to be a part of Harmony's life when I found out about her."

"How noble of you."

Mark's eyes flashed, but he didn't take the bait. "The situation is complicated. Harmony's father—the man who raised her—hated that she didn't belong to him."

Anne listened, processing. She was mesmerized to find that while she felt upset and shocked at Mark, she could still feel sympathy for Harmony. Anne pictured her own babies, thought of them being raised by a parent who held no love for them. It made her queasy. It brought back those three days when she'd walked out on her own family. Only she'd been granted the opportunity to walk back in, and she'd never forgotten the gift she'd been given.

"When Angelina died, her husband wanted nothing to do with Harmony. He kicked her out of the house and made it difficult for her to get what was rightly hers from the will."

"That's unfair."

"It is," Mark agreed, "but she's still a child. She has no money to hire a lawyer. What could she do?"

"What did *you* do?"

"I helped Harmony find an apartment. It's in my name, and that's where I've been going on Tuesdays," Mark said. "We spend a little time together. I bring her groceries now and again. She likes to cook. We play cards. She tells me about school—she's enrolled in college for next year and wants to declare a criminal justice major."

Anne hesitated. "She sounds like a nice girl."

"She is. You'd like her." Mark gave a long pause before leaning forward. He grasped Anne's hands in his and stared imploringly into her eyes. "I should have told you everything. I just never knew how."

"It was right of you to help her," Anne found herself saying graciously. "But I don't know what else to say."

"I don't expect you to say anything."

"Maybe you should have expected more from me. I was your wife."

They both paused at her use of the past tense.

"You still are," Mark finally said, his voice a whisper. "Would you consider remaining my wife?"

"Are there any other secrets you're keeping from me?" Anne asked. "Anything at all?"

"No."

"Nothing." Anne's heart deflated. "Not a thing?"

Mark stared into her eyes. "About another woman? I promise you, Anne—"

"I'm talking about us, Mark. Me and you. Things that could jeopardize our family. Our lives."

Mark sat back in his seat, his eyes flashing with a hint of calculation. They were soft as they studied her, a siege of resignation taking place in his expression. "You know about the money."

Anne felt her heart cracking into shards. "You wouldn't have told me if I didn't find out for myself."

"There was no need for you to know. There still isn't. It was a one-time thing, and I was trying to keep you safe."

"Roman knew," she said softly. "He was going to turn you in."

Mark blinked. "Roman Tate?"

"And now he's dead," Anne said. "It's eerily convenient, don't you think?"

"I didn't—" Mark stopped talking, then looked at Anne. After all they'd discussed, this was the first time fear had entered his gaze. "Anne, you didn't..."

"Me? You think I killed him?" Anne's mouth dropped open in

shock. "You're the one who didn't come home that night! How do I know *you* didn't find out about the blackmail?"

"This is the first I'm hearing about it! The night Roman died, I fell asleep on Harmony's couch while she cooked dinner," Mark said. "We were going to watch a show with our food, but the second I sat on the couch, I knocked out. I'd worked overnight the day before and was exhausted."

"Very convenient."

"When I woke up, hours later, I panicked. I went to work the next day and mumbled something to you about working overtime. Your mother was with the kids, so I didn't worry about them. I hoped you were too tired after your night out with the girls to notice…"

"I guess I'll just have to trust you," Anne said. "And you'll have to trust me. I didn't kill him, Mark. In case you were actually wondering."

"Anne…"

"I could have. He blackmailed me over what you'd done. He took everything from my 401k."

Mark's brow furrowed. "If you'd come to me—"

"What would you have done?"

"You tried to keep us together," Mark said. "Despite everything. Through what you thought was an affair and blackmail and everything else."

"You are my husband. The father of my children." Anne's voice rose. "I'm a housewife with no credentials and a decades-old résumé. I couldn't afford to do anything but keep us together."

"Is that why?" Mark asked. "Or do you still love me?"

"Why did you do it?" Tears streamed down Anne's face. "Why did you take the money?"

"Extenuating circumstances!" Mark shot to his feet, the outburst too loud for their quiet conversation. He paced back and forth before turning to Anne. "It was a month before the twins were born. You remember that time, don't you?"

Anne thought back. She'd been huge with pregnancy and wildly uncomfortable. The other children were going through rough phases. Money was tighter than ever. Mark was working long hours, and their marriage was holding on by a thread. They'd hardly been an example of a happy family.

"I was on the drug unit at the time."

"Working lots of hours," Anne said. "I remember."

"I was *trying* to make ends meet. We had two babies on the way and could barely afford the two we had. I borrowed money from a friend to pay the mortgage a few months running. I didn't tell you about that because I was embarrassed. What sort of man can't support his family?"

"What sort of man hides things from his wife?"

Mark sat down in response. "One night on the job, we had a huge bust. Keep in mind, I'd been chasing these guys for months. Going on a year. During that time, I'd been shot at twice. Once, they stabbed me in the leg—almost hit an artery. The hell I'd been through to get these assholes..."

Anne remembered that part well. The phone call, the hospital visit. The pit in her stomach as she wondered if her husband would survive his injuries.

"I was back on duty by the time we moved in for the final bust and demanded to be present. These idiots had almost stolen everything from me—my wife, my children, my life—and I was determined to put them behind bars. I never expected we'd find money on the scene. These guys don't usually keep money on them."

"But you did find money."

"There was over $1.2 *million*." Mark let the number hang there. "Over a million dollars in drug money. I saw it, and I grabbed a stack. I didn't bother counting it. Didn't think twice about it. I couldn't, or I would have put it back."

"You should have."

"In that moment, all I could see was red. I was so angry at these thugs, so worried about you and the kids. Gretchen was going to need braces. Sam needed those special shoes. The hospital bill for the twins' deliveries was going to use up our savings. We deserved that money."

"It was illegal, Mark. So, so illegal."

"Don't you think I know that?" He raised his beer, finished it off. "I regret it. I regret taking the money. Hell, in a sense, I almost regret getting away with it. But I don't regret doing what I thought was best for my family."

Anne's breath hitched as her husband locked eyes on her.

"I would do anything for you, Anne. For the kids." His other hand fisted in his lap. "It's probably good you didn't tell me what Roman knew, because I might have done something I regretted."

"Apparently someone else did it for you."

Mark didn't look all that upset at the notion. Anne's frazzled mind ached as she stared at the man she'd thought she'd known better than anyone else on earth. And she wondered if it was true. The true murderer hadn't been caught yet. Anne was convinced Eliza hadn't done it...so who had?

Is it possible? Mark had already lied so much...

"Why was Roman looking into me?" Mark asked suddenly.

"I hired a private investigator to tail you." Anne tried to keep her chin up. "I'm not proud of it, but I had to know. The PI then sold the information he turned up to Roman. It's a long story. My question is how did the investigator find out? Does someone at work know? Are we in danger?"

"There's an account," Mark said dully. "A banking account I opened up and didn't tell you about, and if the PI is any good, he would've found it. There's more money in there than I should ever have earned to date. He could've dug around, matched the deposits up with my work history, and connected the dots."

"You still have money left over?"

"Yes. It's how I've been able to afford Harmony's apartment. To make ends meet during months it should never be possible. I'm sorry I never told you, but I just couldn't explain how the money got there."

"What does this mean for us?" Anne asked finally. "What am I supposed to do?"

"You can turn me in," Mark said, his eyes glancing up toward hers. "I wouldn't blame you. Not in the slightest."

Anne forced her doubts about her husband to take a back seat. Just for a moment. *Suppose he is telling the truth?* What would that mean for their marriage? If Anne didn't give him the benefit of the doubt, just once more, would she regret it?

"We all make mistakes."

"We do," Mark acknowledged. "That doesn't excuse them."

Anne stood, pushing her empty bottle toward Mark. "I have to think. Alone."

"Take as much time as you need. You know where to find me when you're ready."

The couple walked silently through the house. It had gone from an awkward first date to the tired, exhausted reality of a couple married with four children. They had marched through hell and back. They had both made mistakes. There were pains that needed to heal. Wrongs that couldn't be righted.

Anne slipped her shoes on, paused in the doorway. "Mark…"

He stepped closer, his breathing thin and fragile. "Yes?"

Anne licked her lips, swallowed. "I've been thinking… The vanity I threw out the other day…the garbage man didn't take it, and I didn't get around to burning it."

"You want me to get rid of it for you?"

"Actually," Anne whispered, "if you have a spare minute, maybe you could fix the drawers?"

THIRTY-EIGHT

Three Months After
May 2019

P enny waddled down the hall and let herself into the casting office. She knew, of course, that this job was only temporary. That it wouldn't last. The idea of asking about paid maternity leave—or maternity leave in general—was laughable. Benefits weren't even on the horizon.

The previous week, Penny had picked up an application at the grocery store down the street from her apartment. It had pained her physically to write her name on the form. But her hospital bills wouldn't pay themselves.

As it was, Penny had enough savings to get through a month, maybe two, of self-made maternity leave. She'd already cut every cost she could—she'd given up all her writing classes and patched her car's bumper with duct tape.

She'd stashed every cent she could muster into a savings account that would give her a tiny buffer once the baby arrived. But after two months' time, she'd be back to work. At a grocery store. She'd moved to Hollywood to find herself and, in the process, had lost everything.

"Penny?"

It took a moment for Penny to remember that she was at work. Her eyes shot up from the sign-in log at the casting company's front desk while she registered the sound of a familiar voice. Penny couldn't quite place it until she laid eyes on a face she hadn't seen in...almost nine months.

"Ryan!" Startled, Penny gulped down a breath of air. "How...um, how are you? What are you doing here?"

It was a stupid question, since Penny could see the headshots he carried in his hand. The moment was embarrassing for both of them—for Penny because she was employed by a crappy company peddling hope to wannabe actors, and for Ryan because he was knowingly visiting said crappy company on the fumes of hope. Both their careers were obviously floundering.

"Are those your headshots? I can get you signed in." Penny stood, flummoxed, wiping her hands on her umbrella of a dress. "I hadn't realized you'd be in the studio today."

Ryan had bigger problems, it seemed, than his sad excuse for a career. He was staring with a glazed look at Penny's stomach. His face scrunched up, and it became painfully obvious that he was trying to do math. His lips moved as he counted backward.

"How far along are you?" he asked finally. "Congratulations, by the way."

"I'm due any day."

Ryan blinked. "Why didn't you tell me?"

Penny dropped the hand that had been extended to collect Ryan's headshot. "I'm not sure we should discuss this here. Do you have a minute? We could go somewhere. Somewhere close."

Ryan took a step back. "I think that's a good idea."

Penny tugged at his elbow, pulling Ryan from the studio. She paraded him downstairs, out through the gated front door where she glanced hungrily up and down the street for something, anything, that would work.

"Let's get some Froyo," she decided. "There's a little shop around the corner."

Ryan followed Penny's every move. He mimicked her motions as she served up a bowl of yogurt for herself. Penny didn't pay attention to the flavors she selected, but she did keep the serving sizes small. She couldn't afford Froyo.

However, when Ryan offered his credit card at the register, Penny nearly gasped with relief. She made a noncommittal noise of protest, but he waved away her offer to split the bill. Clutching her bowl, Penny followed Ryan outside to a shaded patio. They took seats opposite each other at a warped, rusty table and equally misshapen café-style chairs. They were blissfully alone.

"Is it…" Ryan glanced at Penny's stomach. "Is it mine?"

"He," Penny confirmed. "It's a boy."

"If you're nine months, and I'm counting right…"

"You're counting right," she said softly.

"Why wouldn't you tell me you were pregnant?" Ryan shoved his spoon into his yogurt and let it sit there. "Did you stop coming to class so I wouldn't notice?"

"I'm not sure the baby's yours."

"But nine months ago…"

Penny dug her spoon into her bowl and took a bite. The edges of the frothy, bright colors were starting to melt into a brownish soup while she waited for poor Ryan to put everything together. He looked incredibly perplexed. He didn't seem to sort out what Penny was saying until she winced. Then she nodded, and he sat back in his seat. His fingers toyed with the edge of his spoon.

"You think the baby is *his*."

"I'm sorry," she whispered.

Ryan eventually sighed. "I suppose that doesn't matter now."

"What do you mean?" Penny said. "What doesn't matter?"

"We can still be together," Ryan said. "I've wanted to be with you since the day we met."

"But that's—"

"The other guy isn't still in the picture, is he?"

"Er, no. He's not. He's, ah, dead."

"So it was Roman."

"I don't know what else to say. I'm sorry."

"If there was a chance the baby was mine, you should have come to me, too."

"I didn't think the chances were equal!" Penny leaned forward, her hands gripping at the table with her outburst. She recovered, sat back. Continued quietly. "I went to Roman first because I figured there was a bigger chance it was his. I...um...saw him more than you."

"You *hoped* it was his."

"For a moment, maybe. But I was wrong. Very, very wrong."

"When he died..."

"We weren't together. I broke things off in October of last year."

"That's one short-lived romance with one long-term consequence."

"You're telling me."

"Does your family know? Anyone else?"

"A few friends," Penny said. "That's it. My family doesn't know. I didn't know how to tell them."

"We can tell them together."

"What are you talking about?"

Ryan steeled his face. "Roman might have been an asshole, but that doesn't mean we all are. If there's a chance this baby is mine..."

"I don't know if it is," she reiterated. "I would have to do a paternity test to know for certain. That's so embarrassing. I never thought I'd be the type of girl to have to say those words."

To her surprise, Ryan leaned forward and grasped her hands. He looked into her eyes. "Penny, you're the type of girl I haven't stopped thinking about for months. We can try this again, the right way this time."

"Don't be ridiculous. We went on three dates."

"Sometimes, you just know."

"And sometimes, you *don't* know," Penny said firmly. "What if this turns out to be Roman's child?"

Something flashed through Ryan's eyes. "I don't need to know for sure. The chance that it's mine is enough."

"That's crazy."

Before Ryan could respond, Penny hunched forward and gripped the table hard. Ryan's eyes narrowed in concern.

"Oh shit," she said. "My water just broke."

THIRTY-NINE

Four Months After
June 2019

Eliza waited in the same small, concrete room where she'd waited several times before. She'd met with Anne, with Penny, with her lawyers. Her routine was comforting, which was somewhat alarming, considering she was still in prison.

Marguerite's voice rang quietly through the room. "Eliza?"

Glancing up, Eliza noted the bestselling author looked preened and professional. No more wild hair and wilder accessories. She wore simple black slacks topped by a crisp, white shirt. Her hair had been tamed into a sleek bun.

Eliza smiled across the table, which had the funny side effect of making the author cringe. Finally, Eliza Tate knew the rules of the game.

"Hey," Marguerite said softly. "How are you?"

Eliza stared directly into Marguerite's eyes. The funny thing about being arrested for murder was that nothing really scared her anymore.

Marguerite's eyes flashed as she looked wildly around the room, scanning to see if someone was listening. Maybe they were. Eliza couldn't be sure. She didn't care.

"You've always been a sucker for a good publicity stunt," Eliza said. "Getting me arrested for my husband's murder is your best yet, I'll admit."

"I don't know what you're talking about."

"Coming forward after Roman's death, laying out the pieces of the puzzle for the police—it was a good PR move, I'll give you that. Get ahead of the rumors. Start playing Marguerite the victim. It's probably what I would have told you to do."

"I was just telling the truth."

"You were playing Nancy Drew for the public," Eliza said. "Sharing in all those interviews about how my poor business was floundering, and didn't I need Roman's life insurance payout to stay afloat? Or maybe I killed him out of rage because he'd gotten one of his students pregnant. You didn't hold anything back, did you?"

Marguerite swallowed hard but didn't deny any of it. "If you're so innocent, why are your fingerprints on the murder weapon?"

"I don't know," Eliza said. "Did you put them there? It's possible, you know. There were two wineglasses missing from my house."

"Why would I take a wineglass? I have plenty of money."

"To go with the cake knife," Eliza said. "It's possible to transfer fingerprints from one surface to another; I looked up the technique. The prints probably weren't even usable, but that doesn't matter, because my DNA would have been on the knife, along with remnants of Roman's blood, and that's the really important bit anyway."

"I hope you realize how far-fetched this all sounds."

"It's simple actually. Brilliant. You set me up for it," Eliza said. "On the afternoon of February 13, you even suggested that I'd kill Roman with a knife. But when I didn't take your bait, you marched in and did it yourself. You were so sweet to keep me involved, though… leaving all traces of evidence pointing my way."

"Not true."

"Maybe not. You did leave a little evidence toward Anne and Penny, just for kicks. But it was me you wanted. Why?"

"I didn't kill your husband."

"Well, we both know I didn't kill him," Eliza said. "I mean, what sort of criminal would dump a murder weapon—with their own damn name *printed on it*—in the alley behind their own house? How idiotic do people think I am?"

"It's not—"

"I would have had weeks to dispose of it. Why didn't I drive to the Hoover Dam and toss it over the railing? Throw it in the ocean? Bury it at the top of Runyon Canyon?" Eliza paused for dramatic effect. "Apparently the world thinks I'm stupid enough to throw it out with my leftovers. As if that weren't coincidental enough, a Good Samaritan just happened to walk by that same night and see a bloody knife. With my name on it."

"The truth has a way of coming out." Marguerite's answer rang hollowly through the room. Even she didn't look convinced. "They arrested you. Not me."

"I'm well aware."

"I don't have to be here and listen to this."

Eliza raised her eyebrows. Marguerite didn't make a move to leave. They waited at a standstill.

"Why did you do it?" Eliza said. "Ego? Did you actually love him?"

"I didn't kill your fucking husband, okay?"

"Okay."

The simplicity of Eliza's answer seemed to irk Marguerite further. She stood. "I came here as a friend. I have been nothing but supportive of you, Eliza."

"Thanks for your support," Eliza said with a half smile. "Really. In a way, you did set me free. And then you took it all away when you had me locked up."

"I didn't do any such thing."

"I suppose a part of me is envious of you," Eliza said. "You did what I never could have done. You pulled it off, too. Got away with it. If I thought I could have gotten away with killing Roman, would I have done it myself?" Eliza bobbed her shoulders. "I'm not sure, to be honest. What does it feel like, killing someone?"

Marguerite turned on her heel and stormed to the door. She knocked, and the guards moved to let her out.

"By the way," Eliza called after her, "congratulations."

"On what?"

"I saw you hit number one on the *New York Times* bestseller list with *Be Free*." Eliza gave a dark chuckle. "I guess that's the one I should read next, huh?"

"I'm glad you can joke about this."

"It was genius, how you pulled it off. It's true—the best PR of all time is getting your publicist arrested for the murder of her husband."

Marguerite's eyes narrowed to slits. "You really think I'm the kind of person to do that?"

"Let's just say…" Eliza glanced down at her nails, "you're welcome."

FORTY

Five Months After
July 2019

Penny dragged herself up the stairs to her apartment. It had been a long day at court, and she was exhausted. Or she'd been exhausted until the drive home, when she was overcome by the buzz of nervous energy.

Crawling through Los Angeles traffic on autopilot, Penny's mind whirled through the twisty, twisty trial happening all around her. The strange contradictions, the parts that didn't make sense. They were all missing something. Something so close, she could almost touch it...

Eliza's prints are on the murder weapon.
Penny had the murder weapon in her possession.
Who stole the murder weapon from Penny?
Evidence pointed toward Anne, Eliza, Marguerite—but why not Penny?
Was Mark lying? About what?
Motive, motive, motive... Who was the deadliest of them all?

It hit Penny as she swung a right onto La Cienega. The puzzle pieces ground into place, and Penny knew—without a doubt—who had killed Roman. She wondered how she'd missed it all along.

It's the motive, Penny eventually surmised. She'd been so focused on the women who'd been angry at Roman that it had blinded her to everyone else. For months, she'd assumed one of the women in her book club had grabbed the nearest knife and plunged it into Roman in a fit of rage. God knew they'd all had reasons to be angry with Roman Tate.

But what if that wasn't the case at all? What if Roman's murder had been planned—not for minutes or hours but for days or even months?

On a hunch, Penny pulled over at the first turn and parked in a fast-food lot. The scent of fries drifted over her as she climbed out of her car and moved to the hood. It took her half an hour of poking around, prodding every which way, before she found it. A little GPS tracker attached to the underbelly of her crappy car.

Another twenty minutes of research turned up a second bug, this one fastened to the inside of her purse. The fabric in the bottom of the bag had been cut—a tiny incision that Penny only discovered because whoever had made the cut had stitched it up with thread that didn't quite match. Penny's blood chilled. Roman's murder had been no accident.

Penny needed to phone Eliza—or her lawyers—or the police, but before she could do that, she needed to get home and see her baby. Sweet Peter, her precious boy, who would be waiting for her embrace. Once she had him in her arms, she would take care of the rest.

Parking in a handicapped spot outside her new apartment complex, Penny shuffled from her vehicle to the front door. This building had a key card lock out front. A definite upgrade in living space, one she'd only been able to afford because she'd moved in with Ryan just after the baby was born.

Ryan had been there for her from the very beginning, from the second Peter was born, and from that moment onward, they'd been a makeshift family. He'd helped care for Peter, and in the intensity of those newborn days, Penny had assumed Ryan was an angel sent straight from the heavens to watch over her. He'd rocked Peter to sleep when Penny's eyes drooped. He'd cooked healthy food, encouraged mama and baby to eat well. He'd rubbed Penny's back and wiped Peter's drool. He had been everything Penny had imagined in a partner. How could she have turned him away?

And it was Ryan who opened the door before Penny could even insert her key into the lock.

"There's Mama!" Ryan raised the tiny baby's hand and gestured toward Penny in an assisted wave. "We love Mama!"

"Hi, baby," Penny said, going in to nuzzle her son. "I missed you."

"What about me?" Ryan swung around and headed into the kitchen, ignoring Penny's outstretched arms. "Didn't Mama miss me?"

"Of course. I always miss my boys."

"Good." Ryan swooped behind Penny and locked the door behind her. "That's the right answer."

"Man, I'm tired." Penny yawned. "Let's put the baby down and have dinner."

"A little quiet time for Mommy and Daddy? That sounds nice."

"It's just what the doctor ordered after the day I've had."

Penny walked over to the kitchen table and set her bag down, then continued into the nursery. She looked into the baby monitor with a pinch of dread. How long had he been watching her every move?

Ryan followed Penny into the nursery and went straight to the crib. He set Peter down on a cotton dinosaur fitted sheet and moved toward Penny with an exaggerated, seductive swing of his hips. "What do we think about getting a start on baby number two?"

"Peter's not even six months old. I'm still recovering from his birth. It will be a while before I'm ready to think about another."

"That's not what I wanted to hear." Ryan frowned. "Peter needs a sibling."

"I can't fathom another child. I can't even fathom a full night of sleep."

"Come on, darling." Ryan crossed the room, rested one hand on Penny's shoulder. "Me and you, we're meant to be together. Meant to have a family. How do you think we ended up like this? It was fate. All the obstacles we had to overcome just to be together..."

"What obstacles?"

"Oh, you know..." Ryan shrugged. "The other man primarily."

"Roman wasn't an obstacle. I broke up with him."

"He was an obstacle, but now he's not." Ryan seemed completely unaffected by the fact that the man in question had been murdered. "Isn't life so much better now that you're completely free?"

"I *was* free," Penny said. "At least I thought I was."

As she spoke, her blood began to chill. He knew. He knew that she knew, and she should have guessed that he'd be prepared. She should have been more careful. She should have known he'd been watching, watching, watching.

"Aw, honey." Ryan tsked. "I can see it in your eyes. You don't trust me. It's that stupid trial. You don't believe anyone anymore. It's ruining you."

"I think you might be right."

"Well, you never have to doubt me. We are meant to be together. You can't fight fate."

"Not even if you orchestrated fate?" Penny murmured. "You made me believe that we were destined to be together when I was most vulnerable. Pregnant, single. You held my hand when I went into labor, made me believe we were a family."

"We *are* a family."

"Families don't have to kill to be together."

"Sweet Penny." Ryan shook his head. "You are so naive, darling. I love that about you."

Penny backed away, inching toward Peter. Ryan stepped between her and the crib and raised his hand. He grasped her chin between his fingers, hard.

"I hoped it wouldn't come to this. I was prepared to come clean about what I'd done for you, for us...but only when you were ready. You're not ready yet."

"You murdered a man just to be with me?"

"Roman was a sad excuse for a man. He didn't understand the word 'commitment.' When I found out you thought he was the father of your child, I had to do something about it."

"You planned his murder for months."

"God, you ladies made it easy. You talked point blank about killing him. I couldn't believe my luck—it was too perfect. Apparently, the lawyers thought so, too. That court case is a fucking mess."

"How…"

"One little listening device sewn into your purse, and I heard everything. Unfortunately, I know you found the bugs this afternoon. The trackers. You shouldn't have touched them, Penny. I saw you, heard you. I'm always listening, watching."

"How'd you do it?"

"What, kill him?" Ryan smiled. "I'm not proud of the murder— that bit is messy. But the rest of it was perfect, I have to admit. The knife's availability was made possible by you, darling. You and your filthy little habit of stealing. Yes, I know you stole the knife from Eliza. I know you also stole wineglasses from her. I would have bought you those things new, but you didn't let me."

"You're the one who took them from my apartment?"

"The knife was easy. I held on to that for a while. You didn't notice it was missing, which was a small relief."

"You were biding your time."

"I didn't plan on the big event being the eve of Valentine's Day, but it's fitting, don't you think? He didn't deserve romance. That afternoon, when I heard y'all talking about murder, I couldn't hold back. I listened and waited, like I'd been doing for months, and it paid off. Talk about destiny. It had already been planned, and then you all tied it up with a big, fat bow. There was a nice sprinkling of evidence and motive for everyone. Plenty to go around to muddy the waters."

"You went into Eliza's house? How?"

"It's easy to get through the door when it's left open. Eliza left in such a rush, she didn't bother to close it. Quick jaunt upstairs and voilà. Roman was naked in the shower, rinsing off his latest conquest, when I got to him."

Penny winced. "That is awful. He didn't deserve to die."

"He did."

"That wasn't your choice to make."

"You're welcome. I made a difficult decision, but it was for the best, Penny. For us. I'm telling you it was fate."

"Fate is not an excuse for murder."

"It was too easy to do it. It was destiny. The rest, after the murder, was a fucking cakewalk. I just had to plant a little seed of doubt in everyone's mind to point the attention away from us. Y'all wanted Roman dead, so that part was easy. You know it's true. Even you doubted your closest friends."

Penny didn't respond, because that bit was true. She'd wondered if Eliza, Mark, Marguerite, or even Anne had been guilty over the course of the trial. Had she truly believed one of them had done it? That was hard to say.

"I decorated the murder weapon with Eliza's fingerprints— transferred from the wineglass, easy peasy, thanks to you. Anne's a nutcase who hides it well. All I had to do was turn up her issues with postpartum depression and booze. It was a bonus people thought Mark did it. But that man doesn't have the balls to do what I did."

Penny's skin crawled. She'd moved in with this man. She'd thought they could be a family, that he could be a father, maybe a husband. Had she ever gotten it wrong.

"Don't go feeling sorry for him," Ryan said. "Roman was the scum of the earth. I couldn't risk you ever going back to him. I knew you wanted him to be the father. I waited for months— *months*—for you to tell me about my own child. I had to watch from a distance as you grew our baby, and I had to pretend to be surprised when you finally came clean to me."

"I didn't know what to say."

"I had to walk into that ridiculous office that you called a job opportunity and *pretend* to run into you. Pretend to count on my fingers back about…oh, nine months. How thick do you think I am? You should have told me about my son. What you did was fucking rude, Penny."

"I'm sorry. I should have told you, but I didn't know who the father—"

"The baby is mine. I know it."

"How can you possibly know?"

"I told you, it's fate," Ryan said. "We're destined to be together. We always were. From the day you walked into class, I knew I'd have you. One way or another."

"It was all an act. The nice guy. Letting me go out with Roman."

"I am patient. I am a talented actor, even if the world hasn't realized it yet. I am intelligent—far more intelligent than that imbecile Roman. I was patient. Watched, waited."

"You mean you stalked me. Spied on my every move."

"The four of you women talked about how to murder a man in your book club. You wanted it; you set me up. Who the hell cares if the courts never get a conviction? Roman's out of the way, and that's what matters. Everyone's better off for it—you, Anne, Eliza, Marguerite. You should all be thanking me."

"It's not your job to play God."

"I wasn't playing God. I was just helping to scoot our destinies along in the right direction. A gentle touch, if you will."

"A knife to the heart isn't very gentle."

"No, but it was pretty damn poetic. Not bad for a struggling actor."

"What now?" Penny pressed. "How do you expect to get away with it?"

"I expect we'll get away with it together. You won't say anything. If you do, I'll be forced to…take Peter under my wing. As a single parent."

"You wouldn't kill me."

"I love you, sweetheart." Ryan had dropped his hand from Penny's chin, but at his declaration of love, he grabbed her by the back of the head and pulled her against him. His tongue burned against hers as he shoved it into her mouth. He pulled away, whispered hotly against her cheek, "But I won't go to prison for you. My son needs me."

"He's not your son," Penny said. "He's my baby. Just mine."

"I wish it didn't have to come to this, but I planned for all scenarios. Bottle of sleeping pills, a note of postpartum depression from the doctor. It was all too much for you, the baby, the trial… It tipped the pretty Penny Sands right over the edge."

"You're right," Penny said finally. "This is fate. You and me. Maybe you were right all along."

"It's too late for that." Ryan clucked his tongue. "You don't love me anymore."

"I meant this." Penny nodded toward the baby monitor. The one that had belonged to Anne once upon a time. The fancy-schmancy device that streamed live to an app. "Ironically, you gave me the idea."

"The idea?" Ryan sounded unsure for the first time. "What idea?"

"You've been watching me for months. Creepy, Ryan. Creepy. So I figured you wouldn't mind if I reciprocated."

"What are you talking about?"

"Anne still has the app to this baby monitor on her phone—it was her hand-me-down. I called her on the way here, and she's livestreaming everything we say. Recording it, too. In the car with her is her husband. Mark is a cop…but I'm sure you know that. You know everything, right?"

Ryan's eyes widened. "You're bluffing."

"Am I?" Penny used the element of surprise to her advantage and jerked her knee upward, connecting with Ryan's groin. "Sweet dreams, asshole."

Then Penny marched to the crib and picked up Peter, deftly avoiding a groaning Ryan. By the time she made her way to the living room, the door had burst open, unlocked by the spare key Penny had left downstairs with Anne and Mark.

Mark burst into the room first, his gun drawn. Anne was just behind him, her face white, her hand clutching a cell phone where the livestream was still happening. Ryan's groans echoed from her phone, giving an eerie surround sound to the man's agony.

Behind Mark and Anne poured in more cops, some plainclothes detectives, others in uniform. Penny didn't pay them any mind; she just held Peter close and huddled against Anne as Mark arrested Ryan.

When Mark appeared, leading Ryan out of the apartment in handcuffs, she met Ryan's gaze head-on.

"You bitch," he said. "I did this for you, for us. And this is how you repay me?"

"Take charge, asshole," Penny said. "Never underestimate book club."

An excerpt from an article in the *Iowa Times*

August 2019

By: Penny Sands

Earlier today in Los Angeles, Eliza Tate was released after spending months in prison for a crime she did not commit. In related news, Ryan Anderson has confessed in a plea deal to the murder of Roman Tate.

When asked for a quote, Eliza said, "For the full story, you can buy my book."

Eliza Tate's first nonfiction book, *Taking Charges*, will be out in May 2021.

READING GROUP GUIDE

1. Which of the three main characters did you find the most interesting? Who did you identify with the most?

2. How did you feel about the courtroom interludes? How do you think they changed your perceptions of the rest of the book?

3. Eliza tells Anne: "You shouldn't live your life like me. It will only get you in trouble." Given the way the book turns out, what do you think of her advice?

4. Anne seems guilty and upset when she consults Luke Hamilton. Would you ever hire a private investigator? How comfortable would you be?

5. Marguerite's vegan, gluten-free, wholesome lifestyle is a facade she keeps up to capitalize on trends. Do you think most modern-day influencers are like that? How does that reflect the progression of social media?

6. What did you think of Ryan when he was first introduced? By the end of the book?

7. If Marguerite's book was condoning, or even recommending, murder, would you consider her responsible for deaths that might

result? How much can an author be expected to control the way her books are interpreted?

8. What did you think of Penny's "hobby?" Is it as harmless as she thinks?

9. Eliza, Anne, and Penny all lie in some way to keep up appearances. Do you think they have good reasons? How do these lies hurt them?

A CONVERSATION WITH THE AUTHOR

Eliza, Anne, and Penny have followed three very different paths in life. Are they inspired by women you know? Do you see yourself in any of them?

While my real-life relationships and experiences have always inspired my work, I tend to avoid having a single person in mind as I create my characters. I like them to be unique individuals, a combination of traits from people I've met or read about over the years. I fill in the rest with my imagination.

If anything, I see myself in my characters more than any other person. Little bits, here and there. Penny's dreamer-like attitude. Anne's hectic mom-life. Eliza's desire to work hard and succeed. I hope many women can relate to at least one of the characters in *Three Single Wives*, if only a glimmer.

Anne's postpartum depression is integral to the way that other characters treat her. Did you do much research on the topic?

I did do a fair amount of research prior to writing Anne's character. Postpartum depression isn't something that is discussed a lot publicly, but it is a very real, very scary illness that affects many women. I think by talking about it and researching it, we can bring the subject to light. The end goal is to bring awareness to women and help one another recognize that there is help available.

When you started writing, did you know who the murderer was? How did you map out the courtroom scenes throughout?

I thought I knew who the murderer was when I started writing, but as it turns out, I didn't! The first ending I wrote isn't the same one that is in the book now. After writing the first and even second draft, I did a hefty set of revisions that included changing the murderer, and I feel the book is much stronger now.

As for the courtroom scenes, I added those in after the rest of the novel was complete. I mapped out a chronological timeline of the events as they unfolded and then peppered in little bits of information each time we visited the courtroom.

Do you have more fun writing righteous characters defending their own, like Anne, or characters who take whatever they please, like Roman?

I think it's important to have a wide mix of personalities. If everyone were the same—in reality or in fiction—life would be boring! By having a slew of characters with various motives and dirty secrets and differing moral codes, and then mixing them all together—it creates quite an explosive plot.

With *Three Single Wives* following *Pretty Guilty Women*, you seem to a have a flair for ensemble casts of women. What draws you to those kinds of stories?

I find fascination in how we, as women, deal with the issues we are faced with every day. Between societal pressures, our roles as wives, mothers, caregivers, employees, chefs, etc., there's an almost suffocating list of things expected from us. Each woman handles these pressures differently, and I think we all long for others who understand what we're going through—not only the good, but also the bad and even the ugly. Who wouldn't want to have a group of friends who have their back...no matter what?

Where do you start a book? A scene, a character, a corpse?

I start usually start a book with a title or a question. In the instance of *Three Single Wives*, however, I started with characters. I started with Penny moving out to Los Angeles, then Eliza and Roman. Anne naturally fitted into the equation, rounding out the three perspectives I wanted to explore in the novel. I built the story around each of their secrets.

You chose an apt setting for this story. What drew you to LA?

I'm fascinated with LA and Hollywood, and the fact that the entertainment industry seems to exist in a world of its own. I moved to Los Angeles after college and lived there for six years, and it does feel different to live in the middle of it all. There's a very eclectic, creative ambiance, and I credit living in Los Angeles for kickstarting my desire to write. I now live in Minnesota with my husband and family, but I will always be grateful for my time spent on the west coast. Not least of all because I met my husband there and brought him back to Minnesota!

Are you a self-help reader yourself? What kinds of books appear on your bedside table?

I don't read a lot of self-help, but I have read a handful over the years. I read across almost every genre. As I have an eleven-month-old son, I currently have a couple of parenting books on my nightstand. I always have a slew of mystery and suspense books that I'm trying to catch up on, though my TBR will be forever endless!

What's next for you?

I am currently working on my third suspense novel that will be in the vein of *Pretty Guilty Women* and *Three Single Wives*. You can expect more bodies, more secrets, and more women with complicated lives and even more complicated decisions before them. I have several additional series that are currently available, and you can find my entire catalog at ginalamanna.com. There, you can also join my newsletter to be kept up to date on cover reveals, news, and release dates.

ACKNOWLEDGMENTS

I am beyond grateful to the wonderful teams at Sourcebooks and Little, Brown and Company. In particular, a very special thanks to the wonderful Shana Drehs and Rosanna Forte. It is a dream come true to work with editors as talented as you both.

To my agent, Sarah Hornsley, for everything you do. This book wouldn't have been possible without your guidance and support. Thanks also to Jenny Bent and the Bent Agency for your absolutely fantastic work. I appreciate all you do.

Thank you to my husband, Alex, and to my son, Leo. You two are my entire world, and I love you both so much.

Thank you to my mom, my dad, and my sisters, Kristi and Megan. Thank you for helping make this book possible by playing with Leo so I could get some work done!

A huge thanks to Rissa Pierce, Katie Hamachek, Michelle Foss, Kim Griggs, and Nicole Boelter for always being there for me over the years.

And a huge thank-you to Stacia Williams. I don't know where I'd be without you. Thank you for your incredible friendship.

ABOUT THE AUTHOR

Gina LaManna is a *USA Today* bestselling author. She has written more than thirty novels that include *Pretty Guilty Women*, *Sprinkled*, and *Shades of Pink*, among many others. She lives in Saint Paul, Minnesota, with her husband and son. Visit the author online at ginalamanna.com.